Anelthalien

Anelthalien

Written and Illustrated
By
H.A.Pruitt

ELM HILL

A Division of
HarperCollins Christian Publishing

www.elmhillbooks.com

Anelthalien

Published in Nashville, Tennessee, by Elm Hill, an imprint of Thomas Nelson. Elm Hill and Thomas Nelson are registered trademarks of HarperCollins Christian Publishing, Inc.

Cover and interior illustrations are created by and copyright of H.A.Pruitt. Used by permission

Elm Hill titles may be purchased in bulk for educational, business, fund-raising, or sales promotional use. For information, please e-mail SpecialMarkets@ThomasNelson.com.

Library of Congress Cataloging-in-Publication Data

Library of Congress Control Number: 2019913440

ISBN: 978-1-400327522 (Paperback)
ISBN: 978-1-400327539 (Hardbound)
ISBN: 978-1-400327546 (eBook)

TABLE OF CONTENTS

For my Maker, my Father, who always keeps His promises.

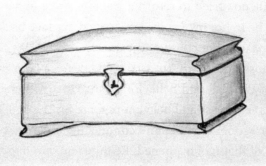

A Flawed Demise

Blenda gazed around her spacious throne room. It was the same as every other day, and yet it was unsettlingly different. The vast peacock blue floor in front of her usually contained a wide variety of people—townspeople, castle workers, travelers paying her respect, and numerous others—but not today. Today the giant room created for containing all sorts of activity lay quiet and empty before her. Blenda slowly surveyed the beauty of the room that she hardly ever saw through the normal constant human crowd. She swept her eyes across the shimmering blue floor and noticed how the light from the glass dome above made it dance like water. Then she moved her gaze over to one of the rich mahogany walls. Slowly she counted the number of doors spread across the wooden wall and then lowered her eyes back to the shimmering floor. Blenda was about to move her stare to the opposite wall to see if it held the same amount of doors, but a small movement to her right made her jump and clutch the golden arms of her throne.

"Oh! So sorry, ma'am. Did I scare you?" A little girl had emerged from one of the doors Blenda had just finished contemplating. She grinned in the funny way she always did—with her teeth bared and nose wrinkled. Blenda relaxed and smiled at her awkward grimace that was meant to show a friendly greeting.

"No, dear, you didn't scare me. It's just so quiet today, and I wasn't expecting you yet." Blenda tried to return a friendly smile to her little apprentice but heard the lie in her own voice and turned her face back to the opposite wall to try to resume her count of the doors.

Edaline closed her smile but wrinkled her nose even more and tried to make sense of Blenda's odd behavior today. Usually Blenda came to wake her up before the sunrise and help her prepare for the day. Then they would go to the throne room together and conduct the kingdom's business. Today, though, none of that had happened. Edaline had lain in bed and only once she couldn't stand to stay in her bed any longer had she begun to wander the halls to find Blenda. Edaline had noticed that the castle was strange today too; never once during her search had she seen a single person when on most days she couldn't find a room that didn't contain three or four people bustling around. And now Blenda was saying funny things and staring at walls. Edaline tilted her head and wondered what could be happening today.

"Are we having a party?" she asked, still standing by the wall. Blenda slowly spun her head back around to the little girl.

"What?"

"A party. Like a surprise for someone? Is that why everyone is hiding?"

"No, dear. No party."

"Then where is everybody? They have to be somewhere. Are they hiding? Or did everybody sleep late like me? Oh! Is everybody asleep still? Should I go wake them up?" Edaline spewed the last few thoughts out excitedly. She loved to roam about the castle and discover all of the rooms, and the opportunity of doing that made her giddy.

"No, Edaline," Blenda curtly replied. Then, realizing her harsh tone, she spoke gently to Edaline. "Do come and sit down, dear." She extended her hand toward a now dejected Edaline and beckoned her over to the smaller throne at her side. Once Edaline began to slide over to her side, Blenda sighed heavily and apologized, "Now I am sorry for becoming short with you, dear, but I have much on my mind."

"Like what?" questioned Edaline as she slipped into her miniature throne. Blenda avoided her question and instead decided to try to explain the emptiness of the castle.

"Today we are going to have a quiet day. A quiet day for just you and me. Does that sound alright?"

Edaline tilted her head and wrinkled her nose again. She wanted to ask why or say no—the quiet did not really suit her—but out of fear of stirring Blenda's reproach again, she simply nodded.

"Good." Blenda smiled down at her little apprentice and then reached down on the other side of her throne and brought up a small, golden book. "Here, Edaline." She put the book into her small hands. "You can read this for now. It has much wisdom you'll find useful when you take my place." Edaline let the pages fall open and smiled her grimace up at Blenda. Only half satisfied with her shoddy job of appeasing the girl, Blenda forced her attention back to the quiet room. She shifted her gaze back and forth from wall to floor, then floor to wall, but never let her eyes touch the enormous doors that lay straight ahead of her. Her attempt at avoiding them, though, failed after several minutes of examining every other detail in the room. As reluctantly but longingly as a mouse drawn to cheese on a trap, she let her eyes settle on the huge wooden barrier between her safe haven and the rest of the world. The main doors were crafted from the same thick, luxurious reddish wood that the walls were crafted from, but the sweeping gold floral curves that wove their way up each panel made it hard to avoid their beauty for long. Blenda traced the gold paths in her mind, not caring where they took her as long as they did not come to an end. She rested her elbow on her throne, leaned forward, and laid her chin on her hand as she continued her wanderings.

This shift caught Edaline's attention, and she stopped pretending to rifle through her book. She peeked at Blenda from the corners of her eyes and examined her face. She knew today was different somehow and was sure that some sort of surprise was coming. She kept watching Blenda in what she thought was a sneaky way to see if her actions showed any signs of the surprise. Without realizing it, Edaline slowly leaned forward too and fully stared at Blenda's mesmerized face. The little girl watched the queen's eyes smoothly drift up, around, over, down, and every which way. She broke her stare to also look at what Blenda was watching, and the second her eyes flicked to the door, a low rumble—not just audile but felt in the soles of

3

their feet as well—rolled over the quiet room. Edaline's eye snapped back to Blenda, but she was not met with the anticipated comfort that the calm adult usually gave to her. Blenda's eyes had stopped their quiet journey and now were slightly widened and locked on one spot, straight ahead. Edaline frowned at the fear she saw.

"Ma'am?" she said softly, "Wha—"

"Edaline," Blenda cut her off without moving an inch, "listen to me." Another, slightly louder rumble shook their ears and nerves again.

"What—" Edaline tried again, this time in a frantic whimper.

"Edaline, listen to me." Blenda kept her eyes straight forward but laid a hand on Edaline's arm and gently squeezed it. "Go to my bedroom. Under the bed is a loose floorboard. Find it and move it aside." Another tremor broke out like raging thunder overhead, and Edaline let out a terrified moan.

"Ohhh! What?!"

Blenda finally turned her face to Edaline and looked straight down into her wide, green eyes. "Under that board is a little box. You bring that box here. Understand?"

Edaline tired to open her mouth but couldn't find words.

"Did you hear me? Do you understand?" Blenda was trying to keep her voice calm, but it came out rushed and hot. Edaline nodded vigorously and shook her arm free of Blenda's increasingly tight grasp. Blenda watched her black hair fly out like a sheet of night behind her as she fled out the same door she had come in earlier. Just as the door snapped shut, the tiny click was drowned out by another now deafening roar. Bits of sawdust and wood slid down from above and dulled some of the glittering blue swirls before her. Blenda tried hard to keep her stare on those tarnished spots, but the lure of what was coming dragged her eyes back to the huge wooden doors before her.

The din of the last rumble completely died, and she was left alone in silence once again. Then the doors began to crack open, and out of a strange mix of adrenaline and bravery, she stood to her full, impressive height to meet her adversary.

As the doors opened, a great light silhouetted the figure standing between them for a moment. Blenda squinted and turned her face a fraction away, but never let her eyes leave the form. Her mind began to race as the doors swung shut and the small figure of an otherworldly woman materialized in front of her.

"Blenda darling, it's been…," the small but fully grown woman smiled and showed a row of dangerously pointed teeth, "ages." She took a few steps forward, and Blenda was met with the full oddity of this woman. She could not have been over five feet but was very curvaceous, dressed in a form-fitting bloodred gown that spilled into a puddle over her feet. Her skin was the purest white Blenda had ever seen, even more bright and unblemished than snow, and her brilliant orange locks curled and twisted as if on fire. The most shocking feature was on her beautiful, porcelain face, though—her blind eyes. The two holes where eyes should have been were cloudy white orbs of nothingness, but they seemed to be looking right into her own blue eyes. Blenda couldn't help but frown in disgust at the odd sight in front of her.

"Clarice," she said with disdain.

"Oh, good! You've remembered," the woman gushed in a deep, rich voice with mock excitement, and Blenda frowned even more. The low purr that emitted from Clarice did not fit her small frame and added to her sinister image. "I really had thought you'd forgotten all about little me."

"Of course not. You are quite unforgettable."

"Oh, well, how flattering. I feel I should blush," Clarice playfully sighed and began to step closer. Blenda shifted her weight anxiously, and Clarice immediately halted, turning her ear toward Blenda. Then she let her eyes slide back onto her and smiled again. "Why so troubled dear, dear, Blenda? Am I unexpected? Surely you did not think I was gone for good?"

Blenda said nothing.

"Because so many did," Clarice continued. "I heard all sorts of nasty rumors about the terrible, evil queen being vanquished, lying down and dying, just giving up and letting the wonderful queen Blenda have her time. Isn't that sweet? Your people do love you, Blenda."

"Stop stalling and do what you've come to do. Go ahead and kill me," Blenda snapped at her, greatly disturbed by all Clarice seemed to know.

"Oh my, no need to become hasty, my dear. I'm not going to kill you—at least not yet." She grinned again. "We do have some time to catch up and chat, and isn't that what you enjoy—to surround yourself with lovely little people and have nice little chats?" Clarice's sickly sweet pretense was beginning to succumb to her true, malevolent self. Blenda shifted uncomfortably again, and Clarice twisted her head like a bloodhound catching a scent. "Ooh, struck a soft place, have I?" she hissed happily. "You of all people should know, Blenda, that I did not just fade into the night never to be seen again. You should have known I would appear before our time ended. You see, Blenda, *darling*," she vomited out the word this time, "even though I did not show my face to every living soul to assure them that everything was *all right* and *as planned* as you felt the need to do, I was still very well aware of the passing time and what was happening in all of Anelthalien around me. That is where we are so different, my dear. *You* believe that you should surround yourself with people, so many people, that in the end will simply let you down, and—"

"All of my subjects are loyal," Blenda heatedly interrupted. "You cannot make me believe one of them betrayed anything to you—you vile harpy."

"Oh, dear. That did sting," Clarice dryly commented with an unaffected face. "Anyway, you surround yourself with all your lovely subjects who trip over themselves to drink up your thin reassurances, and I choose to work entirely alone. And see where we both are now?" She spread her hands out and gestured around the huge, empty room. "We are each completely alone. Except I chose this way and you did not. So do tell me, what are you going to do now?"

A long, tense silence opened up like a chasm between them, and Clarice crossed her arms and tilted her ear toward Blenda again.

"I can wait, my dear."

"No, you can't.

"Oh yes, I can."

"You have as little time as I do."

"And how I spend it hinges, as you know, on how you spend it," Clarice slowly responded, letting each word sink into her mind. Blenda swallowed and tried to gage the time. Her day had passed so differently that she was unsure of just how much time they did have. Her thoughts were cut short when a small snap made both women twist their necks toward the wall. Edaline stood in front of the same door she had exited earlier, staring terrified at the newcomer and clutching a small wooden box.

"Ah!" Clarice purred, "And who do we have now?"

"No one," Blenda darkly replied to Clarice. Then she motioned for Edaline, and the little girl quickly scurried to her side and buried her face and treasure in her skirt.

"I'm scared," she whimpered into Blenda's dress, and the queen ran one hand over her small head.

"Shh, shh," she sighed down at her as she pried the box from Edaline's trembling fingers. "You will be fine. Just stay by my side."

"Oh, no, no, no," murmured Clarice brightly, "we must become acquainted, young miss. Do tell me, what is your name?"

Edaline unburied one eye for a moment, whined, and then dove back into her hiding place.

"No need to be shy...," Clarice began as she started forward again, but at the sound of her steps, Edaline let out an earsplitting bawl that echoed through the hall, and Clarice stopped her progress.

"She's an awfully noisy thing, isn't she?" Clarice grumbled with disdain, but Blenda didn't hear her comment over Edaline's extended wail. Clarice frowned as she tried without luck to distinguish any other sound through the girl's crying. "Blenda," she called angrily, "make that wretched child stop or I will!"

"Hush, hush!" whispered Blenda over her apprentice's head as she tried to detach her from her dress. Edaline ended her vocal wails but gripped Blenda's skirt tighter and kept her head hidden away in it.

"Now we really are running short on our time." Clarice suddenly took a quick, impatient tone, leaving all playfulness aside. "You feel it as well as I do I am sure, so Blenda, oblige me one small favor and tell me who that loud child is."

"No one you need to know of," Blenda insisted. Suddenly, Blenda swayed as she felt the room spin and knew she had to act quickly.

"Oh, dear. That is quite unfortunate," Clarice menacingly whispered. Blenda regained her balance as she watched Clarice turn her unseeing eyes up and then raise her white arm up also as if to sense how far the ceiling sat above them. In a second, she brought her arm down like a bolt of white lightning and another terrible rumble shook the whole room as a blinding light pounded the great skylight above. More sawdust and wood splinters tumbled down and rained on them all.

"I can bring this palace down upon us all, and you'll have no chance at carrying on your line—" Clarice began, but Blenda cut her off.

"Do what you've come to do—take my life and leave it at that." At this statement, Edaline began to screech again.

"Noooo! Noo-oh-oh-oh!"

"Cease, you obnoxious demon!" raged Clarice as she swayed back and covered her ears.

"NOOOO! NOO-OH-OH!"

Clarice raised her arm again, and this time when she brought it down, the thick glass above cracked like a thousand whips and a million lines spider-webbed across its surface.

"Take me and leave everyone else, Clarice!" Blenda yelled over Edaline and the thundering din.

"Oh, do not put on your show any longer!" Clarice snapped back as she brought down another fist and cracked the glass overhead even further. "I know who the child is and what you've brought her here for." Clarice swayed slightly and put out her arms to steady herself. As Blenda watched her, she felt the same dizziness shake her own body and felt a chill dance up her spine as she realized Clarice had never intended to kill her. She was definitely here for Edaline.

"No," she softly murmured as she closed her eyes to focus her balance. Clarice, though, did not hear her small plea and recovered her senses quicker.

"And now is the time to tell you my plan." Through fuzzy eyes, Blenda saw Clarice raise her pale palm and beckon. "You hand that child over to me and she becomes my heir."

"NOOOOO! NOOOO! NO-OH-OH-OH!!" At Clarice's words, Edaline increased her volume and began to shake her hands, causing Blenda to twist and completely lose her balance. The pair fell, and the wooden box tumbled out of her hand. Edaline had lost her breath as she fell, and so her wailing ceased. As the box hit the floor, its heavy clang rang out loud and clear.

"What is that?" hissed Clarice and turned her head jerkily back and forth to detect the noise. Blenda threw a hand over Edaline's mouth to keep her quiet. When Clarice received no answer, she became enraged. "WHAT IS THAT?!" she screamed and brought down another bolt from the sky. This time, the bright light completely shattered the glass canopy and rained blazing glass shards down on them all. In the midst of the chaos, Clarice darted forward and grabbed Edaline around the middle and began to drag her toward the huge doors. Edaline burst out with even greater volume right in Clarice's ear.

"YAAAAAAAA! NOOOOO! LET ME GOOOOOO!" the little girl screamed. She thrashed with vicious might, but Clarice held her with a ferociously tight grip. Blenda watched the pair slowly make their way to the doors and tried to raise herself up off the floor. As Clarice yanked Edaline's twisting and flailing figure further away, though, Blenda felt her strength fade even further. A thousand thoughts rushed in her mind as she continued her struggle against her failing body—had she waited too long, had she chosen the right path, would anyone come to see her before her life ended? Blenda closed her eyes and shook her head, trying to shake away those thoughts that didn't matter. Another wave of fatigue gripped her, and before she could shake off her stupor, her hand slid across the floor and would have slid completely out from under her if it had not hit the little wooden box. In the second her hot skin connected with the cool wood, her eyes popped open, Edaline's cries became muffled, and Clarice spun around. Blenda looked steadily ahead, right into Edaline's wide eyes, but curled her fingers around the box and brought it to her side.

"What are you doing?" yelled Clarice over Edaline's attempts to keep screaming through her hand, which she had slapped over the girl's mouth. "I can hear you, Blenda! Answer me! What—OW!" The hand that Clarice had been holding over Edaline's face suddenly shot in the air, and then before Edaline could suck in breath to take up another round of her wailing, it came back down, knocking violently into Edaline's skull and bringing another terrible rumble with it. Blenda kept watching, hardly believing her eyes as she saw what had been the cause of the thunderous roars. Straight down through the gaping hole in the ceiling, a gigantic pillar of fire twisted and then exploded when it slammed into the floor. It broke into a million scalding tongues that shot in every direction and began to devour the beautiful wooden throne room.

"WHAT IS IT?" Clarice was still screaming at Blenda from across the enflamed room. Blenda broke her eyes away from the destruction around her and squinted to see Clarice through the smoky black and bright orange haze. Clarice was still standing and facing Blenda, but her posture was beginning to give way to the weakness of oncoming death, and she was struggling to drag a now limp Edaline back toward the enormous doors. Still with her eyes set on the pair, Blenda pulled the little wooden box into her lap and passed her hand over the lock.

"Open" she whispered and then let out a terrible cough. The smoke from her burning castle was speeding her oncoming demise. She let out another horrible cough and then took her eyes off Edaline and Clarice to focus on the picture of hope tucked in the tiny velvet interior. She breathed in one last gasping breath and then spread one hand over the open box and coughed, "Send us help."

From across the room, Edaline rolled her head around, dizzy from Clarice's blow. She pulled open one eye to see the floor dancing and shimmering with light as never before. Edaline smiled, rolled her head to the side, and saw Blenda sitting in a crumpled heap on the floor with the little wooden box open in her lap. She tried to call out but found the air impossible to breathe. After a fit of coughing, she forced her eye up again and saw a light shine up out of the little box, illuminating her queen's face one last time. As the small glow faded, Blenda slowly slid sideways onto the floor and Edaline's eyelid dropped, and she slid back into darkness.

KINDLE

K indle stared out the window and watched another car slowly cruise down the street outside. She quietly sighed and snuck another look at the clock by the classroom door. It was still ten minutes until three o'clock. Dropping her head into her hand again, she stared back out the window. She had thought that high school would be so much better than junior high, but so far the first day of ninth grade proved otherwise. All day each teacher had done nothing but talk them through the rules and brief them about all the things they would learn just like every other first day of school that she had sat through since kindergarten. Kindle was quite irritated at the fact that high school was just like every other grade. She had imagined it more like college, where the teachers talk for a while and then let the students go free. Very early that day, though, she had found out that this year would be nearly the same as eighth grade—classes that were filled all the way to the bell with the teacher talking. The history teacher—who was standing at the front of the room, carrying on with his monotone lecture of why history mattered—was especially boring, and Kindle was beginning to wonder how she was ever going to stay awake in this class. She wanted to take another look at the clock but willed herself to still the urge and try to stare at her teacher, Mr. Franklin, and try to act like she was paying attention for the last few minutes of class.

"And you never know when or how it's going to repeat itself," he was saying, announcing every word slowly in the same tone and pitch, "so be careful to listen to our ancestors' responses to adversity and choices because you may one day be in the same situation as they once were. Now, does anyone have any questions? We're almost out of time, but I can answer any questions you have about the class, or we can discuss any current events that are on your minds." He stopped, crossed his arms, and peered around the classroom through his old, squinted eyes. "Any, any questions?" he mused almost to himself. Without taking her head out of her hand, Kindle examined the other students around her. No one seemed a bit interested in Mr. Franklin or anything he had to say; almost everyone else had assumed a similar posture that she had—their head propped up on a hand or torso slouched down in a chair, losing the battle to stay awake.

"Ahem," Mr. Franklin coughed, and a few of the lethargic students stirred. "I need you all to remember that class will not always follow this pattern. We will not outline the rules every day and therefore I expect tha—" Suddenly the bell rang, cutting off Mr. Franklin, and brought forth blissful life from every body that was nearly unconscious a few seconds before.

Kindle pulled her notebooks and purse into her arms, hopped up with everyone else, and galloped into the packed hallway. Despite how eager everyone had been to run out of class, what seemed like a million groups of teens now congregated in the hallway and refused to budge. Kindle slipped through the crowd until she felt a hand grab her elbow. Retightening the grip on her belongings, she twisted around and saw her best friend, Mallory, grinning at her.

"Kindle!" the little brown-haired girl squealed and locked her into an awkward, one armed, notebook-filled hug. "Girl, I haven't seen you in weeks! What's your schedule? Do we have anything together tomorrow?" she quickly spouted in one breath and then began searching through her belongings for her schedule. A large boy walked by and bumped Mallory's armload to the floor.

"Sorry, freshman!" he called over his shoulder as he kept walking.

"Ugh, boys!" Mallory fumed and bent down to gather her scattered folders and papers. Kindle knelt down to help.

"Have you been getting that?" Mallory asked Kindle as she snatched a syllabus from under a senior's foot.

"Getting what?"

"That whole 'hey little freshman' thing," she mimicked in a ridiculous, deep voice.

"No, nobody's really said anything to me except you." Kindle felt her face flush in embarrassment. Even though it was true that she had hardly any friends except Mallory, she really hated to admit it. Kindle longed to have a whole fleet of friends she could talk to and hang out with, but she just couldn't manage to weave her way into any of the groups of girls in her grade. The two girls finished their scramble and Kindle stood up and pushed Mallory's things back into her arms.

"Thanks, girl," she sighed and hooked her short, thin hair behind her big ears. "Hey, you are going to Emma's tonight, right?" she asked as they started to make their way to the freshmen lockers.

"What?" Kindle rifled through her thoughts, trying to remember who Emma was and why she would go to her house tonight.

Mallory put a hand on her forearm. "Do not tell me you don't know! Emma Anthony—you know, like everybody loves her and she's way cuter than anybody else, Emma—is having a pool party tonight at her huge house, and everybody is going. Well, everybody who's cool enough anyway." Mallory once again said her whole thought in one breath, and Kindle looked down at her wide eyed, taking in all she had exhaled.

"And we're invited?"

"Uh, yeah! In science, she totally asked me if I was coming, and I told her yeah and you were too, and she was like 'That's cool.' Isn't that awesome?" Mallory and Kindle had reached their lockers and Kindle opened hers before she answered.

"Um…yeah," she slowly mumbled, visualizing herself in Emma Anthony's pool laughing and having a great time with all of the coolest kids in the school. "Yeah, that's awesome," she finally agreed and grinned down at her friend who returned an eager smile.

"Oh, I'm so excited!" Mallory sighed as they closed their lockers and worked their way to the nearest door.

"Yeah," Kindle replied, happy for once that Mallory inserted herself into everyone else's business. "I can't wait to go. When is it?"

"Right after school. Oh, girl!" Mallory suddenly stopped and grabbed Kindle's arm again. "And you know who's going to be there?"

"All the cool kids. You said that alrea—"

"No, no, no! Well, I know, but I mean like somebody specific, like you-know-who." She whispered the last few words and gave Kindle a sly look. Kindle felt her blood rush to her face again in embarrassment.

"Oh, yeah," she mumbled.

"Yeah—Jeremy."

"Shut up, Mallory, I know who you mean, and I don't really care...." Kindle scanned the parking lot for her mother's van and hoped she could escape soon. She really wasn't interested in allowing Mallory to tell everyone about her chronic crush, Jeremy Linton.

"Oh, you do!"

"There's my mom. Bye," Kindle breathed with relief and jogged away from her friend. She pulled open the sliding back door and flung her purse and then herself into the window seat behind her mom.

"Hi hon, how was your first day as a high schooler?" Her mom gave her a smile in the rear-view mirror as she shifted the van into motion.

"It was okay." Kindle twisted around to see if Mallory was talking to anyone else in the parking lot, but couldn't find her in the crowd. She slumped back into her seat and tried to think of something to satisfy her mom's question. "It was really pretty boring. We just went over rules and stuff like every other year."

"Well, that's necessary. And it's only one day," her mother thoughtfully replied. "Do you have any classes with your friends?" she asked as she turned into a fast food restaurant parking lot.

"Are we getting dinner here?" Kindle asked, looking out the window, ashamed to admit that she didn't have any friends and glad to have an excuse to ignore the question.

"No, Kin, we're picking up your brother's cake," she said matter-of-factly and pulled her purse out of the passenger seat. "Are you coming in or staying in the van?" she asked as she opened the door. Kindle just stared open-mouthed at her mom—she had completely forgotten about her brother's birthday party tonight.

"Oh, Mom, Emma Anthony is having a pool party tonight at her house. Can I please go there instead of Mikey's party?"

Her mother gave her a look that made Kindle almost sorry for asking. "Kindle, you know we celebrate your brother's birthday after the first day of school every year."

"Yeah Mom, but Emma Anthony has never had a pool party on the same day, and Mikey won't care if I don't come. He never wants me around," Kindle protested.

"No, you can't go," her mother responded with finality. "I need your help at the party, and right now I need to pick up his cake. Are you staying in the van or coming in?" she asked again with one hand on the door and the other on her hip.

"Van," Kindle huffed and her mom tossed her the keys.

"Roll the window down if you get hot." She snapped the door shut, and Kindle slumped back in the seat and laid her head back on the hot, fuzzy headrest. Just minutes ago she had thought she had finally found her way into the elite circle of popularity and friends, and now she was doomed to a house full of sixth-grade boys revved up on sugar.

"Ugh, stupid Mikey," she grumbled and pulled herself up to the driver's seat to roll down the windows. She turned the key in the ignition and depressed the window button. The breeze from outside, even though it was warm summer air, blew relief into the smothering van. Kindle maneuvered her way into the passenger seat and spread her legs across the middle compartment onto her mom's armrest. Her mind churned as she thought of all the arguments she could try to convince her mom to let her go to Emma's pool party instead of her brother's birthday party.

When she saw her mother balancing the large ice cream cake across the parking lot in the side mirror, Kindle swiveled her feet down in front of her and leaned across the seats to open her mother's door.

"Oh, thank you. Can you hold this?" Without waiting for an answer, she pushed the giant, cold cake into Kindle's hands. Kindle started to place it on her lap but jumped at the chill it sent down her bare thighs and decided to balance it up on the armrest. As her mom restarted the van and let out an aggravated sigh at the time that illuminated below the dashboard, Kindle prepared to pitch her best argument.

"Mom, I know you said I had to go to Mikey's party to help, but what if I just did whatever it is you need help with and then went to Emma's?" She let it out quickly so her mom couldn't interrupt.

"Kindle." Her mom used a tone that made her name a whole sentence. "I already told you that you are not going to that girl's party. And who is this girl anyway? Emma? I don't think I've ever heard you talk about her before."

Kindle lost her tact and dove into a plea. "Please, Mom, this is *the* place to be. Everyone's going. Everyone! And if I don't go, I won't ever be cool or have any friends or any kind of life." She sighed heavily and then gave one more push. "Please, Mallory already told her we would be there."

Her mom sighed too, but it wasn't one of resignation. "No, Kindle," she said without taking her eyes off the road.

"Ma—om," she whined and let her head fall heavily back against the seat. "No wonder I don't have any friends."

"Kindle, don't be ridiculous. You have friends, and not going to this girl's party is not going to determine your social life."

"Yes it is!" Kindle picked her head back up, ready for an argument. "Mom, it is! If I don't go, then I'll be the loser who had to go to some dumb kid's birthday party instead of—"

"Kindle Marie," her mother interrupted her with a low but deadly voice, "you do not call your brother dumb, and you are going to his party. This is the end of the discussion. I do not want to hear one more word about that girl's party. Understand?"

Kindle didn't answer but huffed and glared out the window. She watched as a row of neat houses, all very plain and almost exactly alike, rolled by and thought how she was so much like them—just one plain face in a crowd that never caught anyone's attention. She changed her focus to her reflection in the side mirror. Her face was really nothing special—she had never thought of herself as ugly, but she also had never been called pretty by anyone besides her family. The blue-green eyes that stared back at her from an oval face surrounded by straight brownish-blonde hair annoyed her. They and every other feature she could see were just so obnoxiously average. Only her freckles that barely dusted her cheeks and gave them a slight blush were unique. She huffed again as she thought how everything about her was normal—she was average height, weight, build, even shoe size.

Kindle's mom softened when she heard her sigh and tried to soothe her. "There will be other times when you can hang out with your friends, but today is just a special day for Mikey, and I want you to share that with him."

"I'm a nobody," Kindle quietly replied as they pulled onto the road that ran in front of the middle school.

"Oh, Kindle, no you're not. You are very special to me and your father." She glanced over at her, bit her lip, and then added, "And Mikey. You're special to Mikey too, and that's why I want you at his party."

Kindle didn't reply; she couldn't bring herself to tell her mother what was really bothering her. Truthfully she didn't care about the pool party so much as the fact that she was just going to continue to be a normal, average, overlooked nobody. She didn't feel like letting her mom know, though, since she already didn't seem to understand why she was so deflated. Pulling her eyes off her plain reflection, Kindle saw Mikey and two of his best friends hurtling toward the van. They slammed into the side of the vehicle and ripped the sliding door open.

"Yah-hoo!" Mikey yelled as he swung across the seats and landed behind their mother.

"Mikey!" she called over his and his friends' yelps, "Mikey, Devon, Toby! Settle down, boys, or nobody is getting any cake."

"Cake?" Mikey grabbed his mom's seat and stuck his nose inches away from his cake. "Ice cream cake, Mom?! Really?!" He thudded back into his seat and high-fived Toby and Devon. "Yessss!" they all hissed together.

"Now I mean it, boys," their mom warned in her serious voice, "settle down and buckle up or else your father and I are going to share this whole thing along with your burgers."

"No, Mom, we'll shut up," Mikey quickly spouted and then slugged Toby for snickering and attempted to whisper, "Shut up, Toby."

"Michael, stop saying that."

"Saying what?" He smiled as he tried to trick his mother. She gave him an evil eye in the mirror and authoritatively clarified, "You *know* what. Devon, that seat belt is there for a reason."

Kindle heard the click of three seat belts and rolled her eyes. An afternoon with just the three boys behind her would be irritating, but she was going to have to endure a whole mob of them. As they drove home, Kindle continued to stare out the window at the different houses and wish she was going to Emma's party instead of her brother's. She knew, though, that she couldn't persuade her mother to give her freedom from what she guessed would be a very loud, obnoxious evening. The whispers, laughter, and random noises from the backseat made that very clear.

The van finally pulled into Kindle's driveway, and as soon as the engine died, she slid the cake onto both of her hands and dashed toward the house. An explosion of noise erupted behind her as the boys escaped from the confines of the van but soon melted away as she balanced the cake into the house and flipped the door shut with her foot. She took in the pleasant silence for a moment and then realized that the frozen cake was starting to numb her fingers. She swiftly carried it into the kitchen and laid it on the counter so she could rearrange the refrigerator's contents to make it fit. An irritated sigh escaped her as she popped open the fridge to find it stuffed full of everything her dad would need to make burgers later. Kindle pushed the door shut and stared glumly at the ice cream cake.

"Guess you're just gunna to have to melt then," she grumbled at it and headed toward the back door. Kindle pressed her face against the glass to see if her dad or any boys had invaded the backyard yet. Her father's grill was pulled up onto the porch, open and ready for charcoal, but no one was in sight. She cracked the door to get a better look around, and then after confirming the all-clear, she jogged across the porch and yard so she could reach the wooded area behind her house unseen. Even though it only was a three-tree-deep barrier between their house and the next, Kindle thought of this place as her own forest. These few pine trees had given her a place to play when she was young, and now it gave her a retreat of solace whenever she wanted to hide away from the rest of the world. She settled down on some roots protruding up from the thin soil and picked up a nearby stick. Tracing the outline of her flip-flop in the dirt, she laid her head on her knees and wondered to herself what all the other kids in her grade were doing at Emma's party. After going through several disheartening scenarios in her head in which she became the unknown loser of the town, Kindle heard a loud yell from her backyard. She looked up from her daydreaming and dirt tracings and saw that more of Mikey's friends had arrived and they were all invading the back patio. Kindle frowned. She wanted nothing more than to disappear and avoid her little brother's party and monstrous friends. A thought ran through her mind that if she climbed a tree right now, perhaps no one would be able to find her, and she really could skip the party. Kindle peered up into the branches above her and searched for a solid series of limbs that she could climb. As she scanned the dark canopy, a small glitter of light caught her eye. Dropping her stick, she pushed herself up out of the dirt and squinted to see just what had sparkled above. She caught sight of the glitter again and threw her arms around a branch on the tree in which it had appeared. She heaved herself up, rescanning the maze of wood above every few seconds to make sure she was heading the right direction. The little glitter kept shining for her, but she couldn't tell exactly what it was.

Finally Kindle reached a branch on the same level as her glitter, and she stretched herself flat out across it so she could bring her eyes nearer to it. Now she could see that it was a gold necklace tangled in the many twigs and needles sticking out of the end of the branch. The chain was brighter and finer than any other gold she had ever seen—it looked as if flecks of glitter had woven themselves together to create one long string of sparkles. Kindle hugged the branch under her tightly with one arm and her legs and reached out to touch to beautiful chain. As her fingers bumped it, the pine needles around it shifted, and the jewel on the end of the gold chain slid into view. Kindle caught her breath and wrapped her outstretched arm back around her supporting branch. She was terrified of sending it down onto the roots below and breaking or losing it. As she planned her next move, she tilted her head to examine the oval jewel that was now hanging below the branch's fingers. The flat back of the oval was made of the same glittering gold as the chain, but the jewel embedded in it was unlike anything she had ever seen. It was a fiery red and smooth with little striations like a fingernail that had just been polished, and right in the center was a little golden dragon. Even though the dragon wasn't any larger than a bottle cap, it was an incredibly realistic painting—the miniature eyes seemed to see her, and the unfurled wings appeared ready to fly.

Another yell from her backyard startled her, and she almost lost her grip on the branch supporting her. Kindle glared in the direction that she knew her brother stood and then returned her eyes to her newly discovered treasure. She sucked in a gasp of breath as she saw that her latest movement had freed even more of the necklace and now it hung on just one small twig. In one swift, impulsive movement, she threw her hand out to snatch the chain and kicked her foot against the tree behind her to propel her arm far enough to reach it. As her hand closed around the small oval on the end of the chain, she lost her balance and slid off the branch. She tensed her leg that was still wrapped around the branch and lurched to an uncomfortable and scratchy but thankful upside-down stop. Kindle threw her arms wildly around her head to determine if she could reach any branches and pull herself back upright. After hitting her wrist on the tree, she ended her flailing and slid the necklace around her neck so she could try to grab something and pull herself to safety. As the chain fell against her skin, though, she felt her leg slide away from the branch, and the world around her became a blur. She let out a scream in her terror and waited for the impact of the hard dirt and gnarled roots below.

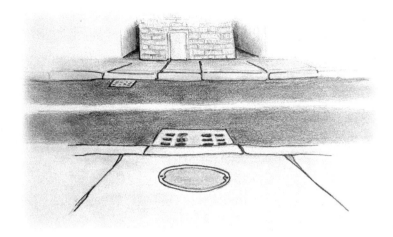

ANDREW

Andrew scanned the lunchroom, hunting for the best place to sit. This was the first day of school, and so no one had claimed their lunch table yet. In this moment he had to select a place he knew he would want to sit at all year and that no one else would want to sit at all year. He strategically decided upon a vacant table near the teacher's table and cafeteria door. No one ever wanted to sit at this table since it was right by the very humans that most of his classmates wanted to keep their business hidden from, and so it was the perfect table for him. Andrew—unlike most eighth graders in his school—wanted to sit alone and as close as possible to the teachers at lunch. He enjoyed the quiet and knew this would be the ideal position to deter Rob from coming anywhere near him. Rob was and always had been a bully, and due to his small, wiry frame, fair hair and skin, and his quiet, intelligent nature, Andrew was the favorite bully victim of Rob.

He carried his tray through the mazelike lunchroom and dropped it onto the empty table. Before he had a chance to sit down, though, someone else did the same directly across from him.

"Hi, Andrew," a short, chubby, brown-headed girl cheerfully greeted him and plopped down behind her tray. Andrew did the same and gave her a half smile. She eyed him as he began to twiddle with his fork.

"So how was your summer?" she asked, trying to be conversational, but Andrew sensed something else was on Natalie's mind. He shrugged and made a noise, which apparently satisfied her.

"Yeah, mine was good too," she replied, picked up her sandwich, and then drove ahead to the reason for invading his solace. "Um, so you know that we get to be in quiz bowl this year, right?"

"Yup," he mumbled, taking a stab at his tater tots.

"Yeah, and we get to go to the competitions and really compete." She blinked down at her sandwich. "Oh…that sounds dumb, but you know what I mean. We'll actually get to go on the trips, and we'll have a shot at winning."

"Yup." Andrew dipped a tater tot in his ketchup, examined it, and then popped it in his mouth. Students in seventh grade on the quiz bowl team weren't allowed to travel to the state competitions, and so not many people—only he, Natalie, and one other seventh grader named Brian—had ever showed up for practice. He knew that Natalie remembered that he was the one answering most of the questions and now wanted him to carry the team to glory in the competitions.

"So are you going to be in it this year? I think the first practice is next week. We get to start earlier because we actually have a reason to practice." She peered at him eagerly, still holding her uneaten sandwich over her tray, but Andrew simply stared at her as he put another tater tot in his ketchup.

"I'm going, and Brian said he's committed to the team if you are." Her voice pushed for an answer. Andrew dropped his eyes to his tray and found it all much more unappealing than it was minutes before. He had enjoyed being on the team last year because it was something he actually did well. Andrew hardly did anything well except being smart—he failed miserably at most sports, and all his attempts at music or art led everyone around him to cringe—and he truly wanted to be on the quiz bowl team this year but knew he couldn't. This year, unlike the last, the team would travel and that would cost money, something he knew he couldn't get. Ever since the end of the last school year, when his mother had died in a car accident, he and his father didn't seem to have much of anything, especially money. She had been the main worker in their house and, as a doctor, kept them pretty comfortable on her own. Until she died, though, Andrew had never realized just how much she brought to him and his father. All summer they hardly talked, and the happy family moments disappeared. His father, who had been a writer for a journal, had completely wilted after the accident, fell into a state of depression, and lost his job due to lack of good stories. Now his father was struggling to pay the rent and buy groceries, and Andrew knew that asking him for any amount of money was out of the question. He wasn't about to pour his story out over his and Natalie's lunch trays, though, and instead decided to pretend that he wasn't interested in the quiz bowl team.

"I don't think I want to this year," he sighed down to his sandwich.

"What?!" Natalie cried loud enough that a few of the teachers peered over at them. She blushed and then continued with a lowered voice, "But you *are* the team, Andrew. You are the best one we have."

"We've only ever had three people," he pointed out, and Natalie stared blankly at him for a few seconds. "You'll have more people this year," he quietly assured her and decided to try to finish his tater tots, even if his stomach wasn't hungry for them. Natalie kept staring at him with frustration on her face as he began eating again.

"Yeah, but you're *really good.*"

Andrew knew she was playing up his ego, but after years of Rob's bullying, he didn't have much pride to inflate. "I'm not."

"Yes, you are! You're the smartest kid in our grade—you know more than anybody else, and we *need* you on the team," she pleaded. "If you aren't on it, then we'll lose every time."

"Maybe I'll come to practice," he mumbled just to stop her arguments. Andrew knew that he wouldn't go to any of the practices or events, but Natalie didn't have to know that right now.

She perked up at his words. "Oh, good! Then maybe you'll decide to go to the competitions too." Natalie glanced at the lunchroom clock and commenced shoveling down the contents of her tray as quickly as possible. Andrew was grateful for her silence, even if it meant she had transformed into a messy garbage disposal, and also dug into his lunch.

For the rest of the school day Andrew's classes kept his mind busy, but as he walked home that afternoon, his conversation with Natalie crept back into his mind. Her last attempt to convince him to join the quiz bowl team had deeply jabbed him. He couldn't forget her voice saying, "And we *need* you on the team. If you aren't on it, we'll lose every time." In his mind, he knew she was probably right. Last year, Natalie and Brian had proven themselves almost incapable of answering questions that didn't relate to the current pop culture. They really did need his help to win anything, but he knew what his dad would say if he even tried to ask.

"We just don't have the money," Andrew mimicked his dad's words in a whisper at the sidewalk. He let out a sigh and picked up his gaze to peer left and then right before crossing the street. Even though it was just after three o'clock, the pavement on both sides was empty. This didn't come as a surprise to Andrew, though, since his apartment was in the older part of the city where not many people ventured unless they had specific business there. He put his head back down to stare at the sidewalk as he trekked on past the tall, dingy brick buildings. Some were and had been abandoned for years while others still held dying businesses or multiple cramped families. Very soon after moving into their apartment in the middle of the summer, Andrew had decided that he hated it and the whole neighborhood around it, but he knew that his father couldn't afford their old place just outside the city that they had rented before his mother had died. He had once begged his dad to let them go back, promising that he would find a job and help pay the bills, but his dad said the only phrase he seemed to know now: "We just don't have the money."

Andrew turned down another street, which was even more decrepit than the last, and readjusted his backpack. The load was heavy, but the weight was worth it because it meant books were coming home with him. A small grin picked up a corner of his mouth as he thought of how he would stretch out on the floor and forget the small, ugly, dirty apartment around him as he read about faraway or imaginary places. Andrew had always really loved reading, and over the depressing summer he had found if he could find a good enough book, he could forget about his mom dying, his dad losing his job, and the awful apartment around him.

A noise pulled Andrew up from his musings, and he lifted his eyes to see a terrible sight heading toward him. To anyone else, the kid riding his way on the old blue bike would just look like an oversized teenager in a sleeveless t-shirt and holey, faded blue jeans, but Andrew saw torment and pain radiating from a devilish smirk and those narrowed, gleaming eyes. This hulk of a boy was Rob.

"Hey, lemon head!" Rob called as he stood up on his pedals and popped his bike off the sidewalk and into the street. Andrew didn't answer but put his face down and proceeded to ignore him and walk as quickly as possible home. Out of the corner of his averted face, he watched Rob sail past him and then reappear next to him, pedaling slow enough to match his pace while sitting straight up with his hands in his pockets.

"Hey, lemon head," he repeated, "didn't ya hear me?"

Andrew said nothing; he had been harassed by Rob too many times to feed his fire. Rob leaned over his handle bars and took a long side look at him.

"Are you deaf, lemon?" he asked quietly, but Andrew kept ignoring him. "Hey!" Rob suddenly yelled and propelled his bike onto the sidewalk in front of Andrew, causing him to stop and stare directly into his enemy's squinty brown eyes.

"I heard you," Andrew muttered and tried to walk around Rob's bike. Rob pushed off the ground with his feet and sent his back wheel into Andrew's shin.

"Aw, man, did my tire get you?" Rob spouted with feigned apology as Andrew stumbled into the street and picked up his shin to rub it. The sorrowful look dropped off his face as Andrew dropped his leg and began limping forward to his destination again. Rob snickered and took up a new line of attack.

"Didn't see ya at school, lemony. You ain't switched out, have you?" Rob allowed him a few seconds to answer and then went on, "'Cause that would really make me sad to not have a wimp like you to see every day." Andrew was sure that a bruise was already forming on his leg but tried to walk even quicker. He was almost to his apartment building and knew he could shake Rob if he could just get inside. Andrew peered sideways to check Rob's position, and just as he realized that he couldn't see him or his bike, a sudden tug from his backpack jerked him a few steps in reverse. Rob had twisted a hand around his backpack's top strap to stop him and now began riding circles around him so that he had to pivot on his toes to keep upright. After three pirouettes that brought braying cackles out of Rob, Andrew forget his internal vow to remain silent regardless of what annoyance Rob delivered.

"Quit! Will you quit?!" he shouted and groped behind him to find Rob's meaty fingers. Rob only guffawed louder and continued his circles.

"Why you dancin', lemony? You should be a ballerina! You already look like a little lemony girl!"

"Quit, you idiot!" Andrew yelled and jolted to a halt.

"What did you say, you fairy?" Rob threw him down to the sidewalk, and Andrew's elbow mashed against the concrete. Andrew tried to pick himself up, but before he could scramble away, Rob jumped off his bike and came at him.

"What'd you say?" he demanded, grabbing his strap again, but Andrew decided that speaking was not a good option anymore. He wriggled his arms free of his backpack and began to sprint down the sidewalk, willing his throbbing leg to move faster. In only a few seconds, though, he heard Rob's huge tennis shoes beating down the sidewalk behind him and knew that he couldn't escape by outrunning him. When he was sure the flap of the bully's shoes was right behind him, Andrew darted to the right and watched Rob tumble past him with an outstretched arm. Andrew didn't wait to see if he turned around but quickly scurried over to Rob's bike and swung himself up on the seat.

"You pipsqueak, get off my bike!" Rob roared at him as Andrew began to try to work the pedals into motion but to his horror, found that the bike was not created for someone as small as him. Andrew jiggled his bum leg back over the bike to desert it in the street, but before he could break himself loose, Rob collided with him.

"What about that?!" Rob boomed as he sent a direct blow straight into Andrew's jaw. He tumbled backwards, falling on both his elbows this time, and grimaced at the shock of renewed pain that shot up his already damaged arm.

"Yeah, you little lemony. See what happens when you mess with me? I think *you're* the idiot." Rob let another gorillalike fist slam into the other side of Andrew's face, and he twisted onto his stomach.

"Ugh," he moaned and reignited Rob's glee.

"I bet you'll think now before you mess with me, huh?" Rob gloated.

Completely worn out of self-control and knocked out of better judgment, Andrew retaliated. "You're already enough of a mess without my help," he spat and immediately regretted it as the toe of Rob's thick rubber shoe smashed into his ribs and flipped him over again. Andrew, dizzy and gasping for the breath that had just been knocked out of him, blinked up at Rob. His squinty brown eyes glared down at him and his bottom lip slid sideways into an ugly u-shape. Andrew threw an aching arm over his eyes just in time to feel the wet glob of spit hit it instead of his eyes.

"Stupid lemon head," he heard Rob sneer and then heard his shoes flap away. Andrew kept his defiled arm over his face as the sounds of Rob picking up his bike, jumping onto it, and then cruising away played around him. Finally, sure his enemy had really gone, Andrew carefully slid his arm away from his eyes and watched it drop onto the ground beside him. He grated his skin across the rough sidewalk to wipe away as much of the spit as possible and then lay still for a few moments to catch his breath.

As blood started to flow through him at a slow, even pace again, he chanced sitting up but immediately collapsed back down on one side. The area that Rob had kicked felt as if it were shooting thick needles of pain through his whole torso, and the agony left him breathless again. Andrew didn't dare to look at the source of the pain, but gingerly put a hand to his right side and let his fingers carefully brush the skin. Bringing his fingers before his eyes, he examined them for blood but to his relief found none. He knew that as long as he wasn't squirting blood everywhere, he could lay here as long as he needed. The thought that maybe Rob had broken his ribs crossed his mind, and then he groaned thinking of how much the hospital would charge to mend something like that. Andrew picked his head up and twisted it to see if he could diagnose his side wound. Seeing nothing except the beginning of a bruise under his blue t-shirt where Rob left a dirty shoe print, Andrew let his head sag back to the ground. A bruise wouldn't be hard to keep hidden from his dad. So far, he had never found it necessary to tell his dad about Rob's bullying and wanted to keep it that way. Andrew knew his dad already had a heavy load weighing his mind down and didn't need his little problems adding to it. Not wanting to give his dad any reason to suspect something was wrong, Andrew resolved to get up so he wouldn't seem late coming home. He wedged his left arm under his body and slowly began to push himself up into a sitting position, but a shimmer on the sewer grate in front of him caught his attention, and he ceased his difficult ascent. A twinge from his bruised side brought his focus back to his task of picking himself up, and he broke his eyes away from the twinkle to finish it.

Once he was sitting upright with his legs stretched out over the curb, Andrew searched for the glimmer again. He found it—a thin bronze string draped over one of the sewer grate's bars. The sight didn't make sense to him, and he tried to reach out for the sparkling, clean string on the grimy metal, but his side immediately protested against any attempt to lean forward. Andrew groaned, put a hand to his side, groaned again at the pain created by his impulsive gesture, and planted his hand back down on the ground beside him. He closed his eyes and bit his lips together until the pain ebbed away and then stared up at the blue sky far above. An idea hit his mind, and he looked around to find his battered backpack. It was close enough to wrap a finger around and drag near him without reigniting the pain in his side. He pulled it up on his lap and dug around until he found the right object—a pencil. With the new, unsharpened pencil, he guessed that he could reach the sewer grate and pull up the shiny thread to see what it was. Andrew carefully reached forward with the small tool and could almost touch the glittering bronze. Out of fear of moving his side, he brought his arm back and readjusted the pencil so that he held it tightly around the eraser. Andrew tried again and this time could dip it down and loop the string around the pencil's tip. He dug his short fingernails into the eraser and slowly lifted his arm. The thin bronze string was much heavier than he expected, and he began to wonder if it was more than just bronze-colored. He pursed his lips together and flicked his eyes back and forth between the tilting pencil and the end of the thread. When he was almost sure that he couldn't lift his arm any higher without dropping the pencil, the end of his treasure came into view. Quickly and smoothly he yanked his arm back and let the pencil and thread drop onto the sidewalk in front of him. Andrew stared down in wonder at what he had fished up out of the sewer, completely awestruck by his discovery.

The thread wasn't a thread at all but a chain that connected to a thick, intricately decorated oval of bronze. In the middle of the oval was a domed yellow gem too smooth to be a diamond but just as brilliant as one. The jewel's brilliance was interrupted by something on it, but the shine radiating from it hid it from his vision. He picked it up by the chain and dangled the pendant in front of his eyes. The sight piqued his curiosity and wonder even further—a tiny picture of a long snake, or maybe a dragon, was painted on the stone. It was a marvelously lifelike painting, and the bronze dragon seemed to swim back and forth on the stone as it slowly rocked in his palm.

Andrew placed it back on the sidewalk and put his pencil back in his bag. Staring down at it, he suddenly felt a small stab of sadness. Surely this necklace belonged to someone, and if he took it, that person might find him and accuse him of stealing it. He chewed his cheek uncomfortably, unsure of what to do with it now. He began to pick it up and then snatched his hand away to hold his backpack strap. After a few more seconds of pondering if its owner would even know where to look for it or be able to find it in the huge city, in one motion he grabbed it up, slung it over his neck, and tried to stand, but the hurt in his side resurged. He let out a pained gasp as the ugly city around him blurred and the sidewalk seemed to drop out from under him.

ELLA

E lla spun around to scan the busy, candlelit room spread out in front of the long wooden bar. Her eyes danced from table to table, checking each patron for signs of need—a face peering her direction, an empty plate, or a raised mug—but at the moment everyone seemed appeased. The concentration on her face faded, and a smile took its place as she gathered up the dirty mugs on the bar and whisked them into the back room to be washed.

"Oy, where you bringin' all these mugs from, girl?" joked a plump, ruddy woman standing beside the large sink where Ella dumped her load. "We got a full house out there then?"

"Yes, seems like the whole kingdom's here tonight." Ella's smile grew wider as she spoke. She was thrilled that tonight her father's inn, the Lighthouse, was packed with customers. Almost every wooden table in the front dining area held at least one person, and most were occupied by groups of townspeople who had recently made the Lighthouse their regular haunt. The steady increase of customers was due to the downpour that had begun a few weeks ago and since then had refused to stop. The incessant rain had driven all of Garrick Kingdom indoors and many of them into the Lighthouse. Even though Ella desperately wanted to see the sun again, she was glad that her father profited from the dreary days and she kept busy with her work.

"Go on then, Miss Ella," called the woman at the sink, pulling Ella out of her elated distraction, "if they's all out there, then you best goin' and seein' about them."

"Alright Sara." Ella laughed and hurried back into the dining hall. As she swung open the door, she began to assess her tables once again. She almost decided all was well, but a mug rocking back and forth on a table in a dim corner caught her eye. After catching up a pitcher of tea, she agilely slid through the mazelike room to the swaying mug. Even though the cup was active, the man holding it was not. Drawing near him, Ella sighed as a familiar ragged torso and shaggy head slumped over the table crept into view. Ella stood over him for a moment shaking her head and then placed a finger on his mug to stop its motion. She felt the cup pitifully jerk a few times, and then the dirty hand holding it slouched away from the handle. It slid across the table and dragged the man's limp, greasy locks away from his face so his eyes could squint around to see the reason for his mug's new resistance.

"Oy, Miss Ella," he slurred up at her when he finally found her. The man placed both hands on the table to push himself up. "Wha ya doin' wi' me cup?"

She smiled sympathetically down at his blurry eyes and flushed cheeks. "Oh, Barnes," she sighed, "you are drunk, aren't you?"

Fabin Barnes, the very dirty, drunk man before her, came alone almost every day to the Lighthouse and quite often drank himself silly. He had always been a melancholy man who tended to try to drink away his depression, but once the unending rain began, he had drifted into an eternal state of gloom and attempted to drink himself to sleep at this table nearly every night. Ella felt sorry for him since she knew his sadness flowed from his inability to find a job and care for his family, who now had left him, and tried very hard each night to rouse him out of his stupor.

"Ah, oh…." He drifted to the left and then pulled himself center again. "No! No, not drunk. No. An' I think I haven't got any in me cup." He pulled his mug under his nose to check. "Nah, lookie there, I ain' got a thing to be drunk."

"Barnes," Ella said firmly and he gazed up at her open-mouthed. "You have had too much. I'm not giving you any more alcohol."

"Oh, Mis' Ella," he groaned, "don' do tha' now. Just gimme one fill more an' I won' ever ask ye for another thing, I promise." Barnes shakily held his mug under her elbow and prodded her with it. "Jus' one more." He continued to quietly beg as she stared sadly but sternly down at him.

"No, you don't need it and…." She pushed his mug to the table and leaned down so she was at his eye level. "You already owe my papa more than you can pay him." She stared steadily at him and tried to determine if he had understood. Unsure if his blurry eyes had captured what she had implied, she tried a more direct approach. "Barnes!" she loudly called, making him jump and stare wide-eyed at her. More quietly Ella continued, "You have no money. I can't give you any more to drink if you cannot pay for it."

"Ah." He bowed his head and patted his coat pockets. Ella straightened up and watched his sad search.

"You can't stay here, Barnes," she quietly informed him after a few moments, "you'll drink yourself dead."

"Aye. An' maybe I'll be better off 'en," he mumbled as he shrugged. Before Ella could rebut him, she heard a mighty yell from behind her.

"BARNES!"

The whole inn fell quiet, and all eyes turned to the source of the shout. A short but very stocky, red-faced man was huffing through the crowd toward Barnes' table. Even though his head was losing hair, his cheeks and chin were hidden behind a thick, bright orange beard and mustache, and they made him appear even more irate than he was. He began to shake a meaty fist at the decrepit man as he neared the table, but Ella put her hands out and caught his shoulders to stop his approach.

"Papa," she cooed gently, "please don't throw him out. He's got nowhere to go." Her husky father tried to push her hands away, but she was quicker than him and kept returning them to his heaving chest.

"He owes me too much money to be comin' in here and drinkin' me dry," he growled, trying to see around Ella. "Barnes!" he shouted over her shoulder and pulled a paper out of his apron pocket. "Barnes, you see this?! This is your tab for the last month! Just the month! And you haven't paid me a single coin of it!"

"Papa, please," Ella begged, still holding him away from the wide-eyed Barnes.

"No!" he yelped into the air, shaking the paper. "No! You have worn my charity too far, man! You pay or you get out!"

"He doesn't have any money, Papa," Ella interjected in a whisper. "Please, if—"

"NO!" he roared again, refusing to listen. "If you have no money, you have no service! Get out of my inn, Barnes!"

"Ey, Marin, come now, don' be puttin' me out." Barnes protested from his table, and Ella turned and gave him a tight-lipped look to tell him to stop. His drunken mind didn't understand, though, and he simply squinted at her questioningly. Ella blew out her cheeks and returned her face to her father before he could explode again.

"Can't he stay just for the night, Papa? He's terribly drunk and has nowhere to go—I'm afraid if we push him out, he'll die in the street."

Marin gave Barnes one last threatening look and then spun and tramped away toward the bar. Ella followed him and kept up her appeal for the poor man.

"Or perhaps he could work in the washroom to pay his tab?"

Marin still didn't reply as he pushed his way through the swinging doors into the back room.

"Papa!" Ella cried in frustration and he finally stopped. "Why did you make such a scene as that anyway? Now all of Garrick knows poor Barnes' troubles."

"I had to make it known," he turned to face her, now with a somber face, "tha' no one would cheat me out of my service."

"But like that? Yelling and shouting?" she incredulously asked.

"Yes, like that, my dear. I have to let the people know they must pay for what they get. I know old Barnes doesn't mean any harm, but I just can't let him have his fill every day and night without payin' for a thing!"

"He could work it off—work here in the washroom." She spread her arms out and looked around.

The woman at the sink peered at them and scoffed, "He ain' comin' back here with me, the lout."

"Sara!" Ella flapped her arms down in frustration.

"Well he ain't. 'E wouldn' work!" She shrugged matter-of-factly and went back to rinsing dishes.

"Yes," Marin affirmed, "he would not work. Child, that is why he's in his mess—he won't pick himself up out of his mug and work. I can't let him go on. He's got to get out." Marin threw up his hands to curb any protest she could bring. Ella dropped her shoulders and fell quiet. The sound of the rain pounding on the wooden roof above filled the silence, and soon jovial voices from the dining room crept in as well. Marin turned to plod away to the kitchen, and Ella took the opportunity to catch him off guard.

"Can he just stay the rest of the night?" Her words made Marin stop and tense his broad shoulders.

"Oh, 'ere we go," murmured Sara.

"Just to sober up, Papa. So he won't catch an illness or run out in front of a cart or—"

"Serve 'im right it would," Sara chortled.

"Hush!" both Ella and Marin shouted at her.

"I was only sayin'," she defensively replied and kept eyeing the two to see the outcome. Sara was usually the lone witness of Marin and Ella's arguments and enjoyed commentating on the spectacle.

"I won't give him anything but hot water," Ella quickly assured her father. "He just needs some time to come to his senses, and then I'll send him on his way."

Marin's shoulders heaved up and then slowly back down. He made a low growling noise and then broke. "Urg, you soften me too much, my girl," he grumbled, still facing the other way. "Let him stay the evening then. But only till he's sharp enough to keep himself out of the gutter!"

"Thank you, Papa," Ella gladly sighed and then to cover up Sara's snickers, added, "I'll go tell him of your kindness."

She spun and headed out the door as her father let out an agitated bellow. "Don't you be tellin' tha' Barnes I got any kindness for him!" She smiled to herself and left him to face Sara's newly erupted laughter.

As Ella reentered the front of the inn, the murmur that had been swelling hushed and many uneasy eyes peered over at her. Knowing that all was well, she found the uncomfortable silence amusing and couldn't stop her face from cracking into a grin. She laughed, whisked a pitcher off the bar beside her, and hoisting it in the air, cried, "Who needs some more?"

The whole room caught her elation and burst into jovial calls. As mugs jumped into the air and hands beckoned, Ella diligently swept the room, taking inventory of each need, and then dove in among her customers. Dancing from table to table, she quickly filled orders and mugs, collecting many more tips than usual. Her father's threat apparently hadn't fully left the buyers' minds. Before long, the whole room was filled with hearty chatter and brimming mugs once again. Ella smiled at her expeditious work and then sighed as she remembered Barnes. She took up a water pitcher in both hands and carefully carried it to his corner. He had slumped back down over the table, and for a moment she feared he really *had* died, but when she finally reached him, he stirred.

"Hello, Barnes," she gently greeted him as she poured steaming water into his mug. "Papa's going to let you stay until you sober up."

"Uh?" He picked up his head to watch her pour the water. "Wha's this?"

"Careful!" She caught his wrist to stop his eager hand. "Barnes, it is very hot water and—"

"Water?" Tha's it? Tha's a bad joke on me, Mis' Ella."

"Yes, water. And it's all you can have."

He squinted up at her. "Wha' now?"

"The water is free," she slowly explained. "Papa says it is all you can have unless you come up with payment for your tab."

"Ah." He turned his deflated face to his mug. "Ah."

"And it's hot, so be careful."

"Ah," he sighed and then fell silent. Ella began to turn away from his pitiful figure, but he spoke again.

"Can we 'ave a song?" He was still staring at his cup, but she knew he was talking to her. When the rain had begun and dreary faces filled the Lighthouse each night, Ella had taken up singing to keep her spirits aloft while doing her duties. One night while she was carrying a tune around the inn, a woman had requested that she sing a song for the whole company. Ella, glad to cheer her neighbors in any way she could, had obliged by climbing onto the bar and singing the tune the woman had suggested. Ever since then, she piped out happy melodies almost every night and on occasion long into the night. Barnes, though, despite his routine attendance at the Lighthouse, never had joined in the gaiety. For him to ask for a song was quite uncharacteristic, and Ella repeated his request to make sure she had heard him right.

"A song?" she asked in disbelief.

"Aye." Now he finally turned from his mug to peer up at her. "Do ye know anythin' sad, Mis' Ella? Anythin' tha' woul' match me sad heart?"

"Oh, Barnes…," she began softly as her chest filled with compassion.

"Do tell me ye do." He stared off into space again. "I jus' need ta know I ain' the only…," he trailed off and Ella waited, wanting him to finish.

"Barnes?" she finally prompted, but he kept his face turned and voice silent. "Yes, Barnes," she gave in, "I know one. Do drink your water. I'll go and sing it." Ella turned and made her way through the room, not really hearing or seeing it. A faded memory from a long time ago was filling her mind. An old, old woman's blurred face that felt like leather under her small fingers was all she could see and feel from the memory, but the words that the woman sang were clear. Ella sat the pitcher on the bar and then pulled herself up on it. Even though she didn't announce herself, the crowd was used to this motion and soon hushed. She waited until the beating rain was the only sound and then let her own voice sing the old woman's song:

You have no love, you have no home,
Child you were made to always roam,
You have no love, you have no light,

Child you were made to hide your face within the night
Oh-oh-oh, oh-oh-oh,
Child of whispers, child of woe, you have nowhere to go,
Child of sorrows, child of fate, oh the world turns its face,
Into the night you must go, run far away from home,
Here you cannot stay, for death is on its way,
Oh child of whispers, child of woe, you have nowhere to go,
Oh-oh-oh, oh-oh-oh, oh child you have no love.

Ella sang the mournful tune once and then again, staring not at the inn but into her memory, trying to wipe the mist away from the old woman's face. As she finished the second round, though, Ella gave up the effort and brought her focus back to the bemused and solemn faces gazing up at her. She nodded to indicate that she was done, climbed down from the bar, and wove through the silent room to Barnes. He didn't look up at her but spoke up when she reached him.

"Thank ye." The slur in his voice was fading now. "It does me heart good ta know I ain' the only soul tha's so full o' sorrow." He tapped his mug handle, and Ella noticed he had drunk the water.

"You're welcome, Barnes."

"Who tau' ye tha' one?" he asked, still tapping.

After a few moments, she murmured, "I don't know ... I heard it a very long time ago when I was very young."

"Aye. They stay wi' ye, them sorrowful ones. They don' leave."

"No." Ella blinked hard and cleared her throat. "No, they do not."

Barnes abruptly ceased his tapping and shoved his hand into his coat pocket. Ella eyed his rummaging until his hand reemerged as a fist and jumped onto the table between them. He rapped on the wood a few times and then stared straight at her.

"Ye done me much goodness," he told her with difficulty and then—quicker than she knew he could move—Barnes stood and slouched to the door. Ella watched his silhouette hunch against the rain outside and then disappear. She kept her eyes on the door as it swung shut and heaved a sigh. The weight of telling Barnes he had to leave was lifted from her heart, but the knowledge that he really had nowhere to go replaced its heaviness. Ella dropped her face to his table so she could clear it, and a whole new emotion shot through her. Lying where his dirty hand had been just moments ago was a sparkling copper mass. She stared at it with surprise, almost afraid to touch it, but curiosity urged her fingers to slide across the shining metal. The touch nudged the copper, and Ella saw it was a long, fine chain as it fell away from the lump it covered. Unable to restrain her wonder from the newly uncovered gem, Ella slid her fingers under the brilliant emerald oval and made it dance and catch the candlelight. It was a strange thing—the necklace she examined. Even though the smooth green oval surrounded by the beautiful copper was as lustrous as a gemstone, it was opaque and so smooth that Ella wondered if it was a stone at all. More curious than the green oval, though, was the tiny painting upon it. Ella ran her thumb over the small copper reptile posed in mid-stride, and a smile pulled up a corner of her mouth. She had heard tales of dragons in Anelthalien and so, although she had never seen one, knew this must be what they looked like.

Suddenly remembering the inn around her, Ella dropped the necklace into her long vest pocket and swung her eyes around to check the state of her customers as she gathered Barnes' empty mug. No one seemed to have noticed her distraction. In fact, she sensed that most faces were purposely averted from her. Ella felt her cheeks heat and shook her long auburn hair back from her face to try to assume a more cheerful, easy demeanor. She dodged through the tables toward the washroom, collecting a few more dishes along the way. When she finally burst through the swinging door, Sara mumbled, "Easy now" and raised the corner of her mouth in a smirk. Ella sighed the feigned cheer off her face and dropped her armload into Sara's sink. The washwoman used the sleeve of her rolled up shirt to wipe some suds from her chin and looked Ella up and down.

"Wha's wrong with you?" she questioned in her usual rough, untactful manner. "You look all bothered, girl."

Ella knew Sara well enough to understand that even though she sounded insulting, her comment was out of concern.

"Erm…." Ella wanted to release all the emotions swirling inside of her but wasn't sure how to go about it, especially since Sara was known to gossip about everything she could. Before Ella could decide, Sara nodded down at her pocket.

"Wha' chu got there?"

"Hm?" Ella followed her stare down to the copper chain peeking out of her pocket. "Oh!" she exhaled and thought about trying to quickly hide it but knew Sara would persist. "I think it's how Barnes means to pay us." Ella reluctantly fished the necklace out of her pocket as she spoke. "He left it on the table."

Sara let out a gasp when the emerald oval slipped from its hiding spot. "Why, ain't that right pretty!" She wiped her sudsy hands on the towel slung over her shoulder and caught the jewel between two fingers. Ella gripped the chain tighter as Sara examined it.

"Barnes left it, eh?" Sara let it go and crossed her arms. "Did the ol' man say what it's worth?" she slyly questioned and then without waiting for an answer, interrogated, "Or where he got such a thing? 'Cause knowin' him, he probably pinched it."

"Sara!" Ella cried reproachfully and balled the necklace into her hand.

"I was jus' sayin'." She put her hand up defensively. "You know he ain' got a coin to his name, so how's else would he go about gettin' somethin' like that?"

"I don't know, Sara, but that's awfully presumptuous—"

"Not really."

"And anyway," Ella continued, ignoring her interruption, "he's given it to me, so—"

"Wait—to *you*? I thought you said it's his payment."

"Well, yes, but—"

"But this, but that," Sara flippantly chortled, "but wha' did he say when he handed it over?"

"Nothing, Sara," sighed Ella, exasperated from Sara's questions. "I told you, he just left it on the table."

"So he's left then?"

"Yes."

"And he left that behind?"

"Yes."

Sara's eyes glinted greedily. "Well. I 'spose it is yours then. Unless you're givin' it away to Marin."

"Yes," Ella resolutely replied, "I'm giving it to Papa." She tried to stuff the necklace back into her pocket, but Sara laid a hand on her forearm to stop her.

"Now, don' be so hasty there. Let's have a see of how it looks round your neck."

"No, Sara. I'm giving it to Papa. I have no business wearing it."

"I ain' sayin' keep the thing there forever, child. I just want to see how pretty it can sparkle with them green eyes you got."

A small smile lifted a side of Ella's face, but she dropped her eyes to the impartial floor to search for a decision. The wooden slats didn't help much, and the compliment pushed aside her reluctance to indulge Sara. The grin spread across her face, and she retracted the necklace from her vest. "Do tell me how it looks."

"That's my girl!" Sara laughed heartily and stood back to view Ella. "Is like it was made for you, that gem, matchin' your eyes an' all. Just be a shame not put it on, even if only once," Sara began babbling, "An' you know Marin, him and his soft heart to you, he'll probably let you have it anyways."

Ella lifted the necklace over her head and saw Sara smile and open her mouth to gush about how she looked in it, but Ella never heard the words because as soon as the delicate chain hit her skin, the washwoman and washroom blurred out of sight.

Tad

A dark-haired, dark-skinned, tall, athletic-looking boy slouched slowly across a beach, kicking rocks and sand into small explosions in front of him. He had spent much of his time at this lonely place over the summer, just wasting away the hours. It was one beach that none of the Florida tourists were interested in due to the great amount of rocks and weeds buried in the sand, but he liked it. The ugly beach's ability to repel most people attracted him to it. Its loneliness made it quiet and peaceful—two things he couldn't seem to find anywhere else. Every other place he went to was full of people yelling at him.

As he meandered forward, he readjusted his messenger bag that was slung over one shoulder and frowned down at it. The bag was old and worn out, but it was the only thing in his house that he wasn't embarrassed to carry around school. Even though it was only the first day of school and he didn't have any books in it yet, the strap was fraying at both ends and threatening to drop the bag. The only aspect of it that he didn't find ugly was the word he had scrawled across the flap in sharpie marker. It was his name: Tad. He scowled down at the shabby lump and punched the air out of it.

"Stupid bag," Tad muttered under his breath as it exhaled. He returned his attention back to his slow trek over the rocks and, seeing that he was running out of beach, veered off toward the shoreline. He didn't really have a destination but simply wanted to go anywhere except home. Tad tilted his head back and huffed into the air. Even though he would never admit it, he would even rather stay at school than go home, but the school day had ended—just like every day would all year—and now he had nowhere to go but his house. Still wandering along the rocky beach, he thought seriously of never going home and actually finding somewhere else to live. The idea of running away had always tempted him, but fear had always stopped him. Now, though, he was sixteen, a sophomore, and nearly old enough to drive and live on his own. It wouldn't really be running away from home—that was for kids—it would just be moving out. A half grin climbed onto his face, but he sniffed it off and bent down to pick up one of the small, smooth rocks. While tossing it in his hand to assess its weight, reality crept into his mind and assured him that he was never going to move out, run away, or be able to do anything to get away from his grandma and sister. The two women were the only people he lived with, and he despised them both. His little sister, an annoying preteen named Jamie, was just a whiny brat, and he could stand to live with her for a few more years, but not his grandma. As the emotion attached to her surged through his mind, Tad clenched the rock in his fist and then chucked it as hard as he could out over the ocean. He watched it spin through the air, skip once, and then drop between the rough waves. Glaring at the unaffected water, he let the scene that he knew would ensue once he arrived home play out like a movie in his mind.

He would come in, and his grandma would start to yell at him. According to her, he was a loser and a failure who could never do anything right. He could almost hear her voice shouting at him.

"Where have you been? Out up to no good? I bet you didn't even go to school today, you worthless, stupid…."

Tad slammed his tennis shoe especially hard into the ground and sent sand granules up into a cloud.

"Stupid sand," he hatefully grumbled as some settled into his shoe. Carefully balancing on his other foot, Tad emptied the shoe of sand. Once he finished, he decided to strip off his other shoe and his socks as well to avoid any more sand attacks. He dropped his bag on top of his footwear and resumed his walk closer to the ocean now that he didn't have to worry about the tide soaking his shoes. As he watched his bare feet, his mind slid back to his mental movie. His grandma would keep berating him, letting him know how much of a waste he was, and Jamie, who would probably have come straight home from school to watch TV, would join in the shouting. His sister yelled no matter what she said, and it was highly obnoxious.

"Yeah!" He knew she would take his grandma's side. "He didn't go to school me-maw! I never saw him! I bet he skipped!"

Then he would push his luck and yell back at her, "Shut up, Jamie! Nobody asked you! You don't even go to my school!"

"Now you shut up!" his grandma would yell, "I won't have none of your mouthing off! You don't talk to your sister like that!" Then he would give up the fight because he never won against his grandma and stalk off to his room and slam the door. His grandma would continue to belittle him through the wood, bang on the door a few times, and then start yelling at Jamie to quit watching cartoons, but Tad wouldn't hear it. He would have already shoved his earbuds into his head to drown out her raging. And he would spend the rest of the night locked in his room with nothing except his music to keep him company.

Tad stopped and stared down at the water rhythmically hiding and revealing his feet. He really wished that it wouldn't happen that way, but it always did. Every night was always a shouting match won by his grandma. She always won because he and Jamie were afraid of her. Neither of them would ever say it, but he knew it. He and his sister had too many times been the victim of her physical anger to fight back. Her violent rages were the reason why Jamie yelled—Tad had watched his grandma frequently club her head to convince her to stop crying—and why Tad locked his door every evening. His grandma had always acted like they were a thorn she wanted to yank out of her side. Ever since his mother had left him on her front porch and then had done the same thing a few years later with Jamie, his grandma had let them live with her but never let them forget that if the state wasn't paying her good money to keep them, she would kick them right out into the street. Tad was sure that she hated both of them and only kept them around so she didn't have to work. He squatted down to pick up another rock, flung it into the water, and started searching for better rocks to skip as he thought even harder about leaving his grandma's house. It had never really occurred to him that moving away would be the best way to return the many blows she had dealt him. His absence would mean that she would only get half as much money. Tad smirked as he found a particularly smooth, flat rock and sent it hopping over the waves. He nodded to himself; he was definitely going to make sure that he was out of that rotten hole as soon as possible.

Now confident in his ability to skip a rock over the restless water, Tad snatched up another rock without looking, and was about to send it spiraling away when he felt a warm tickle on his wrist. Quickly, he thrust out his arm to see what had brushed his skin and saw that a long, thin chain was dangling from his fist. He moved it closer to his eyes to inspect it and saw that it was extremely clean and shiny. It was silver like most jewelry chains, but something about the way it glittered made him think it wasn't some cheap metal. He flipped the chain into his palm as he fanned open his fingers to see what it was attached to. Tad blinked at it, surprised to see not the rock or goofy charm that he had expected, but a large, brilliant blue gem. He ran his finger over the surface to affirm that it really was as smooth as it looked and then traced the woven silver loop that encircled it. Both looked real, but he doubted anyone would leave anything valuable lying around the beach. How it came to the woebegone beach in the first place was a mystery to Tad. Of the many times he had walked over this shore, he had never seen another living thing besides a few seagulls. He swept his eyes all around just to make sure he hadn't missed anyone while he was busy kicking the sand and skipping the rocks but found no trace of any person. Turning his attention back to the jewel in his hand, he peered closer at the picture in the middle of the rounded surface. It showed a tiny dragon, and Tad noticed that whoever had painted it must have spent much time on the details. He could see each scale on the monster's arched back, the flare of its nostrils emitting brilliant orange flames, and the tensed muscles surrounding its deadly claws. A huff of wonder escaped his lips, and Tad almost let his imagination tell him that it was something from a fairy tale, but then he shoved back his childish awe and stuffed the necklace into his shorts pocket. He knew better than to get his hopes up about anything, especially something as silly as kid stories. It was probably just some cheap necklace, he told himself, not worth anything to anybody. Tad paced back over to his pile of shoddy belongings and slipped his feet back into his socks and shoes, taking care to avoid getting sand in them. He slung his bag back over his shoulder and began to amble toward the street above the lonely beach.

As he ascended onto the pavement and looked around, Tad saw that the sun was already sinking. He had spent more time than he had realized drifting along the beach. His grandma would be furious, but she always found something to be angry about no matter what time he finally slipped in the door. Shoving his hands in his pockets, he quickened his pace. Even though he didn't want to go home, he did want to make sure his grandma didn't call the police to bring him home. She had done that a few times before, and the aftermath was never fun. Unconsciously, he began toying with the necklace in his pocket. Its smooth surface attracted his fingers to it like a bee to honey. The small round bump was almost calming to rub. Tad continued to slide his thumb back and forth over it his whole journey home.

Once he reached his house—a decrepit, grungy cube—he decided to try to sneak in his room and pretend he had been there for hours. Tad kept one eye on the front windows while using the other to navigate the sidewalk. Glad to spy no movement, he slunk into the alley between his house and the neighboring one. As he reached the side of the house, he crouched down and dashed under the windows. Silently he curved around the back of the house and straightened up. Only two windows looked out over the backyard—his and Jamie's—and he knew neither would have anyone in them to see him. The windowsills were higher than the ones in front—just about level with his chest—but he knew this height wouldn't cause a problem. Tad had used his window as a secret entry and exit many times and so had no problem quietly jimmying the screen loose and sliding up the already partially open glass. Now the hard part came—getting in without making any noise. He decided to push his bag through first and ease it down onto his low futon cushion. A slow puff of air told him that he was successful, and he let the handle drop inside as well. Next, he jammed the screen through the hole. The old screen had suffered through this treatment several times and took it as well as possible. Once it fell through, he sucked in a deep breath. Then in one smooth motion, Tad threw his arms over the sill, pushed himself up until he could throw a leg inside, and let the momentum throw him onto his bed below. He grunted as his back ground into the corner of the screen and quickly fished it out from underneath him. Kneeling on his bed, he swiftly returned it to its home and then flopped down on his back. The entrance made more noise than he would have liked, but he could hear Jamie's television shows blasting and knew that he was safe.

Tad pulled his old iPod and headphones out of his bag and proceeded to pump his music into his ears. To settle down in the most comfortable position possible, he mashed his messenger bag into a lump for a pillow and kicked his legs up against the wall. The necklace he had found slipped out of his pocket and settled on his futon beside him. Tad felt it knock lightly on his side and picked it up. He stared at it for a while, examining the dragon on it, wondering where the weird piece of jewelry had come from. When he became tired of holding it up, Tad laid it on his stomach and closed his eyes. Sleep slowly spread over him and shut his mind down.

A sudden loud yell shook him out from his leisurely position, and he rolled off his cushion onto the floor.

"What do you mean you don't know?" his grandma's loud voice rang out. Tad pulled out his earbuds; they were silent now. He tossed them and the iPod that had apparently reached the end of the playlist onto his bookshelf.

"How am I supposed to know where he's at?" Tad heard Jamie yell back. It was her typical loud way of talking, not an agitated yell.

"Ooooh, when he comes through that door, I am gunna kill that boy!"

Still on tensed all fours on the hard floor, Tad waited for more. The silence extended, though, and he began to wonder if he should emerge from his room or stay hidden. Either way he knew his grandma would not be happy when she did see him. He closed his eyes to think and decided that it probably was best to show his face now rather than let her anger fester. Dropping his head in defeat, he opened his eyes to see the necklace lying under him. He huffed out an angry puff of air—the thing's persistence to be noticed was really starting to bug him. Just to keep it from bothering him again, he snatched it up and swung it around his neck. He had planned to get up and make a nonchalant appearance in the living room, but suddenly his room blurred and standing became impossible.

DANICA WOODS

Kindle's scream echoed around her as adrenaline tensed her muscles. She waved her arms over her head to try to find a branch to grab and suddenly smashed her elbow into the ground. Immediately her scream ended and her eyes popped open. Moss lay just inches away from her nose. Kindle dropped her flailing feet and arms down on the squishy green carpet, and her mind began to race as she tried to manage her breathing. Somehow she hadn't felt the impact of her fall. Kindle anxiously put a hand on her head and wondered if she had been knocked out. Slowly propping herself up on her elbows, she assessed her condition. She didn't feel dizzy—that was good—and she didn't feel any pain. The thought to check her hands and knees occurred to her, and she quickly examined her palms for any sign of a scratch, but they held no mark. Kindle flipped off her stomach and sat up. Her legs also showed no sign of injury. She frowned in confusion then irritation as she followed her legs down to her feet and saw that one of her flip-flops was missing. Looking up, hoping to find it stuck in the branches she had fallen from, her eyes grew wide. She slowly brought her frozen face back down and let her eyes dart back and forth. This was not her backyard.

Not one tree looked even vaguely familiar. In fact, a whole forest lay around her full of sights she had never seen before. The soft, spongy ground under her was less like moss and more like a million tightly curled blades of thick, soft grass, and as she peered closer, she saw that each one seemed to be a different shade of green. Bright neon sprigs melded into dark olive curls and then into bright emerald as the little plants twisted across one another. This strange grass covered every inch of the ground in the clearing around her and even climbed up and around the giant roots protruding from the dirt at of the edges of the circular area. From their exposed, mammoth roots to their towering height, the trees surrounding her were completely unlike the evergreens near her house. The roots that gracefully arched up from the green sea and dark soil were as thick around as Kindle and were covered with the same glossy, mahogany bark as the hulking trees towering between them. Kindle turned her round eyes up again, following the massive trunk closest to her. As she craned her neck, she wondered if they were redwoods but at the same time knew this place could not be California. With her eyes, Kindle traced the maze of giant branches higher and higher until they faded into the thick canopy of dark green leaves. The lofty, dark ceiling and huge trunks continuing in every direction made her feel very small and alone. Fear began to creep into her throat as she wondered where she was. All she knew was that she was not in her backyard or anywhere near it. Kindle drew her bare legs against her t-shirt to hug them.

"Hello?" she attempted to call out, but only a squeaky whisper escaped. "He-hello?" she tried again with slightly more success. Kindle wasn't sure if making her presence known was wise, but she had no idea of what else to do.

"Hello?" This time she managed to let out a loud voice, and when no answer came, she gained more confidence.

"Hello! Anybo—ahh-oo!" Kindle sprang up and tumbled backward into one of the enormous roots. A boy had just appeared from nowhere right beside her. She slung an arm over the root to steady herself and gaped at him. He was a thin, pale, blond boy and was likely just a little younger than her. Kindle couldn't make out much more about him due to his odd position—he was frozen in a sort of hunched crouch, as if he was in the middle of standing up or sitting down. Suddenly he collapsed to his knees, groaned, and put his hands down to stop his face from hitting the ground as well. Kindle jumped, but fear kept her tied to her root. She watched him for a few moments, unsure if she should help him or run away. Too curious and scared to move, she did neither.

"Hey," she cautiously called, "hey, are you, uh, okay?"

The boy didn't say anything but tilted his head to see who had spoken. The movement apparently hurt because he quickly dropped his forehead onto the moss and wrapped an arm around his chest. Another groan issued from him, and Kindle gripped her root tighter, still uneasy about him.

"Hey, um ... what's your name?"

"Whe—Rob—" he panted just loud enough for her to hear, and Kindle relaxed slightly. Knowing he had a normal voice and name eased her anxiety about his strange appearance.

"Rob," she said loudly and slowly, "are you okay?"

"Na—Rob—" He waved his free hand. "An—drew."

Kindle was confused now. She decided to just not use his name, whatever it was. "Um, are you going to be okay? Are you sick or something?"

"Go—home." The boy tried standing again but only succeeded in sitting with his knees bent in front of him and propping his elbows on them. Now Kindle could see him clearly. She grimaced; Rob—or whatever his name was—had a nasty bruise on his face, and the front of his t-shirt was dirty as if he had been rolling on the ground. The thought that he had probably just come from a fight blossomed in her mind, and her stomach dropped. She impulsively began scanning the area for his assailant, but the gigantic forest around them was utterly silent and still. Another groan from the boy brought her attention back to him. He was trying to stand again.

"Maybe you should just stay there," Kindle warily advised. She was worried someone else was lurking nearby and didn't want him making noise to give away their location. The boy didn't seem to hear her, though, and carefully stood, mashing his eyes shut against his pain.

"I need—" he breathed heavily, "to go—home."

Kindle released her secure root and edged toward him. "Where do you live?" She had no intention of wandering around to find this boy's house but very much hoped his answer would tell her where they were.

"An old apartment." He pointed past Kindle "1843 on Bradford." Kindle started at him with wide, skeptical eyes and slowly craned her neck over her shoulder in the direction he was pointing. Just as she had expected, the mahogany trees still towered behind her as far as she could see. She raised her eyebrows at him and watched him rub his forehead with his fist.

"Seriously?!" Kindle couldn't help but loudly rebut.

Her sharp remark shook him alive, and he raised his head up and frantically waved his face around. His turning suddenly stopped, and a look of awed terror melted over him. Slowly, he let his eyes take in everything, gazing up and down the titanic trees just as Kindle had minutes ago. When his wide eyes met Kindle's, they flicked down to her feet and then back up to her face.

"This isn't Jersey," he said matter-of-factly and then in the same tone, "You only have one shoe." She gave him a suspicious look, and he averted his face from her to instead take in every other object around them.

"Yeah," replied Kindle, unable to believe that was all he had to say. From the unaffected way he spoke, it seemed as if maybe he was accustomed to popping up in strange forests. With no idea of what to make of him, Kindle simply watched him continue his examination. His eyes were extremely quick—darting up and down, this way and that, taking in every detail. They never stopped but just kept moving as if they were reading everything. Kindle noticed, though, that he took special care not to allow his eyes to travel near her. Feeling ignored, she shifted uncomfortably.

"Where are we?" she asked, trying to get him to talk to her or at least look her way. His eyes ceased their investigation but remained focused on a tree in front of him. He quickly shrugged and immediately sucked in his breath. A hand instinctively flew to his side, but he arched his back to avoid its touch.

"Are you…," Kindle began, but the necklace that now freely dangled in front of his curved chest stole her words. It was similar to the one she had discovered—a glittering oval on a long, fine chain—only different colors. Her fingers floated upward to check for the gold chain that she presumed was still hanging from her own neck. As she touched it, the odd silence created by her unfinished sentence finally pulled the boy's attention her way.

She watched his eyes peer at her from their corners and then follow her fix-ated stare to the necklace hanging under his chin. Very gradually, hesitant realization melted over his face. His eyes, slightly dangerous and nervous now, flicked back to her. Straightening himself up again, he wrapped a fist around his yellow gem. The boy worked his jaw, as if he wanted to say some-thing, but kept silent.

"Where'd you get that?" Kindle quietly asked. For a while he simply stared at her fingers toying with the necklace and continued to nervously move his lips. Sensing the tension between them, Kindle uncomfortably shifted her weight. She wished he would say something—her mind was fly-ing down a million trails, trying to answer all of the questions she had, but just kept tumbling into even more questions. When she was about to burst out another, more rude inquiry, he opened his mouth.

"I'm Andrew."

Surprised, Kindle automatically responded, "I'm Kindle."

A less tense air rose between them.

"You don't know where we are," he stated. Kindle gave him a strange look, unsure of how to reply. Andrew had spoken as if he was telling her a fact, but the sentence was a question.

"No, I don't know," she decided to slowly answer.

"But you put that on to get here."

"Well yeah, but." Kindle crossed her arms in agitation, thinking maybe it was better for him to not talk. "But I didn't know that this was what would happen. It was in a tree, and I had to put it on so I wouldn't drop it. If I had known I'd end up here, I would have left it alone."

"You just found it?"

"Yeah, that's what I just said. In a tree." Kindle was enjoying snapping back at him, but when his cheeks flushed and he turned away, she felt a pang of guilt for her sassiness.

"Well, what about you?" she asked, now trying to be polite, "Did you find yours in a tree or, like…." Kindle stopped herself from asking if he had fallen out of a tree. She doubted that would coax a laugh out of him.

"I just saw it on the street," he mumbled with a shrug.

"Okay...and then you popped up here, right?" Kindle was determined to keep him talking. To her frustration, Andrew nodded.

"So, um, do you know where *this* is?" Kindle clarified by waving a finger around. "You know, like, where we are?" Again, Andrew answered nonverbally by shaking his head. Then he slowly eased himself back down onto the spongy turf. Annoyed, Kindle let her sauciness return.

"You're not being very helpful," she snapped.

"I don't know anything, okay?" Andrew suddenly retorted and then glared at her. She tried to mirror his angry stare, but guilt attacked her again. An apology was on the verge of escaping her lips when a small sound distracted her. It reminded her of something like a tinkling giggle, but as Kindle swung her head around to scan the forest, she saw nothing except the giant mahoganies stoically standing around her. Wondering if Andrew had created the sound or heard it, she covertly watched him for a few minutes. His focus was completely on his side though. Andrew kept gingerly poking his t-shirt near the footprint, wincing, and then testing a different spot. Kindle observed him repeat the odd cycle a few times before she became convinced he neither had uttered nor detected the tiny noise. Taking her eyes from him, she squinted around again. Everything stood perfectly still, almost eerily quiet and still. No birds or bugs flew by, and no wind shook any of the branches or leaves overhead. The trees that extended in every direction and then faded into blackness were the only living things in sight besides Andrew. Now unsure if she had really had heard anything at all or was only scaring herself, Kindle sighed and melted down onto the ground as well. As soon as she did, though, the same giggle—only louder this time—sounded from nearby. Andrew questioningly glared at her, and relief twisted into her apprehension as she realized he must have heard it also. To wave aside his silent accusation, Kindle shook her head. She crawled closer to him, causing him to wrinkle his nose and lean away from her.

"No—hey," Kindle whispered, shaking a calming hand, "listen, that's the second time I've heard that. Somebody else is here, like watching us or something."

Andrew stared at her blankly for a few seconds and then without turning his head, pulled his eyes as far left and right as he could.

"Where?" he whispered back.

"What? I don't know where. But didn't you hear that laugh—I know you did." Kindle peered between the trees as she spoke.

"Yeah." Andrew nodded, but then a strange expression washed over his face.

"What? Did you hear it again?" she breathlessly urged. Although Andrew didn't say a word, Kindle understood the reason for his slightly alarmed stare when she turned her head to follow it.

A woman was floating behind her. The fact that she was levitating, though, seemed banal compared to her bizarre appearance. She was no more than two feet tall, and instead of one long torso, two round, black and yellow striped bulbs joined together to form her body. Two thin black arms that ended in pointy hands protruded out of the sides of the top bulb and matching twiggy legs extended from the front of the lower one. Also strange was her hair, or really, the lack of it. It seemed to only sprout from two points on the back of her scalp and was gathered into two tight dreadlocks that raced forward over her crown then broke away from her forehead and swayed in the air above her. Out of her entire body, the woman's head appeared most human; besides her pointy chin and shiny, jet black color, she had a normal face. The expression the little woman wore was also strangely familiar, as if she was a distant aunt who was ready to pinch her beloved niece and nephew's faces. She made no move but simply grinned merrily down at Kindle and Andrew as they gaped up at her.

"Oh!" she suddenly squeaked, putting her thin fingers on her cheeks. Kindle and Andrew both jumped at her high-pitched shriek, and the woman let out a tinkling laugh. Then she dropped to the ground, clasped her hands together, and recommenced to fondly smiling at them. Now Kindle could see how she had been floating. Two large oval pairs of wings, now immobile, poked out of her back. Altogether, the tiny woman resembled an overgrown bee. Kindled sensed Andrew trying to stand up behind her and did the same. At once the bee woman ran toward them with outstretched arms squealing, "Eeeeee!"

Kindle instinctively side-stepped, not realizing that she left Andrew fully exposed to the woman's approach. He had almost straightened fully upright when she tackled his legs and sent him back down onto the ground.

"Urff!" he groaned and clutched his side.

"Sorry!" Kindle gasped and nervously bit her lip.

"Sweet, sweet children!" cried the bee woman, squeezing Andrew's legs. "Oh, we've waited so long! So long!" Her wings buzzed behind her as she hugged Andrew tighter. Kindle hesitantly took a step toward them. Now that she knew the odd creature could speak and was almost positive she was friendly, Kindle decided to talk to her.

"Um, hi." She waved awkwardly as the woman's face turned to her. Andrew grunted and attempted to free himself from her choking embrace.

"Oh, um, I think you're hurting him. You uh … yeah, that," Kindle mumbled as the bee woman released Andrew.

"Oh, so sorry. Sorry so. I just—oh!" She sprang into the air right in front of Kindle's face. "So happy!" she shouted and placed her hands on Kindle's ears. Ducking back, Kindle tried to grin but felt disgust show on her face. Suddenly the thought that this woman might know where they were crossed her mind, and she swallowed her discomfort.

"Do you know where we are?" she quickly asked and received a bemused stare from the woman.

"Where we are?" she repeated, and then her silly grin snapped back on her little black face. "Where you are, and I, and he, and we are is…," she twirled up in the air and then swept her arms out with a flourish and finished dramatically, "is Danica."

"Danica," Kindle blandly repeated. She had never heard that name. She tried to catch Andrew's eye to see if he had recognized it but saw he had lain back down on the soft grass.

"Danica," she said again up at the woman. "And where is that at?"

The little black face stared down at her, and the woman dropped to the ground. "What do you say, child? Where do you say is Danica Woods? It is where it has been for always."

"What state?" Andrew groaned from his back, and Kindle nodded in understanding.

"Yeah, like, what state are we in?"

"State? I know nothing about the state of things beyond the woods."

"What country?" Andrew tried again, his voice a little more hesitant, and Kindle felt his nervousness; she was slowly realizing that they could be very far from their homes and possibly America.

"Country!" the odd woman cried and her small black legs danced. "Oh surely, yes, yes, children, you I do understand now! Danica Woods is in the west of Anelthalien!"

Kindle stared blankly at the gleeful little woman. She wanted to ask where or even *what* Anelthalien was, but fear of the answer kept her silent. She glanced at Andrew for help but saw that he had flung an arm over his eyes. The woman started making short, high-pitched sounds again, and Kindle deeply sighed as she turned to her.

"E-e-e, o-o-o," she chirped to herself as she jigged in a circle. Noticing Kindle watching her, she stopped and grinned. "Sooo happy!" she squealed and in a second sprang aloft to hover close to Kindle's nose.

"But you are not, I do see," she mused, and the silly joy evaporated from her voice as it softened. "So why child? Surely this meeting of I, and you, and he is happy and so good. But child, the face you wear is sad. So why?" She continued to hover in front of her face so closely that Kindle could see her distorted reflection in the woman's black eyes. Deep discomfort ran through her, and she took a step backward.

"Where are we?" she shakily cried and then, hearing the fear in her own voice, lost all the bravery gathered in her. "I want to go home. I don't know what this stupid place is, but I want to go home, okay?" she half-shouted her plea at the bee woman, who simply blinked at her. "Is it this?" Kindle heard Andrew stir as she grabbed the charm hanging from her necklace and shook it. "I put this thing on and now I'm here! Why? Can you tell me that? And he's got one too!" Kindle pointed an accusing finger at Andrew. She could feel her fear and anger heating her face and pushing tears to her eyes, but she blinked them away. "What is this place? Why are we here? And what are these?" she demanded with finality and shook the red gem at the woman again. Receiving nothing but a shocked, agape mouth, Kindle commenced to searching for the clasp on the necklace so she could remove it. She thought that surely if putting it on had caused her home to suddenly disappear, taking it off would bring it back. That was how this sort of thing always worked in movies. To find the clasp, she wildly spun the chain around and around her neck until it became painfully clear that no clasp lay on it. Feeling the others' eyes staring at her, embarrassment crept on her, and she ceased her search but kept her fingers tightly on the thin metal. Determined not to look up and face the tiny woman's probing stare, she locked her eyes on the glittering gold and let her mind slow so her growing fear wouldn't overwhelm her. Then, Kindle remembered that she had never clipped the necklace on but had slipped it on. She closed her eyes, sure this was the way to return home, and blew out a sigh of relief as she brought the necklace up and over her head. Her hair cascaded through the chain and fell around her neck. Now Kindle was positive that when she opened her eyes, she would be in her backyard under the familiar pine trees.

"Questions you have are so many. I have no answers," that tiny voice squeaked.

Kindle slowly opened her eyes and turned her defeated face to the small woman, who was looking quite helpless herself. When their eyes met, Kindle immediately shifted her gaze to the strange moss still under her feet. A few moments of silence passed through the group as Kindle attempted to shut the others out of her vision. Cutting them out of her sight made her feel as if she could be alone and that gave her some shelter from the insane reality that she was trying hard to ignore. As she closed her eyes against the woods, an odd sound pulled her away from her solace. It was a low buzzing noise gradually increasing in volume. When Kindle cracked open her eyes to search for it, she saw Andrew was squinting up at the bee woman as if he suspected the sound to belong to her. The little woman saw him staring at her and flew to his side.

"Child! So sorry I am. Not thinking—do you hurt?" she apologetically blurted as her tiny hand flitted over him.

"No—shhh," he whispered, and she dropped down on her knees by him, still patting him lightly.

Now sure she wasn't imagining the noise, Kindle also knelt down beside Andrew and murmured, "What is that?"

Andrew propped himself up on his elbows and scanned the space around them. Seeing his actions, the little woman mimicked him then waved her hands in excitement and eagerly asked, "Oh what?"

"That sound—do you hear it?" Kindle cautiously whispered.

"Noise? Sound?" she chirped and Andrew hushed her again.

"Buzzing," he breathed, and suddenly the woman perked her chin up like a dog that had caught a scent.

"Bu—oh! Ahh!" she cried as she shot into the air at the same time the noise became clear and a black blur slammed into her. Andrew and Kindle both let out a gasp, exchanged alarmed glances, and then scrambled away from the now very loudly buzzing tangle at the foot of a tree.

"Missi!" a male voice cried from the black heap, and another bee creature, that except for his slightly larger size looked almost identical to the woman, sprang away from the tree's roots. Realizing the two were obviously acquainted, Kindle stopped her and Andrew's fearful retreat.

"Missi!" he yelled again, this time much more sternly. "I thought you had ... I told you not to wander! Too young! You are too young to be out on your own! I told you to stay with me, and then—gone!" the little man ranted in a parental manner, shaking his finger down at Missi, who was sprawled wide eyed over the tree roots. "I have told you again and again that the woods is dangerous—"

"Ah Misson!" she broke through his words, "Worry, worry over me you do too much."

"No, no, no," he quickly retorted, "we had *orders*—directly from Rex himself—to stay *close* and stay *together*. You broke orders, Missi, *you* should be worried, not me." He crossed his black arms across one of the thin yellow stripes on his chest.

"Oh, not mad! No, not mad Rex will be!" Missi cried, and Kindle could see she was grinning again. "So happy he will be when we show him my findings!" She buzzed up to Misson's height and caught his face between her hands. Andrew chuckled, and Kindle flashed him a quick grin—she could tell he was also glad to see someone else caught by Missi's excitable hands.

"Oh quit!" Misson grabbed her wrists and pulled her arms down. "What, Missi? What could you have possibly discovered that would remedy your insolent behavior?"

Missi smiled wider and pranced in the air. Then in one movement she stilled her feet, leaned forward, and whispered, "Heroes."

Kindle felt her brow scrunch and, taking a sidelong look at Andrew, saw she wasn't alone in her confusion. "Us?" she dared to breathe his way. Andrew simultaneously shrugged and nodded.

"Heroes?" Misson bluntly responded. "What heroes, Missi? What are you babbling about?"

Missi shook a hand free and pointed a tiny finger at Kindle and Andrew. Misson's head slowly swiveled their way, and before either of them could move, he set his eyes on them.

"Guh!" he shouted, flew backwards into a tree, and then darted to Missi's side and began to pull on her shoulder.

"Missi! Those are humans! *Humans!* Come, we must hurry to the Tunnels!" He continued to paw at her, but Missi slipped out of his reach and flew between Kindle and Andrew.

"No, Misson, we have no need to flee." She placed a hand on each of their heads as if to keep them from escaping. "Heroes, these children are. Heroes so long awaited for! And Misson, I have found them, so to Lord Rex and Lady Luna we must all go."

"Yes, Missi, they are children," Misson cautiously replied, almost as if he were reassuring himself. "Why you are calling them heroes, though, I have no idea."

"And neither do we," Kindle quickly chimed in, and the bee woman turned a surprised expression to her.

"Guh! It speaks! Oh, Missi, stop your silliness—we must go."

"So rude, Misson!" Missi snapped back at him. "Children speak of course! *You* are full of silliness." She darted to the middle of the clearing but then hung there, looking at each of them with a pleading face. "Oh, but children, you are," she insisted, "you must be the heroes we have awaited so long for."

"Missi! Stop it!" Misson wagged his pointy finger at her. "Stop saying that. *They* do not even know what you mean." He sighed angrily and started toward her, but she zigzagged out of his reach. "Missi, stop. We are going back to the Tunnels."

"No, no, Misson, you *do* know—the heroes of the good kingdom—the ones who teacher Gustin tells so much of."

"Oh, Missi, no. Not one of old Gustin's legends." He shook his head and banged a fist on his forehead. "You know those are just stories he tells. Not a one is true."

"It is!" she cried. "You do not ever believe him, Misson! Nothing you do not say is ever true, you say, but he tells truths!"

"What makes us heroes?" The question from Andrew silenced everyone and put all eyes on him. Missi flew near him and gazed at his face.

"Child so silent, so deep," she murmured, touching his lips, and then said so they all could hear, "Gustin tells many stories, but truth he promises of only one. He tells that when the time is near, heroes summoned by a fallen queen will come bearing the marks of the four makers of Anelthalien." She looked to Misson. "And these marks they have." Missi turned back to Andrew and pulled on the chain around his neck so that the yellow gem fell into her hands. Kindle watched the irritation on Misson' face slowly dissolved into wonder. His awe at Andrew's necklace sparked her curiosity, and she slid her red jewel into her palm. Misson's eyes immediately moved to her.

"Hux?" he breathed, and Missi let out a joyous squeal.

"Oh, you see now, Misson! It is true you see!" She darted to him and encased him in an embrace. "See now why they must come with us to Lord Rex and Lady Luna?" Before he could say a word, she charged Kindle and lovingly grasped the necklace between her hands. "And, child, they will answer your questions, I know it. They are wise."

"Missi?"

"Yes, Misson?" she spun to face him but kept Kindle's necklace tightly in her fists.

"I believe we must do as you say." Misson's hesitant, quiet tone let them all know how difficult the statement was for him to utter.

Missi spun upward, shrieking with glee and then zoomed to one of the trees behind Andrew.

"Come, children! We will together go!"

"Go where?" Kindle questioned, suddenly aware of her fear to leave the clearing. She was sure that if they wandered away through the trees, she would never be able to return home.

"The Tunnels, our home," Misson answered, his confidence back now. "We must present you and the marks you carry to our lord and lady. They will know what to do."

"What do you mean 'to do'?" Kindle asked. She was resolved to stand firm until she knew what was going to happen.

"You are here to save the land, these necklaces prove," Missi excitedly spouted as she buzzed over their heads. "But how, we do not know."

"She means that we and our people, the Cifra, do not need heroes—we know of no trouble here in Danica." He paused to frown and look away. "Few of us know what lives beyond the Tunnels, though."

"Yes, so to Lord Rex and Lady Luna we go," chirped Missi, unaffected by Misson's gloom. "Answers only they will have." She flashed them a silly grin and then transformed into a black, buzzing blur as she zipped away between the trees.

"Come!" they heard her distant voice squeal.

"Missi!" fumed Misson, "Missi, return! They cannot fly at your speed!" When no answer or woman came, Misson folded his arms and glared sideways at Andrew and Kindle. "Will you come, bearers of the ancient marks?" His voice was serious, but Kindle couldn't help feeling as if he was mocking her. She was considering saying something sassy in return when Andrew spoke.

"Sure," he mumbled and shrugged.

"Then follow," Misson commanded as he began to trace Missi's direction at a much slower rate. Andrew slowly started trudging after him but stopped at the edge of the clearing.

"They want to help. And I think they can," he told Kindle, who was trying her best to give him an irritated glare.

"Yeah, well, all you care about is your sore side. You don't know anything more about them than I do," she grumbled angrily.

"But I will," Andrew murmured just loud enough for her to hear and then resumed following Misson. After only a few seconds, the sounds of buzzing and his steps faded. Kindle sighed, huffed, and crossed her arms in agitation. She was annoyed with him for answering for her and now leaving her alone. She wanted to run after them but was still unsure about following two strange, giant bug people to some place probably just as weird as them. Somehow, she felt that if she stayed right where she was, she still had a chance of reversing whatever magic had swept her away from her backyard. The fear of leaving the spot, though, was giving way to the fear of staying. The more she considered how she was now standing completely alone in an absolutely foreign place with no idea of where to go or what could be lurking nearby, the more will she had to move. A sudden noise shocked her out of her indecision, and she quickly dashed in the direction that Andrew had gone. Once she reached the trees, she found that due to the gigantic roots twisting up from every which way and her still bare foot, her nervous gallop had to slow to an awkward horizontal clamber. Bending under and high-stepping over the wooden hurdles as fast as she could, Kindle soon heard the dull buzz of Misson.

"Misson!" she dared to call as she threw a leg over another root, "Hey, Misson, I'm coming!" The buzzing ceased for a moment then began to grow louder, and in a second Misson appeared above her.

"Oof!" Kindle dropped over a root and tried to hide her humiliation by smiling up at him.

Misson returned a grimace.

"I'm coming, so wait for me. Okay?" she told him as she hauled herself up.

"Not too nimble, are you?" he sardonically chuckled.

Kindle ground her teeth together to keep from snapping at him. "Which way to the Tunnels or whatever?" she mumbled instead.

"Follow," he replied and gracefully flew up away from the tangle of roots. Kindle, even though she was annoyed at him and embarrassed by her bumbling, kept winding over and under the roots to keep up with Misson. As they slowly progressed, nothing seemed to change; the deep red trees all stood the same height, spanned the same width, and shot the same number of twisting roots out of the ground. Soon Kindle noticed that even though she was trying to carefully weave through the tangle of roots as fast as she could, Misson grew steadily smaller each time she peered up at him. She was just about to call for him to wait when she straightened up from a crouch and saw Andrew's blond head like a star glowing in the dim forest. Then she spied Misson hovering just beyond him, gazing lazily back her way. Another surge of embarrassment grasped Kindle, and she ducked out of his sight. She knew that crawling under the roots was not the easiest or most graceful way to them, but at least Misson couldn't make fun of her if he couldn't see her. Just as that thought left her, she heard a buzz overhead.

"What are you doing?" Misson's voice sighed, and twisting her neck around, she saw him frowning down at her. For a second she simply squinted at him, trying to think of something to say that would not sound ridiculous and give him more reason to taunt her.

"Crawling…," she slowly answered, still thinking, and then lamely finished, "It's the best way to get through." Once she had given her answer, Kindle turned back to the dirt and kept inching forward.

"Hmpf," Misson haughtily sniffed, "Humans."

Despite feeling absolutely silly, Kindle stuck to her difficult crawl until she reached Andrew's feet. Then she popped up and set the most cheerful smile on her face that she could with the sting of the hard ground still causing her palms and knees to ache.

"Oh, good," Misson said flatly and flew off the branch he had settled on, "you've finally reached us." He immediately buzzed ahead, putting several feet between them and himself.

"Ugh." Kindle rolled her eyes over to Andrew. "He hates us."

Andrew pointedly turned away from her and silently began to weave away around the roots. Kindle wanted to scream at him—the way he kept ignoring her was driving her crazy—but she let her anger out in an agitated breath and hurried to catch up with him. Unlike her, Andrew was somehow easily winding his way through the maze of roots without ever ducking or climbing. Kindle carefully examined his path and mimicking it, found maneuvering around the roots easier. Following his swerving and turning trail, Kindle came close enough to Andrew that she noticed he wasn't at all looking where he was going but steadily staring at his feet. Kindle, wondering if something was fascinating about the ground, also peered down and saw that a very thin, shallow rut was worn into the dirt. Surprised, she stopped to stare at it. With her eyes, she traced it back the way she had just traveled and then forward to where Andrew had just trod. Delighted at her discovery, Kindle's enthusiasm bloomed, and she jogged the path until Andrew's slow pace blocked her from hurrying forward. When she came near him, his shoulders tensed and Kindle fell back slightly. As she watched the back of his head, the fear that he was angry at her slid into her mind. A sudden desire to make amends pushed words out of her mouth.

"Hey, I'm sorry for what I said," she clumsily sputtered. Andrew jolted at her sudden words but kept walking. Kindle tried to think of something else more redeeming to say. "You know, back there. I guess it wasn't very nice."

"No," he immediately but quietly agreed. Kindle wished he would say more.

"I mean, like, I know you were just trying to help and ... and I do care about your side too. *Really.*"

"Okay." His reply wasn't tinged with any emotion, and Kindle didn't think that he believed her.

"No, I do! What happened anyway? Did you get in a fight or something? Your face is pretty bruised up, you know."

At her last comment, he put a hand to his face to feel for the damage and when he found it, sharply inhaled.

"Yeah, it's bad," Kindle assured him, wrinkling her nose. "Did you get punched by like, a semitruck or what?"

"Sort of."

"You got hit by a truck? Really?"

"No. Just really hard—I thought you meant did I get punched hard by someone huge, and ... I did."

Kindle had to shake off her feeling of stupidity and the surprise of him speaking so much before she could answer.

"Oh, yeah—I knew what you meant."

As Andrew turned around a root, she saw his expression and knew he could see past her lie.

"So who won?" she asked, eager to help him forget her error.

"What?"

"The fight." Kindle rolled her eyes—he seemed about as skilled at conversation as a tree. She tried to keep her voice from showing any annoyance. "Who won the fight?"

Andrew kept silent as she peered at him eagerly, trying to judge his expression for an answer. After a few minutes of quietly curving back and forth, he finally uncomfortably shrugged and mumbled, "It wasn't a fight. I don't want to talk about it."

"Oh, okay." She was disappointed that he still seemed unwilling to talk to her. Hoping he wasn't even more agitated with her, she tried again. "Uh, sorry … I didn't know. Um, where'd you say you were from—I mean, you are from, like, earth, right?"

He gave her a sour glance as if she had insulted him. "Jersey."

"Huh?"

"*New* Jersey."

"Oh, like up east! Cool!" Kindle was relieved that he was from America too. "I'm from Missouri," she excitedly told him. A new urge to befriend him pushed her to apologize again. "Hey, Andrew, I *really* am sorry for, you know, being like that. Can we be okay and, like, get along?" She waited just for a second and then became nervous at his silence. "I mean, we really don't know what *he's* up to," she jabbed a finger at Misson, who was too far ahead to hear them, "or where he's taking us or anything but—"

"Yeah," he interrupted.

Kindle smiled, glad to finally know he didn't hate her. "So are you gunna talk more?" she carefully asked.

"I don't talk much," he replied matter-of-factly, and now that Kindle knew he wasn't just trying to annoy her, she accepted his odd answer with a nod. The pair fell silent as they twisted their way through the roots, intent on following the tiny trail to the place that Misson called the Tunnels.

The Night Watchmen

A s Kindle and Andrew wound their way through the sea of roots under
the shade of Danica Woods' massive trees, the afternoon sun slowly
slipped down the curve of the sky, taking its warmth and light with it. The
changes snuck around them so silently and gradually that Kindle didn't
immediately sense them, but once the air had chilled enough to cause her
to shiver in her thin t-shirt and shorts, she lifted her eyes and noticed that
the woods had changed. The trees had remained exactly the same during
their entire walk, but the shifts in the atmosphere high above had stealthily brought the darkness hiding between the distant trunks much closer.
Blinking around the dim woods, Kindle became even more aware of the fact
that the heat had evaporated and the thin trail she had been watching and
the nearby trees were almost invisible.

"The trees are gone…," she quietly mused, realizing from her hoarseness
just how long they had been traveling in silence. Andrew made a questioning noise from a short distance ahead, and Kindle darted around a few roots
to catch up with him.

"Andrew," she said, reaching for his shoulder. He hadn't broken his gaze from the trail or stopped following it. Kindle caught a handful of his shirt, and he abruptly halted and swung his head around to frown at her.

"What…," he began in irritation, but his voice trailed off as his eyes began to roam. "The trees *are* gone," he whispered as if just realizing what Kindle had said. The trees, of course, had not really vanished, but the darkness had crept up and swallowed everything except the nearest few trees. They squinted around for a few moments, testing how far their eyes could see, and Kindle's stomach tightened with fear.

"Can you see Misson?" She tried not to let her anxiety show in her voice. "What if we can't find him? We'll be lost forever," she moaned and looked to Andrew for an answer, but he blankly stared at her.

"What?" Kindle unintentionally snapped and then clasped her hands over her forehead and groaned, "Ugh, sorry, sorry, I'm sorry, it's just—"

"Let's follow the trail," Andrew calmly cut short her apology. "I can still see it, and it was going the same way as Misson."

"Oh, yeah. Yeah." Kindle let her hands flop down to her sides and stared down at her feet. She felt incredibly silly for panicking and forgetting the path. Hearing Andrew's footsteps, she also began trekking on behind him without lifting up her reddened face. Now that they knew the darkness was creeping closer, robbing them of sight, they tried to quicken their pace but found that speeding up only made the trail more difficult to see through the gloom.

"Can you still see it?" Kindle asked with rushed breath.

"Yeah. Barely." Andrew seemed to be panting, and Kindle looked up at him. Although he wasn't running, she could tell he was struggling to breathe. Then, all at once, he let out a horrible gasp, doubled over, bounced to an oddly bent stop, and Kindle smashed into him.

She squealed and immediately jolted backwards, ramming her back into a root. Gripping it with both hands for balance and security, she gasped, "What?! What?! Are you okay?! What happened?!" Even though she was almost sure something terrible had finally decided to attack them, Kindle reached out one hand toward the gleam of his blond hair. "Can you see me? Andrew? Can you see me?" She waved frantically but he didn't answer. Kindle drew her hand back and squeezed the root. "Say something!" she shouted anxiously and stomped a foot. A deep groan issued from where he still stood slightly atilt, and Kindle bit her lip. She was still convinced a wild animal had him in its grasp, but a rush of concern for her only companion and possibly only way out of the woods pushed aside her fear, and she jumped forward to rescue him. Kindle leapt to his left, caught his arm, and pulled him away from whatever had immobilized him. They landed in a tangle heap in the dirt.

"Off!" Andrew grunted, and Kindle, realizing her elbow was somehow in his stomach, squirmed around until she was crouching beside him.

"Oh, sorry!" she cried and squinted down at him, expecting to see a gaping wound but saw nothing. "What? You're okay?" She turned to where he had just stood and still saw no sign of anything. "What happened? I thought some—some *thing* got you."

"A root," he breathed.

"Huh?"

"A root. I ran into a root."

"What? That's it? No, um, thing eating you?"

"I think my rib is broken."

"What? No!" Kindle couldn't believe he had run into the root hard enough to crack a bone. "How do you know?"

Instead of answering, Andrew drove the heels of his hands into his forehead and drew in a slow, shaky breath. He squeezed his eyes shut and released the air with the same difficulty. Kindle's brow twisted with unsure concern as she wondered if he really had broken something. Half agitated at him and half terrified for him, she deeply sighed and bit her lip. She knew that the longer he lay on the ground, the darker the woods would grow, and so she decided to try to talk him into moving.

"C'mon, Andrew, I don't think anything is broken—you're breathing and not bleeding or anything." She tried to smile and sound positive, but when he didn't answer, her face slid into a pout. "You've got to get up," she whined and then attempted to pull up his shoulder, but he let out a yelp of pain, and she dropped him. His eyes slowly opened and glared at her. Kindle felt her cheeks redden and she mumbled an apology as she quickly stood and turned away from him. She really wanted to be angry with him for being stubborn but now felt terrible for not believing that he truly was in pain and for hurting him even more. Deliberately avoiding the sight of his motionless body and staring into the blackness did not help—it only reminded her of the darkening woods. With all of her emotions stirring around, Kindle felt as if she was going to burst out in tears when Andrew softly spoke.

"Misson."

"Huh?" She glanced down at him and saw the dim shine of his eyes staring off into the woods. Realizing what he had said, she hopefully squinted in the same direction.

"Did you see him? Did you see Misson?" she questioned as she searched the vast black surrounding them. Andrew pointed a pale hand directly in front of him, and Kindle stuck her neck out and squinted harder. After a few seconds of seeing nothing, a small, yellow light blinked. Kindle gasped happily and, forgetting her fear of the woods, cried out, "Misson! We're here! Here!"

The light blinked again, closer this time. Kindle beamed down at Andrew but saw he was not smiling.

"He's coming, Andrew, didn't you see him?" she asked and then looked back up to find the light, sure it and Misson would fly out from behind another tree soon.

"Misson?" she called, and then the tiny light blinked beside her shoulder. Kindle jumped back in surprise but when she saw what it was, groaned, "Ugh, it's just a firefly." She sighed heavily. "We are never—"

"Hero?" a quiet but very commanding voice chirped, and Kindle froze. The firefly flew nearer to her face and lit its body. Now Kindle could see that it wasn't an ordinary firefly but the same sort of bug-person as Misson and Missi. Instead of being made of two bulbous orbs, he had one long, slender black body with limbs to match and wore a bright red vest. He looked quite like a firefly except for his black human head and limbs. Also, unlike the fireflies Kindle knew, he held a lantern from which the yellow light was emitting.

"Are you one of the heroes Misson spoke of?" the tiny man asked Kindle, holding up his lantern to shine light on her face. She couldn't help but stare at him for a few moments, too dumbfounded by another human-bug to say anything.

"Yes," Andrew groaned at her feet and caused the man to swing his lantern back and forth, searching for the speaker.

"Oh, yeah." Kindle woke up from her speechlessness. "Uh, sorry, I am a—uh what, um, Misson was talking about." Kindle still felt silly being called a hero. She watched the man discover Andrew with his light just before it flicked off. He quickly flipped his wrist and the yellow glow reappeared.

"I mean, *we* are," Kindle anxiously blurted, pointing at Andrew, then herself. "Both of us were with Misson. We were following him, but he got too far ahead, and it got all dark, and—"

"Yes," the firefly man interrupted her brightly. "He and Missi arrived at the Tunnels' gate after dark, not too long ago really, and explained everything to us."

"Us?" Kindle wondered if he was a little loopy or if more Cifra were flying around unseen. He picked his eyes up to her and smiled sympathetically.

"Missi said you seemed lost and confused. I really must introduce myself. I...," he announced grandly, holding out a hand for her to shake, "am Lucer, Sergeant Lucer. Head officer of the Tunnels' night watch."

"Um ... okay," Kindle hesitantly replied and, as well as she could, shook his extremely small hand with two of her fingers. "I'm Kindle...."

"Kindle! Fantastic name," Lucer heartily cut in. Kindle gave him a half grin.

"Uh, yeah ... and that's Andrew. Can you get us to a doctor or something? He's hurt." She gestured at Andrew, and Lucer let the lantern drop light over him.

"No, I did not think he was well," he seriously murmured. Then he raised his lantern with spirit and cried, "Watchmen! Show our heroes the way to the Tunnels!" Immediately a thousand tiny lights exactly like Lucer's appeared all around them.

"Whoa," Kindle gasped. It was as if someone had sprinkled the entire woods with Christmas lights that could float and bob on their own. As she gazed all around at the scattered lights, they rushed together into one glowing line that curved through the branches overhead.

"Well done, men," Lucer called to them then flew to Kindle's side and proudly whispered, "My men are really quite efficient." Kindle nodded but didn't take her wide eyes from the twinkling, levitating path.

"Fall in with concealed lights once we pass. Understood?" Lucer called to his men and from a million voices received a resounding, "Sir!"

Lucer buzzed under the illuminated path and turned back to Kindle and Andrew. Waving his lantern, he cheerily called, "Now your road to the Tunnels is clear, heroes. We will arrive there expeditiously."

"Uh…." Kindle glanced down past her elbow at Andrew, who was slowly drawing breath in and out with closed eyes. "I don't think so, um, Mr. Lucer." She peered up apologetically at the small man. "I don't think Andrew can walk. Like I said, he's hurt. Bad."

The important little man flew back to them to examine Andrew and furrowed his brow. "Man down," he murmured, and Kindle rolled her eyes at his back.

"Yeah, like I said, he's hurt *bad*."

"My ribs," Andrew gasped, and Lucer flew down right in front of his face.

"Son!" he yelled. "You conscious? Aware?" Lucer waited a few seconds then barked, "Answer, hero! Give a sign!"

"Murb," Andrew groaned.

Kindle knelt down to them. "Mr. Lucer, he really doesn't talk much. Maybe you could get somebody to help him walk—I mean, I tried to help him up, but I think it just made it worse."

"I think—" Andrew panted, "—broken ribs."

"Ribs," Lucer murmured and spun around to scan his body. He appeared to be in deep thought, so Kindle quietly waited. After a minute, though, the small officer's lantern darkened and he huffed in frustration.

"What are ribs?" he questioned, giving his hand a shake to relight his lamp. "Where are they?"

"Huh?" Kindle couldn't believe that this firefly, who seemed to be an adult, didn't know what ribs were. He huffed again then flew up to her.

"We Cifra hardly ever deal with humans or their parts and systems. Exoskeletons." Lucer emphatically pounded his chest with his free hand. "Wings, antennae—that's what we have, not those hidden bones and things."

"Oh, sorry—I uh … didn't know." Kindle had learned about insects and their exoskeletons over and over in school but had never thought about insects never learning about human bones. The idea of bugs going to school amused her, and she couldn't help but smirk as she ran her finger up and down her own rib cage. "Here—all along here in front of our lungs."

"Hmm … broken in the middle."

"Uh…." Kindle began but decided correcting him would not help the situation.

"Quite out of my forte really," Lucer continued to murmur to himself and then shot up above Kindle's head. "Officer Lio!" he called to the glittering line that still obediently hovered nearby. One small light separated itself and zoomed straight to Lucer.

"Yes, sir!" Lio shouted when he snapped to a halt. He looked much like Lucer except he was smaller and held a slightly dimmer lantern.

"Fly fast to the Tunnels and fetch Medara—" Lio drew in a sharp breath at the name, but Lucer ignored him. "—we have a man down. Hurt badly."

Lio's eyes darted from Kindle to Andrew several times before he finally yelled, "Understood, sir!" Then, in a blink, he zipped away. Lucer watched him disappear with a smug smile before turning to Kindle.

"Lio's my runner—the fastest night watchman I've ever brought to the team." Lucer flew down to Andrew as he kept boasting. "Yes, I have the best on my team—an a-one man for any job. Lio will return to us in no time with Medara, and we will patch you up posthaste, son."

"Sir!" Lio's voice rang out, causing Kindle to jump and blink at Lio, who was hovering in exactly the same place he had been seconds ago.

"Officer!" replied Lucer in the same tone as he flew up, shaking his lantern. "What of Medara? Did you fly ahead? You know that protocol—"

"Sir, may I report!" Lio interrupted him in one breath then threw a quick glance over his shoulder.

Lucer eyed him with a stern look but nodded and slowly cautioned, "Make it count. Report."

"Sir, I reached the Tunnels in a moment and set straight for Medara's ward, but our lady herself motioned me to a stop—and you know, sir, I cannot refuse Lady Luna's summon—in order to inquire as to the reason for my rush, and so in a quick way I informed her of our immobile hero to which her nonnegotiable reply was to—" Lio had divulged every word in one rushed breath but now hesitated to inhale and then gush out, "—come herself."

Kindle watched as Lucer absorbed what Lio had related. His agitation melted away and was replaced by awed apprehension. Lucer blinked his bulging eyes several times and in disbelief asked, "Here? Lady Luna coming here?"

"Sir, I tried to dissuade her...." Lio peered over his shoulder as his voice drifted off. The two watchmen fell silent and gave Kindle a chance to think over what Lio had explained.

"Oh!" she cried louder than she had intended when she suddenly remembered where she had heard Lady Luna's name. Both Lucer and Lio turned wide eyes on her, and Kindle bit her lip.

"Sorry—I, uh ... isn't Lady Luna, like, your queen? Missi said she could tell us where we were and what's going on and stuff."

"Yes." Lucer's expression was still stupefied, but his bright, direct tone had returned. "Lady Luna and Lord Rex are the most powerful and wise of all the Cifra. She reigns over the night creatures and he presides during the day. The two exclusively execute their rule from the Golden Hive, though— the lady in particular never leaves."

"Sir!" Lio cried to grab his attention. "Lady Luna was flying to the Gate already! I never would alter orders, sir!"

"Lio!" Lucer barked, shaking his lantern to a whole new brilliance. "I know you're a true man of the watch. Gather you senses and reposition in line!"

"Sir!" Lio yelped and dashed back to the mass of fireflies so quickly that Kindle's eyes couldn't keep up with him.

"Probably that Misson and his bees riling up the Lady," grumbled Lucer just loud enough for Kindle to hear. "No order, no regard to policy...," he continued to grouch to himself. Kindle didn't really care to hear his complaints. She was excited to see this queen and kept her focus on the illuminated path. Having only encountered queens in fantasy stories, she only held a small idea of what to expect but imagined the queen would be a beautiful woman with a gorgeous dress and shining tiara. For a moment, Kindle felt self-conscious when she remembered that she was dirty, half barefooted, and probably frizzy-haired, but her uncomfortable nervousness faded when she caught sight of who she knew had to be Lady Luna. The woman approaching them *was* quite beautiful, but other than that, nothing about her matched Kindle's expectations. Even from far away Kindle could see that she was an incredibly large Luna moth. Under the yellow lantern light her outspread, translucent, lime-green wings swept closer to them like quiet, soft silk gliding through the air. The tails of her wings blew out gracefully behind her, twisting lazily with each turn. As Lady Luna neared them, Kindle could see that she was much more humanlike than any Cifra she had met so far, but still very much resembled a Luna moth. Her head was white and without hair except for two golden braids that traveled over her crown and then curved up into branched antennae. What seemed to be soft purple fur covered the back of her neck then thinned to two stripes that ran over her shoulders and connected to her upper wings. When she landed in front of them, her wings draped down her back like a glowing cape, and Kindle could see that the rest of Lady Luna's human figure was covered by a long, creamy white dress that was so glossy and soft it seemed more like milk than cloth. Through long side slits in her dress, Kindle could see that her arms and legs, which were not spindly insect legs but full human limbs, were also covered with the velvety purple fuzz.

For a few seconds, Kindle and Lucer simply stared at her in silence. Everything about her was so strange and ethereal that she was captivating. Lady Luna also said nothing but stared back at them with an expression that made her look half asleep but somehow also entirely alert. Suddenly Lucer bent forward in a bow that teetered on a somersault and apologetically whispered, "Lady Luna, it is an honor." He gave Kindle a brisk, commanding glance, and she realized that she should bow as well. She tipped forward slightly but refused to take her eyes off the queen partly out of fear, partly out of wonder. Even though Kindle was almost positive everything that was happening was real, she still felt that if she closed her eyes for too long, it would all disappear.

Lady Luna inclined her head to them as well and then, in a soft, musical tone, said, "Thank you, Lucer." Her lime-green eyes turned to Kindle, who averted her own. "Young hero, you know my name, so please grace me with yours and—" she peered around Kindle to see Andrew and concern filled her sleepy eyes, "—your injured friend's."

"Andrew," Kindle sighed as she turned to him, glad to have somewhere else to direct her attention. "He's Andrew and I'm Kindle. Can you help him? I think he's got a broken rib, so he can't really walk." Talking somehow alleviated her anxiety, and so Kindle continued, "Like, I don't even know if he can stand up or anything. He ran into a root, but he was already hurt. I think—"

"Shhh," Lady Luna gently broke into her rambling, and Kindle felt embarrassment color her face. "All will be well," she assured her in a voice so like a comforting lullaby that Kindle believed her. "Lucer, I will see that Andrew reaches Medara. Please escort Kindle to our mender's tunnel and we shall meet there."

"Understood, my lady!" Lucer promptly replied and saluted her. Lady Luna gave him a gentle nod and then spread her beautiful, glowing wings.

"If you would pardon me." She tilted her head to Andrew, and Kindle unwillingly sidestepped away from her.

"You really are going to help us, aren't you?" she asked as Lady Luna lifted off the ground. "I mean…." Kindle wanted to be sure that these Cifra were not monsters but was also terrified to offend them. "Just where *are* we and when are you going to tell us anything?"

"All will be well," the moth's caring voice repeated. "I will meet with you soon." With those words, she glided down beside Andrew, gently shifted a wing under him, carefully slid him on to her back, and then turned and flew away under the lantern-lit path. Kindle and Lucer watched her until she evaporated from sight.

Lucer exhaled a large puff of air. "Hooo! Never thought I would see the lady in the forest. Or carrying a boy!" He shook his head and shone his light on Kindle. "I suppose I've seen a lot tonight I never suspected I would, really."

Kindle stared at him, feeling as if he had much less right than her to talk about seeing weird sights. "Yeah," she mumbled.

"Well now, I have orders." Lucer shook his lantern awake and gestured with it to the path of light. "To the Tunnels, young hero!" he proclaimed and headed forward. Kindle, not wanting to be left alone in the forest again, followed him. She still felt uneasy about everything happening, but Lady Luna's words had reassured her enough to give the odd bug-people a chance.

As they traveled under the brigade of fireflies, Kindle could hear a million indistinct murmurs from the watchmen above, and she gazed up at them. They each looked much like Lucer but were smaller like Lio. Every few seconds one of them would snatch a glance at her between his whisperings or vigorously shake his lantern to keep it aglow.

". . . says they're heroes...," she heard one voice whisper. Kindle sighed heavily and tried not to hear any more of their murmurings. She felt incredibly irritated that she seemed to be the only one who had no idea of what was going on.

"Lucer—uh, Mr. Lucer?"

"Yes?" he chirped.

"Why do you all keep calling us heroes? I mean, I know Missi said it was because of our necklaces or something—"

Suddenly the low buzz above them broke out into a clamor of exited voices and clanging lanterns. Just as abruptly, Lucer halted and yelled, "Watch-MEN!" Silence rippled through the trail of light. "Watchmen," Lucer repeated in a quieter but still stern tone, "you are on special duty tonight, but that is no cause to disregard routine protocol. Really men, keep your heads and maintain some dignity."

A chorus of "Sir" and "Yes, sir" broke out for a few seconds, but then the forest became quiet. Lucer resumed his flight, and Kindle stepped up beside him.

". . . like a hive of buzzing bees, really," he grumbled in a low voice and then nodded at Kindle. "Excuse their actions. My men are trained to conduct themselves better," he apologized with quiet disappointment but then brightened. "But as to your question, young Kindle, every Cifra knows the marks of Anelthalien's makers, and you wear the emblem most dear to us."

"But how does that make me—us—heroes?" she argued, trying not to grow more irritated. "I just found this thing—" she tugged at her necklace,

"—and Andrew did too. Like, I know Missi said some stuff about a queen and these 'makers' but, ugh, I dunno, I just don't get how it makes us heroes." She ended her sentence in helpless frustration, and Lucer quietly eyed her for a few seconds before staring straight ahead.

"I am sorry, young Kindle, that I do not understand much about all this," he began seriously. "My duty is head officer of the Tunnels' night watch, and so until, well, earlier this night really, I did not concern myself with whispered tales of ages past. My duty is to efficiently execute orders, not ask questions." He paused to relight his lantern. "And I have orders to collect the four heroes who I will know by the ancient marks."

"Well, then, you know what this is, right?" She held out the red gem to him.

"Yes. The mark of Hux," he proudly reported, and Kindle huffed in frustration.

"Okay. Thanks," she acquiesced, deciding that questioning him was futile.

"Of course, glad to help, really." Lucer smiled, oblivious to his uselessness.

Kindle rolled her eyes and noticed that even though the fireflies had ended their conversations, they were all still staring down at her.

"Are there more of you guys?" she asked, keeping her gaze upward, hoping Lucer would at least know about his own people. "Like, are Cifra just bees and fireflies, or are there other, um...," she wasn't sure if using the word "bug" would offend him.

"Oh, yes!" he quickly chirped, "All kinds of insects! Moths, mosquitoes, beetles, butterflies, every kind of flying insect really." He gave her a smart look. "That's what we Cifra are—the flying insects transformed and commissioned by Hux to protect the skies."

"So, were you not always, um, part human? Like did, um, Hux," she felt odd saying the name without knowing who or what Hux was, "make you like this?"

"Ah, I see why you have so many questions about our history, really." He folded his unoccupied arm behind his back in a soldierly manner. "A very long time ago, I believe right around when the four makers created most of the people and creatures of Anelthalien, Hux decided to create brave workers to help him guard his domain—the sky. He chose the flying insects as his workmen and charged them—our ancestors from all over the land—to care for the sky. So young Kindle, to be direct, I and all the Cifra now in the Tunnels have always been Cifra, but our ancestors were common bugs changed by Hux." Lucer smiled proudly again and shook his light. Kindle stared at his lantern and toyed with the chain around her neck as she soaked up his explanation.

Finally she hopefully asked, "So will I get to meet Hux? Does he live with you guys?" She was very curious about Hux and was sure that Lucer would now make it his duty to let her see the mysterious maker, but when she saw his face, her hope sank. A very strange expression—something like puzzlement and frustration—had twisted away his proud grin.

"Sorry," she couldn't help saying, feeling like she had upset him, "I didn't mean to…."

"Oh no, young Kindle, no apology necessary," he interrupted, maintaining his challenged face. "I am sorry to say that you will not meet Hux. He does not live in the Tunnels."

"Oh, that's okay—" she began even though she was quite disheartened by his words.

"Not sure where he lives, really," Lucer kept pondering out loud, "Or if…ah!" Lucer suddenly triumphantly barked and caused Kindle to jump. He sped forward, and Kindle watched as he flew to one of the gigantic trees and slapped it with his tiny hand.

"Well done, men!" he shouted back in her direction. "Now, back to your routine posts for the time!"

Before Kindle had time to turn around, all of the watchmen scattered in every direction from right behind her, causing gusts of wind to sweep past her. Instinctively, she threw her arms over her head for safety. Once each firefly had disappeared into the dark woods and Lucer's lantern was the only source of light or sound, Kindle dropped her arms and stepped over a tangle of roots to him.

"They are good men, really," he was mumbling to himself.

"Is this the Tunnels?" Kindle asked, trying to squint through the darkness to see anything besides trees. The night kept her from seeing much, but she could tell that the tree Lucer was still patting was sandwiched tightly between two others.

"Not quite. This is our outer gate," Lucer brightly informed her as he smacked the bark particularly hard. "The Tunnels lie below Danica Woods."

Kindle stared down at the forest floor and frowned at the sight of her dirty bare foot. She turned an uncertain face back to Lucer. "Like, under the whole forest? Are we over the Tunnels now?" She felt uneasy about standing on hollow earth.

"Almost the entire woods." He flashed a smile at her. "We have some excellent diggers." Lucer stopped slapping the tree and drew in a deep breath. "Hoo!" he exhaled then pressed his lips together and murmured, "This *is* the Gate. Likely those flighty bees on duty." He wound up for another impressive hit, but an odd crunching sound began, and he relaxed.

"Due time!" he barked as he flew past Kindle to the crevice created by the tree and its neighbor. "Really." He shook his head. Kindle tried to catch sight of what was making the sound, which was growing louder, when she noticed that the bark right in front of her was moving. Taking a step back, she could see the trunk of the massive tree was slowly rotating to her left.

"Lucer?" she breathed in awe, unsure if something amazing or awful was happening.

"Come, young Kindle." He beckoned her to the crevice where he hovered. "It will open here ... *soon*." He grumbled the last word in agitation and began to knock sharply on the tree.

"Come now! Look alive! Really! On duty!" he shouted but with no success. The tree kept its leisurely pace until a small slit of light appeared.

"Ah, it's you, Officer," a slow, sleepy voice said. "Come on in. Sorry for the wait."

"As well you should—your action was slow and sorry," Lucer chastised. "I am on a serious mission; one to be carried out swiftly—"

"Then come in, Officer, don't hold yourself up now," the sleepy voice retorted, and Kindle cracked a smirk as Lucer sputtered and shook his lantern.

"I don't know why you're coming through anyway, why you couldn't *fly* over the gate if you're in such a rush," the voice continued to babble through Lucer's angry noises.

"Are you uninformed?!" Lucer shouted when he finally found his voice.

"I just came on night shift—"

"I am escorting a *hero*," Lucer declared importantly.

"Hm?" the voice grunted loudly, and then a head—much like Lady Luna's except smaller and a soft brown—poked out from the slit. He blinked a few times, and then his black eyes grew wide before his head disappeared.

"That's a human," the brown moth whispered in alarm.

"Yes, Tyren," Lucer snapped, clearly annoyed, "Young Kindle is a guest of Lady Luna. Now, quickly crack this gate open so she may pass through."

For a few seconds nothing happened, and Kindle wondered if the fearful moth would allow them through the gate. Lucer, though, stuck his head into the opening and cried, "Come now, Tyren, do your duty!"

"Urgh, yes, sir," Tyren replied in the distance, and the tree trunk began to turn again. Lucer retracted his face and shook it at Kindle.

"Apologies, young Kindle," he huffed.

"It's okay" she replied, trying to sound and look as serious as Lucer. Truthfully, Kindle was enjoying the attention and thought that Tyren's reaction was comical. Lucer continued to disappointedly shake his head until the trunk stopped its rotation.

"Come, young Kindle," Lucer commanded as he flew forward, and Kindle eagerly followed. All of the strange bug-people were growing less creepy and more fascinating each time she met one. The Cifra, though, suddenly seemed insignificant as Kindle stepped into the trunk. Even though she had been surrounded by the large trees for quite a while, Kindle had not realized just how massive they were until now. The trunk had been hollowed out into a large cylindrical space that was easily bigger than her living room in her house. The one continuous wall, which was light pinkish-yellow and covered in thin ruts twisting and climbing in millions of curved patterns, rose high above their heads then slowly curved into a dome. As she examined the intricate wall, Kindle noticed that thousands of small lights, which resembled Christmas lights without the green plastic casings, sat snugly in the ruts. Not only did the sight of the strange but beautiful hollow trunk entrance her, but the smell—a rich, woodsy aroma that reminded her of a lumberyard—also struck her when she entered. Kindle inhaled deeply and smiled at the familiar scent. Then she noticed Tyren leaning on a strange wooden contraption in the middle of the rutted floor. Besides Lady Luna, Tyren was the biggest Cifra she had seen, not only in his height but in the burliness of his limbs. He was almost as tall as Kindle but had much thicker, fuzzy brown arms and legs. Everything about him appeared soft and brown except for his eyes, which peered warily at her from under his bushy antennae.

"Come along, young Kindle," Lucer prompted as he flew to Tyren. "Make your way to the middle here so we may speed this mission."

Kindle, still gazing around, nodded and began to walk toward them, but Tyren let out an uncomfortable whine.

"No, you just stay there, alright? That's alright," Tyren nervously told her then leaned harder on the wooden handle under him. His brown wings fluttered, and he puffed, "I turned this thing—" he sucked in and blew out a blast of breath, "—with those beetles in here once. Hrrm." When Tyren grunted, the whole hollowed space around them jolted, and Kindle instinctively bent her knees and spread her arms to steady herself.

"Well done, man!" encouraged Lucer to Tyren, who kept pushing and grunting. Then, as the handle slowly gave way to his effort, the trunk began to turn. Kindle watched as the slit of forest behind her narrowed away into nothing and the opening she had just passed through slid neatly over a concave wall carved into the adjacent tree.

"Lucer?" Kindle called to him as she admired the pattern of ruts also on this wall. "How'd you guys do this?" she asked, tracing the curves with her finger. Lucer flew over her head and patted the wall.

"All these here?"

"Yeah, they're so pretty—how'd you guys make them?"

"Termites!" Lucer grandly cried, and Kindle couldn't help but show her repulsion on her face.

"Ew! Termites? Really?"

"Affirmative, young Kindle," he replied, laughing. "The termites in the Tunnels are the finest woodworkers in all of Anelthalien. They whittled our whole Gate." Lucer sounded very proud, but Kindle did not like the idea of tons of termites everywhere. She shook in disgust.

"Did they, like, eat the middle out of this tree?"

"Correct! And the rest of the Gate!" Lucer cried triumphantly as a sliver of darkness appeared near them. He sped back to Tyren to congratulate him, and Kindle stepped closer to the growing view of the Tunnels' Gate.

THE MENDER

Kindle expected to see a giant dirt tunnel and so was surprised when she realized that a forest clearing lay in front of her. She had just enough time to take in the wide oval of springy moss softly illuminated by many of the fireflies' lanterns before she heard a high-pitched squeal and saw a black dart shooting right at her. Even though Kindle tried to sidestep, Missi still collided with her shoulder.

"Sooo happy!" she continued to squeal. "You children I thought were gone—lost. Oh, my flying I am sorry was fast, but sooo happy now!" Missi cried while clinging tightly to Kindle's arm.

"Come now, woman, really!" Kindle heard Lucer shout. "Grab a hold of your emotions!" He flew into Missi's embrace and, even though he was so much smaller than her, pulled one of her arms away from Kindle.

"What's the meaning of this, Missi? Where's your propriety? And why are you up here—the day is done." From Lucer's impatient tone, Kindle could tell that he was quite irritated with her.

"Oh, so sorry I am," Missi pleaded as she engulfed both of his hands in her own, "the children's safety I only wanted to see."

Lucer shook free of her and frowned. "So now you see young Kindle and that she is in capable hands. Now please, retire from your watch."

"No not on watch! Never take your watch would I, good officer. Just waiting to see the heroes. Andrew I saw on Lady Luna, so you I knew would soon come." Missi smiled at them both, clapped her hands, and glided nearer to Kindle, but Lucer quickly flew between them.

"Missi," he firmly cautioned and she bowed her head.

"Yes, I will go now, sir," she sighed and buzzed off to the opposite side of the clearing.

"Bees, really," grumbled Lucer as he flew out of the tree trunk. Kindle turned to see Tyren one more time, waved and thanked him, then jogged to catch up with Lucer.

"She was okay. She wasn't hurting me or anything," Kindle tried to explain as she welcomed the soft green curls under her feet.

"Ah, no young Kindle, I didn't believe Missi could harm you. She was against regulations by buzzing around the Gate after dark." He placed his hands behind his back and authoritatively continued, "You see, every Cifra group has its own area of work so that every branch of the Tunnels runs smoothly. As I explained, the termites are expert woodworkers, and so they efficiently complete all woodworking tasks and encroach upon no one else's area of expertise. Those carpenter bees are the day watch since they are quick and *usually* communicate with succinct precision. Their duty at the Gate ends when night falls, though, and since they are not nocturnal, remaining on watch after the sun fades is a hazard and against our standing laws."

"Oh. Okay," Kindle simply replied. She still didn't think Missi was hurting anything but didn't want to argue.

"Yes, each Cifra does the job he was created to do. It's a fine system we Cifra have made, really. When every man follows the system, that is," Lucer kept bragging, but Kindle didn't care to hear more about the grandness of the Cifra's organization. She was too interested in surveying the incredible view around her. The sea of springy grass was surrounded by a ring of the mammoth trees that had somehow grown right next to one another. As Kindle snatched glances of the trees illuminated by passing fireflies, she realized that each one had been eaten down so that they formed one long, continuous wall. Peering up, she saw that even the branches on the inside of the gate had been devoured. For the first time since she had abruptly left her home, Kindle could see the sky. No moon hung in her circle of vision, but an explosion of tiny stars dotted the dark dome above them. Kindle heard Lucer say her name and brought her eyes down from the sky.

"Huh?" she asked and when she realized Lucer was not in front of her, stopped to search for him.

"Young Kindle," he repeated, and she found him shaking his lantern awake not too far to her left. "Come this way. You have no wings, so we must traverse the ramp."

Curious about what he meant, she peered over her shoulder. Only a few steps ahead of where she had stopped walking, the ground ended and a black void took its place. Following it, she saw that the hole ran along most of the long side of the oval, but as the gate's walls began to curve, the ground reappeared.

"We're going down there?" she nervously asked while staring at the darkness beside her.

"That is our destination," Lucer buoyantly replied as he flew away along the curve of the hole. Kindle trotted after him but carefully maintained her distance from the edge of the drop-off. Going along, Kindle saw a dirt slope gradually rise from below and was glad that she would not have to jump down. Lucer u-turned over the dirt surface once it connected to the level Kindle still stood on. He watched her, waiting for her to catch up, and once she did, breathing a little noisily from his quicker pace, Lucer tipped his head.

"My apologies—I became fervent to complete my mission and flew speedily. Do call out if you fall behind again."

"Uh—" Kindle wanted to argue that she was not slow, but Lucer was already floating down into the black hole.

"The Tunnels are dark and vast. It is essential that you keep with my light," he informed her so seriously that Kindle forgot her argument. As they descended down the ramp, the Gate's dim illumination soon vanished and they were surrounded by complete darkness and, except for the rhythmic slap of Kindle's single flip-flop, total silence. She hadn't realized that the forest above had been filled with a symphony of night sounds until they had disappeared and now felt very unsettled by the lack of noise.

"Is it always so dark down here?" she asked, wanting to break the quiet. "Or is it only this dark at night?"

"Well, young Kindle, it *is* always dark in the Tunnels, but during the day I and my watchmen hang our lanterns on the walls. We carry on our usefulness at all times and serve the day Cifra, who need light much more than night Cifra. You see, we night Cifra find light more of an accessory than a necessity," Lucer explained in his authoritative tone.

Kindle wondered if anyone had ever told Lucer he was a little arrogant but knew better than to speak her question. "So we're really in the Tunnels now?" she asked instead, "Like, this isn't a gate or entryway or something?"

"Yes. We are traveling along one of our main tunnels, Fyrst Way. It connects our gate to most of our minor tunnels."

"Do they have names too?"

"In a way. We call them by their function. That is the Wasp tunnel—it leads to the wasp hive. There is the Honeybee tunnel, that is the Honey tunnel…." Lucer swished his lantern left and right as he named each tunnel they passed. Kindle followed the lantern even though its glow was not strong enough to reach the sides of the large Fyrst Way tunnel.

"Ah, young Kindle! This is the Mender tunnel," Lucer suddenly announced as he flew to the right and then stopped to hover in front of the outline of another tunnel. It was much smaller than Fyrst Way but still big enough for her to easily walk through.

"So this is where Lady Luna brought Andrew?" she asked as she spread out her arms and let her fingers brush the cool dirt walls.

"Correct," Lucer replied.

"And where all the doctors or, um, menders are?"

"Not exactly," Lucer sighed thoughtfully and then folded one of his thin arms behind his back. Kindle rolled her eyes but giggled at his mannerism because she knew it meant he was about to lecture in his important voice.

"Young Kindle. I have told you that we Cifra are descended from the flying insects chosen as guardians of the air, correct?"

"Yeah."

"So, you see, we Cifra are a distinguished race—set apart from all other insects by our transformed features and our wings. And due to our different way of life and distinct mission."

"Okay," Kindle mumbled, unsure if he was just going to endlessly brag again or answer her question.

"We Cifra now all live here in the tunnels, separated from all ordinary and wingless insects." Lucer heaved another great breath, but it sounded annoyed rather than thoughtful. "Except—and now I greatly disagree with breaking our code of life—" he quickly exhaled, "except for our one single mender."

"Oh, uh, Medara?"

"Yes—Medara is the only wingless insect among the Cifra. It is a shame, really, to let down our—"

"What kind of bug is Medara?" Kindle excitedly asked, now very interested in what Lucer had to say. Lucer cleared his throat but remained silent, and Kindle dropped her eyes.

"Sorry ... I didn't mean to interrupt. I just wanted to know. Sorry," she mumbled.

"No matter, young Kindle. I know our decorum is new to you," he stiffly answered. "We are not far from her tunnel, really. You will meet her soon."

Even though Kindle wanted to continue asking Lucer questions, she quietly followed him down the dark, silent tunnel, too abashed to speak. After only a few minutes, Lucer halted and held out his lantern to illuminate the surface ahead of him. Kindle leaned around him to catch a better look at it and realized that it was not dirt like every other surface around them. She had no idea exactly what it was but thought it looked like beautiful, shiny silk. As she squinted at it and tried to decide if it was silver or black, Lucer's voice distracted her.

"Through here you will find Medara's tunnels and your friend. By Lady Luna's orders, we are to wait here for further direction." Lucer kept his arm pointed at the strange curtain but didn't move. After a few seconds, Kindle took a step forward.

"Can we go in?" she shyly asked, "I mean, like, it's okay to see Andrew, right?"

"You may enter, young Kindle, but I will wait here according to orders," he crisply responded then flew above her head, gave his lantern a jiggle, and hung it on a hook sticking out of the dirt wall. He settled on the earth below it and nodded back to the end of the tunnel. "Go on if you would like. I see you are anxious about your friend."

"It's okay? I mean, I don't want to miss Lady Luna or make you stay here alone or anything." She was afraid Lucer was still upset with her and so was glad to see a reluctant smile lift one side of his face.

"Young Kindle, I am a night watchman—this is my honorable duty. You are not a night creature and require restoration. Medara will have accommodations for you. Really now, go rest."

Kindle smiled at him. "Okay, thanks," she finally assented, relieved. She started toward the curtain, but Lucer made an odd noise that caused her to hesitate.

"What?" She turned back to see he had a strange look on his face.

"Remember, young Kindle, Medara is not like us. She is not a Cifra," he said slowly and emphatically enough that Kindle continued to stare at him, trying to determine if he was suggesting more than he had said. She shrugged off his foreboding tone as just dislike of Medara.

"Okay, Lucer, I'll remember," she flippantly replied with a nod and then returned her attention to the shiny curtain. Expecting it to feel just as luxurious at it appeared, Kindle was surprised to find that when she touched it, the curtain felt more like coarse nylon than silk. Kindle pulled it aside, also surprised by its lightness, and was immediately blinded by the brightly lit room that she stepped into. After a few seconds of furious blinking and eye-shielding, she was able to survey the bright circular room. The wall was a large dirt circle with tunnels shooting off in every direction, but the flat floor and ceiling were woven from the same shiny material as the entry curtain. In the light, Kindle could see that the strange fabric was definitely silvery white and especially glittery. The massive amount of light that was making everything sparkle was emanating from tiny glass orbs that seemed to float near the ceiling. Kindle carefully took a few quiet steps further into the room and gazed at the amazing baubles. They appeared almost like the lights she had seen inside the giant hollow tree except they held bluish white flames instead of yellow pinpoints. They all hung perfectly still, and just when Kindle thought she had caught sight of a thin string connected to one, a friendly, elderly woman's voice filled the air.

"Hello."

Kindle quickly scanned all of the tunnels in front of her but saw no one. She pivoted to check the opening behind her and froze. Clinging to the wall just above the curtained opening was an enormous black spider. Kindle had never liked spiders, and so this creature, whose body alone was as big as her, terrified her. She desperately wanted to scream and run, but a dizzying numbness had washed over her whole body. All she could do was stare at it as it gazed back with all eight of its eyes. Unlike each Cifra she had encountered, this spider was exactly like a normal spider—eight-legged and fanged—except humongous.

"Hello. Who might you be?" it asked, but Kindle still couldn't find any unfrozen muscle in her body to respond. The spider blinked a few eyes and clicked its fangs. "Can you understand me?" it asked as it scuttled down to the floor, and Kindle suddenly felt hot blood rush through every inch of her. She screamed and sprinted to the nearest tunnel, but before she reached it, a tall, bowed spider leg spiked in front of it. Kindle skidded to a halt and dashed toward another opening.

"Calm down, dear," the spider almost laughed, and Kindle watched as it easily leapt over her to block her way again. Kindle quickly turned and ran for the tunnel she knew Lucer was hovering in, but the spider once again beat her to her escape.

"Be still, human," she forcefully commanded, and Kindle, seeing she had no way out, obeyed.

"Please don't eat me! Don't eat me!" she pathetically whimpered.

"Oh goodness, dear, is that what you're fussing about?" the spider sympathetically chuckled. "Don't worry over that one bit. I found out humans aren't worth biting into a long time ago."

"Then why were you chasing me?" Kindle defensively retorted.

"Well, dearie, you were running around my home like some lunatic. What would you do if a stranger walked into your house and took off like that when you said hello?"

Kindle had no idea how to answer the monstrous arachnid—she very much wanted to tell her that she was creepy and shouldn't expect people to stay calm when they meet a giant spider, but Kindle also very much did not want to make her mad.

"I dunno—I guess … I dunno. Sorry," she replied and frowned at her feet.

"Oh, it was just a question. Don't you fret over it," she said, laughing as she waved one of her long legs. "Now tell me your name and what you're up to here. It's been a long while since I've seen humans down here, and now to have you little people popping up is a bit much."

"What? Are you Medara?" Kindle asked in disbelief.

"Yes, dear."

"So you know where Andrew is?"

"Ho, dearie, slow down. I need to know who *you* are before you go tossing names around."

"I'm Kindle, but is Andrew okay? Where is he?" Kindle swung her head around the room as she spoke.

"Calm down, calm down." Medara sighed and shook her head. "Goodness, you're an excitable little thing, aren't you? Well, Kindle, Lady Luna told me to expect you and your one bare foot. She said you and that banged up boy are a couple of heroes, but I don't know about all that. You two look more like lost chicks to me."

Kindle shifted uncomfortably and hugged her arms across her chest.

"Oh, hoo. Don't be insulted by the truth. But it doesn't matter what I think, does it? No. Now let's go see how that friend of yours is patching up—it's high time I checked on him anyway." Without waiting for a response from Kindle, Medara scuttled away to one of the tunnels. Kindle stared at the black hole she had disappeared down but didn't move. Every muscle in her itched to run as fast as possible back the way she had came, but curiosity and concern about Andrew kept her from fleeing. She looked back to the shiny curtain, which she now realized had to be made of Medara's silk, and almost stepped toward it, but some distant noises coming from the way Medara had gone made her stop. Quietly she swept across the room to the opening and stuck her head in it. She still couldn't hear any clear words but determined that the sounds seemed fairly peaceful. Believing that she would probably be safe but still wary of being eaten, Kindle slipped her single flip-flop off in case she needed to run and then took a deep breath before walking down the tunnel. Immediately she found that it was steeply sloped but very short, and so she soon reached the room at its bottom. The circular room appeared to be exactly the same as the one she had just left except beds instead of tunnels lined the wall. Medara was standing over a bed on the right side of the room and even though the spider was blocking the person in it, Kindle was sure it had to be Andrew.

"… and what about this, dearie?" Medara was saying, "Can you feel that? Does it hurt?"

Kindle, trying very hard to keep quiet and unseen, carefully eased into the room until she could see past Medara. She smiled when she saw Andrew sitting up in bed staring down at the black spider leg poking his torso. Medara kept prodding, and Andrew continued to shake his head until the mender nodded and settled onto her back four legs.

"Well, good, good. It seems I've sewn you up quite well. I don't know the last time I mended a human—I've certainly never spun up anyone quite as damaged as you. I don't know what tossed you around, but hoo!"

"I feel fine. Thank you," Andrew said and tried to toss the bedsheets aside, but Medara pinned them down with three of her legs.

"Oh, ho, ho! I'm not ready to let you go just yet. No, dear, you may feel fine, but you're all wrapped up with spider's silk—if not for it, you'd still feel that pain. No, no, I am the mender and you are the patient, so be patient. You need to stay here at least a few more days. And have you seen your eye there?" She caught his head between two of her legs and gently rotated it. "Oh, dearie, that eye. That needs some work."

When Medara turned his head, Andrew was able to see Kindle. She smiled and excitedly waved, and he, though much more calmly, returned the gesture. Medara looked back and forth between the two and released Andrew.

"Oh, good, dear, you're here. I was sure you shot away as soon as I turned around." Medara neared Kindle and bent down to her. "Keep him in that bed, please. I need to fetch something, and I can't have him up and about."

Kindle, holding her breath out of terror, quickly nodded and then exhaled as Medara moved past her and out of the room. As soon as Kindle was sure the spider had crawled out of earshot, she hopped on the end of Andrew's bed.

"Isn't she creepy? Did she really heal you like she said? How long have you been here?" Kindle rambled, not expecting him to answer every question but thoroughly excited to talk to another human again.

"Yeah, she did," Andrew answered and rolled up his t-shirt to show Kindle that his entire torso was wrapped in Medara's silk.

"Ugh!" she groaned, half disgusted, half amazed. "What's that feel like? Is it hard to move?"

"No, spider silk is really stretchy—see." Andrew stuck his thumb under the edge of the material and pulled it down to show her his darkly bruised rib cage.

"Oh, that's gross." Kindle squished up her face but kept staring at the discolored patch of skin. "What's that?" she asked as she pointed to what looked like shiny stitches.

"It's where she sewed my skin back together," he nonchalantly replied. "She had to cut my side to get to my ribs."

"Ugh—oh, that is *really* gross! You let her?"

Andrew just shrugged. "Yeah."

"Eh—" Kindle shuddered. "So was your rib broken? How'd she fix it? I thought people, like, died when they broke their ribs."

Andrew smirked slightly. "She just made a cast with her silk. Spider's silk is really strong—some people say it's as strong as steel," he explained as he pulled the woven sheath back up and let his shirt fall. "It also has antibiotic properties."

"So it really will help," Kindle mused and Andrew nodded. For a few moments she wondered how he knew so much about spiders, but then her thoughts returned to the Cifra. Staring seriously at him, she asked, "You think these guys—I mean, the Cifra—are okay? Like, do you think they really *do* think we're heroes and all that? I mean, they seem okay, but I dunno…."

Andrew shrugged. "They've been pretty helpful."

"Yeah, I guess so." Kindle brought her legs up on the bed and yawned.

Sitting on the soft surface made her suddenly realize how tired she felt. "Do you think they'll know how we can get home?" she asked as she pulled her legs against her chest and laid her head on her knees.

Andrew turned his eyes away and quietly stared at the floor. Kindle was too tired to mind, though, and closed her eyes.

"You know, I tried taking the necklace off and that doesn't work." She yawned again and picked up her head. Clumsily she unfolded herself and lumbered over to the next bed. "I just hope we get to go home soon," she sighed and heard Andrew utter a vague noise in return as she plopped belly down on the soft bed and almost immediately fell asleep.

ARRIVAL OF WHAT IS ANCIENT

K indle was home again. She ran across her backyard to Mikey, who was eating his birthday cake. She grabbed him in a hug and then ran to her mom and dad and tightly embraced them as well. Wanting to tell them about the necklace she had found, Kindle tried to find the chain around her neck, but it was gone. When she looked up, her parents and Mikey were running into the house. Kindle tried to run after them, but her legs couldn't find ground to run across, and she realized that she was riding a giant spider through a maze of trees. Andrew, who was riding a giant moth, flew up beside her for a moment and then sped past her and the spider. Suddenly Lucer, who was juggling all of the tiny lighted orbs, appeared on her other side. He smiled, bouncing all of the lights, then began talking. Kindle leaned forward to hear him. Then, all at once, Lucer stopped juggling and let out an enormous shout.

Kindle gasped as her fists tightened around wads of bedsheet. Her heart racing, she let her eyes spin around the room and realized that she had been dreaming. She rolled over on her back to see the bluish-white baubles hanging from the woven ceiling and reminded herself of reality: she was still in one of Medara's beds in the Tunnels where the Cifra lived. Kindle sighed loudly, looked over to Andrew's bed, and grimaced. He had fallen asleep, but Medara had apparently first tended to his bruised face. It was half covered by gray goop. Wanting to get a better view of the disgusting glob, Kindle tried to sit up but ended up slipping down between the two beds when a loud, angry shout echoed off the curved wall. She peeked over her bed to search for who had make the racket but ducked as another awful yell bounced around the room. Then a very rough, deep voice bellowed, "You insulting human! Get back here!"

Another voice broke out in a stream of cursing, and Kindle's eyes widened in shock. She craned her neck to see Andrew, who amazingly had not stirred at all.

"Human filth! Urgh!" the deep voice boomed, and a heavy thud resounded.

"Back off, stinkin' bug!"

"You *will*—" a series of grunts and foul words exploded, "—stay here," the first voice panted triumphantly. "You *will* remain here until the lady sends for—"

"I don't care about some stupid lady! Back off me!"

"Disgraceful!"

Another loud thump sounded, then an odd scratching noise began, and Kindle chanced a glimpse of the scene. A large Cifra, who seemed to be wearing a full suit of shiny, boxy armor, was disappearing behind the dirt he was flinging into the opening of the tunnel. Kindle felt her heart sink into a pool of fear. They were trapped.

"Stupid bug," she heard the second voice grumble and pulled herself a little higher to see who it belonged to. A boy was sprawled out in front of the tunnel also watching it transform into a wall of dirt. Kindle couldn't see much of him besides his shaggy black hair and faded t-shirt. As she walked her elbows onto the bed, his head snapped around and his shockingly bright blue eyes glared at her.

"What?!" he very rudely and loudly spat.

"Um ... uh," Kindle stammered and blinked.

"*What?!*" he angrily barked again and swiveled on the floor, stood up, and stalked over to the other side of the bed. Now that Kindle could clearly see him, she couldn't decide if he was completely repelling or captivating. She could tell that he was older than her but definitely not by much—he was tall and lean, but his face still held a softness of younger years. His skin was an interesting caramel tone and between it, his soft black hair, and odd but amazing blue eyes, he could have been good-looking, but his hateful sneer and old, baggy clothes erased most of his attractiveness.

"Do you have a staring problem?" he asked darkly, and Kindle dropped her eyes to the bed between them. He let out a brief snicker, and Kindle glared back up at him, but the boy had caught sight of Andrew.

"What's his problem?" he asked as he made a repulsed face.

"That's Andrew." Kindle stood up and crossed her arms. "And he doesn't have a problem. He's hurt. Don't you know this is a hospital?" She tried to sound sassy, but since she wasn't really sure if they actually *were* in a hospital, Kindle's tone slid into uncertainty rather than derision.

"Pft. No. I don't know what this stupid place is, Miss Know-it-all."

Kindle gave him an ugly glare, but he began to glower up at the strange lights. She wanted very much to spit something condescending back but was even more avid to learn if he was wearing a necklace like hers and Andrew's.

"Really, you don't know what this place is?" she asked, still glaring. He raised an eyebrow at her then returned to sneering at the ceiling and very sarcastically replied, "Nah, I come here every day."

"So you, like, really don't know where you are?"

He sighed, "C'mon, are you stupid? No. N. O. I don't, okay?"

Kindle recoiled at his defensiveness and huffed, "You don't have to be such a jerk! It was just a question."

"A stupid question." He smirked slightly.

"Ugh! You're a jerk!" Kindle exploded and defiantly plopped down on the end of Andrew's bed, trying to face the wall but still let the boy see her angry frown. She heard him quietly snort at her and whipped around, ready to engage in a screaming match if necessary. A thin metal chain lying across the back of his neck, though, snatched away her vehemence.

"So did that necklace get you here?" she slyly asked his back. He said nothing but tensed and gave her a confused grimace over his shoulder. She watched one of his hands brush over his collar, discover the thin metal strip, and then pull it away from his skin so he could examine it. Turning back to her, he fished the rest of the chain up from his t-shirt. They both saw that a brilliant sapphire-colored oval hung at the end of it before a loud noise pulled their attention upward.

"What the—!" he shouted and quickly slinked back against the far wall as a long black spike jabbed through the ceiling. Kindle also jumped back as she realized that the spike was a spider leg. It slashed across the beautiful silk with ease, and Medara effortlessly swung through the long slit. Then all of her terrible legs went to work and in seconds mended the long gash. Medara made a satisfied noise and then gracefully flipped to the floor.

"My, my, that is the last time I let those dung beetles...," she murmured and scuttled over to where the tunnel opening had stood. "Hmmm...," she calmly mused and then suddenly fiercely stabbed the dirt with her front two legs. "Oh, goodness!" she exasperatedly cried as she retracted her legs and turned to Kindle. "Oh, there you are, dearie. Do you know, I think that beetle filled the whole tunnel. Oh my, they are overzealous—I'll be making him dig it out, that's certain. Oh, dear, don't look so excited now, I'll get you two out another way." Medara—to Kindle's horror—patted her on the cheek before she turned to Andrew.

"And how is this one?" She peered at his face with each eye and then delicately lifted away the disgusting gray mush pile. Kindle was surprised to see that his face had completely healed.

"Ah, fantastic," Medara sighed and flung the grey mass aside. "Now, he should wake.... Ah! Hello dear, how's it all feel?"

Andrew blinked awake and squinted blurrily at her. "Huh?" he mumbled, rubbing his eyes in the crook of his arm.

"Oh, come now, sit up, sit up," she encouraged as she pushed him up herself, "and let's see how you are." Medara began to poke Andrew all over his torso, but he didn't seem to notice. Finally he looked up from his arm and stared around the room. His eyes stopped at the boy, who was still pressed against the opposite side of the room. Andrew quickly made eye contact with Kindle, then Medara, and finally turned his eyes back to the boy. Medara followed Andrew's gaze and stopped poking him.

"Oh ho! Now who are you? Another one of these frazzled heroes?" she joyfully laughed at him, but her friendliness did not sweep away his silence or murderous stare.

"Oh, goodness, you humans are skittish. Now, I know you can hear me, so let's have your name." When he simply glared harder at her, she sighed and shook her head. "Oh, dearie, I know I'm a bit shocking, but I will not eat you or do whatever you humans are so startled about." She looked back around at Kindle. "Is that what you said, dear?"

Kindle nodded and then bent around her to see the boy. "She really won't eat us." She said the words much more confidently than she felt about them. "She's a mender—like a doctor."

"Oh, ho, ho. How thoughtless I am. They didn't tell you about me, did they now? No, those beetles aren't masters of formalities. Ha hum. My name is Medara, dear, and like Kindle said, I am the mender for the Cifra. And this, you know, is Kindle," she informed him as she gestured to her, "and this one is Andrew. Now, we've been civil, so return us the favor, dear."

They all stared at him, waiting for his response. For a few seconds his eyes darted over them and the room as if he was searching for an escape, but finally his blue eyes bored into Medara.

"Tad," he answered. "What is this place and what is this?" He nimbly pulled the chain away from his neck with his thumb and switched his glare to Kindle.

"You knew I had it. What is it?"

"I—I don't know," she said weakly, "But I've got one and so does Andrew." She pulled up her own necklace for him to see and pointed at Andrew, who nodded and showed his also.

"When we put them on, we just, like, appeared in the forest, so I figured that's how you got here too."

"I didn't put this stupid thing on," he defensively interjected, "I…." His eyes shifted to the side, and his nose wrinkled in thought. "I don't know, but I didn't put it on." With that he lifted it off his neck and flung it down. Immediately Medara scooped it up and dangled it before all of her eyes.

"Oh, ho, ho now, dear. Where did you get this?" she asked in a faraway voice. Tad glared at her and frowned.

"I found it. What's it matter?"

"This is old, ancient." She glanced back at Kindle then Andrew. "Never saw those but…." Medara faced the blue gem again. "I know this one. Where did you say you found this, Tad?"

"I didn't."

Medara laid the necklace back on the floor as she looked hard at him.

"Perhaps, perhaps," Kindle heard Medara faintly whisper. The spider shook her head. "Now, what am I going on about—Lady Luna is waiting at my door for you three, and I'm chatting." She flicked the blue necklace to Tad's feet.

"Put that on, dear—I think you'll need it." She clicked her fangs a few times then sighed, "Now, I really hate to do this, but that bull-headed beetle—" Medara ripped a gash through the floor and easily sprang onto the ceiling.

"Just slide down the silk. Alright dears? Oh, Andrew, yes, you are clear to leave. You just keep that silk skin. Come on, now, after me." Medara spun and furiously knitted her legs to fashion a thick strand of silk as she lowered herself through the hole. Once she disappeared, Andrew pushed himself out of bed and carefully stepped to the middle of the room.

"Dude! Are you nuts?!" Tad scoffed as Andrew curled his hand around the ropelike strand. Andrew ignored him and half smiled at Kindle.

"You think it's okay?" she quickly asked. Andrew ran his eyes up and down the silk, gave it a few tugs, nodded, and then wrapped himself around it and slid out of view.

Kindle gasped and ran over to the opening, trying to see through it, but as soon as it had swallowed Andrew's yellow hair, the edges had sprung back together.

"Dude is nuts," Tad grumbled and finally eased a few strides away from the wall. Kindle glared at him.

"Shut up. At least he's smart enough to not stay trapped here." She grabbed the silk and slid away from Tad before he could spit something back at her. Just a second later, she landed on something soft at the edge of a room almost exactly like the one above. Every detail seemed the same, except the beds against the wall were tiny. Kindle checked and saw one of the beds, which was just big enough to hold her folded legs, was the soft surface under her.

"Good, good, now let's hope that Tad comes on his own," Medara chuckled from the middle of the room, "It might shock him out of his wits if I have to go up and bring him along."

Kindle tried to fake an accommodating laugh but instead choked out an awkward noise as she stood and sidled past Medara to the tunnel opening where Andrew stood.

"She's so creepy," Kindle whispered to him, but he merely shrugged and kept gazing up at the slit they had dropped from.

"You think he'll come?" she asked, staring at it also. "I hope not," she quietly grumbled so Medara wouldn't hear, "He's a jerk." Andrew smiled very slightly but remained silent.

"Goodness," Medara impatiently huffed. "Well, go on now, you two, up that tunnel and just out the door. Lady Luna is waiting for you. That one will be along soon I'm sure." She scurried over to the silk strand and expertly climbed out of sight. Kindle heard a clamor from above and grinned. She wished she could watch Tad run in fear from Medara, but Andrew was already trekking away from her. As fast as she could up the steep tunnel, Kindle jogged to catch him and then slowed to his pace. This walkway was much longer than the one she had traveled down earlier, but they still did not have to wait long before they emerged into the room with the shiny curtain.

"Here, this way!" Kindle excitedly cried and jumped in front of Andrew to the exit. Looking over her shoulder, she pulled back the light woven silk and barreled into someone.

"Sorry! I'm sorry!" she yelped and spun around to see Lady Luna forgivingly smiling at her. Andrew, much more carefully, slid into the dim tunnel.

"Ah, Andrew, correct?" she softly asked, and he nodded to his feet.

"Do you feel better?"

Again he nodded at the ground.

"Good," she breathed and then silently smiled at each of them then the curtain. As the seconds passed and she continued to slowly turn her beautiful face back and forth, Kindle began to feel awkward in the silence.

"Uh, Medara said you were waiting for us?" she finally decided to mumble.

"Yes, but I believed three heroes to be with her. Perhaps the boy with Tarus has not come yet?"

"Oh, no, um—I mean, yeah, he's in there, but ... but he's really angry."

Lady Luna gave her a confused look. "Angry? Why? Oh, was Tarus rough with him? I was worried when Strin called for him."

"Yeah, that guy who was with him wasn't very nice ... but *he* wasn't very nice either."

Lady Luna sighed deeply and closed her eyes.

"My Lady, if I...," a hesitant voice chimed in, and Kindle smiled.

"Lucer!"

"Yes, hello young Kindle." He quickly flashed a grin back and then cleared his throat into seriousness. "If I could assist in any way, my Lady...."

"Yes, Lucer, thank you." She turned to him. "Please find Tarus. Let him know I must speak with him before dawn."

"Yes, ma'am! I will!" he heartily cried and grabbed his lantern.

"Oh, Lucer," Lady Luna put up a hand, "could you leave your light for us?"

"Certainly!" He nodded at Kindle. "The heroes must see!"

"Thank you, Lucer. I will have it at the Golden Hive for you."

Lucer bowed in the air and then shot down the dark tunnel. Lady Luna stared after him for a few moments before she laid a hand on Medara's curtain.

"Is the boy alright? Did Tarus harm him?"

"Oh, no, I think he's fine, just mad. And...."

"Yes?" the moth's voice encouraged Kindle to finish.

"And, well, he didn't really want to listen to Medara when she told us to come meet you. I think he's scared of her."

Lady Luna nodded understandingly as she let her hand slip the curtain aside. With only a second to process the shape hurtling at them, Kindle and Andrew scattered as Tad barreled into the tunnel. He smashed against the wall, spun, and let out a laugh of triumph.

"Stupid spider!" he yelled while blinking to let his eyes adjust to the dim light. The smirk on his face curdled into a grimace, though, when he noticed Lady Luna.

"Not more of you freaks," he growled and defensively hunched his shoulders.

"They're not freaks—they're Cifra. And she's their queen," Kindle quickly shot at him. Tad menacingly glared back at her.

"I am truly sorry for the way Tarus treated you, young man." Lady Luna's musical voice pulled Tad's eyes to her and slightly softened his face. "His conduct was much too harsh. Please, young hero, what is your name?"

Tad gave her a stupefied stare. "What?"

"Your name—what is your title?"

"It's Tad," Kindle impatiently chimed in and earned another sharp glare from Tad before he returned his wary eyes to Lady Luna.

"What did you call me?"

"Hero. You bear the mark of one of the makers of Anelthalien, but—" She raised a palm and sighed heavily. "I would like all of you to come with me to the Golden Hive where Lord Rex and I can help all four of you understand."

"Three," Andrew very quietly corrected, still looking down.

"Yes, the three of you, but our last hero has arrived as well and is already waiting for us at the Hive. Come." She pinched Lucer's tiny lantern from the wall and gently shook it. "We have much to discuss before dawn."

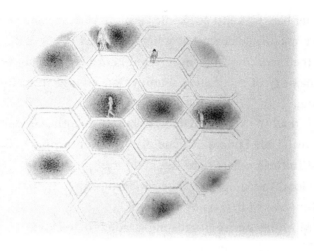

THE GOLDEN HIVE

Kindle, Andrew, and Tad silently trailed behind Lady Luna's beautiful wings as she led them through tunnel after tunnel. The quiet and blackness surrounding them didn't seem so overwhelming to Kindle now that she was among the odd group. Somehow, just as she had in the forest, Lady Luna created a strange ease in Kindle and transformed all of her earlier anxiety into sleepiness. She let out a huge yawn and caught Andrew smirk. He was right at her shoulder, so she could faintly whisper to him without disturbing the peaceful quiet.

"What? I didn't get to sleep very much like you."

He shrugged but kept his small grin, and Kindle shook her head. Out of the corner of her eye, she snatched a glimpse backward to see if Tad was still following them. He was barely inside the circle of lantern light but was indeed stalking slowly forward. When Lady Luna had first directed them to follow her, Kindle had been surprised he had so readily complied and was convinced that he would bolt at any second. Kindle wasn't sure exactly how long they all had been walking but hoped they would stop soon. Her lack of sleep had left her tired, and the hard dirt floor was beginning to hurt her bare feet. Just as Kindle began to wish she hadn't lost her flip flops, Lady Luna turned down a new, lighted tunnel. A few of the firefly watchmen with their clinking lanterns hovered here and there above their heads, but the majority of the golden illumination poured from the opening ahead of them.

"Is that it?" Kindle excitedly asked, "Is that the Golden Hive?"

"Yes," Lady Luna warmly replied without turning to her, "It is the heart of the Tunnels, where Lord Rex and I live."

"Good morning, my lady! Good morning, heroes!" cried one of the watchmen as he flew up beside them.

"Morning, Luke? Has the night faded so quickly?"

"No—and yes," he bumbled. "Well, we've passed midnight anyway ... ah, anyway, the hero you requested to be brought here—Lord Rex had awakened and summoned her to the throne room. He, uh, hopes it's, um...."

"That is fine, thank you," Lady Luna assented, smiling to him.

"Ah, yes, alright, good!" He nervously flitted near them a few seconds longer then flew back to the tunnel wall. Kindle heard Tad condescendingly snort behind her, and she looked back to see him mockingly sneering around at the fireflies. She rolled her eyes as she turned away to gaze around herself. A quick scan of all the watchmen told her that Lucer was nowhere near. The archway at the end of the tunnel caught her attention, and she tried to peer through it, but the closer they came to it, the more Lady Luna blocked her line of vision. Just a few feet from the opening, Lady Luna stopped and placed Lucer's lantern on an empty hook.

"Watchmen, this is Lucer's light," she informed the long tunnel behind them, "Please, when he arrives, direct him to wait here with it. I shall be back before morning."

"Yes, ma'am!" the group of watchmen enthusiastically boomed in unison.

She began to step forward but halted to peer over her shoulder.

"Kindle, Andrew, Tad, please follow me carefully. The Golden Hive is not considerate of those who walk."

"Huh?" Kindle softly wondered, but Lady Luna had already entered the golden room. As Kindle hurried through after her, she heard Andrew murmur, "Watch your step."

In one moment the warning and the golden glow, which now surrounded them, instantly made sense. They had stepped into the bottom of a humongous hive-shaped honeycomb. Enormous hexagons—some filled with marvelously shiny honey, most golden caverns that faded into black holes—covered almost every surface. Kindle saw, as Lady Luna easily glided across the floor, that the narrow yellow bars between the combs were the paths they would have to navigate to reach the opposite wall. Nervously spreading her arms for balance, Kindle carefully began her journey. She kept her eyes glued to the golden strip below her as she progressed. It was a little wider than her shoulders, and Kindle knew she could walk across a much thinner balance beam, but the deep pits on either side of it incited her fear. Every few steps, she peeked ahead to Lady Luna, who was waiting for them where the honeycombs sloped up into the wall, and soon ended her dangerous balancing act beside her. Lady Luna took her hand, and Kindle blinked up at the queen.

"I'll keep you steady," she breathed in her calming voice, and Kindle eased. Lady Luna lifted her eyes, and Kindle followed them to watch Andrew and Tad maneuver across the broken floor. Tad was nearing them steadily, using the same method of stability as Kindle, but Andrew still hung in the tunnel archway.

"Come on, Andrew!" Kindle cried, beckoning with her whole arm. Tad swayed then lifted two ire-filled eyes at her.

"Oh, sorry!" she apologized and slapped her hand over her mouth. He huffed and waved his head in agitation but wordlessly returned his concentration downward.

"Are you going to have to go get Andrew?" Kindle whispered to Lady Luna, who shook her head.

"No. He will come on his own."

When Tad reached them, he sat on the thin walkway and hung his legs over the empty combs.

"Come on, you wimp!" he yelled then let out a laugh. Kindle gave the back of his head a disgusted glare and was tempted to kick him off into one of the holes.

"It's not so bad," she called, choosing to ignore Tad instead. "It's really not a long way." Kindle smiled when Andrew dragged his hand from the dirt wall. "See, he's not a wimp," she fiercely breathed to Tad.

"Pft—whatever," he grumbled and they all watched as Andrew slid a foot onto the nearest golden beam. He, unlike Kindle and Tad, very unsteadily inched sideways with bent knees and arms, looking like he was preparing to dive. Kindle bit her finger to keep from shouting; she wanted to tell him the easiest path across but was terrified he was going to topple out of sight if her voice distracted him. Every few moments Andrew began to wobble and would spin his arms wildly, causing Kindle to hold her breath and Tad to snicker, but each time Andrew somehow regained his balance and finally stood next to Tad.

Lady Luna released Kindle's hand and said, "Now our way will be easier." She stepped up onto one of the combs and swept a hand around the room as she spoke. "As the Hive rises, each layer of honeycombs sits further back. We can walk along them until—" her hand stopped and pointed about halfway up the enormous cavern at a particularly large, hollow honeycomb, "—we reach the throne room."

"Then are you gunna tell us what's going on?" Tad suspiciously asked, still seated and still blocking a very annoyed Andrew. Lady Luna stared silently down at them, and for the first time Kindle saw hardness in her expression and heard it in her voice.

"Douse your anger. Trust." She aimed her words at him like melodic darts, then tight-lipped she quickly began her ascent.

"What's her deal?" Tad grumbled and carefully stood to follow Kindle up the makeshift stairs.

"Maybe you should just shut up for a while and quit being such a jerk," Kindle whispered back and heard him make an angry, defiant sound. She grinned to herself at his lack of a comeback, but her small victory faded from her mind as she focused on the narrow, uneven ledge beneath her feet. Despite what Lady Luna had said, the climb proved difficult for all three of them. Where two vertical honeycombs met, the ledge dove in a sharp slope and then shot back up to a higher level, and so they found themselves sliding and jumping more than walking. In one especially steep junction, Kindle attempted her routine escape hop but instead slipped back into the vee. She tried again, with the same result, and then plopped down into a tired, frustrated heap. Before she could finish her exhausted sigh, though, she heard Tad.

"Move," he commanded from above, and she twisted around to glare up at him.

"No!" she rudely shouted, but her angry face broke into a pout and she whined, "I can't get out. I need help."

"Hmm, too bad for you." He shrugged and slid down next to her. Kindle angrily swatted his legs as he stepped over her. In one swift move, though, he bounded up and heaved himself onto the higher platform.

"Heh, heh," he condescendingly chortled down at her then disappeared.

"Ugh! You butthead!" she fumed and pounded her fist against the wall, but Andrew's voice quelled her fit of rage.

"You need help?" he asked her while sending a disgusted look in Tad's direction.

"Um, yeah," she admitted with embarrassment.

"Come back up here and get a running start at it." He motioned and carefully inched backward so she could follow his direction. Kindle climbed to him then spun and attacked the pit just as he had advised. The next second she triumphantly stood where Tad had mocked her moments ago.

"Hey, thanks, that was smart," she said as she caught Andrew's wrists and helped him mount the incline.

"Yup," he mumbled and deliberately stared away from the now very deep drop-off on their left. "Let's go."

"Oh, yeah." Kindle gave him a smile before returning to the trek she had momentarily forgotten. They didn't have much further to climb and soon hoisted themselves onto the ledge where Lady Luna and Tad were waiting.

"Ugh! I'm so tired," Kindle sighed and leaned against the wall.

"Yes, you all do need rest," Lady Luna sympathetically agreed. "But first we all have questions and answers." She stared into the tunnel created by the large honeycomb that stood open beside them. "Come, we are very close," she breathed as if speaking to herself more than to them and then strode into the golden passageway.

"This better be it. I'm sick of walking," Tad complained but followed her with Kindle and Andrew right behind him. To Kindle's relief, the tunnel was short and the room that opened at the end of it, even though it was honey-colored and hive-shaped, was much smaller than the last space and had a smooth, unbroken floor. As they walked into the glossy, sweet-smelling room, Kindle watched Lady Luna glide over to a seated Cifra who was undoubtedly Lord Rex. He was as tall and just as humanlike as Lady Luna but was completely different from her in almost every other way. All at once he reminded Kindle of a monarch butterfly and a millionaire who lounged around in his expensive silk housecoat. What must have been his four wings were wrapped loosely around him to form an elegant orange and black robe, and his black face wore an easy, somewhat smug expression. When Lady Luna reached him, he stood and held out a black arm to receive her hand. She took it then said something inaudible to him that caused his bright, amber eyes to turn toward Kindle and a brilliant white smile to flow across his face.

"Ah! Come in! Come in!" he called cheerfully to them as he beckoned with his free hand. Kindle glanced sideways at Andrew and Tad before they all started slowly approaching him, but Lord Rex didn't wait for them to come near. He unfurled his wings to reveal a rich red-orange robe and leapt to them in one arching bound.

"Heroes!" he heartily exclaimed while clapping Tad's shoulder and grabbing Andrew's hand to shake. "I am honored to welcome you to our home." He stood back, crossed his arms, and fiercely smiled again. "Ah! This is wonderful!"

"Rex—" Lady Luna began with a bit of sternness, and he nodded back at her.

"Yes, yes—introductions, formalities, yes, my lady. But we must arouse out final hero first." He gave them one more enthusiastic grin then flew back beside the throne carved out of the golden honey that Lady Luna sat in. The tall butterfly crouched down to shake someone awake then stood again, helping up a girl with him. Kindle couldn't help but stare in surprise as Lord

Rex brought her around the front of the two thrones. She had been certain that the girl would be from America, just as she and Andrew were, but upon seeing her, Kindle highly doubted she was even from planet earth. The girl was very much a normal human and seemed not too much older than her, but her outfit—a long, brown leather vest over a long-sleeved olive-green tunic, brown leather leggings, and short, flat, floppy boots—was far from anything she had ever seen anyone her age wear.

"Come around, heroes," Lord Rex called and eased into his throne so he could smile at all of them at once. Hesitantly Kindle, Andrew, and Tad finished crossing the room to stand beside the yawning girl. She finished her sleepy gape, brushed her long, dark auburn hair away from her fair face, and smiled at them.

"Hello," she quietly greeted them, but before they could respond, Lord Rex spoke.

"Heroes! I am Lord Rex, king of the day Cifra, and this is my lovely Lady Luna, queen of the night. This is wonderful, to have you four gathered here in our home. Please, tell us your names and titles." He eagerly leaned forward and stared at each of them.

"What?" Tad finally grunted with disgust.

"What do they call you, young man? Where do you hail from?"

"Ella," the oddly dressed girl interjected, "of Garrick Kingdom."

"Ah, yes, thank you, Ella!" cheered Lord Rex then gestured at Kindle, Andrew, and Tad to speak.

"Kindle, from, um, Missouri."

"Andrew. Jersey."

"Tad, Florida—okay? This is stupid. She already told her my name," he defensively grumbled, and Lord Rex's face slid into confusion as he glanced at Lady Luna.

"Rex, these are not from Anelthalien. We have much to explain," she gently told him, patting his wrist.

"Where are these places you speak of?" he asked, now serious.

"America, earth, the *world*," Tad snorted and spun a finger in the air. "What stupid planet are you on?"

Lord Rex blinked, apparently taken aback by Tad's rudeness, and wordlessly looked to Lady Luna, who sighed and nodded. "Young man, show some manners. You don't seem to understand that you are in the presence of royalty," rumbled Lord Rex but just received a glare from Tad.

After a few moments of tense silence, Kindle felt as if all of her questions would never be answered and burst. "Um, sorry, uh sir, Lord Rex, but, um, like, we don't know where we are or what's going on or why you're calling us heroes or anything." Her voice started to break, and she took a deep, steadying breath.

"And that is why you are here," Lady Luna calmly said and then touched Lord Rex's arm. "I will tell them." She paused to stare into each of their eyes. "You are in Anelthalien—a land that is its own world, far removed from the places you know, and until now, I believe our two worlds have never crossed. Anelthalien has rested here a very long time, since before a time anyone could remember. No one knows when it began, but how, we Cifra at least are certain. Four makers—the four makers whose marks you each bear—spun and wove this land together with their powers over earth, sky, water, and fire. They filled it with beautiful creatures—animals of all kinds in each of their domains—and lived as rulers and guardians of all they had created."

"But then men came," Rex said darkly. "They came on boats from beyond the seas that surround Anelthalien. Perhaps they were lost ... but it does not matter. They came and ventured out on the land as if it was theirs—cutting, digging, and so on—tearing the world and catching animals the makers had guarded for so long. That led the makers to see a need for something more in Anelthalien. Each of the four makers created ... well, something like a ... hmm...." Lord Rex held his chin in thought then turned to Lady Luna. "What were they called?"

"Elemental spirits. Each one fashioned from the element of its maker's domain."

"Yes, that! Thank you, my Lady. So the makers created these spirits that were and at the same time guarded whichever element to which they belonged. And those necklaces you each have—those were the connections between each maker and its spirit." Rex smiled as they peered down at the gems.

"Really?" Ella gasped, "Is that true? I've heard many stories about how Anelthalien came about but…." She shook her head.

"Nearly true." Lady Luna's eyes fell to the floor as she continued, "The beautiful jewels you wear were not always necklaces. When the makers brought the spirits into existence, they did so by pouring much power, strength, and life into those colored pieces and implanting them in the hearts of the spirits. That is where the connection lived."

"Yes, now I recall it!" Lord Rex snapped his fingers. "And the spirits drew all of their life from the makers, depended on them for everything and faithfully returned the favor by using their power to guard the domains."

"So how do we have these?" Andrew quietly asked, staring down at his yellow gem.

"Ah! We are getting to the thick of it now!" Lord Rex shook a fist and grinned. "So as time passed, these four spirits learned that they could draw power from the makers' marks within them and began to pull more and more. They became so powerful that they separated themselves from their element. Think, heroes—water, air, fire, and earth walking through Anelthalien. What a sight it would have been!"

"They formed bodies for themselves. Humanlike ones," Lady Luna added and Rex nodded.

"Yes, and that was the beginning of the reason you four are standing here. The spirits saw how powerful and independent of their maker they could be and ripped those stones out of their souls."

Kindle gasped and Ella whispered, "Did they die?"

"No." Lady Luna's voice was tinted with ice. "When the spirits separated themselves from their makers, all of the power that they had stolen resided in the marks, which they encased in precious metals and hung on their necks." She looked away to the wall. "They gained the freedom and power they wished … and then lost so much."

Silence opened around them as they waited for one of the royal Cifra to continue, but neither spoke.

"And then?" Ella urged, "What happened then? Was that the cause of the Great War? Were—"

"War?" Lord Rex asked and sent a questioned glance to Lady Luna, who shook her head at him.

"No, no war ensued."

"Ah, I did not believe so," he mumbled then turned back to Ella. "No, you see, when the spirits liberated themselves, they stopped acting as the guardians they were meant to be and, hmm … took their own paths I suppose you could say."

"They wanted more power," Lady Luna seriously sighed to Lord Rex.

"Yes," he admitted then shrugged. "But the Cifra—our ancestors—only saw the beginnings of that all. Once the makers vanished, our people built the wonderful home we have now." Lord Rex finished proudly, and Kindle was reminded of Lucer's bragging in the woods.

"Lucer told me that!" she excitedly cried and received a mix of surprised stares from everyone. "Um, sorry," she lowered her voice. "I just, um, remembered … Lucer said that you guys made the Tunnels after Hux made you. He said Hux was one of the makers."

"Yes, Hux was our maker," Lady Luna replied and smiled at Kindle. "After creating the animals of the sky, he changed the winged insects into his special race of helpers."

"And we—the Cifra—were the guardians of the sky long before that spirit … what was his name…? Ah, it does not matter!" Lord Rex enthusiastically grinned and banged the armrest of his throne. "We Cifra are much better sky guards than he was."

"But…." Andrew scrunched his brow at Lord Rex. "You live underground."

"Yeah! Why are all you flying freaks underground?" Tad laughed.

Lord Rex's grin instantly dropped from his face. "Ah, well, you see, when the makers disappeared and Hux was nowhere to be found, well, without direction the Cifra couldn't very well guard the sky."

"Rex." Lady Luna shot two very steady eyes at him. "Do not be proud."

He stared back at her for a few seconds then lowered his face. "Fear," he confessed simply, and Lady Luna placed her hand on his arm.

"Our ancestors fled from the skies in fear when Hux disappeared. They dug deep in the earth where no danger could touch them. Many, many years have passed since then—enough that few Cifra know anything of the past or anything outside of the Tunnels. And still we remain removed from the sky and the whole land below it. Still afraid."

"It's more complicated than that. We have an established—"

"No, Rex, it is not," Lady Luna sliced into his words and silenced the monarch.

"Excuse me." Ella bent into a slight bow. "Lord Rex, Lady Luna, I still don't understand why we have these necklaces. Perhaps I miss—"

"We don't know," Rex interrupted with agitation. "We could unravel every moment of Anelthalien's history but only until the Cifra hid underground. After that, we know nothing. We can tell you only what those necklaces are, not how or why they came to be yours."

"Then why are you calling us heroes?" Kindle asked in exasperation and turned to Andrew. "What did Missi say? In the woods, remember? Didn't she say why she kept calling us heroes?"

All eyes turned to Andrew, and his fell to the floor. He seemed to be thinking, but Kindle couldn't help but prompt, "Like, wasn't it something about a queen?"

Andrew nodded. "Yes. A fallen queen would summon four heroes who had the marks of the makers."

Rex shook his head and sighed, "Missi … Missi is unlike any of our other bees. A good worker but … well, she is not all there sometimes."

"Now, Rex, be kind," Lady Luna softly chided and Lord Rex shrugged. "Is she not?"

"Excuse us, heroes. What Missi told you is a story our schoolmaster Gustin enchants all of the children with. He tells them that in a kingdom just north of Danica Woods lived a good queen who watched over all of Anelthalien to make sure all of the people in the land were good."

"Oh, yes, I've heard stories like this!" Ella smiled in excitement.

Lady Luna nodded and continued, "Gustin tells the children that the four makers were pleased with the good queen and gave her gifts—each of their marks—that she could use to protect Anelthalien. And then, just as Missi told you, one day the queen found herself in trouble and used the marks to call for heroes who would rescue her and the whole land."

Tad sniffed loudly. "No. I'm not gunna save anybody. This is stupid." He pulled the necklace over his head and held it out. "Get somebody else. I'm not helping anybody."

"Excuse me?" Ella leaned forward to see him past Andrew and Kindle. "You are a *hero*, chosen by ancient magic. You can't refuse—"

"Yeah, well, I am. I'm not doing all this messed-up fairy tale junk. This is stupid. I'm outta here." With that he flung his necklace down and started toward the exit.

"Oh." Ella shook her head and trotted after him. Kindle spun to watch, hoping she would punch him. When Ella reached him, though, she simply stood in front of him and crossed her arms.

"You are not leaving."

"Yeah, I *am*." He tried to sidestep, but she matched his movement.

"Didn't you hear what she said? You—out of apparently every person in your world and mine—have been chosen as one of the four heroes who will save this whole land."

"So?" He tried to maneuver around her again but to no avail.

"So?! So if you leave now and refuse this responsibility, people could die."

"Calm down. She said it was just a story."

"Then why are you here?" she strongly retorted and silenced Tad into stillness. They angrily stared at one another until Ella suddenly softened her face and said, "You have some purpose here, and it very likely ties to the fate of some of Anelthalien."

"I don't care." He tried to wave her back, but she caught his wrist.

"*I* care. This is my home, and I would be grateful if you stayed to help it before you go back to yours."

Tad yanked his hand away and gave her an odd grimace as he rubbed his wrist.

"Okay, whatever. I'll stay, but not because I want to help you," he sneered, but she lifted a corner of her mouth and replied, "Thank you."

The pair walked back over to the golden thrones and took spots on opposite sides of Kindle and Andrew. Tad stooped to retrieve his necklace and as he put it on, asked, "So what? Do we go talk to this queen to see what she wants?"

"Well, ah—" Rex cleared his throat, obviously just as surprised at Tad's question as everyone else. "No. You see, the queen—and the whole story—may not be true, and even if it is, the queen may not be alive still. We can really only point you in the right direction … and as long as we've existed, no city has laid north of our Woods. I thought we made it clear, heroes: we do not know why you are here."

"But Rex." Lady Luna suddenly seemed deep in thought. "We do know of someone who would."

He energetically shook his head, "Oh, no. No, no, *no*. I am not dealing with that man again. We have a pact. We made an agreement—"

"They could go on their own."

"Hm. Yes, well. Heroes, a man named Azildor lives north of our woods. We believe he could help you further. That is where you will go."

"Tomorrow," Lady Luna added and Lord Rex blinked at her. "Yes, Rex, tomorrow. Now you four must rest."

"Ah, of course, rest. Yes, I'll call some bees—they should be along soon." Rex rose and offered a hand to Lady Luna. "It is almost morning, my Lady, I can manage them if you would like to retire."

She took his hand, stood beside him, and said, "Thank you. Provide them with food as well."

"Yes, yes. Go and do not worry—I will see them cared for."

"Wait!" Kindle said before Lady Luna could leave, "I can't stay here—I need to go home. I mean, I've gotta go to school and stuff." She looked at Ella apologetically. "It's not like I don't want to help, I do, but … you know, my parents are going to worry, and I dunno, I don't want to make them mad. Maybe I could just go home for a little bit and tell them not to worry?" She tried to smile but was worried that Ella might explode at *her* now. To her surprise, Lord Rex spoke.

"Ah, I suppose that is not out of the question. Nothing wrong with informing her parents of her whereabouts, hm?" he asked, gazing around the group for affirmation.

"You know how to get me home?" Kindle felt delight arouse her tired mind at the thought of being in her own house.

"Hm? Know how?" Lord Rex turned to see Lady Luna's reaction; she was slowly shaking her head.

"No, Kindle, we do not know from where you came and do not hold the power to return you there. When you leave Anelthalien, I believe, is a decision that the mark around your neck will decide."

Kindle's joy sunk away as she asked, "We can't go home? Will we ever get to go home?"

"Who cares?" Tad mumbled.

"For now, rest," Lady Luna comfortingly spoke over him, "We will see that you meet Azildor before the night falls again this day." She turned her sleepy green eyes to Lord Rex. "Wake them at midday. That will ensure their journey's success."

"I will see it done." Lord Rex nodded then waved at her. "Now sleep, my Lady."

She nodded then spread her lovely wings and silently glided away.

"Oh, she's beautiful," Ella whispered as Lord Rex motioned for them to follow him through the same tunnel. He led all four of them back down the uneven golden ledge but stopped when they were still far above the daunting floor.

"Young ladies!" He searched the small group to find Kindle and Ella. "If you would follow this comb, you will find an accommodating cell at its end. I will send one of my trusted workers to wake you when the sun is at its highest, so sleep sound until then. Young men, a cell that will fit you is a bit further." Lord Rex jauntily led the two boys further away, leaving Kindle and Ella staring at the dark hole in front of them.

Finally Ella sighed, "I can't wait for a good bed." Then she crouched and disappeared down the tunnel.

"You sure it's okay?" Kindle called after her.

"Come along, you must see this!" Ella's voice cheerfully echoed back. Kindle sighed, snatched one more glance around the hive to see Lord Rex directing Tad and Andrew down another passageway, and then bent to travel along the one before her. When she reached the end of the tunnel, Kindle straightened up and relaxed her nervous shoulders. The little domed space was much cozier than she had expected. It was dug out of the rich, dark soil rather than built from golden honey and so was dim and cool. The only light came from a tiny lantern at the apex of the room and was just bright enough to illuminate what had to be beds hanging on either side of it. The two contraptions looked to Kindle like inverted sleeping bag hammocks, and she would have taken her chances sleeping on the floor if Ella hadn't already climbed into one.

"These funny things are terribly comfortable." She smiled as she swayed, half wrapped in the soft pod. "Go on, see for yourself."

Kindle nodded and pulled herself into the vacant bed.

"Isn't it lovely?" Ella prompted, "I wish we had beds like this at the Lighthouse."

"Huh?" Kindle squirmed around in the plush hammock so she could see Ella. "You live in a lighthouse?"

"Oh, no." She twisted to see Kindle. "The Lighthouse is an inn. A place with food and drink and rooms for travelers."

"Yeah, I know. Like a hotel."

Ella blinked curiously at her. "A what?"

"A hotel—you know, like a really tall building with tons of little rooms on every floor?"

"Are you really from another world?" Ella replied, and Kindle nodded. "Is it much like Anelthalien?"

"Um, well, I dunno. Is Anelthalien all like this—like bug people and forests?"

"Oh, no. I've lived my entire life without hearing even a whisper of these Cifra—and I hear a lot at the inn. No, Anelthalien has some forests where no one lives … and the mountains; no one lives in the mountains, at least the southern ones anyway. Most people live in towns scattered all over. I live in Garrick Kingdom, the largest city in Anelthalien."

"What's it like?"

"Well, it sits by the sea and it's one of the only settlements in the east, so we get all sorts at the Lighthouse—men traveling and trading from all around. They come to Garrick because it has so many artisans, shops, and craftsmen—blacksmiths and ship makers and such—that make wares they can't find anywhere else. The woodworkers craft truly exquisite goods. They gather most of their wood from the forest to the south of the city, and it's all black."

"Black trees? Really?"

"Yes. A few men say they're cursed, but I've never seen the forest myself. I've never been outside the kingdom's walls, but I have been to the docks to buy fish, and I saw the sea! It was beautiful and just went on endlessly."

"Cool." Kindle smiled as she settled into her hammock. "So you don't have, like, cars and fast food and stuff?"

"Well, of course we have food," Ella laughed, "Like I said, we live by the sea, so we have plenty of fish. My papa usually goes to the market at the docks, though, since he's the cook at the Lighthouse. But I never have heard of a car. Is that something in your world?"

"Yeah. You don't have cars? How do you go anywhere?"

Now Ella stared at her with a questioning grin. "Are you fooling me?"

"No," Kindle replied, unsure if she should be embarrassed. "Just ... if you don't drive a car, how do you get anywhere?"

"Why, I walk or ride a horse or cart—is that what you mean? But tell me about your world and the car you have."

"Um, well, I don't know. Cars are like big metal things with wheels that you put gas in so they move. And they're a whole lot faster than walking everywhere."

"Oh, you are fooling me! Big metal things that just roll around on their own? No!"

"Yeah! Really!" Kindle couldn't help but laugh at Ella's disbelief. She sat up and began to construct visual pictures of every technology that she thought would amaze Ella. Kindle was desperately tired but found Ella's wonder and repeated cries of disbelief in her strange, subtle accent too enjoyable to trade for sleep. Finally, after Kindle had finished trying to explain microwaves to Ella, she threw her head back against her pillow and let her eyes drop.

"A whole dinner in five minutes? I just can't—I just ca...." Ella's giggles broke into a yawn. "My papa would love it," she murmured, then Kindle heard her pillow puff as well. "G'night Kindle," Ella gently said, and Kindle managed to grunt back before she surrendered to sleep.

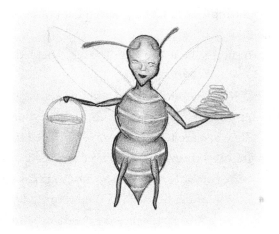

PREPARATIONS AND GIFTS

"Hoo, hoo," Missi cooed, hovering inches from Kindle's face. The little bee woman shot across the room a few times then froze above Ella's nose. "Ooo, ooo," she sang as she patted her pale forehead. "Oh children, hard to wake up they are," she mumbled and frowned at both of the sleeping girls. An elated grin suddenly lit her face, and Missi started buzzing laps around them, squealing like a whistle. Immediately Kindle and Ella shook into consciousness. Ella jolted up in her bed and covered her ears against the awful noise, but Kindle's limbs spun wildly as she flipped onto the floor.

"What is that horrid sound?!" Ella yelled into the air, and Missi ended her shriek. Before Kindle could shake off the dizziness of her fall, Missi collided with her head.

"Awake heroes are! Children sleeping sound now awake!" she shrilled in Kindle's ear, and Kindle tried to swipe her away.

"Missi! Get off me! You're screaming in my ear!" Kindle shouted and to her relief, Missi obeyed.

"Sooo happy! Awake now and to go!" As Missi clapped her tiny hands and bobbed around Kindle's head, Ella lowered her palms from her ears and climbed onto the floor.

"Have you two met?" she asked Kindle as she helped her untwist her foot from the bed.

"Yeah. Thanks." Kindle stood and she and Ella stared at Missi, who was still jigging through the air. "She's Missi, uh, the one Lord Rex said was, you know…," Kindle whispered, and Ella slowly nodded in understanding. Missi suddenly halted and threw her arms over her head.

"Oh! Before we go, you eat! Lord Rex says honey cakes you eat and like." She zipped to the mouth of the tunnel and then returned balancing a stack of what appeared to be golden pancakes on one hand and toting a pail in the other.

"Here! Here!" She pushed the soft, warm cakes into Kindle's arms and shoved the top one right into her mouth. "Good?" she asked, grinning as she loaded the pail in Ella's hand. Kindle nodded; to her relief the mouthful that Missi had force-fed her was incredibly delightful. It tasted like the most perfectly internally fluffy and externally crispy honey-flavored pancake imaginable. Still chewing, Kindle twisted to offer the pile to Ella.

"Good! See?" Missi laughed and took one for herself. Before she bit into it, though, she waved it at the pail. "And nectar too is good. Special nectar only made in the Tunnels."

Ella gave Kindle a smile and shrug, then tipped the pail to her mouth. Ella's eyes brightened, and after wiping away her liquid mustache, she said, "This *is* delicious. Missi, what is it?"

"Oh, pollinators and cooks know but don't tell other bees. Special things they keep secret," Missi replied then dug into her honey cake. Ella and Kindle sat on the ground and unloaded their arms so they could enjoy their meal. Kindle picked up the pail and saw that the nectar looked creamy and pale. The taste surprised her—it was somewhat like ice cold milk infused with a symphony of fruity and floral threads. She drank another gulp and held the sweet liquid over her tongue to try and experience every flavor.

"Mmmm," she hummed and sat the nectar aside so she could eat another honey cake. "Thanks, Missi, this stuff is really good."

"For heroes Lord Rex says give the best, and I did. Honey cakes and nectar are best," she happily chirped, but a call from the tunnel removed her smile.

"Missi! Missi, stop wasting time! We have a long journey!"

"Misson!" she yelled back, "Heroes are needing to eat!"

"No, Missi, they can eat on the way!" Mission griped as he flew into view. "No, no, no. Gather all this up, the heroes must leave *now*. Hurry now—the boys are waiting below." He hovered over them as the girls snatched all of their newfound delicacies. "Ugh, Missi…," he moaned as he smacked his face onto a hand, "they need a sack and … ugh … did you think of nothing they would need? Look—she does not have any shoes."

"Food, Misson, Lord Rex said to give them, not sack," Missi defensively answered.

Misson sighed, "Oh, Missi. Just take them down to the boys. *I'll* find them supplies." Misson immediately buzzed away, and Ella chuckled, "A grumpy sort, isn't he?"

"Misson is unhappy at heroes. Humans are bad he says. Cause trouble they do," Missi pouted.

"Why does he dislike humans?" Ella questioned as they followed Missi out of the small room.

"Scared, I think, he is of humans. He was unhappy to lead you to the farmer. He is not happy at the farmer also."

"The farmer?" Kindle wondered.

"Is that the man Lord Rex told us could help us? Wasn't his name … Azildor?" Ella enthusiastically questioned, and Missi nodded.

"The farmer named Azildor is at the north edge of Danica Woods where we go. He can give you help."

"Are you and Misson taking us there?" Kindle hopefully asked. Despite Missi's tendency to attack her head, Kindle was becoming quite fond of her.

"Yes, Missi and Misson to the farmer we will lead you. And before sunset we must, so sitting to eat makes Misson unhappy. Now we hurry, children," Missi said and quickened her flight so much that Kindle and Ella had to use all of their energy to climb along the valleys of the descending ledge. It was easier traveling downward, but Missi's repeated calls for them to hurry made the trek much more strenuous. When they finally reached the dirt tunnel where Andrew and Tad were waiting, Ella and Kindle sank down and passed the nectar and honey cakes back and forth. Missi buzzed over to the opposite wall where Andrew was by himself gazing up at a lightning bug's lantern. She hugged his hand and then began babbling and fluttering around him. Kindle watched the pair for a while before noticing that Tad, who appeared particularly disheveled and grumpy, was eyeing them as they ate.

After a few seconds, he caught her staring at him and snapped, "What is that stuff?"

"Food," Kindle retorted just as saucily as she made a face at him. Ella, though, swallowed her bite and tilted her head up to him.

"Did Misson not give you anything to eat?"

"Does it look like it?" Tad spread his arms to show his empty hands. "That stupid bug didn't give us anything."

"Well, here," Ella said and handed a honey cake up to him.

"Give me that," he growled as if she hadn't offered it at all and snatched it. Without even glancing at the cake in his hand, he ripped half of it off into his mouth.

"If a panpake," he asserted through a mouthful.

"Honey cake," Kindle gladly corrected him, and he sneered at her.

"And he hasn't eaten anything either, I suppose," Ella, ignoring them, mumbled to herself as she plucked a few cakes from Kindle's pile and popped up to carry them over to Andrew.

Kindle sipped another drink of nectar, and Tad demanded, "What's that?"

She just glared at him, unwilling to share the delicious liquid but also unsure if she could keep it from him. Finally he sniffed and grumbled, "Whatever." Kindle smiled as he began to stalk away but heard him mutter, "Stupid brat." Her face snapped into sour anger, but before she could do anything, Misson appeared with a group of bees trailing behind him.

"Here they are," he called lazily to his fellow Cifra. Misson halted and gestured at each of them. "Four children, load each one with gear. Emmit, that's the one with no shoes." Misson hung back while the bees dispersed, dropping items at their feet. The bee who Misson had called Emmit flew to Kindle and tossed a sack down beside her.

"For your feet," he directed, pointing at the lump. Kindle suspiciously peered at him, then reached into it and fished out a pair of flat boots. Even though they were black, she immediately recognized the material as Medara's woven silk. She looked up to thank Emmit, but another bee had replaced him and dropped a shiny, round container by her.

"Water," he quickly said before dashing away. Kindle pulled the heavy canteen closer to examine it and felt sure it was completely composed of welded bug shells. She frowned at it, somewhat disgusted, then set it aside so she could stuff the honey cakes into her sack. When Kindle lifted her eyes again, she realized that all of the bees except Misson and Missi had disappeared.

Misson clapped his hands importantly and called, "Pack up, children. We do not have time to waste standing here."

"We're not kids!" snapped Tad as he slung his sack's strap over his head. Misson flew back slightly as he looked Tad up and down then spun and waved to them.

"Missi, I'll take the lead, you bring up the rear. Just *keep up*, alright?" he emphasized to her over his shoulder as he began to fly down the tunnel.

"So rude, Misson, you are! Kindness to the heroes you should show!" she cried and darted to his back to angrily poke it. "Do not help Missi and the heroes if you do not like to."

To Kindle's surprise, Misson stared at Missi with hurt eyes and quietly spoke to her. Kindle yanked on her amazingly well-fitting boots and plucked up her gear so she could near the pair without seeming nosy. As she approached, trying to act busy with her canteen, she heard Misson say, "… don't want you getting hurt." When he saw Kindle and the others coming closer, though, Misson fell silent.

"Misson, Missi, I believe we're all ready," Ella cheerfully told them.

"Heroes now ready, Misson." Missi poked her chin at him. "Do what Misson says they should."

Misson, clearly humbled by Missi's reproach, lowered his eyes. "We will all remain together. We must exit the Tunnels and travel north through Danica Woods. It is important we make good time and reach the edge of the woods before sunset," he explained and then after nodding at Missi, began to lead them along the tunnel. Kindle, Andrew, and Ella followed the two bees without hesitation, but Tad hung back. Ella shot him a stern glare, but he still didn't move.

"Why's it matter when we get there, huh?" he questioned.

Misson, without stopping, called back, "The man you four are bound to is neither accustomed to nor accepting of guests. So it is best that you do not encounter him after dark."

"What? Is he some kind of creeper? I'm not doin' that," Tad scoffed, and Missi emphatically shook her head and buzzed back to him.

"Come, hero!" she begged, tugging his arm. "All about the farmer I will tell if you come."

"Okay, whatever," Tad snapped as he tried to peel her tiny hand off him. Missi let out a squeal of joy at his defiant assent and kept yanking his arm until he caught up with the group. They had reached the first crossway of tunnels now and Kindle could see that, just as Lucer had told her, the walls were lined with lanterns that were perfectly spaced to light every inch of the dirt passageways. As Misson led them to the right, Missi returned to his side but flew backwards so she could see them as she spoke.

"At the edge of Danica Woods, Gustin says a farmer—"

"Missi," groaned Misson, shaking his head, "please do not repeat Gustin's stories. The chil—heroes do not need to hear such rot."

"Rot, Misson! Not rot what Gustin, wise Gustin, says. Jealous you are that he knows more," Missi fumed at him.

Ella waved a hand as if to wipe away their tiff. "Tell us, Missi. We want to know."

Misson sighed heavily, but Missi beamed at Ella's encouragement and launched into her story.

"Gustin says living just north of our woods is a farmer growing food and animals. The land animals that walk on four hooves and eat much grass he has and food that shoots out of dirt like grass. But not an ordinary farmer he is. He is a magic farmer!"

At her exclamation, Misson groaned and Tad let out a deriding chuckle as he mockingly asked, "So is that why he lives all alone? He's some crazy guy?"

"No, no! Never said the farmer is alone! Gustin says the farmer has a whole magic family. A big family to all be farmers and make the earth happy. Makes food and animals grow their magic does."

Kindle realized the silliness of Missi's story and felt herself smiling sympathetically but doubtfully at the excited little bee woman. "Um, Missi—" she felt obliged to interrupt, "you know farmers don't, like, *make* stuff grow. They plant seeds and use fertilizer and stuff, but...."

"Soil, water, and the sun cause plants to grow," Andrew finished her thought for her, and she nodded. Missi stared back and forth at them in confusion then shook her head.

"No, he is a special farmer, Gustin says, one that comes from the trees."

"Oh, Missi, no." Misson dropped his forehead in his hand as he turned down another, much larger tunnel, which Kindle suspected was Fyrst Tunnel.

"Oh, Misson, yes!" she smartly retorted, "Yes! The magic he has is from the trees. An elf the farmer is. And his family as well—they all come from trees."

Tad laughed and muttered, "Seriously?"

Misson, though, covered Tad's incredulousness with his own disgusted reaction. "Missi! Stop! You know, you *know* that no elves still live in Anelthalien." He turned to address the four behind him, "Elves are not real. This is nonsense."

"But weren't they?" Ella suddenly passionately burst out, "Did they not fight in the Great War? That's what I learned and have always been told—the witches and the elves battled one another." Silence rose around them as Ella searched for support.

The only help, though, came from Andrew, who said, "Lord Rex and Lady Luna didn't know about that either."

Ella, slowly nodding, murmured, "No, they didn't." She stared squarely at the back of Misson's head. "Do you only believe what you see? Surely your eyes haven't seen everything." She paused as Misson uncomfortably rolled his shoulders. "I believe elves exist ... at least, they did once."

Missi, totally unaware of the tension hanging around them, gleefully clapped her hands. "Yes! Gustin says the only elves in all of Anelthalien left are the farmer and his family. Come from trees elves do, so good farmers they make. They grow animals and food where no other man can, so alone they live, very far from any towns or cities."

"No map I've ever seen has any sort of settlement west of the mountains and north of this wood," Ella thoughtfully commented.

"So we're going nowhere?" Tad groaned with disgust.

"Maybe no map shows where the farmer lives," Andrew suggested and Ella smiled at him.

"Yes, I think it's just that … Andrew, right? That's your name?" He nodded, and she turned to Tad to brightly say, "I've never seen these tunnels plotted on a map either, but, well, here we are."

"Oh yeah, great. We don't know where we are or where we're going—super awesome," he sarcastically snapped under his breath.

Kindle heard him, though, glared at him, and hissed, "Quit being a jerk."

He rolled his eyes away from her to sneer at the dirt wall. She huffed in annoyance at being ignored, but when she saw a pair of Cifra floating toward them, her mood shifted to wonder and fear. The two Cifra were new to her and completely unalike. One was a thick, mean-looking red hornet and the other was a slender, shiny dragonfly. When they saw Misson and Missi, they perked up and altered their course to block them.

"Hal-loo!" cooed the dragonfly, who—now that Kindle stood close to her could see—was completely covered with glittery flecks of green and black. Even her human face shone with the pieces. "Misson, Missi, good to see you both around here. Not on regular guard, hmm? Who are these with you? Humans?" She spoke to the bees but kept craning her head around them to stare at Kindle, Tad, Ella, and Andrew.

"Excuse us, Velitra, we are still on duty, and we do not have time to waste," Misson coldly replied and tried to fly around her, but the hornet, who was also ogling the four behind Misson, obstructed his path.

"These those heroes everyone's all twisted over?" he questioned in a gruff voice.

"Heroes, yes, and hurry we must to the farmer north of Danica before night," Missi spouted, and both of the newcomers turned their prying eyes to her.

"What's that? Oh, Missi, the farmer—whatever for? Why do you need to go meddling around with him, hmm?" Velitra quickly interrogated.

"Ugh," Misson groaned, "We do not have time for this. Missi, don't talk to them. *Good day*," Misson finished forcefully and shoved past them. Along with the others, Kindle followed suit, trying to ignore the intent stares of the hornet and dragonfly.

"Real humans," Velitra breathed as Andrew tried to slip by her. Then she reached out to stroke Tad's hair, but he deftly smacked her delicate hand away before she made contact.

"Oh! It touched me!" cried Velitra, sounding half horrified and half giddy.

"Probably best you take those humans away from here," the hornet threatened as he flew behind them, "They'll fit right in with that stubborn, coarse man." Kindle glanced back at him, curious to know why he and Velitra seemed to dislike the man who was supposed to help them. Missi and Misson, though, refused to give the hornet another word and kept buzzing further away from him.

When Kindle finally could spot no trace of Velitra's glittery body, she said, "Misson, they acted like the farmer was real."

"I never said I did not believe he existed. If that were the case, I would never have agreed to this trek," he quickly defended himself. "I know he resides at the edge of our forest, but as to his being an elf…." He peered slyly at Missi before falling silent.

"And they didn't seem to like the farmer. They got all weird when Missi mentioned him," Kindle continued.

Andrew nodded as he added, "Lord Rex didn't like us going to him either."

"Told you he's a creeper," Tad whispered to himself with a snicker.

"No! Not a creep!" Missi exploded then pushed Misson's shoulder. "Tell, Misson! Tell heroes why no Cifra thinks any good of the farmer."

"Missi, stop," he replied wearily without trying to end her nudges. "We are near the gate now. I will explain when we reach the woods, alright?"

Missi clapped her hands and then began humming to herself. Kindle felt slightly disappointed that she had to wait to hear more about Azildor.

Everything she had learned about him so far hadn't persuaded her that she really wanted his help. She wondered if Tad was right—if Azildor was just some creepy old hermit and they would be better off to stay in the Tunnels. That option didn't appeal to her, though, and so when Kindle spotted a dot of sunlight, her heart leapt in joy.

"It's the gate!" she happily cried and bent sideways so the speck of light grew and blue sky appeared. She heard Tad mock her, but in her delight, she let his negativity pass. Just before they began the ascent up the sloped tunnel, Misson stopped and with a serious face, addressed them.

"I expect many Cifra are above. Regardless of what they say or do, do not speak to anyone. Just make your way through quickly, alright?" Misson didn't wait for them to consent or object but returned to his flight and led them up to the gate.

THE FARMER

As they climbed the tunnel and the bright afternoon opened around them, Kindle squeezed her eyes shut against the dazzling sunshine. She hadn't realized how dark or cool the Tunnels had been, but now that the sun's heat and light enveloped her, she was glad to be above ground and completely disposed of her idea to stay in the Tunnels. When her eyes adjusted, she gazed around the large oval field in amazement. Thousands of Cifra resembling every flying insect she could think of and many she was sure she had never seen hovered and buzzed over the soft turf. If Kindle hadn't walked through the gate the night before, she wouldn't have known the strange green grass lay under them at all. The mob of Cifra was suffocating and extremely distracting, but Missi called for them, and Kindle remembered Misson's strict order. She trotted to their two guides and they dove into the sea of bug people. Worry that they would never be able to navigate through crowd struck her, but the Cifra pushed away from them as if repelled by antimagnetic force. Even though the bugs were obviously adamant against touching them, every eye watched them closely. Some Cifra even jumped and hovered above their heads to catch a better view of them, and soon they were traveling through a moving dome of the bug people. Misson let out a heavy, agitated sigh and loudly grumbled, "Yes, they are humans, they are heroes—you've seen them, now return to work!"

Not one bug seemed to hear him, though; the crowd remained unchanged.

"Around to everyone, news of the heroes must have gone," Missi gushed in excitement as she waved to the eyes that stared past her. Kindle and Ella grinned at one another and followed Missi's example. The rapt attention of the bugs made Kindle feel like a queen parading through her subjects, and their pleasure from her waves pumped even more fuel into her showboating.

Suddenly Tad went off like a bomb. "Quit! Quit staring at me, you freaks!" he shouted, causing Kindle to squeak in shock and the Cifra to scramble away over one another.

"Seriously!" he yelled, shaking his head in anger, and the bugs shrunk further away but began chattering among one another. Kindle whipped around and saw Tad was glaring in every direction, red-faced and tight-fisted.

"What?!" he barked at a group of honeybees still trying to stare at them, and the insects averted their eyes and fluttered further from him. He shook his head again and then locked eyes with Kindle, but before he could open his mouth, she switched her gaze to Ella who was also staring incredulously at him.

"There was no need for that. No one was hurting you," she softly chided him but received only a sniff.

"If I knew that all it would take to move faster was a good scare—" Misson beamed at Tad, but as soon as Tad aimed his deadly blue eyes at him, Misson frowned and lurched back. "Let's continue," he mumbled and did exactly that. Now that all of the Cifra left in the gate had returned to the far ends of the oblong enclosure, they easily made their way to the large, hollow tree that would allow them to reach the woods. Kindle, being careful to stay a good length away from Tad, stepped into the tree first and peered around to find Tyren. The sleepy moth was not leaning against the turning mechanism, though. Instead, a large beetle man, much like the one who had thrown Tad into Medara's home, was smugly lounging against the crank. He sized up Kindle then turned his attention to the others as they entered the tree. Ella and Andrew's eyes immediately wandered to the fantastic wall, but Tad's gaze froze on the beetle. Kindle dropped her face but eagerly peered back and forth between the two fierce faces, wondering who would attack first. Missi, though, broke the tension as she whizzed up to the beetle and patted his cheek.

"Hurry now, we must. Ready to go now that we are all here," she cheerfully said, and the beetle brushed her away as he nodded. He tore his attention from Tad, pumped his arms several times, then threw himself against the crank. The whole trunk violently lurched and threw Kindle, Tad, and Andrew to the floor.

"Idiot!" Tad yelled and quickly picked himself up. Kindle rolled her eyes at him from the floor and waited until the chamber thudded to a halt to stand. Misson floated out into the shady forest and waited for each of them to step clear of the hollow before he silently buzzed off between the trees.

"Keep up this time," he called from ahead, "and steer *around* the roots."

Kindle wanted to toss something equally snide back at him but figured that hiding her past embarrassment from everyone would be much more satisfying. After only a few moments of traversing through the woods, Missi sped to catch Misson's wrist and shaking it, reminded him, "The farmer you said you would tell the heroes about. In the forest you said you would tell."

Misson tossed his head and freed his arm. "I did," he grumbled and paused his flight until the group now lagging behind him stood directly under him.

"What was it you wanted to know?" he asked Kindle but waved away her answer before she could give it. "No, I remember—why do the Cifra hate the farmer Azildor." Misson reset his direction slightly more to the left then sighed, "The truth isn't as exciting as elves ... he tried to cut down our forest. The man wanted to build with the wood or something." For a few minutes Misson led them without speaking, and Kindle finally couldn't wait any longer.

"That's it?" she asked in disappointment. "You guys are all mad because he wanted to cut down a couple of trees?"

"Not all, no." Missi shook her head at Misson. "The whole truth, tell the heroes, Misson."

"Ugh, alright Missi. Now, it was not just a few trees... well, I suppose the whole ordeal began when Lord Rex became the ruler of the day. It was not very long ago when his father passed away and the power fell on him, was it, Missi?"

"Long it wasn't but before the working guard we joined."

"Hmm, yes, it was before we passed our courses. Anyway, that's outside of the point. Whenever Lord Rex took his father's place, he made several changes to the day order. The beetles had always taken charge of guarding the Tunnels under the Monarch—"

"Father of Lord Rex."

"Thank you, Missi," Misson grumbled, obviously annoyed. "But Lord Rex wanted worker bees to patrol the forest. So they did and found a man— this Azildor—encroaching on our territory. And it was more than just a few trees. I don't know—and neither did the bees who reported the human— how long he had been chopping away at our woods, but the reporters said he had destroyed a vast area."

"And home to us is Danica," Missi passionately added.

"Yes, so Lord Rex went to the human with his most reliable soldiers to order him to stop." Misson sighed and patted a tree beside him before flying around it.

"And did he? I mean, like, what happened?" Kindle asked as she rounded the tree as well.

"Well, no one really knows. Lord Rex and the soldiers do, of course, but that was before Missi and I graduated into the working guard, so all we know is what we saw. When Lord Rex returned from the confrontation, he stormed through the gate, shouting that humans were unreasonable, crude creatures that would never enter his forest."

"Decree, Misson!" Missi urged and he nodded.

"Yes, Missi, and the next day he announced that as long as no human ever touched our forest, the Cifra must not go near or harm any human."

Kindle crunched her brow together as she tried to connect everything the two bees had said. "So, you guys don't like him because he wanted to, like, cut down the whole woods?"

"Yes," Misson sighed with relief, but Ella made an offended noise.

"No. How can you say that is what happened when you just a short while ago said you did not know what happened? It sounds like you and all the Cifra are doing much assuming about this man without putting much sense into it."

"You have no proof of anything," Andrew specified, and Ella beamed at him.

"Well put, Andrew," she said to him, causing him to dip his head as if to avoid her recognition. Then she looked around at Kindle. "My papa's always taught me not to listen to gossip, so let's hear Azildor's defense before we soak up any tales."

"Wha—?" Tad shook his head at her. "You were believin' a bunch of fairy tale junk last night, and now you get all wise like you know everything? Pft—are we just supposed to believe whatever *you* say and nobody else?"

"Don't be so presumptuous," she snapped back but quickly removed the chill from her voice. "You know very well that that necklace around your neck was enough proof of all the lord and lady spoke of. Now, I did not mean to rouse an argument, so I apologize for my tone, alright?"

Tad just rolled his eyes, but since he had nothing more to say, Ella bobbed her head to accept his silence.

For what felt like hours the group traveled on without any sounds except Missi's random bursts of humming and Tad's occasional grumble. Kindle gulped another swig of water from her canteen and wished she knew the time or how close they were to the edge of the woods. She checked her comrades' faces to see if she was the only one who was tired and was encouraged by Tad's heavy eyelids and Andrew's dragging feet. Ella, though, still appeared as bright eyed and energetic as she had after their short breakfast. Kindle smiled when she remembered the honey cakes that were still tucked away in her bag. Without stopping, she pulled her pack around and dug out some of the delicious treats. Seeing Andrew's curious eyes observing her every move, Kindle offered him one of the cakes. He immediately took it and began to nibble away at it. She passed one to Ella as well but then stared uncertainly at the two honey cakes left in her hands. Part of her wanted to gobble them up right in front of Tad to show him exactly what his meanness had earned him, but another part of her was afraid of the rage she would probably incur from not sharing with him. Stifling her malicious desire, she turned and held out both cakes to him. Tad stopped and suspiciously eyed her, as if searching for a trap that he knew was hidden somewhere in the gesture.

"Here," Kindle said, stretching out her arm further, and he deftly swiped them. After giving her one more glare, he began to shovel them in his mouth. Turning back to the others who hadn't broken their progression through the tangle of roots, Kindle saw Ella grinning back at her and felt heat bloom in her cheeks. She put her head down and jogged to catch up to Missi so Ella wouldn't see her blush. Kindle wasn't sure what Ella thought, but her sly look reminded Kindle all too much of her best friend Mallory's face when she doted on cute boys. Too afraid at the moment to face whatever Ella thought, Kindle resolved to talk to her about it later. Missi suddenly resurged the melody she was humming, and Kindle, desperate to think about anything other than what the three behind her could possibly be thinking, asked, "What song are you humming, Missi?"

"No song, just music I think of," she flightily responded then resumed her tune.

"Are we getting close? Kindle questioned, still unwilling to be left alone with her thoughts. This time Misson answered.

"I can't tell precisely where we are, but I believe our journey is more than halfway done."

Kindle's face fell. "Ugh, really? Only halfway? But we've been walking for, like, *ever*."

"We have not traveled as long as you believe, hero," he replied, unaffected by her compliant. "The forest is still bright, which means evening is still quite a time from now."

"Can we stop and take a break for just, like, a minute?"

"No."

Misson's short, definite answer reminded her of her mom's tone whenever they argued. Kindle could never budge her mom's final word and guessed arguing with Misson would prove just as futile. She heaved a sigh and bit her lip in agitation—not because of the incredibly long walk or Misson, but because the thought of her mom had stirred up her desire to go home. The Cifra and the woods were amazing, but Kindle was ready to leave them and see her mom, dad, and house again. She stared off through the gigantic trees and wondered if they would look for her or even notice she was gone. A sick feeling blossomed in Kindle's stomach as she pictured her mom arriving at Emma Anthony's pool party, believing Kindle had snuck over to it but discovering that she had not. Kindle continued to run dramatic scenarios of her parents vainly searching for her while her brother tossed all of her stuff out of her room as she walked with the mixed group through Danica Woods. Her mind was so far away that she didn't notice when the light around them began to fade and the gaps between the trees started to grow. Not until one of her companions spoke was Kindle shaken out of her busy imagination.

"Something stinks," Tad complained and Misson nodded.

"That is the smell of animals," he announced with a wrinkled nose. "The farmer's land is not far."

Kindle couldn't locate any stench in the air and so breathed in deeply to see if she could detect it. An oddly putrid but delightfully earthy smell hit her, and she half grinned.

"It's cows—well, I mean, that smell's their poop, but that's what it is—the smell of cows," she explained back to Tad and received a disgusted grimace from him.

"Ugh. Cows are gross," he grumbled and pulled his shirt collar over his nose.

Andrew also hid his nose from the growing odor, but Ella laughed at the boys and said, "Fish smell much worse. It really is not that bad."

Kindle agreed with her; it wasn't bad. In fact, the smell of manure was so common where she lived that it reminded her of rolling green fields of lumbering, dull-faced cattle during the summer and brought her some comfort. Everything she had encountered since putting on the gold necklace had been so alien to Kindle that she hadn't considered Azildor could be anything like the farmers she knew, but the familiarity of the stink around them prodded her to believe that he may not be so strange or bad after all. She was about to ask the bees more about Azildor and his farm when Missi excitedly tugged at Misson's elbow and pleaded, "Close now we are, Misson. To look ahead are we close enough?" He stared at her for a few moments before he hesitantly nodded. As soon as he gave her the signal, Missi let out an exultant squeal and spun away through the trees. Kindle watched her shrink into a small dot before she realized how far the trees had slipped apart. Bending back and forth, she tried to find any slivers of the land beyond the woods and caught sight of one orange beam filtering through the trunks in the distance. The assurance of an actual end to their journey washed relief into her, and she released a glad sigh.

When they had walked far enough that a few more rays of sunset had slid open, Missi came careening back toward them, looking quite pleased with herself.

"Saw a small farmer and spoke to him I did," she joyously called before she tumbled to a halt at Misson's side and continued, "So scared before I spoke to him I think he was, but his father's name I mentioned and calmed him to listen."

Misson shuddered and sputtered, "Guh! Missi! You should not speak to every human you see—" He cast a quick, fearful glance at the group behind him. "Er—um, what did it—he! What did *he* say?"

"Oh, small boy did not say anything but the farmer's name when I asked for him. He ran then away."

She smiled at her report, but Misson nervously rubbed his wrists and asked, "He just ran away? He didn't say what he was going to do or where he was going?"

Missi shook her head, and then Misson copied the motion and grumbled something before sullenly meeting the stares of Kindle and the others.

"You scared?" Tad sneered at the bee's forlorn face then barked a laugh, which spurred Misson to angrily flutter his wings and jet onward.

"Are we close, Missi? Like really close to being out of the forest?" Kindle eagerly asked as she increased her speed to catch up to Missi.

"Near to the end of the trees, yes, hero," Missi replied and clapped her tiny hands.

"What's it like, Missi? Is the farmer's land green and beautiful?" Ella questioned as she reached Kindle's side. Then seeing Kindle's strange expression, she explained, "I've never been out of Garrick Kingdom's walls, and the ground is all dirt there. But I've heard men—traveling men stopped at the Lighthouse—tell lovely stories of the fields of green grass they traverse to gather their goods. And is that what you saw, Missi? Like a rippling sea only green?"

For a moment Missi set her face in thought. Finally she decisively said, "Brown dirt, mostly. Only some green. Lumpy dirt and so much."

Kindle had only a few seconds to imagine what Missi described before she stepped past the last trees in the forest and emerged on the edge of the scene herself. Freshly tilled earth stretched out in every direction uninterrupted except for some blocky shapes in the distance. The dimming sky camouflaged what the shapes were, even when Kindle squinted, but she guessed they were houses or barns of different sizes. Then some movement among the blocks caught her attention, and she strained her eyes harder at it.

"What is that?" she wondered aloud, and Andrew stepped up beside her, shielding his narrowed eyes. "Do you see it?" She pointed for him, but he didn't seem to need her help. Kindle watched his face for an answer, but he remained stoic.

"It's coming this way, whatever it is," Ella breathed and eagerly peered up at the bees. "Can you see it? Is it Azildor?"

Misson was frozen with fear, but Missi happily bobbed up and down beside him and cheered, "A wagon of the farmer is coming! Big and small humans ride on it!"

As they all watched the moving speck grow into a horse-drawn wagon, Kindle felt a desire to dip back into the screen of the trees. Completely unsure of what the wagon was bringing them, she hoped it was good, but the increasing churning in her stomach told her it was not. The horses were swiftly carting the wooden wagon right toward them, though, and Kindle knew she couldn't escape unseen. The outlines of the two bodies atop the cart—one large, one small—shifted into sharp focus, and then, all at once, the thundering brown horses brought the wagon to a shuddering halt inches from them. Kindle impulsively jumped back and before she could feel embarrassed, realized everyone except Missi had as well. Time seemed to stand still as they all silently inspected one another.

Somehow Kindle knew the man holding the reins was Azildor. Even though he was seated and his posture relaxed, everything about him seemed hard and unshakable, like a rock embedded in the ground. His face was shaded by a short, wide-brimmed straw hat, but Kindle could tell it was just as heavily tanned as the rest of his skin and held a rigid expression that would have been emotionless if not for his sharp eyes. Deep brown, like the rich soil under them, his keen eyes roved over them each as if reading their souls. His stare felt so heavy and all-knowing that when it fell on Kindle, she ducked her face. The other occupant of the cart was a much softer, smaller version of the hard man he stood behind. He wore the same sort of hat and dusty brown shirt and trousers as Azildor but was still padded with baby fat and peeked at them with wonder-filled eyes. Kindle tried to smile up at the boy, but he shifted behind his father.

"Who are you?" Azildor demanded in a voice that was just as stern as his appearance. Missi, who was the only one present completely unaffected by his demeanor, burst into a fit of joy then zipped up to his face. Kindle sucked in her breath, sure Azildor would swat her aside, but the only movement he made was to slightly tilt his head back so that his brim didn't obstruct his view of her.

"Sooo happy!" she squealed at his face. "Before sunset we brought heroes to the farmer! Now help can come to the heroes!"

"Who are you Cifra?" he questioned with stern patience. "Tell your name and the purpose you have for being on my land."

"Missi and Misson told by Lord Rex to bring heroes to the farmer, and now you help them," Missi quickly replied as she jabbed her finger around the group, but Azildor shook his head.

"This Cifra does not make sense. Can one of you translate her babblings?"

They all stared up at Misson, but when it became clear he was still too stricken with fear to speak, Ella cleared her throat.

"Sir." She respectfully tilted her head. "Her name is Missi, and the king of the Cifra, Lord Rex, instructed her and Misson to bring us to you. He and Lady Luna believe you can help us."

"They think we're heroes," added Kindle, and Azildor turned his eyes on her.

"Heroes?" he asked in a doubtful tone, "And I am supposed to help you?"

"Yes! Yes! The heroes you can help!" Missi exclaimed, nodding vigorously.

"No. I am a farmer—I have much work to do. Your Lord Rex knows that I have no time for foolish Cifra endeavors."

"But we need help! We don't know why we're here or anything!" Kindle cried in frustration as she saw her only hope of returning home slip away. "Please?"

Azildor gave her nothing but a face as unwavering as stone. By waving his arm, Misson stole his attention and hurriedly told him, "And this all really has nothing to do with the Cifra—these children just popped up in our woods uninvited. The lord and lady only wanted to make sure they trotted off in the right direction...."

"Your woods," muttered Azildor.

"... so we'll be on our way," Misson quickly finished and disappeared into the trees behind them.

"No, Misson!" Missi shouted after him then hung her head and sighed, "Never wanted to help heroes Misson did. Missi cannot help heroes, and sorry she is."

Ella let out a huff, and Kindle saw that she did not share the same dejected face as Missi but wore a soft but set determination. "Sir," she said, stepping up to his wagon, "what Misson said is true: we aren't Cifra. We really did all find ourselves standing in the woods without any explanation, except—" Ella plucked up the emerald oval on the end of her necklace and held it up for Azildor to see. "Except we each have one of these. The lord and lady of the Cifra told us what they are, but why we have them or what we are to do with them, they did not know."

"And they thought you would know," Kindle pleadingly piped in. "We don't want any stuff from you or anything, we just, like, want to know if we need to save some queen or how to get home or you know...."

"What do we do now?" Andrew filled in Kindle's hesitant silence, and Azildor turned his quick eyes on his bowed head.

"Son, what is your name?"

"Andrew," he replied without picking up his eyes.

"Andrew, do you have one of these necklaces as well?"

As a reply, Andrew gave a slight nod and pulled his chain out from under his t-shirt. Azildor made a satisfied sound in his throat then asked, "And is that truly the purpose that brings you to my field? To discover what road you must take?"

Andrew uncomfortably half shrugged and wilted as if he wished he could disappear.

"Son, face me and give your answer." Azildor's voice was slightly softer, but the power in it remained and drew Andrew's face up to him.

"Yeah. What do we do now? What are we supposed to do?" he asked in such an empty, hopeless tone that Kindle felt his sadness fill her own heart. Azildor's eyes darted to each of them, ending on Missi.

"Cifra, you call these children heroes, but you do not know why?"

"Why they are heroes no one believes me. Gustin's story everyone says is only a story."

"Tell me what you believe. Why are they heroes and why did you bring them here?"

"Bring the heroes here Lord Rex said to do—"

"No, Cifra. There is a deeper reason in you than blind obedience. The other bee fled, but you remain here. What is it that compels you to deliver these children here?"

Missi frowned and shook her head like a fussy toddler then burst out, "They are heroes, I know it! Gustin says the story is true of the fallen queen sending the makers' marks to heroes. Heroes to help when the time is near. And see—" she zoomed to Kindle's neck and yanked on the red gem, "our maker's mark it is!"

"Uck! Missi!" Kindle choked and pulled her necklace free.

"Yeah, and those bug people said this is where the queen was—north of their woods—but she's not here. *Nothing's* here," griped Tad then he sneered at Ella, "Told you this was stupid."

"No!" Ella glared back then gazed up at Azildor. "See, we need help. I know we're here for some reason, but no one knows why. Please, if you could help us at all, explain anything—"

He held up a palm to end her plea. "Alright. The light is fading. You four may come to my home where we can talk further, but Cifra, you must return to your home."

"Safe you will keep the heroes? Help to them will you give?" Missi implored with deep concern as she put a hand on Andrew's then Kindle's cheek.

"You do not need to worry over their lives. I have many children and know at the least how to feed them well," Azildor reassured her.

"Oh, heroes, heroes goodbye!" cried Missi as tears welled in her tiny eyes. "Leave you now I must." She commenced to squeezing each of their heads, and only Tad was successful in dodging her small arms. After Missi released them, she tearfully watched as they boarded Azildor's wagon. Tad easily swung himself up first, then Kindle and Ella followed, but Andrew, being shorter and smaller than the others, fell back to the ground after trying to pull himself up. Ella moved to his aid and managed to heave him into the wooden bed. Andrew twisted out of the lump he had landed in and scooted to fit himself between Ella and Kindle. Once they all had settled, Azildor only had to gently flick the reins and cluck his tongue to stir his pair of horses into motion. In just a few quick seconds, the wagon had swept around to face the blocks in the distance and Missi had shrunk to a black fleck barely visible in front of the dim woods. Kindle, with a pang of sadness, watched Missi until she couldn't distinguish her from the shadows seeping out from between the trees. Then, even though she didn't feel like turning her eyes to another strange place, Kindle set her face toward their new destination.

The horses' pace was spritely, so Kindle didn't have to wait long before the stone blocks grew into structures she could make sense of. One that stood at least twice as tall as the others reminded Kindle of a silo, and she was sure that the building nearest it, which was the largest of all, was some type of barn. A few more house-sized squares sat in an unorganized cluster to the right of the barn, but other than those, Kindle began to notice that the rest of the stones were simply fragmented walls. She tried to stretch her head higher to examine the partial walls but couldn't do so without receiving a half disgusted, half exhausted sneer from Tad. In fear of looking silly, Kindle dropped her gaze down to stare at her feet. The view of the boots

Medara had woven for her that ended at her bare knees didn't help ease her embarrassment. The sleek, knee-high silvery-black shoes didn't seem to suit her at all, especially with the bejeweled denim shorts and hot pink t-shirt she was wearing. Something about them seemed so costume-ish—like what a movie actor would wear—that she felt awkward wearing them. Kindle peeled her eyes off them to search for another thought to fill her mind. Not unwillingly, she secretly let them fall on Tad, who was dully frowning back at Danica Woods. As she watched him, she found herself wondering if he did think she was weird or silly, but before her mind could hope that he didn't, she gave her head a shake and reminded herself of how rude he was. Just then Azildor spoke, and the suddenness of his voice interrupting her thoughts caused a blush to bloom on her cheeks.

"I believe you all know I am Azildor Chokmah," he called back, "And this is my youngest son, Adin Chokmah. We would like to hear your names."

"Ella," she brightly replied without hesitation, then Kindle, Andrew, and finally a disgruntled Tad gave theirs as well.

"And whereabouts in Anelthalien do you hail from?" Azildor asked. Again Ella was the first to jump on the question.

"I come from Garrick Kingdom in the east. You know it, don't you?"

His wide hat bobbed an affirmative.

"Yes, and it's as ever bit as grand as everyone says it is. But I'm the only one of us who lives in Anelthalien."

At this, Azildor's head twisted slightly, and Adin, who was still standing so he could cling to his father's shoulder, lifted wide, curious eyes to them.

"It's honest truth," Ella continued as she grinned around at Kindle. "What was it you said—a whole other world with tea-co-lony?"

"Technology," mumbled Kindle as she held back a laugh and Andrew squinted questioningly at each of them.

"Yes, that—it's such clever stuff that does everything you could ever want. But, anyway, they live in another world they call Misery."

Tad released a loud, rude bark at Ella's proud proclamation while Kindle wilted in further humiliation.

"No, it's *Missouri* and it's just a state, it's not the whole world."

Azildor didn't utter a word but eyed Kindle carefully, as if checking her for honesty.

"Yeah, seriously," she snipped, feeling miffed at his suspicion. She nudged Andrew and urged, "Tell him."

"Our world is earth. North America is the continent we live on. It has states like New Jersey. That's where I live," he blandly explained while squinting at the wood by his feet. "I've never heard of Anelthalien."

Azildor shook his head over his other shoulder as he skeptically asked, "And Tad, are you from one of these states as well?"

"Florida," he grumbled.

Azildor made a thoughtful noise in his throat. "Are you all acquainted then?"

"Pft, no," Tad deridingly puffed. "Before yesterday I never saw any of these idiots my whole life."

"You're such a jerk," Kindle hissed under her breath.

"Disrespect is foolishness," Azildor evenly cautioned as he reeled the reins around his fist and the wagon shuddered to a stop. "And arguing produces nothing except strife." He tossed the reins aside, agilely leapt down beside the wagon, and then lifted Adin to the ground. Kneeling down to Adin, he said, "Tell Mommy we have guests. Four guests." The little boy enthusiastically nodded and dashed away as quickly as his short legs could carry him. Kindle smiled as she watched him run toward one of the stone buildings that she had earlier guessed was a house.

"The horses stop here," Azildor told them, motioning for them to disembark as well. Ella hopped out of the wagon just as gracefully as Azildor and received a fleeting thoughtful glance from him before Tad chucked his pack onto the dirt and followed it with a heavy thump. Then Andrew and Kindle unloaded themselves with the help of Azildor's steadying arm. As soon as they had rested their feet on the ground, the two horses trotted the wagon into the nearby barn.

"I must see to the animals for the night," Azildor told them, nodding after the horses. Then he pointed in the opposite direction and instructed, "Trace Adin's path to our house. My wife will undoubtedly extend her hospitable hands to you." He gave them one more penetrating gaze before walking away to the barn. Not waiting a moment, Kindle spun herself around and started what she hoped would be the final walk she would take for the night. Footsteps sounded behind her, and soon Ella and Andrew fell into step with her.

"He doesn't seem as beastly as Misson believed," Ella chuckled with a smile.

Kindle shrugged. "No, I guess not. But do you think he's gunna help us? Like, do you think he really knows what we need to do?"

"Who cares as long as we get something to eat," complained Tad from behind them. Kindle glared back at him to say something just as negative, but the raggedness in his blue eyes swiped the fire out of her.

"Yeah, that'd be good," she replied instead, and Andrew and Ella nodded their consent. While they trekked the rest of the way to the house in mutual silence, Kindle hoped for relief from the long journey. She really did agree that some food would be wonderful; her last bite of honey cake had been quite a while ago, and she could feel her stomach growling. As they passed several structures, she tried to peer inside them, wondering what they held, but didn't stop to examine them. They each appeared empty and forlorn except the one at the far edge of the group. Its stone walls held small windows, some of which were clouded with heat, and melted into a large chimney that was slowly burping clouds of smoke. Instead of a door, a short stone hall sat welcoming them into the middle of the house. When they reached the opening, Kindle began to peer in but, remembering that it was someone's home, backed off to face the others.

"Do we just go in or what?" she asked.

"Nah, let's just sit out here and rot," Tad snickered, crossing his arms.

Kindle turned an ugly face at him before she defensively retorted, "No! Like, there're no doors or anything, and *nice* people knock on people's doors before they go in."

"Adin told his mom we were coming," Andrew said with a shrug.

"Yes, and Azildor said his wife would see to us, so I believe he meant for us to go inside," Ella added then immediately acted on her belief. Andrew ducked into the square entryway as well, and after glancing at Tad, Kindle followed them. The smell of something delicious hit her before she reached the end of the short hall, and the aroma reminded her stomach just how ready it was for food. When the room did open around her, she checked to the left, the side at which the smoking chimney sat, and saw much more than just the food she had expected. Surprisingly, the whole house was one lofty, open room, and the entire left side appeared to be dedicated to cooking and eating. An enormous, long flat rock that likely served as a table lay almost right in front of them and obscured part of her view, but Kindle could still see most of the kitchen behind it. Along half of the entire back wall ran a long stone counter, which was littered with food scraps and metal kitchen utensils and ended at a basin full of water. The counter didn't keep her attention long, though, because Kindle noticed that the far left wall had to hold the source of the wonderful smell. Just as she had suspected when they had stood outside, a fireplace sat at the center of the wall, but it was unlike anything she had ever imagined: it had an archway that vaulted as high as a grown man and contained three separate fires that each blazed under a different sort of pot. Before Kindle's eyes could detect what each fire was cooking, a very red but kind-faced woman stepped out from the chimney. Like Azildor, she was tanner than the animal hide she wore and had dark brown hair and eyes, but her round, cheerful face made her appear much softer and friendlier than her husband.

"Oh, hello!" she called, stepped down from the stone hearth, and approached them with an outstretched hand. "Hello, hello—ah!" She paused to wipe a sooty hand on her apron then began warmly shaking their hands. "My name is Naam, Azildor's wife. My son Adin told me you were coming. Please, come sit down and tell me your names." She led them over to the table and motioned to the boulders around it. Ella settled on top of one first and took the task of introducing everyone.

"My name is Ella, that's Kindle, Andrew there, and Tad."

Naam repeated their names, nodding at each of them in turn, then smiled and sighed, "It is good to meet you all. We'll be eating as soon as Azildor and the children come in from work—you are staying to eat, aren't you?"

"Um, yeah, I guess…," Kindle began, unsure of the right answer.

"Yeah. Definitely," Tad confirmed with finality.

"Good. I was hoping you would. You four look in need of some food," Naam commented then leaned around them and called, "Binah, Adin! Come help set the table. No, it's alright; Sophia will be fine for the moment. Thank you, dears."

Kindle searched behind her for the owners of the footsteps that had begun and saw Adin and a brown-headed little girt trotting away from a big-eyed baby playing on its stomach in the midst of a group of stone chairs covered with various animal hide blankets and cushions. Adin headed straight for the stone counter, but the girl directed her course to the table.

"Hello, my name's Binah. I'm six," she informed them then stood staring at Andrew until her mother reminded her of her job. "And that's my brother Adin and my baby sister Sophia," Binah continued as she wandered over to where Adin was trying to lift more bowls than he could carry.

"Adin, only take a few at once," Naam cautioned and moved toward him, but Ella sprang up and offered, "I can help them."

"Oh, dear, you don't have to. You're our guest," Naam replied, but, as if it were as natural as breathing, Ella swept over to the two children, scooped up the mound of dinnerware Adin had scattered, and began setting the table.

"I want to help," Ella shrugged as she effortlessly doled out bowls and spoons along the table. "And this is really nothing to the lot of tables I usually manage."

Naam, somewhat reluctantly, nodded. "Alright, if you're sure," she consented and returned to the chimney. As Ella and the children continued to set the table, Tad dropped his bag on the ground and his head over his arms on the table. Andrew let his eyes wander around every inch of the room, and Kindle spun on her rock to watch the baby. She had crawled over to a chair and was pulling herself up to lean on it. Once Sophia had achieved this, she switched her stare to the busy kitchen. Kindle waved at her and began twisting her face into different expressions, hoping to entertain her. Sophia finally noticed her and not only smiled but babbled and laughed. Kindle made an especially funny face, and Sophia's babblings escalated into a shriek of delight.

"What the—?" Tad groaned as his head snapped up, and Kindle quickly attempted to appear innocent. Sophia gave another playful squeal, and Tad hatefully frowned at her before he slumped back down on the table. Naam had reemerged from the chimney carrying a large cauldron, which she dropped off at the table before going to Sophia.

"What's wrong?" Naam asked as she knelt down to Sophia's level. "Hmm? What has you all excited?" In response, Sophia bounced and babbled at her, and Naam scooped her up and brought her over to the table.

"Do you want to see our guests? Is that it?"

"Kindle was making faces at her," Andrew informed Naam, and Kindle turned an offended face at him, feeling betrayed, but Naam just smiled and laughed.

"Do you want to play with her? Sophia loves attention."

Kindle, caught off guard by Naam's lack of anger, said the first word that entered her mind. "Sure." In an instant, Kindle found Sophia sitting on her lap, chattering at her and pulling at her shirt while Naam disappeared into the chimney again. "Why'd you tell her that?" Kindle whined at Andrew.

He shrugged. "You were. And she didn't care."

"Yeah, well, I guess," she mumbled as she tried to unlock Sophia's hand from her shirt. Kindle thought babies were cute to look at, but she really didn't like taking care of them. A summer of babysitting had proved they always managed to become wet, sticky, and smelly if you stayed around them very long. To her relief, though, Naam returned after only a few minutes, and after setting down the largest cooking dish Kindle had ever seen, she held out her hand for Sophia and said, "Let's get you set as well, little girl." Naam carried her over to an especially tall rock that had been carved into a small seat with arms and a back. Naam noticed Kindle, Andrew, and Ella watching her and explained, "Azildor made this when we had our first, Masso, so he could sit and eat with us." She carefully pushed the chair forward so Sophia's hands could reach the bowl sitting in front of her.

"How clever," Ella mused before she took the seat beside Andrew.

"It's a highchair," Andrew stated.

Kindle nodded then added, "Yeah, except without the tray thingy."

"Well, I suppose you could call it that," Naam agreed as she considered the chair. "We've always just called it the baby's rock." Naam left them all watching Sophia in her chair to fetch a large platter from the counter where she also directed Adin and Binah to sit as well. Just as they settled beside their sister, Azildor, followed by four more children, appeared in the entryway.

"Daddy!" Binah exclaimed and ran to Azildor, who caught her up into a hug.

"How's my Binah?" he asked as he carried her to the table, and she launched into the story of her day. As Naam finished setting the food on the table and the family around her paced through their regular evening interaction, Kindle grew uncomfortable. She was in the midst of what seemed like a million warm conversations, but no one spoke to her. In fact, she felt completely ignored, terribly out of place, and unwelcome. The longing to be home with her own family swelled up in her throat, and before she could stop herself, Kindle let out a chocked sob. Immediately Naam stepped to her side.

"Kindle, are you alright?" she asked, and all at once, everyone hushed and looked their way.

"No, um, yeah, I'm fine. I just ... I want to go home."

"Oh, dear." Naam gave her a pat on the shoulder. "We can fix that. Where do you live?"

"Don't ask," Azildor interjected, shaking his head. "We'll eat first then speak about other matters."

Naam carefully eyed him but nodded. "Yes, food does a soul much good. Children, come, let's eat."

At her word each family member found a seat but made no move to load their bowls. Kindle wiped away the wetness her sadness had produced as she tried to discover what everyone was waiting for. Then Naam, with a voice full of gratitude, said, "Thank you husband for your hard work to bring us this food and thank you children for helping your father."

Azildor nodded slightly then humbly returned, "And thank you wife for cooking it for us." He smiled at his wife, and then all of their children broke out in a chorus of thanks. Azildor tipped up his head, and all of the voices ceased to listen to him again. "And let's thank the makers of Anelthalien for giving us all that we have." The whole family spoke one last thanks in unison and before Kindle knew what to say, they all stood to fill their bowls from the dishes laid across the table. Ella and Andrew followed suit, and so Kindle, not wanting to miss out, jumped up as well to partake in the buffet. After she had piled more than enough roasted meat and vegetables in her bowl, she returned to her seat and was about to lose herself in deliciousness when she noticed that Tad was still sleeping by his empty bowl next to her. For a moment she watched him, amazed that he could sleep through the clamor, then tapped his head with a finger.

"Hey! Wake up."

"Hrm?" he groaned and lifted heavy eyes at her.

"It's time to eat," she told him, pointing with her fork at the large hunk of meat sitting in front of them. He squinted around as if completely unaware of what was happening.

"Ugh—c'mon, *eat*," she sighed, trying to sound disgusted but couldn't help laughing at his dazed face instead. She forked some of her own meat and shook it into his bowl. He blinked at her then the chunk and, as if finally realizing what she had said, wolfed it down and reloaded his bowl. The talk in the house died to an occasional word as everyone determinedly devoured their dinner. Kindle was glad for the food, which really was every bit as tasty as it smelled, but even more grateful to feel less like a clueless outsider. The simple act of eating with all of the strangers seemed to level them all out and bring them to share the space and time they sat in as one whole body, not just a collection of individuals. Even as their appetites grew sated and the chatter resumed, Kindle noticed that the older children were seeking her attention rather than pointedly ignoring her. Through the strings of conversations, she learned that the oldest of all the siblings, a tall, skinny boy named Masso, was Azildor's main help during the day. The other three who had been outside with them were Yirah and Yirun, who were the second oldest and twin brother and sister, and Navon, who was slightly younger than the twins and looked much like her mother. From the way Yirah and Yirun talked, it became clear that they and Navon only helped feed the animals in the early morning and late evening; they spent the rest of their day with Naam.

"I like reading, though," Navon was saying to her brother, Masso. "Sometimes I like it better than the baydles."

"Well, no matter how much you like it, you still have to help Dad," he replied with a shrug. Kindle was wondering what a baydle was when Yirun's loud voice caught her attention.

"… ran at me really fast! Voom!"

"Yeah, he did. He looked all angry at you," Yirah enthusiastically agreed, nodding to everyone listening.

"And he almost charged right into me!"

"It was pretty scary."

"But I jumped up on the fence—"

"Right before he got you. It was so close."

Yirun held his hands an inch apart to illustrate just how close his sister meant then declared, "But Old Meaty's not as quick as me."

"Nope," Yirah affirmed as Adin chimed, "Old Meaty the big pig, Old Meaty the big pig." The three broke out in laughter, and Naam, also smiling in amusement, rose from her seat to check their bowls.

"If you two are finished, go ahead and start washing."

The twins snapped a quick grin at one another then grabbed up their dinnerware and dashed toward the water basin.

"Yirah, Yirun, be careful," Naam called, and after answering in unison, they slowed their pace. Naam turned back to the table. "Binah, you too, alright?"

"Okay, Mommy," she replied then smiled at Andrew before she slid off her rock to march over to where both of her siblings were now attempting to simultaneously wash their dishes.

"Let Binah dry!" Naam directed before she returned her tickled face to Kindle's side of the table.

"Did you all get enough to eat?"

"Oh yeah, I'm totally full," Kindle replied.

"Yes, ma'am. Thank you," Ella agreed.

"Good. And you boys?" Naam peered at Andrew, who nodded, then Tad, who was still eating.

"Yeah. Good," he grunted and caused Naam's grin to widen.

"I'm so glad you all could stay and eat with us," she said, but her eyes slid off them, and a calculating expression took over her face. Kindle gazed around and saw Naam's attention was pinned on Azildor, who was communicating a silent message to her. After a few seconds of watching his covert nods and gestures, Naam said, "Adin, Navon, why don't you help with the cleaning tonight?"

"It isn't our turn, Mom," Navon politely replied and Adin nodded.

"I know, dear, but we have quite a lot of dishes, and I don't want any of you up late tonight."

Navon and Adin took Naam's answer with a unified nod and began roving around the table, hunting for dishes to gather.

"And Masso, please help your father clear the food," Naam continued as she rose to slip Sophia out of her chair. Masso looked back and forth at his parents then at Kindle and the three flanking her.

"What's up?" he finally asked his father, but Azildor shook his head and urged, "Come, Son, let's do as your mother asked." Masso sent another suspicious look Kindle's way but wordlessly began helping Azildor. Kindle, who was feeling very full and sleepy, was glad that Naam now ended her instructions and instead watched the activity flitting around her home as she softly spoke to Sophia. Once the table was an empty stone slab again and everyone was busy at the counter, Naam slowly meandered behind Kindle.

"Once all the children are in bed, I believe Azildor wants to speak with you all. If the children know, they'll never agree to going off to bed," she whispered then dropped her secretive tone. "Now, he didn't say—are you all staying for the night?"

Kindle, Andrew, and Ella stared around at one another with perplexed faces. Kindle knew that she had no idea how to answer—her agenda was to be in her own bed as soon as possible, but she wasn't convinced that Azildor would or could tell them how to get back home. Sure that Tad would have an answer, she peered back at him and saw that he had fallen asleep again. Rolling her eyes, she resolved to let him stay that way.

"I know you all would like to return home, but the journey to any town is a very long one," assured Naam, obviously trying to persuade them to stay.

"Um, yeah, we'll stay here tonight," Kindle indecisively agreed more to Ella and Andrew than Naam, hoping it was the right answer. "Is that okay?"

"Of course," Naam sighed, "I'm very glad to hear it. I'll make sure you all have somewhere comfortable to sleep." She let one more watchful gaze fall over her family then crossed to the opposite side of the house to lay the now sleeping Sophia down on a skin rug before going to the far corner. Kindle expected her to use the skin at her feet as a blanket or bed, but instead of picking it up, Naam pulled it aside to uncover a square hole that showed the top of a stone staircase. Naam took the stairs and disappeared down into darkness.

Kindle shuddered and whispered to her companions, "You think we're sleeping in a basement?"

Andrew shrugged. "Probably."

"Ugh. That's kind of gross."

Ella gave her a questioning look. "Gross? Why?"

"I don't know ... like bugs and mold and stuff I guess."

"Bugs?" Andrew said in a slightly incredulous tone as he chuckled.

"Yes, Kindle, he has a point," Ella chuckled. "The Cifra were bugs."

"Yeah, well, not really. And they didn't crawl all over the floor."

"Alright," Ella returned soothingly. "I'm sure wherever Naam puts us up for the night will be lovely. Look at the house she keeps. The Lighthouse is never this immaculate, and we have two cleaning ladies ... well, Sara's more of the washerwoman actually."

"The Lighthouse?" Andrew asked, and Kindle, proud to know what Ella meant, answered, "It's where she lives. It's the inn her dad owns."

He nodded in understanding then asked, "You don't have a house?"

"No, Papa thinks it's best to always be at the Lighthouse with all the travelers staying in the rooms at night. He doesn't trust anyone, and sometimes we do get some shifty blokes. But we have the third floor all to ourselves, and it really is quite nice."

Andrew just silently nodded again, but his face seemed to contain a sea of thought. Kindle was so busy wondering what he was keeping from them that she didn't notice Azildor step up and jolted at his voice.

"Follow Naam to your beds. You must sleep tonight. We will discuss your troubles when you are more alert," he definitively said, casting his harsh brown eyes over Tad.

"What?" Kindle groaned with disappointment, "I thought you said you'd talk to us after dinner."

"I did. But now I see you require rest." He paused, ignoring Kindle's whine, to stare at a dark window. "In another case, the morning light will explain much more than I am able to alone." He started to move away, but Kindle hopped to his side.

"You can't keep making us wait! Like, we need to know what's going on so we can just get out of this place!" She hadn't realized how loud her voice was until she ended her plea and the surrounding silence rang in her ears. A quick, hot-faced scan of the room assured her that every wide eye was glued to her and Azildor. Afraid that she had aroused his wrath, she squeaked, "Sorry. I'm really sorry. I just—I—I really wanna go home."

He said nothing but steadily stared at her until, full of embarrassment, she dropped her face. Then to her surprise, he very softly said, "Whether I speak to you now or years from this moment, I do not anticipate that you will see your home for a very long time."

Kindle snapped her wide, fearful eyes back up at him. She wanted to object—to yell that he was wrong—but Azildor's face held only honesty, and she could do nothing but gape at him.

"I am sorry," he whispered. "Please sleep well." He left her standing alone, and all at once she felt terribly hot and chilled. Unsure of what to do with herself, she let her head turn around the room and saw that even Tad was awake to awkwardly stare anywhere except her direction. Ella and Andrew's were the only faces that held any hint of the sad desperation she felt.

"Come along," Ella mumbled as she put a warm arm around Kindle's stiff shoulders. "Let's go bed down." Ella maneuvered them over to the stairs as Andrew and Tad followed. Even though Kindle wasn't keen on the idea of descending into unknown darkness, her numb mind didn't object, and she let Ella guide her down the steps. When they reached the torch-lit basement, Naam pointed out their beds and asked if they were all alright. Kindle mindlessly nodded with everyone else but felt far from alright. Azildor's words kept reverberating in her skull, magnifying and pushing out every other thought. All she could hear was that she was not going home, and even though that one single thought terrified her, she allowed it to continue to fill her whole awareness just so no other horrible realizations could slip in as well. She almost heard Ella say something to her, but refusing to be shaken from her semiconsciousness into reality, Kindle sank down onto her floor mattress and rolled over to face the dark stone wall. Silence refilled the dim room again, and Kindle's one terrible thought began to slip away as the cover of sleep veiled it.

THE TIME IS RIGHT

Noise. Voices talking. Kindle's brain sluggishly, reluctantly crawled out from under its sweet blanket of sleep to sniff at the hints of life around her. It was Mikey's voice. No, it was a girl's. Through her closed eyes, Kindle tried to imagine who could be in her room, but then as yet another voice shushed the other, consciousness flicked her eyes open and reminded her of where she lay. She frowned at the same dark stone wall she had fallen asleep facing and mashed her eyes shut, determined to return to sleep, but the voices hooked her attention.

"If you two can't stay quiet, go back to bed."

"Sorry, Masso."

"We'll be quiet."

Kindle rolled over and saw a cluster of bodies standing in the middle of the room. The tallest one, which she guessed was Masso, broke away from the group and noiselessly slipped between the beds. When he reached the wall and the soft torchlight confirmed his identity, he turned his face up the stairs then back at his siblings. As they took their turn through the beds, Kindle crawled out of her own and followed them. She stopped short of the stairway, though, to hunker behind a mattress. Kindle was curious but not at all committed to joining them. Masso waved his hand at Yirah, Yirun, and Navon, and then they tiptoed up the stairs behind him. Once they reached the top, they all simply settled down on the highest step possible. After a few seconds of silence, Kindle decided that whatever they were up to was not worth losing sleep over and almost returned to her bed when she heard Yirun excitedly whisper, "I can hear Mom!"

Masso socked his arm, and Yirah clasped a hand over her brother's mouth. Now Kindle understood that the four oldest children were eavesdropping on their parents. Sure that Azildor and Naam were discussing her, Ella, Tad, and Andrew, Kindle decided that if anyone was talking about her, she had a right to hear it. She dodged out of her hiding place and up the stairs as well. At first, they all turned flabbergasted and guilty faces to her, but their expressions soothed when she whispered, "I want to listen too. They're probably talking about me anyway."

Masso quickly nodded and hissed, "Just stay quiet."

Then they all turned their ears to the overhead skin to listen.

"... doing well with her reading, but Adin can't sit still long enough," Naam was saying. "All he wants to do is go out and help you."

Azildor chuckled then replied, "He is an enthusiastic worker. I'll talk to him. He needs to learn or he will not always be such help."

"Yes," Naam agreed then sighed, "But how was your day? I don't think I asked."

"Usual."

"Did Yirun really antagonize Old Meaty?"

'Hm?"

"You didn't hear him at dinner? He boasted another close call with that pig."

"The twin's knack for inventing tales is the only thing that is quick enough to harm them."

"Ah," Naam wisely mused as Yirah and Masso hushed an offended Yirun. Once they settled him down, Naam was in the middle of a new sentence.

"Nothing else interesting?"

A long silence opened, but finally Naam spoke again, and Kindle felt them all turn their ears to listen closely.

"What about the children—the four you brought home? Who are they? Where did they come from? I know you too well, husband, to believe that they are only travelers. Your inquisitiveness is much more active than your heart."

"I picked them up at the edge of Danica Woods. Two Cifra were with them."

"I thought the Cifra never left the woods. It wasn't Lord Rex, was it?"

"No. Two of his bees."

"The same as the ones who came before? They didn't threaten you again, did they?"

"They said nothing about land. All they insisted on was that I help the children."

For a few moments, neither parent said anything. Kindle sensed the four pairs of nearby eyes drift to her, hungry for answers. Thankfully, though, another question from Naam captured their attention.

"But why? That—don't the Cifra hate humans?"

"I believed they all did until today. The female Cifra dearly loved them. She begged me to help and care for them."

"That is odd."

"It is."

After another span of silence, Naam carefully probed, "Surely she gave a reason for her request."

"Did you notice the necklaces they wore?" Azildor responded in a quieter but much more intense tone.

"I . . . yes, I did see the dark-headed boy had a chain around his neck, but—"

"They all had one. All four of them. Each one with a different gem."

"Azildor," Naam sounded hesitant but serious, "do you think—?"

"The Cifra called them heroes."

"The time is right."

"I know."

"We must help them. We—"

"Yes," he steadily interrupted then sighed deeply, "I know."

If they spoke more, Kindle did not know because at that moment footsteps sounded overhead and spooked each one of the eavesdroppers down the stairs and into their beds. Kindle dove back under her covers and tried to slow her rapid breathing so she could pretend to be asleep. She rolled over to face the stone wall again, but this time her mind was flooded with thoughts. The conversation had not brought the answers she had hoped for but only more questions, fears, and frustrations. Even with her mind spinning, exhaustion soon took over and drew her into deep sleep.

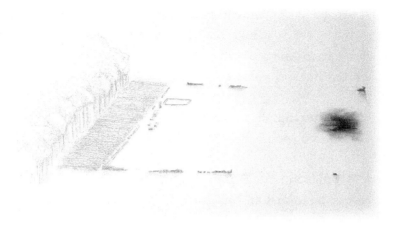

BELLALUX

"Wake up, wake up," a cheery voice urged. As it continued the command, Kindle kept her eyes shut, trying to will the voice to belong to her mom. The voice was just too different, though, and Kindle relented her hopes to reality as she opened her eyes. Naam was standing near her bed holding a lantern aloft.

"Wake up," she repeated more insistently, and Kindle rolled around to see she was gently kicking Tad's mattress. She stopped, shook her head, and then turned to Kindle. "Oh! Good morning! I didn't realize you were awake. Go on upstairs and eat some breakfast before it's all gone," Naam encouraged with a smile as she helped Kindle up. "Did you sleep well?"

"Uh, yeah, I guess so," Kindle mumbled, her sleepy mind still trying to find its balance.

"Good," she responded before turning back to Tad. "Wake up, young man." Interested to see what would happen, Kindle took more time than necessary to slowly wrestle with her boots. The blanket that Tad had buried himself under lay perfectly still, but a groan issued from it.

"Can you hear me? Breakfast is not going to wait on you." Naam leaned over to place a hand on the lump of Tad, but as soon as she made contact, he let out a roar and sent himself spinning onto the floor. Tad punched and kicked his way out of the blanket then angrily glared up at Naam. Something like disgusted confusion replaced his ferocity, though, as he blinked at her.

"Good morning," she very calmly greeted him, "Would you like some breakfast?"

He squinted around the room until he saw Kindle. Then his expression changed again into comprehension, and he finally nodded as he grunted, "Yeah."

"Good. Come on upstairs then," Naam directed both of them. "Like I said, it isn't going to wait on you." Then she took her own advice and carried herself across the room and up the staircase. Kindle, afraid she would reawaken Tad's hostility, stifled her urge to comment on his amusing jolt out of bed and finished pulling on her boots. She was about to flee the basement when Tad stopped her.

"Hey!" he barked, and Kindle froze, prepared her defenses, and then turned an emotionless face to him.

"What?"

"Nah, forget it," he sneered back then brushed past her. At once Kindle regretted her coldness toward him and dropped her callous act.

"No, hey, sorry. I'm sorry. I didn't, um … what was it? What were you gunna say?" she pleaded and he halted. Tad turned his suspicious eyes on her then sniffed and kept heading to the stairs.

"Hey, I said I'm sorry," Kindle, slightly irritated, called and jogged to his side.

"Yeah, well, I don't care," Tad replied.

"Ugh!" she huffed, offended. "Well, you can at least tell me what you were gunna say." To her frustration, he ignored her and loped up into the house. She called him a jerk under her breath then followed his path upstairs.

Unlike the night before when the family congregated around the table to eat, everyone was scattered throughout the kitchen hungrily devouring their breakfasts. Masso and Navon—both looking especially tired—were camping on the raised stone hearth slogging down what seemed to be last night's stew; Yirah and Yirun were noisily chattering on the counter while Adin watched them from the floor; Naam and Azildor were standing apart from the noise, occasionally speaking to one another; and Binah, Sophia, Ella, and Andrew were clustered at one end of the enormous table. Kindle beelined to them, and as soon as Ella noticed her, she waved Kindle to her side.

"Good day, Kindle!" She cheerfully beamed then quietly asked, "How did you sleep? You don't look so lively."

"I'm fine. Tad's just a jerk face," Kindle grumbled as she eyed their bowls.

"Is he up as well?" Ella inquired as she spun her head around to find him. Kindle searched too and found him slouching sullenly in a chair at the other end of the house.

"He's over there being a pouty grouch," Kindle told Ella as she jabbed a thumb over her shoulder. Ella sympathetically frowned at her.

"You two need to learn to get along. You're all thrones and thistles at each other."

"He's impossible to get along with. He hates everybody."

"Oh, he is not," Ella confidently laughed then skipped over to him. Kindle, not caring to watch Ella possibly prove her wrong, rolled her eyes back to Andrew.

"What is that stuff?" she asked, tilting her head at his bowl. He shrugged but put another spoonful in his mouth.

"Mommy calls it mush," Binah informed her without tearing her gaze from Andrew, "And it's meat mush today 'cause Mommy put meat in it."

Kindle nodded at her then glanced sideways at Andrew. "Is it good?"

He dipped his chin. "Better than school food."

"You want some?" Binah suddenly enthusiastically asked then, without waiting for an answer, dropped off her rock chair and trotted over to the pot near Yirah and Yirun.

A few minutes later, Kindle decided mush was not as glorious as honey cakes but was hearty, warm, and satisfying. The oatmeal-like mush rubbed away her grumpiness, and by the time she finished, she had forgotten why she had awoken in such a dreary mood. Kindle was just settling forward over her empty bowl to watch the activity of the kitchen when Azildor's voice called out and reminded her of his words the night before.

"Let's head out!" he shouted above the chatter, and Kindle's stomach sank as all of the children sprang into action. Each of them except Binah and Adin dropped their dishes at the counter then filed out of the house. Naam swept around Kindle and Andrew to gather their bowls and tipped her head at Azildor, who was still standing like a sentinel by the wall.

"He wants you all to go with him today," she briefly notified them before bussing their dishes away to the water basin. Kindle sighed and gave Andrew a nervous face, but he returned a bland look then dragged himself over to Azildor. She considered staying right where she was, but Ella and Tad were also making their way to the farmer. Determining that she didn't want to be left out of whatever was going to happen, Kindle also followed Naam's instruction. Seeing her coming, Azildor ducked through the entry tunnel. As Kindle stepped out into the still dark morning, the chilly air sank into her bare arms and legs, and she desperately wanted to dive back into the warm house, but Azildor was already leading everyone toward the barn.

When they reached the large stone structure, Azildor put a hand on Masso's shoulder and instructed, "Son, make sure your brother and sisters complete their morning chores. I am taking our guests out for a ride."

Masso pushed his chin up with importance. "I will, Dad. Do you want me to hitch the horses to the wagon?"

"Yes—the cart mares—put their feed bags on as well." Azildor followed his son into the barn, and without waiting for an invitation to escape the cold, Kindle did as well. At first, only moonlight creeping in the archways on either end of the barn lit the large space, but Masso quickly lit a lantern hanging on the wall. With its dim light, Kindle could just make out the four cubicles at each corner and the wagon between the two at her right. She made a move for it, but Azildor stopped her.

"Wait outside with your friends."

Kindle frowned at him but trudged outside and huddled beside the wall.

"Are they ready?" Ella asked brightly, and Kindle shook her head, annoyed at how alert Ella could be when it was so cold and so early. Taking a look around, Kindle saw no sign of discomfort from Andrew or Tad either. They both did seem tired, though, and she took some joy in that. She began wiggling her legs in an attempt to warm them and immediately regretted it when she saw a snicker form on Tad's face.

"What?" she hatefully spat at him.

"You cold?" he returned in the same tone.

"Yeah, I am. It's cold out here—or are you too stupid to know that?"

"Kindle—" Ella began to chide, but Tad spoke over her.

"No, you're stupid for wearing shorts."

"You're wearing shorts too, so—"

"I'm not dancing around like an idiot, though."

"Ugh!" Kindle huffed but didn't have a chance to retaliate because Azildor, seated atop the wagon, appeared and eyed them with his hard, piercing stare.

"Sorry," Kindle quickly mumbled as she dropped her head.

"Your harsh words will bring you nothing but anger from others. End them," Azildor instructed down to them with such force that Kindle felt as if she had been struck.

After a few tense seconds, he commanded, "Come aboard." They all silently made their way into the bed of the wagon and were soon bumping away from the barn and then past the house. Azildor gave them no hint of their destination as all of the stone buildings shrank and then blurred into the dark landscape. Before long, nothing but a sea of grass surrounded them. Kindle squinted around to try and detect any sort of landmark but found nothing. What she did notice, though, was Tad glaring at her and sent an evil stare back at him until a cold chill shook her body and a grin crept onto his face. Kindle wanted to defend herself, but she was still shaken from Azildor's earlier rebuke and simply shifted so she couldn't see Tad's mocking smile.

They rode for quite a while without incident, and Kindle wrapped her arms around her legs and turned her eyes to the stars to keep her mind from conjuring up anxious thoughts. She had just decided to try and count them when the wagon lurched in a different manner. Laying a hand on the wooden bed to steady herself and taking a quick scan of their surroundings, Kindle saw that they were climbing a steep, grassy hill. Ella and Andrew were craning their necks as if they anticipated something at the top, and so Kindle tried to as well. Nothing other than the sloped ground lay in her vision, though, and she relaxed back into her former position. As they continued to climb, Kindle turned her gaze upward again and noticed that the stars were beginning to fade from the sky. Excited that the sun was finally going to share its light and warmth, Kindle searched the horizon directly behind them for it. She heard a whisper from Ella and turned to see that they had reached the crest of the hill and Ella was pointing at what sat just a short distance from them.

"It's an abandoned house," Andrew whispered to Ella. Even though the little wooden lump was quite dilapidated, Kindle could tell that Andrew was right—the door hole and slanted roof told her that some time ago this structure had been someone's home. Azildor drove the wagon up beside the ruined house and laid aside his reins. He drew in a deep breath of morning air and exhaled as he surveyed the scene. Tad picked his forehead up off his knee and glared around as well. Catching sight of the old house, he wrinkled his nose and asked, "What's that thing?"

"It was once a home," Azildor replied in a distant voice.

"Is it what you wanted to show us?" Ella eagerly asked as she leaned toward it. "Is it your old home?"

"No, on both accounts. It is nothing to us. Down the hill, all across the plain, is what I brought you here to witness. Come." With his last word, Azildor agilely swung down to the earth and walked back to where it just began to slope. Kindle, Ella, and Andrew quickly dropped down as well and grouped at his side, but Tad merely scooted to the end of the wagon. Azildor cast his hard stare back at him and urged, "I wish you to see this."

"Nah, I'm good," Tad lazily replied.

Kindle was sure—and very much hoped—that Azildor would really let Tad have it, but he simply, calmly said, "Only a fool despises knowledge and instruction."

Kindle, puzzled, glanced at the farmer and wondered if he ever became mad. His comment, just as his other reprimands, held no anger but somehow cut sharp and deep into each of them. Even Tad's angry face held clear signs of defensive injury, and after a few seconds, he slid off the wagon and stalked over to his own spot on the hill. Azildor nodded his way, as if approving his action, then held out a hand over the expanse before them. The sun was barely brimming the horizon, but its light was still enough to show them that the plain held more than grass. Kindle first recognized Danica Woods stretching out to their left and the dirt field they had crossed to reach Azildor's house and barn. What she had not expected to see was the stone path that so distinctly separated the dirt from the grass all around the family's buildings. The stone path ran in a straight line to the hill they stood on then sharply turned right. As Kindle followed it, its shape became clear: she was looking at a huge rectangle. Even though occasional gaps broke its geometrical form in several places, the rectangle neatly enclosed the Chokmah farm and vast grassy area sitting behind it. At first nothing noteworthy except Azildor's few farm structures seemed to lie inside the rectangle, but as the sun gained height, a large black area at the opposite end came into view. Kindle wasn't sure what it could be and was about to ask when Azildor spoke.

"When I met you and the Cifra, she—and you as well, Tad—talked of a queen you believed lived north of Danica Woods."

"That's what those bug freaks said. I—" Tad interrupted in a defensive voice, but Azildor silenced him with his next words.

"What you see is all that remains of her kingdom."

Ella was the first to process what he said and gasped, "We're too late? It's gone?"

"What do you mean by that?" Azildor asked her with a questioning stare.

"The Cifra, well, I suppose it was only Missi really, but she said we were to save this queen and her city."

"That's why she called us heroes, remember?" Kindle added and Ella nodded.

"Yes, Missi was so sure that was why we each had found these—" Ella laid a hand on her emerald gem, "—and why they had brought us here. And it really followed logic, you know, for us to all be right at the kingdom we had to save."

"But it's already gone," Andrew murmured in a hollow voice then asked, "What happened to it ... and to her, the queen?"

Azildor sighed, "The Cifra are not evil, but too often their eagerness outstrips their small knowledge and they pursue wild, untrue ideas. I will tell you what I know of the queen and her city, but first tell me what the Cifra have taught you."

Ella immediately began to unravel the story that Lord Rex and Lady Luna had related to them. Between her quick voice and Andrew's occasional addition or correction, Azildor soon knew all that the Cifra rulers had explained about Anelthalien, the makers, the elemental spirits, and their necklaces.

"… and then after Hux disappeared, Lady Luna said all of the Cifra went down into the Tunnels," Ella finished.

"They made the Tunnels to live in because they were afraid," corrected Andrew as he gave a half smile to Ella.

"Yes," Ella confirmed, smiling back, "and that's all they knew—well, that all and that a kingdom sat here, but I suppose they were wrong about that." The smile fell from her face as she looked out over the ruins. Meekly she asked, "Is any of that true?"

To Kindle's surprise, Azildor dipped his head in a nod. "Yes. The Cifra rulers are more informed about Anelthalien's past than I knew."

"But, like…." Unsure of how to protest, Kindle waved an arm at the grassy plain. "No kingdom."

Azildor closed his eyes then patiently clarified, "A kingdom *did* long ago sit inside the wall you see. I only said the Cifra had supplied you with truth but not full truth. They have gaps in their understanding." He settled down on the grass and motioned for them to do the same. "The Cifra told you that the elemental spirits sought power, correct?" Azildor asked as Kindle, Andrew, and Ella sat between him and Tad.

"That's why they broke their connection and made the necklaces," Andrew replied to affirm his question.

"And even when the four spirits held those necklaces in their possession, their desire for power was not sated. Three took the power of their creators and attempted to build their own kingdoms. They were not their creators, though, and did not succeed. The fourth spirit—the element of fire—set her feet on a different, much more evil path to power. At first she quietly removed herself to the south, but soon word traveled over the land that her desire was to rule all of Anelthalien and that death would find any who opposed her."

"Seriously?" gaped Kindle.

"She was very serious and held the power to carry out her threat, but at that time the land was full of a much nobler people who took action against her dark forces."

"Do you mean the elves and the witches?" Ella burst out. "Was that what really began the Great War?"

"It is. The elves, the guardians of the earth, knew their duty and set out to extinguish the fire spirit and her witches."

"Elves and witches?" Tad snorted from his relaxed position, "No way."

"Actuality is not limited to your belief," Ella snapped at him then looked to Azildor. "Were the elves guardians just as the Cifra were?"

"Did Hux make them too?" Kindle wondered aloud as she touched her necklace.

"Not Hux but Terran, the maker who ruled over the earth, fashioned the elves."

"And the witches? Did the maker whose domain was fire create them?" Ella urged and received a strange, penetrating glance from Azildor before he answered, "No. The witches were the fire spirit's doing. Nothing good lived in them."

"Oh," Ella mumbled and sounded somewhat put off but regained her cheerful tone to question, "Well, what happened? The elves won the war, didn't they?"

"Yes, but not without much loss," Azildor replied and stared out over the valley.

"Did they fight here?" asked Andrew but Azildor shook his head.

"No, when the fire spirit sent out her threat, she was hovelled in the far east, just south of the woods. The elves, led by one of their own named Daniel, took the forest from the north and gained much ground."

"Because their power comes from trees?" Andrew suddenly inquired and everyone turned a surprised face at him. He ducked his head and mumbled, "That's what Missi told us."

"Yeah, she also said *he* was an elf," Tad interjected with derision as he tilted a finger at Azildor.

"I am," the farmer replied nonchalantly, and they all swung their wide eyes at him.

"Like, really? Seriously?" Kindle cried in disbelief. Nothing about him resembled any sort of elf she had ever encountered. She took a second to check his ears for points but saw even they appeared normal.

"Misson said there weren't any elves anymore," Tad suspiciously added.

"Misson? The Cifra who fled?" Azildor asked.

Kindle nodded. "Yeah, was he wrong?"

"Very few half-blooded elves remain in Anelthalien, and as far as I know, my wife, our children, and I are the only full-blooded elves. The war took many lives, and even though the elves won the victory, its effects dwindled them further." He paused as if awaiting another question, but when none of them spoke, Azildor continued, "As I said, the elves became strong in the forest, but once they reached the fire spirit and her witches, the strength they had gathered failed. Witches are monsters of fire, and as a people of trees, the elves could not stand against them, let alone their powerful leader. Beaten down and low in hope, they fell back into the woods, but Daniel would not let them be defeated. He sent his men to find a rock along the nearby shore, and once they brought it to him, he told them that he knew they would be destroyed as they were but not if they relied on their creator's power. His plan was this: every elf in his army would place his power of healing and long life into the stone so that whoever held it would hold its protection from death for a thousand years. His men agreed to their leader's plan; they all knew that it was their only chance against the fire spirit. The elves elected Daniel to be the one who would take the power and defeat their enemy."

"That's incredible," breathed Ella. "Did it work?"

Azildor sent a long, solemn expression her way then answered, "A witch slid from the shadows and stole the rock the moment the elves had transferred their power into it."

Ella and Kindle gasped in unison, and Tad angrily objected, "Nah! You said they won!"

Raising a hand to calm them, Azildor resumed his story. "That was a great loss, but they were not defeated. The witch ran away. Ignalus was his name, and his cowardice gave the elves time to repeat the act. Weak though they were, they hunted another stone from the shore and again poured their power of life into it, but as Daniel held it, they also bestowed their love, wisdom, and goodness into it as well. In that act they ensured Daniel wielded all the power of his creator and their victory."

"What? What about that Ignalus guy? Did he just flake out?" Tad argued.

"When Daniel entered the fire spirit's camp and began felling witches, chaos broke out. The forest caught fire, and Ignalus and the fire spirit disappeared. Once the witches saw their leader had left them to die, many of those who still lived surrendered."

"Pft—he didn't really win if he didn't kill the bad guy," Tad grumbled and lay back down on the grass. "Everybody knows that."

"Ugh," Kindle groaned while rolling her eyes Tad's way, but Azildor gave her a stern look.

"The truth beneath his pessimism stands. Daniel did win the Great War, but that short victory set into motion an eternal battle."

Ella opened her mouth to interrupt, but Azildor raised his palm and said, "I will explain. As I said, Daniel won over the remaining, leaderless witches with his new power. He returned with his men and the witches to the home of the elves in the west—here—and when news of his immortality and great character spread, the elves elected him king. Daniel took the title with true integrity. He built a city—a kingdom—in the valley below us. Bellalux. That was its name. I have been told it was the most beautiful kingdom ever established in Anelthalien."

"But you said he didn't really win!" Kindle erupted, unable to help herself. "That sounds like he totally did."

"And it did seem so to every elf, witch, and man that found Bellalux as his home and gathered around the good king. Daniel built such a stronghold of peace that I wonder if even he forgot his enemy."

Tad with an eager, somewhat evil grin on his face, pushed himself up to better see Azildor, who nodded at him and continued, "Yes, Tad, Ignalus still lived where no one knew, and he was never seen again, but…," Azildor's voice trailed away as he scanned the empty valley. Kindle knew they all wanted him to keep talking, but none of them dared to interrupt. Finally, he shook his head and darkly continued, "But our eyes alone cannot be trusted to tell us the entire, unrefined truth. Just as Daniel lived one thousand years, so did Ignalus. Just as Daniel knew the number of his days, so did the evil witch king. Daniel chose an heir and raised her as his own to rule. When his reign and life ended, she took his throne, which held the stone into which his men had invested their power, and gained the long life and elfish magic herself. I can only assume that Ignalus as well transferred his stone and power to another. I say that because at the end of the good queen's reign, she, her heir, and the whole kingdom of Bellalux were annihilated."

Ella gasped and in a rush, whispered, "And that's what Missi meant, isn't it? About the good queen needing our help? But how long ago—?"

"Almost one thousand years," Azildor calmly answered, and it seemed as if the whole world held its breath. None of them or the nature around them made a sound; even Kindle's mind was empty.

Then Andrew brought them all back to life when he very quietly asked, "Did whoever Ignalus picked do it?"

"Yes, Andrew," Azildor replied. "I believe that whoever succeeded Ignalus on the evil throne was the destroyer of Bellalux and the good throne."

"And the good queen," Ella added in a distant voice.

"Does that mean no one took her place?" Andrew implored, turning his furrowed brow at the grass between his feet.

"Yes," answered Azildor then pointed at the black spot Kindle had almost asked about earlier. "That burnt area marks where the castle of Bellalux and the good throne sat. The destruction of the whole kingdom must have begun there and destroyed the throne in its inception."

"So Ignalus really won, huh?" Tad concluded with an expression that could have been sinister joy or snarling anger.

"No—," Kindle wrinkled her nose in thought, "—it was his heir who won, right?"

"No one is the victor," Azildor corrected them with finality. "But as to who still holds the power of the elves' stone, it is the third ruler in the line of evil. But very soon the fourth will take his place," Azildor sighed and stood. "And that is why I believe you four are here."

"What?" Ella questioned as she popped up as well. "Missi said that the good queen sent these necklaces out for help, but it's too late for us to help her or anyone in her kingdom now. Or—or do you suppose that the evil ruler sent them to us? Is that what you're hinting at?"

"Ella, I do believe the Cifra was correct, but it is not too late. If these necklaces had found you at the moment the queen sent them, you would have been powerless against the evil throne. The one who sits on it will not—cannot—die until one thousand years passes. From all I know, the only way to end the reign of evil is to interrupt the succession and destroy the elves' stone when the time for that is near."

"Hold up," Tad suddenly interjected as he turned on the grass to see Azildor, "You want us to go and tell this indestructible dude to just hand over his stone? Huh—I got news, that ain't gunna work."

Kindle gave Tad a sour face before retorting, "That's du—that's not what he means, Tad."

"Kindle," Azildor's stern voice made her turn nervous eyes up at him, "that is very near the course I believe is set before you four."

"Seriously?!" Kindle gawked then stood and spread her arms in protest. "Like, how are we supposed to do that? We don't even know where the guy is, and even if we did—ugh, like, I have a life I kind of want to get back to. I can't just stay here forever."

Azildor gave her a solemn look, but Ella was the one who spoke in disappointment.

"Kindle … I thought you were resolved to help. I know you have a home and a life, but … but this is my home and the land of so many more, and if you three just go back to your lives and ignore all this and if we do nothing, then what becomes of it all?" Ella turned from Kindle's shocked and guilty face to Azildor's stern one for an answer. "What becomes of Anelthalien?"

He shook his head. "I do not have the answers, Ella. I do not imagine, though, that the next ruler will remain silent as his three predecessors have. Almost every man and creature has forgotten the evil throne's existence, but I feel the land groaning under its influence. I fear that as the next in line takes the throne, he will strike this land that does not remember him. That will make his attack, whatever form it takes, a deadly blow."

Kindle watched Ella shudder and felt somewhat guilty for saying she wanted to leave Anelthalien. Still hoping for an innocent way to return home, though, Kindle asked, "But what do *we* do about it? I mean, like, *can* we do anything?"

"Those necklaces you wear have chosen each one of you for a reason and hold the power of the makers within them. With them you have the ability to complete the task for which you were brought here."

Tad picked up his blue gem and squinting at it, cynically said, "So this thing's gunna get us that stone. And save the world. Yo-kay."

Azildor sent him a disproving eye but replied, "Yes, I believe the marks of the makers have chosen to recapture and destroy the stone that lies in the hands of evil and in consequence save Anelthalien from a bleak future."

"So like, we just go out and look for it or what?" asked Kindle, frustrated her ploy to escape home had not worked at all.

"No, you need much preparation before you are ready for your journey. I will help you as I can. Come, the time you have is limited. You must begin to learn and discipline yourselves today," Azildor told them as he started back to the wagon, but before he climbed onto the driver's bench, he saw that none of them had followed. "We must travel down the hill. Board the wagon," he clarified.

Before anyone could make a move, Tad snapped, "No. I'm not goin' to no school. I'm done with this—" He turned to Ella. "I said I'd stick around until we saw your queen. That's it. And she's dead, so I'm out." Tad grumbled something else about school as he resettled on the grass.

Ella gaped around at everyone in disbelief then cried in frustration, "You cannot just be out of this! Why are you so afraid?"

"I'm not afraid!" he yelled back as he rose to his feet so he could glare menacingly at Ella.

"End this," Azildor sternly commanded as he came to stand between them. "If you do not learn to band together, then nothing I teach you will be of any benefit. Mark this as your first lesson: one that lives against all others in this land will soon find a sword in his back, but one that lives in harmony will find the swords at his side." Azildor turned his face on all of them as if he was searching their thoughts then said, "Now, again I ask you to board the wagon so I may begin to teach you to defend yourselves against your true enemies."

"What? You're gunna teach us to fight?" Tad questioned in a much less hostile tone.

Azildor gave him a nod. "Even though I wish you never find it necessary, I would be sending you four to your deaths without skill in the sword."

One of Tad's sinister but giddy grins crawled onto his face, and he led the way to the wagon. Kindle couldn't help but smile at his sudden change of heart and Ella's renewed bafflement at it.

"Boys are stupid," Kindle whispered to Ella as they started for the wagon as well. Ella gave her a confused look but let a chuckle replace it. Once they had all found their places in the wagon bed, Azildor clicked his tongue, and the horses took up a trot back down the hill. Kindle watched the ruined house sink out of view then curiously peered at Tad. He still wore his strange grin and was squinting away from her at the bright, fully risen sun. She observed him as long as she dared then also turned her eyes to the sky ahead of them.

RESERVING THE LINKS

It wasn't long before Kindle realized that Azildor was taking a different route down the hill. They were heading right instead of left—the direction that would have returned them to the farm. She desperately wanted to know where they were headed but also didn't want to be the one to disrupt the silence, so she occupied her mind by watching the green grass slip by beneath them. A long time passed before Kindle noticed the green sea ebbing away to a dry, black ground. Realizing where they were, she found it impossible to stay quiet any longer.

"This is where the castle was!" she cried in awed discovery. To her embarrassment, though, no one else reacted with the same delight or surprise. As Andrew and Tad gazed at her with bland expressions, she tried to think of how to cover her obviously elementary statement. Kindle hated that she sounded like an idiot but couldn't piece together anything intelligent to say and so was grateful when Ella spoke.

"What have we come here for? Is it where we'll learn to swordfight?" she asked, twisting around to check the barren landscape. "Or are we only on our way?"

"No, I will not teach you here," Azildor replied, "But your training cannot begin until we visit the library."

"Library?" Tad scoffed, sounding greatly disgusted, "What do we need with a bunch of stupid books?"

"Where?" Andrew asked and Kindle was glad for his question. As far as she could see, not even a blade of grass interrupted the flat, black ground spread around them. She felt certain that it couldn't be anywhere close, but Azildor pulled the horses to a stop and assured them that it wasn't far.

"We will go on foot now. The earth is too unsure for the horses," he told them, and they all began to unload from the wagon. Kindle carefully lowered her feet and tested the black ground as if it were ice. It didn't give way like she had feared, and so she cautiously finished her descent.

"Just, like, how unsure is it?" she asked, "Like enough to fall through or something?"

Tad stomped his foot behind her, causing her to jump and let out a terrified squeak. He laughed and she sent him a glare.

"It's not funny," Kindle grumbled so Azildor wouldn't hear, but when she pivoted to stalk away, the farmer stood in her path.

He gave them a warning look—the kind her mother gave when she and Mikey fought—then informed her, "Only the burnt remains of the castle will give way. The rock beneath is solid. You do not need to fear." After he spoke, Azildor strode away, his every step softly crackling. The four of them trailed after him, releasing even more crisp snaps into the air. As they walked Kindle noticed that the ground felt almost squishy beneath her feet and wondered how the charred pieces of what had once been the castle hadn't blown away yet. It seemed odd, but it wasn't as odd as some of the things she had encountered the past few days, and so her curiosity didn't dwell on it for long. Instead, it took up pondering what a library and a burnt castle had to do with learning to swordfight.

She didn't have to wait long for the answer. They had only walked a short distance when Azildor halted, knelt, and ran his hand through some of the black powder. Kindle wondered what he could be doing when his hand stopped, wrapped into a fist, and lifted a ring out of the layer of ash.

Azildor motioned for them to stand back as he stood and yanked a long chain up with him.

"I brought Masso here with me when he was young, and he found this while playing," Azildor said then heaved his strength into one massive tug on the chain. Kindle skittered back as a series of metallic clangs filled the air and a hole that was the length of the chain slid into existence. As the last bang dissipated and the opening halted at Azildor's toes, he huffed, "And I am certain nothing has disturbed it since."

For a few seconds no one moved or uttered a word. Then a curious Ella followed by a much more hesitant Andrew carefully stepped to the edge of the opening.

"What's down there?" asked Kindle, also eager to know but too fearful to approach the hole.

"Come down this way." Azildor nodded at his feet then stepped out over the gap. Fear twisted Kindle's stomach in the millisecond that she assumed Azildor would keep dropping down into nothingness and expected them to do the same, but as his foot touched a step and he gradually sank down a staircase, the fear morphed into embarrassment, and she tried to casually laugh.

"Still jumpy?" Tad snickered as he rounded behind her to head for the steps. She glared at the back of his head but kept her lips together, determined to avoid any further scolding from Azildor. The opening was only as wide as a sidewalk, and so Kindle waited for Ella and Andrew to follow Tad before she joined the descent. Once her head dropped below ground level, Kindle realized the reason for the length of the hole. No light existed in the room below except for what the sunshine from above provided, but since the sun was almost at the summit of its daily climb, the room was illuminated. Kindle could see that the stone room spread out on either side of the narrow staircase and that rows of thin wooden bookshelves occupied most of the space. A few dusty books lay on them, but stacks of old-looking paper and foreign objects took up most of the shelf space. Kindle was so immersed in examining the oddities on the shelves that she didn't notice what else resided in the underground library until Tad's uncharacteristically awe-filled voice echoed around the room.

"Whoa. Nice."

Kindle peeled her eyes away from the closest stack of yellowed papers to search for the source of his amazement and immediately found it. Hanging straight ahead of them, a shining array of weaponry coolly rested all along the wall. A variety of swords, some long and thin, others shorter and hooked or jagged, all with precious metal and jewel adorned hilts proudly sat beside matching shields. As Kindle joined the others to better see the swords and shields, the urge to run her hands over them arose in her. Each piece in the display was so like something in a museum, though, she didn't dare to venture closer.

"Are we gunna fight with this stuff?" Tad asked in hungry excitement.

"You will not begin with these, no," Azildor replied. "These swords were crafted for masters. To wield them you must earn them."

"That's stupid," Tad grumbled, his disgruntled tone returning.

Azildor reproachfully eyed him, but before he could say a word, Andrew asked, "Are all of these yours now?"

"They belong to no one. This was once part of the castle and part of the people of Bellalux ... but now that they are no more, these objects have no owner." Azildor cast a warning look at Tad. "So now they are free for the taking, but only by the able."

Tad sent a sour face at the farmer then stalked up to the closest sword and tugged it up off its hooks. Immediately, the large sword clanged on the stone floor, yanking Tad down into a hunch with it. He tried to pull it up once but without success. Azildor bent and softly said, "Your proud boldness exceeds your strength."

Tad defensively straightened up, kicked the sword, and then tried to hide the soreness of his foot as he trounced over to the steps to gloomily plop down on them. With effort, Azildor returned the sword to its perch then turned to them and said, "None of you are ready to carry these weapons. They are of elfish make and take much strength and skill to carry. I will train you to do so, but today we are here for the other forgotten relics of Anelthalien's earlier days." He pointed at the shelves behind them, and Ella, Kindle, and Andrew squinted around the dusty room.

"What is it all?" asked Ella.

"I do not know. I have never had a purpose to deeply explore this room, but it seems that the reason for your arrival links to the old, forgotten days of Anelthalien, and this is the only place where I know it still lives."

Kindle wrinkled her nose. "So what, all these papers and books and stuff will tell us why we're here and about these necklaces and all that?" she asked, but before she received an answer, her thoughts shifted and she wondered, "But I thought you said we were supposed to go get that stone from that guy. Right? That's what you said."

"Yes, Kindle," he responded, "but I know nothing more than that, and even that is only a belief. A strong belief—but only. How you will accomplish that task or whichever one you are here for may very likely be recorded in this room."

"How likely?" Andrew quickly challenged, and all eyes swept to Azildor.

"Almost certainly," the farmer replied with confidence. "Now—collect what you can and we will return to the farm. In the mornings you will study with Naam—"

"Nah!" Tad yelled in protest as he jumped up. "*You* said we were gunna learn to fight, and now you're saying we're not? That's a bunch of—"

A hard look from Azildor cut Tad off, and the farmer finished his sentence. "And in the afternoon I will train you."

The two males continued to bore holes into one another with their eyes until Ella began chatting to Andrew as she steered him to the aisles of shelves. Kindle trotted after them, eager to escape the tension between Azildor and Tad. As she passed the stairs, she heard Tad quietly grumble, "Whatever. I'm outta here if you're just gunna lie about everything."

Out of her peripheral, Kindle saw him turn and stomp up the steps and before she knew why, ran up after him.

"Hey! Hey, c'mon. Come back," she called as she jogged to catch up with Tad. He gave her a momentary glare then continued to storm away over the black ground. Kindle heaved a sigh and rolled her eyes but darted ahead to block his path.

"C'mon, just go back. Azildor's not that bad if you just listen to him and do whatever he says. You know? Like, just quit arguing," she urged, trying to be helpful.

Tad made a disgusted noise and sidestepped around her so he could resume his walk. Kindle huffed in agitation then shouted at his back, "What?! What is your problem?!"

At her last word, he stopped, spun, and sent her a snarling glare. Kindle felt fear well up in her stomach but punched it back down—if Azildor had heard her, she would already be in trouble for arguing anyway, and she was determined that Tad would not win this time.

"Seriously!" she pushed, now trying to provoke him, "What's your problem? You keep running away every time somebody makes you just a little bit mad!"

"Shut up," he growled in a low, menacing voice.

"Um, no." Kindle tossed her hair, hoping to appear much braver than she felt. "Like, why can't you listen to anybody, huh? You just think you'll go off on your own and suddenly be right about everything?"

"What do you care what I do?" he grumbled with his eyes still narrowed. Kindle glared back but wasn't sure what to retort to his question. She wanted to shout something rude back—the desire to win a screaming match was still pumping adrenaline through her veins—but his voice carried such a bland, uncaring and at the same time genuine tone that she suddenly felt silly and selfish for wanting to argue.

"Well, I dunno—" she ended up sputtering, "I guess I just…I don't think you should leave." Kindle dropped her eyes to the black ground, too embarrassed to take his now puzzled disgust. "Like, you know, I mean, where are you gunna go, and like Ella said, we need your help if we're ever gunna get out of this place." She chanced a peek at him. Tad had turned his eyes away from her.

He snuffed, "That's just a bunch of lies. You guys don't need me."

"What's a bunch of lies?"

"All what Ella and Azildor said and those bugs and everybody. This is just some stupid dream, and we're all gunna wake up, and none of it's gunna be real. I mean come on—elves and magic necklaces and all this stuff is stupid. We're not heroes and we can't save anybody. And this—" He gruffly yanked his necklace over his head and shook it at her, "—this stupid thing definitely isn't gunna save anybody." Tad wound up to chuck the jewel away, but Kindle flung up her arms and darted in his way as she cried, "No, Tad, wait!"

"What?"

"Don't throw it."

"Why?"

"Because," she quickly retorted, hoping a reason would bloom in her mind, but as the seconds ticked, none appeared.

"Because *why*?" he rudely insisted and tensed again to throw it.

"Because, like, I don't know why, just don't, okay? Like, give it to me if you don't want it." Kindle herself wasn't entirely sure why she was so opposed to Tad hurling away his necklace, but something inside of her felt anxious about losing it. "Please?'

"Whatever," he grumbled as he rolled his eyes and dropped it.

Kindle quickly stooped to grab it up and decided to say, "Because I think you'll need it, I guess." He didn't say anything, so she continued in an attempt at a cheerful voice, "I think you'll need it because, like, how could all of this not be real, you know? I mean, I've never had a dream like this and I don't think everybody's lying to us. I don't know if we're really gunna be heroes or anything, but I think we're here for some reason, you know? And I think these'll be important for something, so I'll keep yours for you." Kindle tried to stuff it in her small shorts pocket but couldn't make the entire gem and chain fit. Hearing a snort from Tad, she looked up to see a mocking half-grin on his face.

"It fits good enough," she declared, determined to not seem inept. Then, eager to change the subject, she suggested, "Let's go back and help—"

"No."

"No? What do you mean 'no'?" Kindle incredulously asked.

"I told you I'm not goin' around with a bunch of liars. I'm done with all this junk," Tad resolutely spat then began to stalk away, but Kindle grabbed his elbow. In a flash, he flung her hand off and shouted, "Leave me alone! Why can't you just leave me alone, huh?! Argh! Just get away from me!"

His burst of anger exploded right in Kindle's face, and for a moment she felt so shocked and offended that she wanted to cry, run, and slap him all at once, but the only motion she carried out was a shake of her head.

"No," she choked out, still unsure why she was so determined to keep herself tied to someone so rude and angry. Kindle told herself that it was simply the desire to defy and triumph over him. Just to prove her motive to herself, she shook her head once more and very firmly said, "No. I won't leave you alone."

Fuming, Tad rolled his head back in agitation and grumbled, "Urgh, you are so annoying." He heaved a great, angry huff before growling at her, "Fine, whatever. I'll go back to his stupid house if it gets you to quit bothering me. But I'm not reading any stupid books or doing anything with you idiots. You can do all that fairy tale crud on your own." He pushed past her and headed for the wagon. Kindle, feeling victorious, watched him with a proud grin until he swung up into the wooden bed and squatted down like an irritated gargoyle. Making sure he couldn't see her, she tried one more time to shove the rest of his necklace into her pocket. Relenting to the fact that it simply would not fit, she yanked it back out and slid it down between her calf and the cool, stretchy material of her boot.

DISTANCE MAINTAINED

Naam, Binah, and Adin watched with wide, impressed eyes as the last armload of papers thudded onto the stone table.

"Well, this is quite the unexpected load," commented Naam as she gazed over the numerous stacks.

"What is all this stuff?" Binah curiously asked as she climbed in a chair for a better view.

"Honey, chairs are for sitting, not standing," reminded Naam, and Binah dropped on her bottom.

"What is all this, Daddy?" Adin urged as he also took a seat.

"Many papers with many words that our new friends will read."

Tad snorted at the word "friends", but Binah's question covered it.

"Why?" she sang, and Azildor patted her on the shoulder.

"Because they have a very important job to do, and reading will help them do it."

"That's a lot to read," Adin whispered with fear in his eyes.

"It is, Adin," Naam replied to him and gave her husband a serious face. "And how do you think we'll eat our supper with only half a table?"

Adin tilted his head back so he could see both of his parents. "We got to move all of it, don't we, Daddy?"

"Yes, Son," Azildor responded then sighed as he scooped the pile he had laid down just minutes ago back into his arms. Kindle also gave sound to her frustration. After hauling the majority of the contents of the library up the narrow stairs, pinning them down during the wagon ride, and toting them into the house, Kindle did not feel like moving the papers and books again. She gave an exasperated look to Andrew, who returned a tired face but shuffled up to the table to scoot a stack into his arms. Kindle was on the verge of announcing that she was sitting out when Naam nudged Binah and Adin into action, and the three herded together as much as they could carry. With another groan and a sidelong glance at Tad, who had not yet helped one ounce and was apparently continuing his uselessness, Kindle began her part in the effort to relocate the library into the living roomlike part of the house.

Once every paper had reached the far wall, Kindle plopped down onto one of the skin-covered chairs. Andrew took a seat near hers, and she whispered, "I am so not moving that stuff again."

Before he had a chance to answer, Naam appeared with Sophia on her hip. "Come eat. You two will need some energy for the afternoon," she cheerfully encouraged and held her unoccupied hand out to help Kindle out of the chair. Kindle, though, had no intention to leave the cozy seat she had parked her tired body in and simply stared at Naam.

Hesitantly, she asked, "What do we need energy for?"

Naam's smile melted into slight confusion. "Did Azildor not tell you? He wants to teach you combat skills."

"Yeah, he did," Andrew replied and began to extricate himself from his oversized chair, but Kindle remained unmoved.

"But, like, he didn't mean today, did he?" she groaned.

Naam nodded. "Yes, he did. He already left so he could work a bit while you four eat. He's expecting you soon, so do come and have some lunch." She tilted her head toward the table where everyone else had already congregated around some plates of food then strode over to them.

"Ugh, I wish we could just relax," Kindle complained to Andrew, who gave a short nod. Despite their desire, though, they rose and plodded over to the table. Naam rushed them through their meal and then directed them to meet Azildor in the animal pen at the opposite end of the farm. Ella, Kindle, and Andrew set off in the lead while Tad trailed behind. Sure that Tad would disappear at the first opportunity, Kindle kept checking the entire walk to see if he was still following them. After Ella noticed her compulsive head turns, she too glanced back to see what held Kindle's attention.

"What do you keep looking for?" Ella asked Kindle while eyeing her slyly.

Kindle put on a sour face and explained, "He's gunna bail. I just know it. That's what he was doing at the library, trying to run off again."

"Maybe he just likes to be alone." Ella shrugged, unconcerned.

"Or just, like, hates everybody," Kindle murmured and received a smile from Ella. "What?" Kindle demanded, ready to defend her statement, but Ella shook her head and sighed, "Oh, let it alone, Kindle."

Before Kindle could push further, Andrew pointed ahead. "There's Azildor."

The two girls followed his finger and saw that Azildor was standing among a white, horned herd.

"Aw! Sheep!" Kindle cried in excitement.

Ella gave her a funny look. "Sheep? What?"

"Aren't those sheep?" Andrew squinted at the animals. "Or goats?"

"Those there?" Ella questioned as a grin curled up her mouth. "Those are baydles."

For some reason, the word sounded familiar to Kindle, but she wasn't sure why. "Well, they look a lot like sheep," she finally declared.

"Are sheep animals in your world?" Ella eagerly asked.

Andrew nodded. "Yeah—and they do look like those ... baydles."

"Yeah," Kindle added, remembering how fun it had been telling Ella about things from her life at home. "Sheep are fluffy and white and cute just like those except, like, they don't have those curly horns or super long wool."

"People use sheep for their wool. They're pretty dumb," Andrew continued to explain and made Ella laugh.

"Well, that does sound quite like baydles. At least what I've heard of them." She paused to climb into the pen. "No one in Garrick has baydles, but men come often to trade their wool and horns and always go on about what a foolish lot they are."

Kindle giggled at her remark but suddenly stopped when she saw Azildor catch sight of them and raise his palm. Ella and Andrew halted at her side and the three watched as the farmer led his herd away to the furthest corner. Once the entire group of baydles stood in a cluster by the stone fence, Azildor pulled a rope from one of the short walls to the other so that the creatures were confined to a triangular area. Kindle wondered if the single rope would actually hold the baydles in the corner, but as Azildor left them, the baydles remained grouped together behind the rope. Just when Kindle had resolved that the baydles were too dumb to even notice what had happened, one swung its dull face to Azildor and let out a loud, awful call that reminded Kindle of a hound dog. At once every other baydle joined in the bellowing, sorrowful cry.

"Ugh, they don't *sound* like sheep," Kindle complained, pushing her hands over her ears. The more distance Azildor put between himself and the baydles, though, the less they bayed. When Azildor reached them, the animals had fallen silent and started to munch on the grass at their feet.

"The baydles scare easily. They fear nearly everything except their grass and who they know as their master," explained Azildor. "It will be best for all of you to keep far from them."

"What? Those sheep?" Tad inquired with disgust as he loped up to the group.

"Baydles," corrected Ella but Tad ignored her.

"Are we gunna fight or what?" he sniffed. "'Cause if we're just gunna mess around with a bunch of sheep—"

"Baydles," Ella loudly interrupted, and he sneered at her.

"Patience would do you well," Azildor carefully cautioned then swung his shepherd's rod up and held it like a sword. "We begin with defense." He tilted his weapon behind them at a long stick propped against the fence. "And with sticks. Whoever will learn first, take up the stick there. The others, watch from the fence."

Not wanting to be the first to embarrass herself, Kindle promptly found a seat on the short stone wall. Andrew found a spot on the fence as well, but to Kindle's surprise, Ella, not Tad, snatched up the stick and energetically carried it to Azildor. Kindle couldn't tell if Tad was sour about having to wait his turn or just held his usual sneer as he leaned his elbows back on the stone fence as well. She didn't bother to examine him for his feelings, though; Azildor was already doling out commands to Ella.

"Yes. A bit more. There, do you see?" he was saying, and Kindle wondered if she had missed something important. She set her attention on them to make sure none of his other instructions slipped by her.

"The stance you take and distance you maintain are integral to your safety and success. Too close—" He modeled the actions as he spoke them, "—and your own weapon is an additional hazard. Too far ... and you accomplish nothing but instigation. Here," he directed, positioning himself near enough to Ella so that in one more step, his rod could strike her, "is where you must stand: one step from your enemy."

Ella gazed down at her stick for a moment, and in one swift move, Azildor swiped his staff to her neck and instructed, "Always keep your eyes on your target." He broke his offensive stance as Ella nodded and locked her eyes on him. "Each of you—" Azildor pointed his staff at the wall but took his own advice and kept his face turned to his opponent. "—If you remember nothing more from our time, remember those three: stance, distance, and focus. They alone will rarely earn you a victory but will often save your life."

After those sagelike words, Azildor led Ella through a series of blocks, stopping often to adjust her arm or wrist or to explain the technique to his small audience. Kindle did try to listen but found that the repetitiveness of the display mixed with the increasingly warm sunshine beating down on her created drowsiness in her brain that she just couldn't shake. As Azildor called out the blocks for what seemed like the millionth time and Ella twisted her arm to demonstrate each one, Kindle lost the battle against her heavy eyelids. She would have never known sleep had overtaken her if Andrew hadn't nudged her. Opening her groggy, grumpy eyes at him, he gave her a serious face and tilted his head toward the dueling group. After one look around and seeing that everyone was staring at her, Kindle's mind snapped awake.

"What?" she whispered as covertly as possible to Andrew.

"It's your turn," he replied just as quietly.

Kindle's eyes grew into large circles, and she nervously breathed, "Okay."

Ella was already walking up to hand the stick over, and so Kindle slid off the fence to meet her.

"Did I miss anything?" Kindle hurriedly asked as the mock weapon exchanged hands.

"Stay alert," Ella assured her with a grin, "You'll do fine."

Kindle wanted to argue that she would most definitely not be fine, but Ella had already passed by, and her own feet were still walking to Azildor. Trying to recall all that he had said before her short nap, Kindle realized that where and how she stood was important, but just where and how to stand she could not remember. To extend her thinking time, she milled around as if trying to find a good spot. Suddenly, out of the corner of her eye, Kindle spied Azildor's staff swing up, and she impulsively ducked. It grazed over her head, tousling her hair. She turned her offended face to the farmer.

"You would've hit me!"

"I would not have followed through if you had not evaded my blow."

Kindle didn't respond but let her distrustful stare speak for her as she rose.

"You will never learn to battle an enemy if one is never presented to you," Azildor retorted then returned the tip of his staff to the ground. "Now, show me what you must maintain to fight."

For a few moments Kindle searched her empty brain in vain, but when Azildor began to raise his rod, her instincts kicked her memory into action.

"Focus and distance," blurted Kindle as she shuffled back a few steps.

"And?" Azildor prompted, preparing himself also.

"Um…," Kindle intently watched him twist and slightly bend his knees as if winding up to pounce and guessed, "like, how you get ready?"

"Stance," he corrected. "Give me as small a target as possible."

"Oh," Kindle mumbled, feeling silly, sure this was the bit she had missed earlier. She tried to mimic Azildor's pose and hoped that she appeared just as fiercely ready as he did. To her further humiliation, though, he rotated his free hand and directed, "Put your right foot forward. A sword at your back will render you susceptible to attacks."

Now feeling more idiotic, she corrected her reversed stance. Hoping Tad, Andrew, and Ella weren't watching her miserable attempts, she peered sideways and saw that each of them was avidly following her every move. To her dismay, Tad appeared quite amused. Azildor prodded her arm and brought her attention back.

"Focus," he emphasized. "An enemy could have ended you in your distraction."

Her throat tightened and heat filled her face. Kindle hated that everyone could see how dumb she was acting but was determined to not break down or give up. Gulping back her frustration, she recited, "Focus, stance, and distance."

"Yes." Azildor nodded. "Now parry stomach." Without waiting, he jabbed forward, and Kindle hopped aside while flailing her stick.

"Use your weapon—block. Do not run," Azildor patiently instructed, "Again, parry stomach." He lunged at her again, and once more she dodged the attack.

"Kindle," he firmly warned, "use your weapon."

"I can't help it!" she cried in agitation and hit her stick on the ground, "You just, like, come at me, and I can't help getting out of the way!"

"You *can* help it. You must learn to trust the sword and your skill with it."

"Ugh! It's a stick and I'm awful at this," she whined in protest, but Azildor shook his head.

"No, it is a sword. Now do as I do."

Kindle rolled her eyes but followed his instruction. Just as he had led Ella through the blocks, he now guided her to maneuver her arm and stick to guard attacks to several main areas of her body. Now that he was demonstrating rather than poking at her, Kindle found it much easier to sweep the stick into the proper pose. After a few rounds of practice, the movements began to feel natural, and when Azildor did take a stab at her, she met his rod with her stick.

"Ha!" she triumphantly laughed, and Azildor gave her a very slight smile as he retracted the attack.

"I did it!" gloated Kindle.

"Yes, you have learned a few ways to defend yourself. It is enough for today. Now it is Andrew's time to learn."

Kindle's smile dropped; she wanted to continue now that she wasn't terrible at blocking anymore and had expected more of a congratulation. Knowing that arguing wouldn't sway the strict farmer, she lowered her stick and trudged off to relay it to Andrew.

"He said it's your turn," Kindle sighed as she held it out to him. Andrew squinted at it with a nauseous expression but reluctantly accepted it and slowly made his way to where Azildor stood.

"Is he ... okay?" she asked Ella, "I mean, like, he looked kind of sick."

"He doesn't believe he'll be able to use a sword," she replied, "but he admitted that he's never used one before, so he can't really know."

Tad let out a snort. "Really? 'Cause right now he looks even more pathetic than you."

Kindle took a second to glare at him for mocking her but eagerly returned her gaze to Andrew. She saw Tad was right: Andrew looked more like a little kid trying to play baseball than a swordfighter. Everything about how he tried to stand and hold the stick was so incredibly awkward and unsteady that he was quite excruciating yet at the same time entertaining to watch. As Azildor tried again and again to correct Andrew's pose, he couldn't seem to ever make his arm twist just right, and Ella kept sighing and shaking her head. Even when Andrew did finally halfway model a block, he would cause an eruption of laughter from Tad as he inevitably tripped or dropped the stick. Once, Andrew somehow sent the stick spinning their way, and Kindle's shriek and short sprint melted an already chuckling Tad into a laughing heap on the ground.

"Aw, man, that's great, I needed that," Tad sighed when Andrew came to retrieve the stick. Andrew gave him a blank stare and dropped the stick at Tad's feet before clumsily scaling the fence and walking away.

"You should not have laughed at him," Ella scolded then took off after Andrew.

"What?" Tad defensively said up to Kindle's disgusted frown. "It's not my fault he's a little girl."

"Ugh, shut up," she grumbled, turning back to see Ella and Andrew. Kindle considered following them, but Azildor called for Tad, and her desire to watch him flounder convinced her to stay. As Tad dragged the stick away, she settled down on the stone wall and exerted extra energy to watch and listen. Kindle was sure that she would get to see Tad blunder through the blocks, and so when he reached Azildor and immediately slipped into a seemingly perfect stance, disappointment deflated her expectation.

"Reverse," she heard Azildor instruct and felt a tinge of hope. He had made the same mistake as her.

"I'm left-handed," Tad growled and Kindle lost her hope again.

"Left-handed?" Azildor nodded. "Alright. Show me what you know." Then, without even calling out the names of the parries, Azildor began methodically stabbing his staff at Tad. To Kindle's amazement, Tad was able to block most of the hits. The two fighters seemed to be stepping through a well-practiced routine, and it astounded and mesmerized her. After a few minutes of their synchronized battle, Azildor backed and called, "Down!"

Tad shuffled back but didn't lower his stick or drop his defensive stance.

"Good," Azildor panted in an impressed tone. "You defend well. Do you know the sword?"

Tad shook his head, and Azildor gave him a suspicious look. "How is it you have skill then?"

Tad just shrugged.

Seeing he wasn't going to extract an answer, Azildor shifted and said, "Then let's see your offense." For a few moments Tad remained perfectly still, and Kindle wondered if he knew what Azildor had meant, but just when she was sure nothing would happen, Tad wrapped both hands around the stick and swung it with all of his might at Azildor's head. A shocked and worried yelp escaped from Kindle, but to her relief, Azildor easily blocked Tad's attempt. They momentarily stood locked, but Tad suddenly withdrew his weapon and then began to attack like a madman. Faster than Kindle knew it could fly, the stick lashed at every inch of the farmer only to be blocked again and again. The incredible display of frenzied speed and cool skill continued until a loud crack ripped through the air and the splintered stick flew away from the fray. Kindle watched it arch and smack the ground at least twenty feet behind Tad, but an angry shout pulled her eyes immediately back to the fight.

"Stand down!" Azildor shouted as he evaded Tad's fist. This time, though, Tad didn't obey. Instead, he wound back for another punch and in the instant he swung, Azildor somehow managed to drop his staff, grab Tad's wrist, twist his arm behind his back, and force him onto his knees.

"Stand down means we are finished," Azildor calmly panted. Tad yelled a threat and tried to fling his free fist back at Azildor, who responded by catching that wrist as well and pinning him to the ground. Tad thrashed and shouted even more, but Azildor held him steadily in place like a wrestling champion. Eventually, Tad's energy dissipated, and breathing hard, he laid his cheek on the grass.

"You have much anger. Much rage," Azildor sighed, just loud enough for Kindle to hear. "You must lose it. It will bring you only strife."

"Get off me!" Tad demanded, but Azildor didn't budge.

"I will not release you until you let go of your anger."

"Maybe I have a good reason to be angry!"

"No reason can defend this kind of wild rage. I know you are against the task set before you and far from home—"

"Don't act like you know me! You don't know anything about me!"

"Then I will learn."

"You won't learn squat," Tad growled, and then they sat locked for what seemed like a long time in complete silence. Kindle began to feel awkward. All she had wanted was to see Tad ineptly wave a stick around, but the situation had grown serious. She wanted to extract herself from the heavy animosity but feared that moving would just attract more attention to herself and her unwelcome presence. Gripping the stone under her, she resolved to remain still.

Finally Azildor conceded, "I will release you. Leave your anger here, and we will continue tomorrow." Then, just as he had promised, the farmer rose and gave Tad room to unhinge his stiff joints and slowly ease up as well. Tad didn't give any attention to Azildor but glared off into the distance as he rubbed his wrists and stormed over the fence and past Kindle. Still feeling incredibly out of place, Kindle remained rooted to her seat and didn't take her eyes from the ground. Not until Azildor spoke beside her did she realize that he had moved from the middle of the baydle pen.

"He is a young man very full of anger," he mused, and Kindle picked up her face to see him squinting after Tad with crossed arms.

She shrugged. "Yeah, I don't know what his deal is. He's always like that."

Azildor hummed as if in deep thought then asked, "You spoke with him at the library?"

"Yeah, well, kind of. I mean, we didn't really talk. He just said he was leaving again, and I told him not to."

Azildor raised an eyebrow. "He heeded your words?"

Kindle wasn't sure how to respond. She wanted to tell him that she *had* made Tad listen, but she knew that would be a lie and was positive Azildor would see through it. "Um, I dunno … maybe," she vaguely responded and felt Azildor turn his perceptive stare on her. Kindle wondered if he had the ability to read minds and tried to mentally run through everything that had happened outside of the library. When she was only partially through the memory, though, Azildor mumbled, "Regardless, something has tied him to you."

Sought and Found

A ll the way back to the house, Kindle tried to figure out exactly what
Azildor had meant. It hadn't even entered her thinking that something she had done or said or something about her could be the reason
Tad hadn't actually left, but the longer she walked by herself, the more she
wondered if Azildor's statement was true. She considered that Tad probably
would have left if she had not chased after him, but then her confidence
faltered as she tried to recall exactly what had changed his mind. None of
her actions or words that crossed her thoughts seemed the reason for his
staying. Her stomach twisted in an oddly pleasant way as another explanation ran through her mind, but as soon as she fully realized it, she snuffed it
out; it could not be true anyway. She let her thoughts rove around the new
mystery until she reached the house. Even though Kindle didn't believe the
Chokmahs could hear what she was thinking, she didn't want to chance
revealing all of her ideas to them.

Ducking through the entryway and gazing around, she suspected that
dinner would not be for another few hours. The heat and smell of cooking
food did not permeate the air, and everyone except Naam was lounging in

the living room. Yirah and Yirun poked their heads around one of the chairs and waved her over while calling, "Kindle! Come here!"

Still trying hard to keep her mind blank, she as casually as possible ambled over to them and saw every one of Azildor's children except Masso gathered around Ella and Andrew, who held a short stack of the old library papers in his lap.

"Kindle, come see what we've found," urged Ella as she pulled her to the center of the crowd. "Well, more what Andrew has actually, but look—"

As Kindle settled down in the small space available, Andrew presented an especially large, old paper. Immediately she recognized it as a map, but the place it depicted was unknown to her.

"What is it? I mean, like, what is that place?" she asked and then gazed up at Ella. "Is it *here*?"

"Yes! It is all of Anelthalien." Ella excitedly smiled and pulled the paper into her reach. "See, this is Danica Woods…," she explained, running a finger over the mass of trees on the far left of the funny-shaped island.

"So we live here," Navon chimed in as she stretched to indicate the area above the woods.

"But the city isn't here," Andrew commented and Navon nodded. Kindle leaned closer to the map and saw that it did show a city that matched the outline of ruins that Azildor had taken them to see earlier that day. Right above the tiny rectangle, the word "Bellalux" was written in spidery cursive. Kindle read it out loud, and Ella squirmed with glee.

"That's just as Azildor told us," she breathed. "Remember? This map must have been drawn before it burned down. And that must mean Azildor told us rightly."

"At least about the city," Andrew corrected, and Ella accepted his comment with several nods then leaned over to the right side of the map.

"And see here?" She tapped a small dot that represented a city at the northeast corner. "That's Garrick Kingdom, but I'd dare say it's much larger now."

"How do you know?" challenged Yirun.

"It is where I live," Ella proudly responded, and the twins uttered a noise of understanding in unison.

Navon shook her head at them. "You knew that. That's where Daddy sends things to trade."

"Yeah, Yirun!" Yirah teased and they swatted at one another.

In the time they continued to comb over the map, it became clear that all of the children were fascinated by it but knew very little about Anelthalien. Only Ella could explain any more of the map and the landmarks on it due to the snippets of stories she had heard at the Lighthouse Inn. While Ella rambled on about every city and region, she constantly reminded them that all she knew was possibly fiction, but everyone gulped down her tales as if they were the very air they breathed. Each time Ella's narrative seemed close to exhaustion, one of the Chokmah children would plead for another story or ask for another explanation. For a while Kindle enjoyed all of Ella's half-believable accounts, but soon she grew tired of staring at the same picture and removed herself from the group to play with baby Sophia. She still caught a few strings out of Ella's tales, but since she knew they probably were not true anyway, Kindle didn't bother to pay close attention to them.

The afternoon slowly wore on into evening, and just when the windows began to show tinges of warm colors painting the sky outside, Naam called for the children to hurry to their chores. The twins and Navon trekked out of the house while Binah and Adin crossed into the kitchen to help Naam. Ella sat with Andrew and Kindle for a few minutes but finally gave into her instincts and dashed to work on the dinner settings as well. Kindle watched them prepare until she realized that Ella's stories and her thoughts had distracted her so much, she hadn't noticed that Tad had never returned to the house. She searched the large room again to make sure she hadn't missed him and noticed Andrew was giving her a questioning stare. He didn't have to voice his thought for Kindle to answer it, though.

"Tad's not here. Where'd he go?" she asked.

Andrew's mouth twisted into a frown as he shrugged and returned to the paper he had been reading.

"He didn't come back at all?" Kindle pushed but only gained a head shake from Andrew. She huffed at his obnoxious silence then after a quick decision, pushed herself up, commanded, "Watch Sophia," and then determinately headed for the exit.

Only once she was outside did Kindle recognize how potentially difficult her goal of finding Tad might actually prove. The farmyard alone was vast, and Tad would have had time to travel far from it. Kindle scanned the wide, flat landscape and didn't spot anything, though, so she decided that he was either nearby or so far that she had no chance of discovering him. She mentally limited her search to the stone buildings as far as the baydle pen then set off. While poking her head into the second of the dark, empty squares between the house and barn, Kindle began to wonder why she was even hunting Tad. She stood frozen in the doorway and pushed around all of the thoughts that had suddenly entered her consciousness. Not one of them appealed to her, and she considered ending the search to save whatever would be lost in continuing but then remembered her excuse from earlier; it would be another victory, another point, against him. Kindle nodded to herself, shoved aside her loud string of thoughts, and resumed her mission.

She managed to keep her mind quiet and to check every structure before the sky's light faded completely, but as Kindle peered over the short rock wall of the baydle pen and saw nothing but grass, the light along with her optimism seemed to disappear all at once. Knowing her expedition had failed, she moodily leaned against the fence and heaved a sigh. Not ready to accept defeat by returning to the house, Kindle eased into a more comfortable position so she could watch the sun finish its multicolored descent. While she stood in the solitude, thoughts from the day wove over and between one another. Azildor's comment, though, kept pushing to the forefront, demanding attention, and Kindle grew annoyed with trying to decode its ambiguity.

"Ugh, shut up, brain," she muttered to herself in agitation as she rolled her eyes. At the apex of their roll, Kindle's eyes halted. They had caught sight of a fleck of white high above her in the twilight. When she squinted at it, Kindle realized that the fleck was Tad's tennis shoes. He was sitting on the tip of what Kindle believed was the farm's silo, dangling his feet over the edge. Excitement jolted her stomach, and she pushed away from her repose to jog to the bottom of the tall stone cylinder. She hadn't bothered to extend her search to it because she had been positive that it only held grain, but when she rounded it, she saw an open doorway. Just a peek inside showed Kindle that the structure had to be another abandoned relic of the city of Bellalux. It contained nothing inside except one long, twisting staircase to the top. After cautiously stepping in the tower and turning several times to assure herself nothing lived in it, Kindle started the climb up the stone stairs. As she stepped higher and higher, she saw that slender openings had been built into one side of the curving wall. She briefly stopped to snatch a look out of one, and seeing a nice view of Danica Woods, she figured that what she stood in must have once been a watchtower.

The long ascent caused Kindle to pant and slightly regret her decision to find Tad, but when she finally reached the last step and poked her head out over the roof, a mix of relief and triumph placed a smile on her face. Tad was sitting so his back was to her, but her loud breathing alerted him of her presence. Kindle watched him tense then whip around into a defensive crouch.

"Oh, it's you ... great," he dully grumbled as he relaxed and returned to his previous slouch.

Kindle crossed her arms and saucily retorted, "I don't have to be up here you know, I could just leave."

"Good," he snorted with an unconcerned shrug.

Kindle frowned. That was not the answer she had hoped he would give. Feeling greatly underappreciated by him and wanting to make all of her effort clear, Kindle walked up beside him and demanded, "Do you know I'm the only one who noticed you were gone? And I looked all over this stupid place to find you? And I climbed up all those stupid stairs just to come get you?"

"Congratulations. You want a medal or something?" Tad asked with the same uninterested dullness, and Kindle shook her head with furious irritation.

"No! Just, like, ugh. You're such a jerk."

"For what? Huh?" he snapped and finally turning to glare up at her, yelled, "I didn't do anything to you—*you're* the one who came up here and bothered *me*! Argh! Why can't you get I just want to be left alone? Sheesh!" Tad stood up. "If you're not gunna leave, then I am. And *don't* follow me this time, okay?" he threatened then pushed past her.

Kindle let him pass by without a word. This time she determined she would give him his wish and not stop him. All afternoon she had reassured herself that she actually held the ability to keep Tad from running off, but now she saw reality, and her confident pride was shot. Kindle wanted to continue glaring over the edge of the tower, pretending she didn't care one ounce where Tad stalked away to, but the urge to stop him that had bubbled up inside of her earlier once again swelled. In an instant she dropped her anger and whirled around to catch him, but to her surprise, Tad was standing at the top of the stairs.

"Hey," she began, relieved that she wouldn't have to run down the stairs, "Tad, um…." Kindle struggled to find words that she knew wouldn't make him more furious. "Sorry?" she tried, but Tad didn't reply. His silence bemused Kindle, and she slowly slid up behind him.

"Hey—"

"Shhh!" he hissed, and before she could snap at him, Tad whispered, "Look at that."

Kindle momentarily glared at him but then squinted toward Danica Woods in the distance. The sunset's light had faded now, and all she could discern was the fuzzy outline of the mass of trees.

"What?" she whispered back, sure he was up to something.

Tad's voice was serious, though, when he jabbed his finger straight down and clarified, "*That.*"

Kindle followed his gesture to the ground below and felt her stomach tighten. Not far from the base of the tower sat a dark lump. The night shaded her vision, but as Kindle squinted at it, she could see that it was heavily lumbering back and forth. Its odd movements reminded her of a rabid animal and that scared her; she had heard about how vicious and unpredictable rabid animals were and was not ready to meet one. She felt her palms growing warm and tried to calm herself by claiming, "It can't get up here."

"How do you know?" Tad skeptically whispered.

"It can't climb the stairs—not like that," she replied as the creature tipped again. They watched it stumble around for a few more minutes, and Kindle's fear almost began to ebb away when the creature suddenly halted.

"It's dead," she sighed, but as soon as the words left her lips, the lump righted itself and quickly, smoothly glided into the tower. Kindle sucked in her breath and instinctively latched her hand onto Tad's arm.

"It went in! Did you see it? It, like—"

"Yeah, but you said it couldn't get up the stairs."

"Well, I didn't think it could when it was falling over and stuff, but…." Kindle hesitated to try and test his expression. She was confident that the thing had flown but didn't want to sound crazy admitting it. "You *did* see it get up and…."

Tad gave her an apprehensive glare that assured Kindle they were thinking the same thing. He suddenly knelt down near the staircase opening, and Kindle, whose fear still cleaved her to him, sank down beside him. Following his lead, she peered down into the dark tower below and searched for the creature.

"Where'd it go?" she nervously peeped.

"Dunno."

"Maybe it—huh!" Kindle scampered back across the roof in silent terror as Tad turned a furrowed brow at her.

"What?" he asked in confusion.

"It's coming up the stairs," she mouthed. "I saw it by the little window thing." Panicked, she wildly searched for an escape even though she knew the only way down was the stairs.

"What do we do? What do we do?" she cried out, almost in tears. Tad dully stared at her then crossed the roof and stood in front of her.

"Chill out! C'mon, I don't know what you're so freaked out about," he griped, and Kindle stopped to blink at him. His tone was mostly rude, but something in it almost seemed like concern. Before she had time to think any more about it, though, her attention zoned to the black figure rising over the roof line. She tried to find words but only gaped noiselessly as it continued to creep higher.

"What?" Tad slowly asked as if he already knew but didn't really want the answer. Kindle grabbed his shoulders and twisted him around to see what she saw. Tad sucked in a large breath, and she felt his muscles tighten under her fingers as if he was revving to attack, but they and the creature all froze.

It was not an animal. Kindle could clearly see that now that the black lump stood only a short distance from them. Exactly what it was, though, she did not know. It had the shape of a short, squat child but was completely encased in a black cloak. Even its face was hidden by its oversized hood, but Kindle felt confident that it was staring at them. As they all remained motionless, Kindle realized that the thing was wheezing. Every few seconds a whiny hiss issued from it, and for some reason the sound made her more uncomfortable than the sight of it. Just when she began to hope that it perhaps could not see them and would leave, it began to slowly glide along the perimeter of the roof. Kindle gasped in fear and tightened her grip on Tad's t-shirt, but he remained perfectly still. The hooded figure seemed to float as it circled nearer to them. Kindle bit her lip. Just watching it come closer and closer did not seem like a good idea, but she was sure chancing running to the stairs would also end badly. When it was only feet from them, adrenaline pushed her to flee, but when she dropped her hands to dash away, Tad caught her wrist.

"Don't move," he breathed through his teeth, and she immediately froze. Then, before she knew what happened, Kindle smashed onto the stone and let out an ear-splitting scream. The creature had swiftly pounced on her and knocked her, Tad, and itself into a heap. Kindle tried to untangle her legs from under Tad's torso, but he was upside down and throwing every fist and foot he had into the black cloak.

"Get off! Get off!" she shrieked, pushing against him, but made no progress. "Tad!" she yelled, and he halted his assault to crane his neck around and assess his position. He rolled up and away from the pile, and as he did, Kindle felt her leg twist. Flinging her eyes down to it, she saw that the cloaked creature had wrapped itself around her leg and was thrashing angrily. Kindle screamed again and attempted to wrench out of its tight hold. "It's got me! It's gunna eat me! Ugh!" she yelped and kicked as hard as she could. Her free leg pummeled the creature, but it held fast until Tad charged out of nowhere and tackled it. The pair rolled away from Kindle, taking her boot with them. Without a thought to her bare foot, she scrambled further from them to gain a safer vantage point.

"Be careful!" she cried in a rush, "The edge! Get away from the edge!"

Tad took her cue and jumped back, leaving the black lump struggling to stand at the perimeter of the roof. It picked itself up, chucked Kindle's boot at Tad, and let out a choppy wheeze. Kindle lunged for her shoe and reached for Tad's elbow to yank him to the stairs, but before she could bridge the gap between them, he dove back at the crumpled cloak. Sure he was about to tumble to his death, Kindle shrieked and jolted forward to rescue him but skidded to a standstill when Tad effortlessly punted the approaching creature out into the open night air. They both stood panting as it arched up then down out of sight. In unison they rushed to the edge of the roof to watch their enemy hit the ground but saw only empty space.

"Where'd it go? Where'd it go?!" Kindle shrilled, starting to panic again.

"Kindle! Tad!" a firm voice barked behind them, and they swirled around to see Azildor jogging across the roof. "I heard screams. What is happening?" he breathlessly demanded as he surveyed the scene.

"The thing—that thing—" Kindle gestured uselessly at the spot where it had stood seconds ago. "Did you see it fall? With the black robe? The black thing—did you see it?"

Azildor suspiciously narrowed his eyes as they darted between her and Tad. "A black … thing?" he slowly repeated. "Are you sure?"

"I'm sure! It tried to eat my leg!" Kindle incredulously yelled and caused Azildor to frown and close his eyes.

"Calm yourself," he patiently warned then looked at Tad. "What has happened?"

"Just what she said," he grumbled. "Some freak in a black robe attacked us."

"And where is this mysterious person now?" Azildor inquired in a tone full of disbelief.

Kindle huffed in agitation. "Gone."

"Gone?"

"I kicked him off here," Tad added and Azildor slowly nodded.

"So your assailant will be at the foot of the tower?"

"No," Kindle and Tad replied in one flat voice.

"No?"

"No, it…." Kindle sighed and rolled her eyes. "Okay, I know it sounds stupid, but it disappeared. Okay? It did."

Azildor raised an eyebrow at Tad, who nodded, then rubbed his temple and sighed, "Naam has supper ready. Come." Without waiting for an answer, he started for the stairs but halfway across the roof, bent down and touched something on the ground.

"Tad," he called and summoned him with two fingers, "your necklace."

Tad and Kindle walked over and saw the blue gem wrapped in its delicate silver frame beside Azildor's boot. Tad shrugged, swerved around it, and slouched off down the stairs. Kindle stooped to pick it up and mumbled, "It was in my boot."

"Kindle," Azildor started to reply in a serious tone, but Kindle didn't want to hear what he had to say.

Sliding the jewel back into its snug home and blowing past him, she coldly continued, "I would've said it fell out when that creepy thing attacked me, but that didn't really happen, did it?"

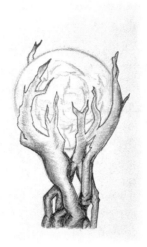

STRANGE THINGS

A tall, thin woman paced across a large, dim room. The only light crept out from the fire held by black torches lining the rock walls. It was unnatural fire—emerald green and angrily crackling yet never charring the black wood below. The torches only lit the edges of the vast room, but since the space was well known to her, she had no trouble finding her way back and forth.

"Anything?" she asked. Her steps sharply clicked as she continued to pace.

"No, nothing. Nothing at all. Not animal nor human anywhere in Ignancia," a small, quiet voice returned lazily. "Nothing ever in the forest, my lady."

"No, and I enjoy it that way." She strode in silence for a few moments then stopped in the firelight and squinted at the other speaker through the darkness. In the flickering light, her skin, which was as pale as milk, seemed sickly green. Her eyes, though, being electric green themselves, danced ardently and menacingly in her thin face.

"And what of the rest of the land?" she interrogated the darkness.

"Not much, no not much," it sighed, "Just the same going-ons as always. Men a-thrashing about, birds a-flying, so on, so on." As the small voice trailed off, a low hissing laugh floated from the darkness, and the woman pursed her lips and spun to face the room. A sneer crawled onto her face and forced her red lips back to show her dazzlingly white teeth.

She tossed her long black hair behind her shoulders and in a low, dangerous tone, rumbled, "Castrosphy."

"Menthoshine," he responded in an airy voice.

"How many times…," she began as she gathered up her long, glistening black skirt and stormed across the hard floor, "do I have to tell you…," she reached a pile of the black wood sculpted into a massive throne and snatched the staff leaning against it, "to stay out of here!" Menthoshine swept the foot of the staff into what seemed to be a heap of rags and watched Castrosphy slump over onto his face. A sneer twisted her mouth as she watched him wriggle on the floor. "Disgusting roach," she fumed. Castrosphy slowly righted himself but kept his face averted. He didn't really have to try to hide himself due to his small size—he came up to Menthoshine's thigh—and his black cloak, which was crafted from the same shiny black thread as her dress and completely swallowed him. Castrosphy was less of a body and more of a lump of black fabric.

"Why are you in here?" Menthoshine placed a hand on the orb at the top of her staff. The globe also began to emit the same vibrating green light and soft crackling sound except slices of lightning danced in it instead of fire.

"Ssspiderss do not sssee," Castrosphy hissed from under his hood. The cloak slowly started to drift away from Menthoshine, but she knocked him over with her staff again.

"What do you mean, Castrosphy? The spiders see more than you do hovelled down here."

He said nothing but let out another cold, hissing chuckle. Menthoshine tightened her grip on the orb, and suddenly a loud crack split through the room.

"Ssstrange thingsss. Ssstrange thingsss come," he hissed and his cloak slid away from her into the darkness beyond her sight.

"Castrosphy!" she yelled after him but heard nothing. He had gone. "Infernal wretch," she spat under her breath and stormed back to the middle of the room. With her staff's light, she could now see who had been talking to her. A thin black spider about the size of her hand was hanging by a thread from the rock above.

"You heard him, Olivar." Menthoshine pushed the light into his many eyes. "What's going on in the land above?"

"I do not know what the creature speaks of." He tried to shield his eyes with his spindly legs. "Neither I nor any of the others have noticed strange things. You know, my lady, how he lies."

"And yet I believe his lies," Menthoshine murmured and pulled herself away from Olivar. Clicking toward her throne, she heard him sigh in relief and stopped.

"Search the whole land until you find these things," she rumbled between her teeth. "Do not come back until you have something to tell."

"Yes, thank you, my lady," the spider chirped, and then the sound of his legs clicking the ceiling told her that he was fleeing. Menthoshine waited until the room was silent before making her way to her throne. She sat, stiff and drumming her long, black fingernails on the armrests. After a few moments, a soft, slow whisper floated through the darkness.

"Men-tho-shine." Her face tightened and she glared around the room. Seeing no one, she wrapped a hand around her staff.

"Castrosphy!" she snapped. "Castrosphy, go find somewhere else to haunt!"

No answer, not even one of his hissing laughs, floated out of the darkness. Menthoshine stood and held her staff up to illuminate the gloom around her, but the green light faded. She stared at her orb, which had never in a thousand years disobeyed her, and saw that it was full of misty grey swirls. Setting the wooden handle on the ground in front of her, she gazed warily at the spinning cloud. Then the voice she had heard just moments ago rang out from it.

"Men-tho-shine! Answer my call!"

"Who is this?!" she ferociously cried out at it.

"You know…my name," the gradual answer came, and she realized who it was.

"Bennickle?"

"Ahhh." As he let out the horse sigh, a chiseled face appeared in her orb. Menthoshine haughtily eyed him. She had never known him to have a face and now looking at it, was very leery.

"You have a shape?" she slowly asked.

"We all do." Even though his sentence was short, he took quite a while to work it out of his mouth. His way of speaking was exactly as the Bennickle's she had met long ago, but it did not convince her that he was the same man. Menthoshine examined him carefully. The bones and muscles under his skin did not quite match up and gave the effect of an angular cliff side to his whole bald head. His eyes were small and dark, the color of rich soil, and he constantly ground his teeth, making his jaw shift slowly as if he were angry.

"You did not last time we met. How is it that you've changed?" she interrogated with narrowed eyes.

"Men-tho-shine," he sighed. "I speak with you." What he said came forth with much effort, but once he had worked it out of his mouth, Menthoshine understood all that he implied.

"Yes." Her mind worked to recall their first meeting. "And so where is that other one, that…that biting one who came with you?" She shivered as the memory of his companion filled her senses.

"Not here," Bennickle calmly replied, and Menthoshine sneered in annoyance. "Far."

"I was thinking of a more exact answer, but if I remember correctly, you never were much for producing anything precise." She rolled her eyes around the room.

"He matters little." Bennickle was unfazed by her comment. "I speak with you—"

"Yes, we have doted on that fact."

"—for Cas-tros-phy."

"What? Why?" she grimaced at the mention of him. "What do you want with him? He's completely worthless, inept, and despicable. I have no idea why you—" Menthoshine heard his soft, broken chuckle and sucked in an angry breath. "Come out from the shadows, you worm!" she called furiously. "Bennickle wants a word with you."

"He sees," Bennickle said, and Menthoshine turned her widened eyes back at him.

"How do you know what he sees? Have you been *listening* to me?" She wrapped a pale hand around the black wood of her staff. "How long have you been spying?" Her voice rose with each question, and suddenly a distant boom echoed above. Menthoshine stepped back from her staff and watched Bennickle slowly lift his eyes upwards and then back to her.

"He sees much. It is his gift." Despite Menthoshine's rage, Bennickle still spoke as if they were sharing a boring conversation.

"Gift?" she spat.

"Ssstrange thingsss," Castrosphy's voice floated from beyond the light of her staff, and Menthoshine squinted around for him.

"Use him," Bennickle quietly directed, and she turned her attention to him.

"What do you mean by that?" she cried in agitation. "Speak plainly, you troll!"

"He knows." The two words escaped Bennickle's rigid jaw, and then his face began to fade as grey mist swirled around it.

"No!" she yelled, "Ben! Bennickle! Do not leave me to sew your threads together! COME BACK!" She let out a furious scream and then closed her eyes and breathed deeply. "Castrosphy. Do you have the slightest idea of what that ogre was spouting?"

"Ssstrange thingsss," he hissed.

"OH! CEASE YOUR INFERNAL SPOUTINGS AND GO! Just go wherever these strange things are, find out about them, and come back *immediately*! Do you hear me? Immediately! And do not show yourself!" She waited for his hiss, but not one sound came. Menthoshine opened her eyes and knew that he had already disappeared. "Infernal wretch," she growled, snatched her staff, and stalked back to her throne.

THANKS

All the way back to the house, Kindle regretted her sassiness toward Azildor. As she walked, she mentally rehearsed a few really endearing apologies until she settled on one that seemed sufficient. When she reached the house, Kindle stopped near the entryway and peered out into the night for Azildor. In her plan, the apology would happen here so she wouldn't have to suffer a guilty conscience through dinner, but the farmer was not right behind her as she had supposed. Kindle crossed her arms and stared all around as she waited. The cloaked figure was still haunting her mind, though, and as the seconds ticked into minutes, she wanted more and more to dive inside. Finally, a distant noise unnerved her, and she jogged into the safety of the warm, well-lit house. No one swung their head her way; Ella, Andrew, and nearly all of the Chokmahs were buzzing about the kitchen, preparing for dinner. Kindle watched them from the wall and noted that Azildor, Masso, and Tad were absent. Taking a glance at the living room, she saw the crown of Tad's head poking over one of the chairs. Not ready to mingle with the energetic, happy crowd, Kindle also slipped over to the cover of the cozy seating.

When she settled down in the chair by Tad's, he lifted one heavy eyelid to check who was near him then let it drop back down. Kindle stared at him, wondering if he was trying to sleep and if she should leave him alone. For a few minutes she tried to remain quiet, but her compulsion to speak was too strong.

"Thanks," she said, still on a quest to be gracious to someone. Tad grunted and knitted his brow.

"Thanks," Kindle repeated a little louder, and this time Tad opened his eyes.

"What?"

"I said thanks."

"For *what*?"

"Oh, um, you know, the whole thing back there," she mumbled, totally unprepared to explain her gratitude.

He shrugged and sniffed, "Whatever."

Kindle turned wide eyes to him, unsure if she should feel offended or not. "I said thank you. You know, you could say, 'You're welcome,'" she told him, trying not to sound sassy. He didn't respond, though, and Kindle rolled her eyes. "I'm trying to be nice. Don't you care?"

"No," he flatly grumbled, and Kindle lost her composure.

"Ugh! Seriously? I try to be nice to you, and you just, like, don't care at all? Don't you care about anything or anybody besides yourself?" she griped, frustrated that he not only refused to return any congenial word but also seemed to be completely unmoved by their shared scare and battle.

"Why should I care about anybody?" Tad emotionlessly retorted, and Kindle almost extricated herself from his presence, but his next grumbled words stopped her.

"Nobody cares about me."

Kindle blinked at him. She wanted to just brush his comment aside, but his tone was serious, and it had jabbed her deeply and painfully.

"Of course people care about you," she argued, attempting to sound lighthearted and breezy, "like your mom and your dad—"

"I don't have parents," he curtly interjected.

"What do you mean?" Kindle slowly asked, still hoping to avoid deep waters. "Are-are they...?"

"I don't know. I never met 'em."

Kindle chewed her lip, trying to figure out how to bring the conversation to somewhere cheery. "But, like, who do you live with? Don't they care abou—?"

"No." Tad interrupted her with such finality that Kindle immediately decided not to push the subject any further. Tad, though, unexpectedly continued, "My grandma and my sister hate me. They don't care. They wouldn't care if I died—my grandma only keeps me around 'cause she gets support money." He paused, and Kindle felt compelled to say something but had no idea what.

"Really?" she finally asked.

Tad nodded and sniffed, "Yeah. She says it all the time. And that I'm a useless ... a useless failure."

"You're not," Kindle quickly objected.

"Yeah I am."

"Ugh. *No*, you're not," she repeated more forcefully, and Tad suspiciously eyed her.

"How would you know?"

"Well, getting rid of that creepy thing was totally not useless," she argued, and Tad shrugged as if her point proved nothing but didn't utter his usual 'Whatever.' Kindle counted it as a win and continued, "And like, I don't know if you noticed, but you were better than everybody else at the sword fighting stuff today. *That's* not useless or a failure." Sure she had proven him wrong, she settled back into her chair and sighed, "*I* don't think you're useless."

Tad huffed, but instead of sounding scornful, it was almost good-humored. "Great. I've got Miss Priss's vote."

Kindle started to snap something rude back, but when she saw one corner of his mouth was lifted in a slight grin, she changed her mind and said, "Yeah, you do."

He turned his partial smile to her, but before either of them could say anything more, Naam called them to dinner. Kindle sprang up from the chair and saw that Azildor and Masso were seated with everyone else around the table. She hurried over to the same spot as the night before and received a wink from Ella. Thankfully, at that moment the Chokmahs began their dinner routine of thanks, and Kindle didn't have to feel her cheeks turn red under Ella's watchful eye.

From that moment on, the night ran its course smoothly and fairly uneventfully. They all dug into their dinner while Yirah and Yirun tried to convince everyone they had found human bones in the barn. Naam eventually ended their tale with the threat of extra chores, and the conversation turned to the true stories of the day. Kindle stayed quiet all through the excited chatter, and when it came time to clean, she slipped away to the basement by herself. For a long while she just sat on her low mattress, staring at the stone wall while all of her thoughts circulated in her head. The quiet, dim room was the ideal place to mull over everything, but Kindle found herself unable to concentrate on any one thought and finally flumped down on her mattress to try to sleep.

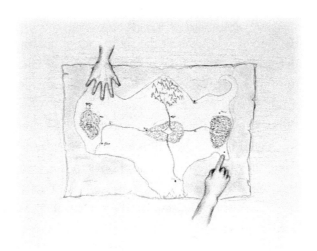

The Chore of Contending

The next morning, Naam woke them up early again for breakfast. When Ella, Andrew, Tad, and Kindle all gathered at the table to eat their mush, Azildor informed them that they would spend the morning searching through the library artifacts for any information relevant to their quest and then after lunch would meet him outside to train just as they had the day before. Ella was the only one to reply, and after she gave Azildor her eager smile and nod, he excused himself from the table and headed out into the dark morning.

"I'm not sitting around reading all day," grumbled Tad. "I don't care what he says."

"Well, the faster we discover our destination, the faster we set out," Ella persuasively replied. "And we'll only do that by perusing those documents."

Tad made an unconvinced noise and shoved another spoonful of mush into his mouth. Kindle, although she didn't want to admit it aloud, agreed with Tad; sifting through endless stacks of words sounded horribly boring.

"But what about that map you found?" she asked, hoping to excuse herself from the task. "Doesn't that have where the evil dude is? I mean, it had Bellalux on it."

"No," Andrew answered. "It only had names of cities and towns—nothing about them."

Ella smiled. "No, I don't believe someone who doesn't want to be found would pin his home on a map."

"Yeah," Kindle sighed, defeated.

"Wha map?" Tad questioned through his mouthful.

"The one Andrew found yesterday," Ella replied, giving him a funny look.

"He wasn't here," Andrew noted to her, and Ella nodded as she stood.

"That's right—you weren't here, you were…." She lingered by the table and crossed her arms then carefully interrogated, "Where *were* you?"

Tad glared at her. "None of your business."

"You're right—it's not," Ella replied, unconcerned, and then strode across the house to retrieve the map. She spread it out before Tad and began pointing out their location. He only gave her time to outline Danica Woods and Bellalux before he interrupted.

"Dude's got to be there," he declared, tapping his spoon on the paper. Kindle and Andrew scooted closer to see that Tad had indicated a small, unlabeled dark spot between the middle and far right forests.

Ella spun the map for a better view, squinted at the spot, and then asked, "There?"

"Yup," Tad confidently replied and caused all three of them to stare at it.

"How do you know?" Ella questioned and Tad barked a laugh.

"I don't. But you believed me! Ha!"

Ella shook her head but smiled. "Yes, I did. But it was more of a hope really." She and Kindle sank back down onto their stones to finish their mush, but Andrew continued to stare at the mark.

"What *is* it, though?" he asked, turning to Ella.

She gulped her last bit of mush then shrugged. "I don't really know what that bit is there, but now it's just this old deserted mine. See—" she pulled it over to her and traced a big circle between the two forests, "—this whole lot of land, men say, is just one big pit. The traders coming up from Turner always grumble about it and not being able to directly travel to Garrick. They say it's a huge, deep, rocky nuisance and nothing else."

"Not a mine?" Andrew quickly questioned.

"No, not now. It only used to be—at least that's what everyone says."

"But it wasn't when this was made."

"Andrew." Ella gave him a playfully serious look. "It is nothing. *Really*. Don't be making it out to be anything more than that."

He ceased his questions but kept running his eyes back and forth over the map. Soon Naam came by to usher them across the room so they could dive into their research while Adin and Binah used the table to practice writing. With Ella right behind him, Andrew immediately rolled up the map and headed for the piles at the opposite end of the house. Kindle, though, hung back when she saw Naam eye Tad.

"Did you eat enough breakfast, Tad?" she gently inquired as she picked up his empty bowl. He nodded then crossed his arms on the table.

"Don't you want to sit in one of the more comfortable chairs to study?" she proposed, and Kindle couldn't help but answer Naam's unspoken question.

"He's not going to. He said he wasn't going to read."

"But your friends need your help," Naam urged with an encouraging smile. "Don't you want to help them?"

"No. I hate reading," he defiantly grumbled, and Naam's mouth twisted in thought.

"Well, you can't just sit here...why don't you go see what Azildor and Masso are up to today," Naam directed. "I know they have work for a capable young man like you. They'll still be around the barn I'm sure."

Tad shifted as if tempted but remained on his stone. Naam gave him an expectant face and said in a very momlike tone, "It's either work out there or study in here."

Tad frowned at her but pushed himself up from the table and lazily slouched outside. Naam raised an eyebrow at Kindle. "Would you like to work with them as well?"

"Uh—no." Kindle pointed at Ella and Andrew. "I was just going over there." Sure that whatever kind of hard, dirty work lay outside was much lower on her fun list than reading, Kindle quickly trotted across the house.

Andrew was already deeply invested in what he was reading, but Ella perked up at Kindle's approach and met her with a stack of papers.

"It's much more comfortable here," she said as she nodded for Kindle to sit on the fur rug. They settled down beside one another, and Kindle plucked the top paper off the stack to examine it. After only a few seconds, though, Ella distracted her.

"That was the least angry I've ever seen Tad."

"Mm-hm." Kindle suddenly realized why Ella had chosen this spot.

"Now, you just tell me if it really is none of my business, but what did you two do all yesterday evening?"

Kindle pretended to read the paper in her hands as she considered what to say. She didn't want to upset Tad by revealing the reason for his disappearance, but she was eager to tell Ella her exciting story.

"I don't know what Tad was doing," Kindle finally decided to half-truthfully admit, "but when I found him on that tower—you know that tall thing by the baydle pen—we saw this black thing on the ground." Seeing she had Ella's full attention, Kindle served her a full and detailed account of the episode. When she finished by hesitantly telling her how the creature simply disappeared, Ella furrowed her brow and let her eyes fall to her lap.

"Well, I mean, it was dark, so we just couldn't see it anymore, I guess," she lied in a clarifying tone, still abashed from Azildor's disbelief, but Ella shook her head.

"No, Kindle, what if it *did* disappear? Wouldn't that be odd?"

"Um ... yeah. It was weird."

"Kindle, I think you and Tad may have actually seen a black ghost," Ella excitedly whispered, and Kindle found it difficult to keep her eyes from rolling.

"No, Ella ... um, I don't think so. It was like, solid. And it breathed. I heard it breathing."

"Yes, why wouldn't you?" Ella smiled, undeterred. "Kindle, do you have black ghosts in your ... earth, wasn't it?"

"Yeah, earth. We have ghosts, Ella, but they're not really real. They're just for Halloween, you know."

"Hallo-ween? Is that a forest?"

"Um, no...."

"Oh, well, because in Anelthalien the only place any man has claimed to see a black ghost is in Ignancia Forest. That's right south of Garrick is how I know. And every man who thinks he's met one comes all pale and chattering to the Lighthouse to tell about it while having a few rounds to settle himself."

"So, like, do you not believe they're telling the truth?"

"Well, ordinarily I don't immediately dismiss any tale I hear from a sober man, but...the honesty of it is that Ignancia is a black wood—it's where the Great War was fought, and after the witches burned the forest, all of the trees have grown back dark as night ever since—and it's not easy to go on believing a man who says he's seen a black creature at night in a black wood. It's too easy for your eyes to slip."

"Oh...yeah, I guess," Kindle mumbled, now more unsure if Ella believed her.

"But hearing you tell about it—Kindle, it must be what you saw. The men have said their black ghosts float and make that squeaky breath as yours did."

"So...you believe me?"

"Yes, of course, Kindle. But do you see now why I said it was odd?"

"Um...." Kindle wasn't sure of the right answer and so shook her head.

"Oh, Kindle, they don't live around here. Black ghosts live in Ignancia Forest, which is all the way on the other side of Anelthalien."

"But I thought you didn't even think they were real. How do you know they only live there? Maybe they live all over the place."

"No, no, Kindle. Let me say it like this: each time—and it has been a rare few—a man has chanced Ignancia, he's come back out with an eerie tale much like yours."

Kindle felt her stomach wriggle in discomfort. "Well, maybe, I dunno, it was just visiting or something." As the comment fell out of her mouth, it sounded silly to her, and she sighed, "I just know I really did see it, whatever it was."

"It was a black ghost," Ella stated with confidence, then as she picked the top paper off the stack to read, she huffed as if the fact perplexed her.

The rest of the morning dripped by slowly. By lunchtime all that Kindle, Ella, and Andrew had slugged through were endless lists of what seemed to be names of soldiers, supply counts, and traded goods and their prices. None of them spoke to one another as they ate their food. Kindle knew her mind felt numb from all of the seemingly pointless research and guessed that her companions' did as well. Even Ella's response to Adin and Binah's eager questions about what they had discovered was sapped of enthusiasm. Finally Naam came to the table to clear their bowls and placed a large basket in Ella's hands. She instructed them to meet Azildor, Masso, and Tad at the baydle pen and to insist that they eat some lunch before continuing with their afternoon. Only after Ella assured the mother that she would carry out the order did Naam allow them to travel out into the warm, sunny afternoon. The walk to the baydle pen swept away much of Kindle's mental grog, and by the time they found Masso and Tad standing by the stone wall of the animal pen, she felt ready to try her stick fighting skills. She stared around for Azildor and saw he was herding the baydles into the corner of the pen. Once the baying creatures were safely separated in their roped triangle, Azildor made his way over to them.

"Naam sent lunch," Ella greeted him as she held out the basket. "She said to tell you that you must eat something."

Azildor fished out a hunk of bread and held it for her to see. "Alright?"

Ella nodded, and then Azildor directed, "Masso, give part of the load to Tad and take the rest for yourself to the barn. Eat and then tend to the fields just as we do each day."

Masso handed some of the provisions to Tad then faced his father. "Dad, can't I stay and watch?"

"No, Son. You have work to do. Do not neglect your work."

Masso frowned but dropped his face and trudged away on his own. Once he had disappeared into the barn, Azildor presented a new, thicker stick and instructed them to take the same places as they had the day before. When Kindle, Tad, and Andrew had seated themselves on the short wall, Ella strode to the middle of the enclosure to face Azildor. This time Kindle watched with rapt attention so none of his instruction would escape her notice. Just as their first practice, Azildor ran Ella through the proper stance then the blocks, but once she had executed each one at least halfway decently, he moved to attacking her without calling out his intention. Kindle squinted at the pair, hoping to detect some sort of pattern so that when her turn came, she could be ready. After a while, though, she abandoned the effort and decided she would simply have to stay alert. Finally Azildor nodded Ella's way and pointed his shepherd's rod to the fence. When Ella bounded over to them, Kindle eagerly sprang up to receive the stick and galloped to take her turn. Azildor smiled as she assumed the proper stance.

"You are much more alert today."

"Focus, distance, and stance," she replied, determined to earn a compliment today. Instead of responding, Azildor chuckled and raised his staff. Kindle bit her lip in concentration, ready to react to his block command, but he swung without uttering a word. Instinctively, she dodged out of harm's way and almost immediately cried, "Ugh, no! I'm sorry, I didn't mean to. Let me try again."

"Remember, Kindle," Azildor calmly replied, "your worst enemy will never meet you as you suspect. Be on guard at all times for all attacks."

"Okay." She quickly nodded and replaced her feet in their solid stance. Azildor copied her movement except he left his sword at his side. Kindle watched it for a few moments, waiting to see where it would fly. Wondering what he could be planning, she let her eyes flick to his face, and as soon she did, his weapon jumped into action. Simultaneously stifling her urge to flee and premeditating where the rod was aiming, Kindle sliced her stick to shield her leg. Azildor's rod met it and softly pushed her stick into her calf, but Kindle still victoriously grinned.

"Yeah!" she celebrated but then hurriedly snapped back into her defensive stance.

"Again, with more strength in the parry," instructed Azildor.

Kindle almost let his comment bash back her glee but mashed it into motivation and sighed, "Okay."

For the rest of her practice, Azildor steadily sent blow after blow toward her, and she just as resolutely attempted to block each one. Even though she didn't succeed in smashing back each attack, her progress of fighting instead of dodging felt like a victory to her, and when Azildor at last indicated that her turn had finished, she proudly carried the stick to her audience.

At first both of the boys refused to even acknowledge the stick. Tad glared off in the opposite direction, and Andrew kept his stare locked on his feet. Ella, who was sitting between them and switching a puzzled gaze at one then the other, urged, "Both of you have to take a turn. Azildor won't allow you to skip this practice."

Kindle rolled her eyes so none of them would see. "Hey," she said, pushing the stick in front of Tad's angry stare. He turned his disgruntled face to her but kept his arms folded. Kindle shoved it closer to him. "C'mon, you know you're really good."

He finally begrudgingly snatched it from her and stalked away from the fence.

"Is he really?" Ella inquired while carefully watching him meet Azildor and raise the stick. Kindle bobbed her head once and then they both set their focus on the pair as a loud smack resounded. Slightly less furiously but just as skillfully and speedily, the two fell into a smooth, exciting battle.

"He *is*," whispered Ella in disbelief. "He really is quite incredible. And he defended like this last night as well?"

"Um…." Kindle shifted, feeling the awkwardness of the previous night, then shrugged. "Yeah, mostly."

"Absolutely incredible," Ella mused and Kindle sighed in relief. She was glad Ella was too distracted by the fast-paced sparring match to notice her reluctance to answer. Kindle thoroughly enjoyed Ella's cheerful personality but was beginning to dislike her inclination to dig into every subject Kindle didn't want to talk about and ability to sense her unspoken emotions. Not wanting to give Ella an opportunity to latch on to her present thoughts or feelings, Kindle returned her full attention to Tad and Azildor. For a long while, they fought without words or a break. Seamlessly Azildor attacked and Tad blocked, their faces so serious that Kindle began to wonder if either of them would eventually step down. Just when she was sure that they would battle until the death of one of their sticks, Azildor, panting, motioned for Tad to stop. Kindle held her breath, worried that Tad would repeat his angry assault, but to her relief, he slouched into a panting hunch as well. Almost too softly to hear, she caught Azildor's voice say, "You did well, my son."

"Don't talk to me," Tad grumbled just as quietly and carried the stick over to Andrew. Clearly not caring if Andrew would take the stick, Tad shoved it into his chest before taking a seat on the ground a short way from the girls. Andrew clumsily gathered the weapon in his hands and, with a sick expression on his face, peeled himself off the wall and trudged over to Azildor. Ella and Kindle exchanged nervous glances before turning their eyes to Andrew. After witnessing Tad's skill, Andrew's terrible lack of ability seemed even more painful than it had the previous evening. Andrew did maintain his stance, but when he had failed to parry Azildor's shoulder attack for the fifth time, he threw the stick down and stomped off to the house. Ella moved to accompany him, but Azildor called to her, "Let him go alone. You have more to learn today."

Ella, Kindle, and Tad traded questioning looks—they each had already finished their turn and had not expected more. Azildor retrieved the stick and brought it over to Ella.

"Andrew's skill is not in combat," the farmer sighed. "It is in the matters of the mind. He has no need to continue wasting his efforts here. Tell him this."

Ella nodded and volunteered to be the messenger then asked, "Does that mean we each do have skill?"

"Yes. I see potential in each of you to become adept with the sword. So today you will venture beyond defense."

"You're actually gunna let us hit something?" Tad asked, his eyes brightening.

Azildor gave him a long, hard stare but finally replied, "Yes. You will learn to attack today, but it is an acquired discipline I expect you to display, not a fit of wild rage."

Tad's smile fell into a snarl, but he silently nodded.

"You are first, Ella." Azildor bent his head to her and they walked to the middle of the pen to begin.

That afternoon and each one after, Tad, Kindle, and Ella stayed with Azildor until the sky grew dark and Adin appeared to call them for dinner. In fact, the entire day's routine remained constant at the Chokmah farm; each morning Tad branched off with the children to work while Kindle, Ella, and Andrew continued their search through the endless stacks of papers. The mornings reading with Ella and Andrew weren't nearly as boring as Kindle predicted they would prove. She and Ella would sit in the midst of the big stone chairs and rifle through a few papers while they chatted about anything that swam through their minds. Kindle decided that she really did enjoy all of Ella even though she was so different from every other person she had ever befriended. Nothing about her seemed hidden or fake; as far as Kindle could tell, Ella was the most open and honest person she had ever met. Even her tendency to sense Kindle's unsaid secrets transformed into a nonverbal, giggling understanding between them. Her good company often caused Kindle to forget Andrew even existed behind them. He never joined in their conversations but silently sat by himself all morning. Kindle counted him as fairly boring but still tried to give him a smile and wave when she and Ella left him each afternoon to meet Azildor and Tad at the baydle pen for practice.

The second part of the day was always much more interesting. Even though they practiced sword fighting each afternoon, Azildor seemed to think up a new challenge each time they met him outside. The first few days she, Ella, and Tad took turns blocking and attacking the farmer, but soon Azildor began matching them up in stick battles against one another. She didn't mind facing Ella but hated facing Tad. He always won and afterward she felt like she had sprinted through a cornfield all day—every inch of her winded and whipped. Fighting him was even more difficult than when Azildor pitted all three of them against one another in a match that lasted until sunset. That sort of fight still wore all of them down, though, and by the time the sun set, they were always reduced to stick-flailing zombies. Despite the type of training Azildor arranged for them, the practice increased in difficulty daily and always felt grueling to Kindle. She found herself sore and entirely wiped of energy at the end of each practice, but under all of her complaints, Kindle really did enjoy the sword practice. She never would have believed that she could fight with a sword, but each day she could tell that her skill and strength increased. Not long after Azildor matched them against one another, she began winning against Ella and sometimes—at least in her mind—she came close to taking down Tad. Kindle especially noticed her strength and ability growing when Azildor finally allowed them to practice with actual swords and hers seemed lighter and more like an extension of her arm each time they met at the baydle pen.

Kindle could not only sense that she was changing and growing, but also saw Ella and Tad transforming. Ella quickly proved the best with aiming and could always satisfy Azildor's specific attack and block commands with more precision than Kindle or Tad. Even though she was deadly accurate, she hardly ever won her matches against the others, and one day Azildor presented her with a slim bow and a quiver of arrows, telling her that her aim would be much better coupled with them. After that Ella would spend only part of the early afternoon sharpening her sword skills but would then disappear to practice with her bow. Azildor did allow Kindle and Tad to test their archery abilities for a few days, but Tad didn't have the patience or desire to stand far from his target, and Kindle gave up after her few efforts manifested as miserable failures. Even though she resolved to stay far from the bow and arrows, Kindle enjoyed watching how adept Ella became with them, and a few times when they actually had time free of work or practice, they tested Ella's skills with every sort of target they could find.

The most amazing transformation, though, was Tad. He was easily the best swordsman—all of the blocking, slashing, and dodging seemed so natural and effortless for him. Kindle expected that much after the first practice, but the slow, subtle morph of his attitude she would not have predicted. His awful, perpetual sneer continued to darken his face, but Kindle noticed that when he talked to her, he didn't sound so hateful, even when he ridiculed her, and that after a few days his backtalk to Azildor ceased altogether. His disrespect and constant rage gradually dwindled, and one night Kindle realized that he had not lost his temper once during practice. It was that night that she went to sleep trying to calculate just how long they had been at the Chokmahs' home.

She had known that the days were passing but hadn't bothered to keep track of them. Until that moment when she had been hit with the enormity of their changes, she had not thought they had spent that many days in Anelthalien. Each one had passed by so similarly as the one before that she couldn't calculate their number. Eventually she gave up figuring out how long they had been in the strange land and let her thoughts roam to her home and life that felt so distant now. Although she still missed her family and went to bed every night hoping she would wake up in her own bed, Kindle had begun to feel at ease in the Chokmah home. They seemed to genuinely like her, and Naam treated her, Ella, Andrew, and Tad so much like her own children that Kindle and Ella referred to her as 'Mom' and even joked one night about tacking the family's name onto their own.

Despite how wonderful the family and Ella, Andrew, and occasionally Tad's company proved, most of the time it could not completely overcome how awful Kindle usually felt. In addition to missing her family and always holding the thought that she might never see them again, every night Kindle lay down on her mattress with her head aching and body sore from the morning reading and afternoon beating. One evening after she had endured a long, tiring face-off against Tad, Kindle lay sprawled over the arms of a chair, trying to forget her pain.

"What are you doing?" Binah's voice sounded nearby, and Kindle lifted her heavy eyelids.

"Ugh," she groaned, "dying."

"Dying!" the little girl squeaked in concern, and Tad's laughter came from beyond Kindle's view.

"You're a jerk, you know that?" Kindle listlessly mumbled.

"At least I'm not a loser," he snickered as he dropped down in another chair.

"Are you okay?" Binah asked, obviously confused.

"She's fine, Binah," Ella comforted as she and Andrew appeared. "Just a little sore. Why don't you go help your mom with dinner?"

Binah stared around at each of them before she wandered over to the stone table. Once she had meandered out of earshot, Kindle grumbled, "I'm not just a little sore, Ella. I'm dying—I really am this time."

"Kin, you say that every night," Ella sighed but gave her a smile. "Now turn yourself up right, Andrew's found something."

"Hm?" Kindle squirmed around to see that Andrew held the map of Anelthalien in his hand.

"What? You finally figured out how much dirt cost?" Tad snorted. Although his attitude had grown more respectful to most of the people around him, Tad still enjoyed bullying Andrew. He had counted Andrew and his job as worthless and often derided him about doing nothing except reading how much people in the past had paid for junk. Andrew gave him the same annoyed frown he did every evening but replied, "No, but it's because of all those trade records I think I know where we need to go."

"Huh?" Kindle suddenly felt awake. "You mean, like, leave here go?"

"Yeah." He grinned slightly.

"He's hatched out where the evil throne is," Ella excitedly blurted. "Go on and show them just as you did me."

"I don't *know* for sure, but it's the only place that makes sense," Andrew humbly corrected her as he spread out the map that by now they had viewed dozens of times.

"Where's it at, huh? Where I told you guys it was?" Tad asked, trying to appear aloof.

"Letum," Andrew announced, pointing to a dot below Ignancia Forest.

"Letum?" Kindle thoughtfully repeated. "How do you know? I don't remember you ever saying anything about that place, Ella."

"No, I haven't—that's the brilliant bit of it. *Tell them,* Andrew."

"I've read over all the purchases and sales in the library, and Letum is the only place on this map that never did business with Bellalux."

"So? What's that matter?" Tad argued. "It's all the way over on the other side. That's why they didn't buy anything from over here, Einstein."

Ella shook her head and replied, "It matters because every other city or town *did* do business with Bellalux, and that must mean no one lives in Letum. Right? Or...oh, just explain it in full."

Andrew took her cue and placed his hand by the tiny word Bellalux. "When this map was made, this was the biggest city, and the population records show it was rapidly growing. They also showed that people were moving here from everywhere else…," he circled his hand over the map before stopping over Letum, "except from here. When I saw that, I figured Letum had to be sustaining its economy from its own resources or commerce, but I never found any records of Bellalux trading with it, and since Bellalux was the biggest city, it had goods no other city had and more than any other city, so it would be the ideal place to buy from. Like I said, though, Letum never did business with Bellalux, so that meant it had to rely on its own resources, but when I asked Ella about the temperature and terrain of Anelthalien, she said the further south, the colder the weather across the land year round."

"Yes," Ella jumped in, "and you see this place here, Turner? That town is frosted to the core. Nothing, not even trees grow that far south. All of the men who travel from there only ever have pelts and fish and medicines to trade. They barter for everything, everything else—they always wipe the fruit market dry."

"Yeah," Andrew reentered the explanation at the first opportunity. "So Turner needs to outsource to get most of its goods, and since Letum is nearly the same latitude, it would have the same climate and also have to outsource … but it didn't."

"And it still doesn't. Never has a man from Letum come up in the Lighthouse. I've never even caught word of the place, and everyone is always chatting about all where they've been."

"So … is nobody there?" questioned Kindle, still trying to process Andrew's logic. She hardly ever heard him say anything, and so her tired mind was reeling not only over the complex, lengthy reasoning he had unraveled but also the fact that he had spoken so much. "Like, I don't get it," she finally concluded.

Andrew grinned. "It *seems* like no one is there."

"So what? Now you're saying it's some deserted town? This is stupid—I'm done. I'm gunna go eat," Tad grumbled, but Ella waved a hand at him.

"Oh, Tad, stop," she chided. "You'll want to hear this."

Tad glared at her but kept his seat. "Hear what?" he demanded.

"It seems deserted." Andrew now didn't try to contain his smile. "But how does an empty, deserted place make it on a map drawn in a city on the other side of Anelthalien?" He paused to let his words sink in their minds then quietly continued, "Whoever made this map knew about Letum and thought it was important enough to be on here. Someone or something is there."

In that second, Kindle's brain caught up to Andrew's logic. "So you mean if it was really deserted, it wouldn't be on the map, but since it *is* on the map, it isn't deserted?"

"Yes! Just that!" Ella happily cried. "And whoever is there has completely cut ties with every other bit of Anelthalien, as if they're trying to be forgotten … as if they don't want anyone to know they're still there."

"That *does* sound like what Azildor said about the evil throne, doesn't it?" Kindle mused in realization. "You know, about that Ignala guy disappearing."

"Ignalus," corrected Andrew. "It does."

They all exchanged curious glances and Kindle saw that even Tad's disbelief was worn down.

"So, what, like, we just go there and see?" Kindle nervously asked, "Or what? What should we do?"

"Well, I think we should tell Azildor after dinner tonight and see what he says. I'm sure he'll know what we should do," Ella replied as she stood and patted Kindle's chair. "Until then, don't stew over it, alright?"

"I'm not gunna stew over it," Kindle grumbled as she also picked herself up.

Ella gave her a knowing look, and once Tad and Andrew had started for the table, she leaned to her and kindly whispered, "If I've learned anything of you, Kin, it's you fret too much, so I'll say it once more: don't stew."

"I won't," Kindle insisted, but even she didn't believe her words.

All through the meal, Kindle's mind boiled over with thoughts. Days ago, when they had first stepped onto the Chokmah farm, Kindle would have been ecstatic to know that she was closer to leaving Anelthalien and perhaps heading home, but now the idea of leaving disturbed her peace. It did not seem fair that she was already away from her real family, and now that the house she sat in was like home and the people cheerfully eating around her were like family, she had to separate herself from them as well.

Kindle began to wonder if she was destined to just be alone her entire life but shook off the thought by reminding herself that they might not even have to leave. After considering that Azildor could say Andrew was wrong or tell them that they couldn't leave because they were not ready, Kindle's appetite awakened, and she was able to push aside her fears while she ate.

Once Yirah and Yirun had cleared all of the dishes and the other children had dispersed around the house, Kindle saw Ella nudge Andrew and he plucked the map up from the floor. All at once Kindle's stomach dropped and her hopes fluttered away; Ella was really going to tell Azildor.

"Azildor?" Ella meekly called down the table, and the farmer raised his eyes. "Could we show you something, or I suppose, tell you? Andrew has found something in all those stacks."

He peered at the four of them in his all-knowing way then said to Andrew, "What is it, son?"

Andrew bowed his head but carried the map down to Azildor and fully but quickly explained his discovery. As Andrew spoke, Kindle tried to read Azildor's expression, but his solemn face remained still.

"Isn't it brilliant?" cried Ella once Andrew had finished. Azildor, though, did not respond but for a long while sat with his eyes fixed on the map and a thumb on his chin.

Finally he turned his stare to Andrew and inquired, "This Letum—did you see its name on any paper other than this map?"

Andrew thought for a moment then shook his head. Azildor sighed and sank back into silence. His eyes roved back and forth across the drawing, and Kindle wished she could know what he was thinking. Not knowing his thoughts bothered her, and the longer he remained quiet, the more anxious she felt.

"Do you think it's *it*? I mean, like, is Letum where we have to go?" Kindle blurted.

Instead of answering her, Azildor asked, "Andrew, do you believe that Letum is home to the evil throne?"

Andrew's eyes darted around as if he was searching for a response, and he shrugged. "I-I thought it was."

"Do you believe it is or not?" pushed Azildor.

"I believe it is," Ella confidently answered as Andrew stiffly shoved his hands in his pockets, "And I know Andrew does as well or he wouldn't have spoken about it to any of us."

Azildor peered between Ella and Andrew as if reading their souls. Finally he gave a satisfied nod to Ella's declaration and commented, "I believe you have found a curious detail, son, but I do not know if Letum is the evil ruler's home."

"So are you not gunna let us go?" Kindle interrupted, trying not to sound hopeful.

"I will not stop you," Azildor thoughtfully mused then turned his hard brown eyes on them. "I know less of this evil throne than you now, Andrew, and if you and your companions trust that Letum is now your destination, then you must make your way to that city. I only ask that you remain here for three more days; I have a few more lessons to pass on to each of you."

As she processed his words, Kindle's head spun and the oxygen in her lungs tied into a knot in her throat. She swallowed the lump so she could try her fearful argument. "But we're not ready. I mean, like, we can sword fight and stuff, but ... but we're just not ready to go out on our own."

Azildor inspected her face, which Kindle knew showed her anxiety, before he carefully responded, "No man is ever ready for the journey he begins until he is at its end. You are not ready because you have not begun. If you never begin, Kindle, you will never reach the end of your quest and never reach your full potential or your home."

"But, but like...," she stammered, trying to find a hole in his solid comment, "what if we get lost or ... or what about food?"

"No. Do not worry," Azildor firmly reassured her. "Tonight, sleep. Tomorrow and the next two days you each will have your answers." With that, he rose from the table and left the four of them. Kindle felt absolutely embarrassed and defeated and so was glad when Ella suggested they all turn in for the night. She was the first to escape down into the dim basement but still lay awake after everyone else's breath had slowed to rhythmic, nasal sounds. Too perturbed to sleep, Kindle glared at the stone wall. Azildor had annoyed her by not supporting her wish to stay, but the majority of her anger lay with herself. It frustrated her that she had not constructed an even remotely convincing argument that would have let her remain in her new pseudo-home, that in only three days everything she had learned to enjoy would be ripped from her again, and that she had lost her composure in front of everyone. Again. She tried to think of a plan to remedy any of her failures, but her tired mind would not allow her to make headway in any direction except toward sleep.

NASAH AND NATZAL

The next morning, Kindle awoke before Naam had descended the stairs to rouse everyone. As she blinked at the sleeping lumps around her, an odd feeling shook her sleepy mind. Then, all at once, Kindle remembered the night before and decided to slip quietly upstairs so she would not have to face all of the people she would have to leave soon.

When she reached the top of the stairs, Kindle wondered how early it really was. The house was unlike she had ever seen it; the only light softly radiated from the large fireplace at the opposite end of the house and left the rest of the space covered in the night's dark blanket. For a moment, she considered returning to her cozy mattress, but a voice stopped her.

"Kindle?"

Following the sound, she discovered Naam's silhouette sitting in a nearby chair.

"Kindle, dear, what are you doing up so early?" Her voice was quiet, but Kindle could still detect surprise in it.

"Um, I don't know. I, uh, can go back—"

"Oh, no no, it's fine, don't worry. It's just that ... well, Azildor seemed to think you would get up early today, and here you are."

"Oh." Kindle nodded, remembering her theory about his mind-reading ability.

"He asked me to send you out to the barn—I don't know what he's got in his head—but you eat some breakfast before you go, alright?"

"Okay," Kindle conceded and followed Naam over to the kitchen. She didn't want to go see Azildor. Truthfully she wanted to avoid him and everyone else, but breakfast was enticing, and so she decided that she would follow Naam's command. Naam led her to the warm hearth, and Kindle noticed that Sophia was nestled in her arms, sound asleep. The mother shifted the baby to one arm and ladled Kindle some fresh mush into a bowl.

"Sit down, eat," Naam invitingly directed as she handed over the warm bowl and eased down herself. Once Kindle had settled on the stone hearth and taken a few bites, Naam softly said, "Azildor told me what Andrew showed him last night. He said you all would leave for a city in the east in a few days."

"Yeah...," Kindle sighed, "it's where they think the evil throne is."

"You don't sound very happy about that."

"No."

"Well ... why not? Isn't it exciting to know where you need to go?" She chuckled, "And to not have to spend all morning reading."

"I guess."

"Kindle, what's on your mind? Something is bothering you."

Kindle took longer than necessary to swallow her bite before she peered sideways at Naam. She hadn't intended to answer, but everything about the mother who was smiling down at her baby was so caring and inviting that she divulged, "I just ... I dunno. It's like I'm not ever gunna see my family again, and then all you guys start to feel like my family, and everything gets okay, but now I have to leave you guys too. It just doesn't feel fair, you know? Like I don't ever get to have a family now." Kindle stopped and stared into her mush. She hoped Naam would have a way to fix everything or at least say she could stay, but Naam didn't say a word. "You know what I mean? Like, I don't sound stupid or weird, do I?" Kindle asked in sudden embarrassment.

Naam turned her warm brown eyes to her. "No, Kindle. I can see why you're upset, and it is completely understandable. Everyone wants a family."

"So … so can I…," Kindle began to ask but forsook her request and simply turned pleading eyes to Naam.

"Can you stay?" Naam finished, and Kindle enthusiastically nodded until Naam shook her head and sighed, "No, Kindle, I'm sorry, but you cannot stay here. Listen, you *do* have a family somewhere waiting to see you again. And you will see them, don't worry over that. I know Azildor said it will be a long time until then, but you can't look at that time as a loss of family. You have to see it as a gaining of one."

"But you said I couldn't stay here."

"Yes, you're right. The family I'm talking about isn't this one; it is Ella, Andrew, and Tad."

"Oh," Kindle groaned, deflated again.

Naam gave her a sympathetic smile. "The four of you have a long road ahead, and you must be a family if you want to make it past our doorstep."

"Yeah, I know. I didn't mean to sound all whiney," Kindle apologized. "It's just, like, not the same, you know? I mean, a family's like a mom and dad and kids like you guys, not … us."

"Kindle," Naam whispered kindly but seriously, "family is not always who your blood links you to but *is* always who you choose to tie yourself to. Those necklaces you four wear have tied you all."

"Does that mean I don't get a choice? Like I have to let them be my family?"

"No Kindle, you do have a choice. The makers of Anelthalien have extended to you the gift of joining their family, and you may deny it, but if you do, know that Ella, Andrew, and Tad will be incomplete along with the entire story of Anelthalien. Your choice to leave us and to go on this journey that you have been chosen to take affects many more than you or I will ever know. You are part of a family and a plan larger than you can imagine, Kindle, but if you stay here and try to hold onto this family not meant for you, you will miss out on everything ahead of you."

Kindle pondered over her words then asked, "You really think so? I mean, that it'll be better to leave you guys and just go off by ourselves?"

"If you are afraid of being alone," Naam replied in an understanding voice, "don't be. You will not be alone."

"Yeah, I know, Ella—"

"No. Closer than your three friends, you will have a tie to the creator whose mark you wear."

"What?" Kindle looked down at her red gem. "You mean Hux? The Cifra said Hux was gone."

"Neither the Cifra nor anyone else has seen him since the early days of Anelthalien, but that does not mean he is gone. He is with you, Kindle. I can't explain how, but I'm sure your journey will show you." Naam suddenly stood and stared out a window. "Oh, the sky's brightening—we've talked too long," she sighed with a chuckle. "Go see Azildor—he's in the barn—and tell him I'm sorry, but it was time well spent."

Before Kindle could consider objecting, Naam helped her up, took her bowl, and walked her to the exit. The morning air chilled her bare arms and legs, but she hardly noticed. All that Naam had told her was still running through her mind. Kindle caught her necklace and squinted down at the little golden dragon, wondering if Hux was alive and was really with her as Naam claimed or if he was real at all. When she entered the lantern-lit barn, Azildor greeted her from one of the horse stalls and pulled her attention away from her necklace.

"Good morning, Kindle."

"Morning," she replied as she wrapped her arms around her torso and walked over to him. She watched him strap a feed bag to the horse's muzzle then begin to check its shoes. "Oh, Naam said sorry it took so long."

"She spoke to you about your fear of your journey, correct?"

Kindle blinked in surprise. "Huh? How'd you know? Did you tell her to?"

"No."

"Can you read minds?" Kindle gave him a suspicious glare, and he met it with a questioning gaze.

"Read minds?"

"Yeah, like hear what people are thinking? Is it an elf thing or something?"

"I cannot hear anyone's thoughts except my own."

"Then how'd you know I was gunna wake up and what Naam said?" she questioned, not convinced he was really telling the truth.

"Your mind was troubled. A troubled mind does not rest. I believed you would rise early, and so I asked Naam to watch for you. I asked her to send you here, but I knew her heart would open to you. I intended this."

"Oh. So like, you didn't tell her to talk to me at all, but you wanted her to?"

"Yes. Did her words put your mind at ease?"

Kindle chewed her lip as she thought. In a way, Naam had stirred up even more mysterious questions for her mind to roll over and over, but the more she considered how she felt, the more Kindle realized that the anxiety from the previous night had dissolved. "I-I guess so. She told me it'd be better to leave here than stay here. Like there's some big family out there or something."

"Good. Are you now willing to travel to Letum?"

Kindle hesitated. Naam had convinced her she would not just keep losing every person she cared about but had not assured her she was ready to survive in a strange land.

"I—yeah, I'm okay with it, but do you really think we'll be okay? I mean, I dunno what we're gunna do if we find a bear and we don't have any money for food and stuff like that."

"I see," Azildor calmly replied and ran his hand along the horse's back. "This is Nasah. She is a strong, dependable horse."

For a moment Kindle just stared at him. She wanted to ask if he had heard anything she had said but stopped herself; Azildor had chided her enough times about her sass for her to know it would not help. Instead she exhaled her agitation into a slow, "O—kay."

"I want you to take her. She can carry much and will serve you well."

"Oh!" Kindle brightened at his words. "Really? You're really gunna give us your horse?"

"Yes. Your journey is far more important than the pace of our work here. We will still have our one cart horse. She is enough."

"Well, thanks," Kindle breathed then frowned. She had only ridden a horse a few times in her life, and each time someone or something had always led it with a rope.

"Nasah must learn to trust you," Azildor continued to explain then noticed her face. "Does she not ease your fear?"

"Um … yeah, well, no. It's just … I don't know how to ride a horse. I mean, I *know* how, just, like, I haven't in a long time."

"Then spend today riding her. It will teach you her ways and grow her trust for you. Do you know how to saddle her?"

Once Kindle assured him that she had no idea how to secure a saddle on a horse, he led her through strapping it on and off several times and then began teaching her how to ride and care for Nasah. That morning Kindle learned everything about feeding and providing for her new friend and spent the afternoon riding her. When she began steering Nasah around on her own, Kindle couldn't help but feel nervous even though Azildor had explained that her own fear would extend to Nasah. For a long while she simply turned Nasah one direction, let her munch on some grass, pulled her in another direction, and repeated the cycle over and over. After the boredom of that repetition exceeded her anxiety, though, Kindle decided to chance slowly riding around the stone buildings. Once she allowed Nasah to saunter about the farm, she found that the horse readily recognized even the slightest signal tug and never seemed bothered to do whatever pleased Kindle. The longer she rode Nasah, the more she enjoyed sitting atop the gentle, well-mannered creature and the farther from the buildings she ventured on her new companion.

Kindle hardly saw anyone while she explored the grassy farmland. Only an occasional Chokmah appeared until the sun had lost its heat and was spilling orange light over the grass. Then she noticed Ella happily skipping toward her. Slowing to a walk beside Nasah, Ella narrated her day to Kindle. She quickly briefed that she, Andrew, and Tad had helped Masso that morning, but once Azildor let Kindle ride on her own, the farmer had taken her bow hunting. Ella excitedly elaborated on every detail, from the arrows she had in her quiver to each tousled hair on the squirrels she had shot. Kindle grinned at most of her narration but tried not to listen to her gory description of skinning the little animals. Blood and dead things made her feel sick. Finally Ella exhausted her story and chased another subject.

"Have you seen Tad or Andrew today?" she curiously asked, and Kindle shook her head. "No? Well, both of them have been in a right ugly mood all day, or at least for the morning time I spent with them they were. Tad's been abominable—just as he was at the Tunnels—cranky and full of protest at everything. He wasn't at all helpful with any of the chores, and Masso finally told him to go be useless somewhere else."

Kindle grimaced at the word 'useless' and groaned, "Really?"

"Yes, and that did not help at all, of course. It was all I could do to convince him to go take a bit of a walk. I thought he would wring that poor boy ... but it wasn't just Tad—Andrew was out of sorts too. He wouldn't say a word to me."

"He never does, Ella, that's pretty normal."

"No, he doesn't go on bantering, but he does talk some to me. He's just a bit shy, Kindle. He has to warm to you before he'll talk to you—but, anyway, he usually says good morning and comments some clever remark about the quality of the mush, but he just would not say a word."

"What do you guys talk about?" Kindle questioned, feeling somewhat left out.

"This and that, nothing too much ever," Ella nonchalantly replied and shrugged. "But never mind that. Isn't it odd that both of them woke up all miffed? Do you believe something happened? Do you suppose they had a row?"

"I dunno," Kindle grumbled, still disgruntled about Ella and Andrew's secret friendship.

"Oh, Kin, don't be miffed as well," sighed Ella. "If you must know right now, Andrew spends the lot of his words complaining about how awful Tad is to him and how much he reminds him of another boy that ridicules him. Other than that and his figuring about all those papers, he really does not say much."

"Oh," Kindle mumbled, now embarrassed by her jealously, "Sorry."

"Don't worry over it, Kin. But did you see them arguing or anything that would have made them so ... odd?"

"No. I haven't seen either of them since last night, and they were fine then," Kindle admitted as she squinted up to the top of the watchtower. She expected to see Tad's shoes dangling over the edge but saw nothing.

"Mmm," Ella huffed then clicked her tongue. "Well, I'm going back to the house. Perhaps Andrew will be there, and I can talk him up to better spirits."

"Yeah," Kindle offhandedly agreed and without thinking, volunteered, "I'll look for Tad."

A grin crept across Ella face. "That is a good idea. Out of everyone, I believe he likes you the most."

"Huh?" Kindle started, but Ella was already jogging off to the house. "Ugh. C'mon, Nasah, let's go to bed," she grumbled and turned her horse to the barn. If anything annoyed her about Ella, it was her frequent allusions to Tad and her liking one another. Kindle was certain that Tad still hated everyone and knew her own opinion of him was far from affectionate.

"I don't like him, and he doesn't like me, and he's a jerk, and even you know it and you're a horse," she angrily whispered to Nasah as she stroked her mane. Suddenly, shouting exploded through the air, and Nasah reared up, whinnying. Kindle wrapped her arms around Nasah's neck to keep from sliding backwards and squealed, "Down, down, down, down!"

The shouting continued, but Nasah obeyed and returned her hooves to the ground. Kindle quickly dismounted but kept a hold on the reins.

"Shh, shh," she nervously chanted as Nasah lightly stomped the grass. Scared of being kicked, Kindle retreated a few more steps and twisted around to see where the ruckus was coming from. Listening hard, she thought she heard Masso's voice and wondered if he was in some sort of danger in the barn. Turning back to her horse, she saw that Nasah still had not calmed.

"Okay, whatever, don't chill. Just stay here, okay?" she ordered Nasah before dashing to the barn door and peering inside. Immediately the shouting made sense; Masso and Tad were kicking up dust as they wrestled and pummeled one another in the dirt. Kindle, thankful that nothing worse was happening, remained outside watching them. Only a few seconds passed, though, before she caught sight of Azildor approaching the opposite door. Feeling relieved of her responsibility to end their fight but curious to know what would happen, she slipped into the empty stall near her and crouched down in the hay.

"BOYS!" Azildor's voice thundered with such authority and volume that Kindle instinctively ducked her head. She heard feet shuffling and running, then Azildor, in a quieter but still powerful tone, warned, "Masso—"

"Dad! It wasn't my fault! He attacked me!"

"You rat!" Tad yelled but Azildor silenced them.

"Stop! Both of you know better than to allow your anger to guide your actions. You know that when you follow your rage, you open yourself to the defeat of your adversaries. Masso, go to the house."

"Dad, he—!"

"Go," Azildor commanded, and after a few seconds, Kindle heard footsteps rush past the stall.

"That's not fair," Tad hatefully spat. "You don't even care what happened! You just think it's my fault! I'm not gunna take that!"

"Tad. I am assuming nothing. Masso will have his turn of discipline. I want to speak with you first," Azildor quickly but calmingly explained. "Tell me, son, did you attack Masso?"

"Don't call me 'son.' I'm not your son," grumbled Tad.

"Did you attack Masso?"

"Yeah, I jumped him, but I didn't start it! Little punk was calling me names like he thinks he's—"

"Tad."

"He was! Don't let him lie to you like he didn't do anything! Or are you gunna believe whatever he says anyway just 'cause he's your kid and I'm nothing but a useless idiot to you?! Huh?!" Tad shouted, and Kindle suddenly felt uncomfortable. She wanted to escape but knew she had to remain hidden or she would also be in trouble.

"Tad, you are letting your anger direct you. You must stop it."

"No! I don't care if I'm mad! What if I want to be mad?!"

For a while Kindle heard nothing but Tad's loud, bullish breathing. Carefully, she lowered herself to her belly so she could watch their feet through the gap at the bottom of the stall. A smaller space than she had expected was between them.

"What fuels your anger?" Azildor asked, then his feet walked to the wall and back to Tad. A shovel scoop and pick head dropped beside him.

"Wha—?" Tad began.

"Your sword," answered Azildor, and then the sound of wood knocking together echoed through the barn before he repeated his question. "What fuels your anger?"

The repetitive clanking of wood ensued, and Kindle watched as Azildor and Tad's feet shuffled and danced to the beat of their makeshift swords. Kindle knew what fierce swordsmen they both were and wished she could see their whole battle, but their steps alone were enough to captivate her. For a long time, they fought without speaking, and she simply watched and imagined what their strikes looked like. Finally an especially loud crack split the air, and one of the long wooden tool handles landed a short distance from the pair.

"Ha!" Tad shouted and Kindle knew he was the victor.

"Good," Azildor panted. "Lay aside your weapon."

Tad's handle also dropped in the dirt.

"You are afraid," Azildor said between breaths, and Kindle wondered if she had missed part of the conversation, but Tad's voice was full of confusion as well.

"What? I beat you! How's that—?"

"Not of this, Tad. Of the journey that lies before you."

"No, I'm not."

"You are. I can see your anger is a product of the fear in you."

"You don't know me!"

"You are correct. I cannot see the reason for your fear. You do not fear an enemy or harm or solitude or anything I can see, but something about this journey ahead of you has spurred the same fear and rage in you that I saw at our first match. Tad, what is it you fear?"

"I'm not scared of anything, okay?!"

"If you deny it, you can never overcome it."

Tense silence spread through the air. Kindle watched Tad's feet shift several times before Azildor spoke again in an uncharacteristically pained voice.

"Do you not wish to be the hero you have been called to become?"

"Yeah, I want to, that'd be great, but I can't, okay? I can't! That's why I keep telling you guys I'm not doing this whole save-the-world thing! Because I can't!"

"Why do you believe you cannot?"

"Because I can't!" Tad yelled in frustration. "Because I'll just fail! I fail at everything—that's who I am—a worthless, useless *failure*!"

"You will not fail, Tad. The makers of Anelthalien bestowed their mark to you; that alone is proof enough of your future success."

"Yeah, well, they picked wrong. I'm not a hero."

"Tad, all that bars you from being a hero is your fear of failing to try to live as one."

"Pft—no. It's not. I can't do anything right. Heroes do everything right. I don't. End of story."

"No, Tad. When the end comes, the hero is not the man who has answers or who is skilled above others. The hero is the man who disregards himself; the man who forgets his own inability, pain, fear, and rage and considers those around him; the one willing to see everyone else's inability, feel their pain and fear, and yet stand in their place. To be a hero, Tad, you must be a shield for others; you must be the very thing that stands between a people and death and stabs back that death. Sacrifice makes a hero."

"What? I have to die?" Tad asked, incredulous.

"Death comes to us all, Tad. Sacrifice is not limited to it, though. Your sacrifice is to fight—to draw your sword for Ella, Kindle, Andrew, and all of Anelthalien and to keep fighting until death or all is won. You have shown me many times that you will never leave a battle, and that is what this journey asks of you. You must stay in the fight, Tad." Kindle watched Azildor's hands gather the tool handles and heads then heard his voice say, "I have something for you." She held her breath as his and Tad's feet approached but relaxed when they veered to the stall on the opposite side of the barn door.

"I meant to give this to you the day you departed, but now is a better time."

"What's—whoa," Tad gasped as the sound of metal sliding across metal sliced the air.

"Its name is Natzal."

"It's got a name?"

"Yes. Its name tells its purpose; it is a deliverer. Many times it has saved its wielders from their enemies. The good king Daniel was the first to use it in the Great War and then passed it on to his most trusted guards, my ancestors, and it has been in my family since."

"Why are you giving it to me then?" Tad suspiciously asked.

"When my father passed Natzal to me, he told me to use it to protect all the good left in Anelthalien and then to pass it on to my oldest son when he was ready to bear that responsibility."

"So Masso gets it," Tad spitefully grumbled.

"No. Masso may be my firstborn of blood, but he only has the spirit of a farmer. You, *my son*," Azildor deliberately responded, "are the one who is ready to be a deliverer and protector of Anelthalien."

Kindle heard the slice of metal again and caught the sound of Tad's voice but couldn't discern what he said.

"Strap it on your right—like that," Azildor directed then very seriously instructed, "Remember, stay in the fight, Tad. Remain in the gap."

"Yeah," Tad mumbled, but if he said anything else, Kindle missed it because a loud whinny interrupted him.

"Nasah?" Azildor wondered in surprise, "What are you doing out? Where is Kindle?"

Kindle closed her eyes and bit her lip. She had hidden so well so long, and now she was sure that Nasah was about to reveal her to Azildor and Tad. In her mind, she willed her horse to lead them away, but she heard Nasah pound the ground inches from her and readied herself to be found.

"Nasah, be still," Azildor crooned, and the hoof pounding ceased. Kindle hunkered down to check what was happening and saw Azildor's feet leading Nasah to her stall. When Tad's shoes also traveled across the barn, Kindle felt like cheering but instead chanced a peek out of her hiding place. Both of their backs were turned to her, so she scrambled outside, took a steadying breath, and then jogged back into the barn.

"Nasah!" she cried, trying to sound relieved and winded. "There you are!"

Azildor turned her way and waved her over. As she closed the space between them, she quickly thought up a believable story.

"Aw, I'm glad you found her," she began, but Azildor, boring through her with his harsh stare, asked, "Why did you leave Nasah, Kindle?"

She balked for a moment, afraid to lie, and compromised for a mostly true excuse instead. "I was bringing her to the barn, but somebody was yelling, and it scared her, and she, like, kicked up, and so I got off and tried to lead her here, but she got away," Kindle related in one breath then, seeing Azildor's frown, mumbled, "Sorry."

"If you truly feel remorse, remember this incident and do not allow it to repeat," he sternly chastised as he began to unsaddle Nasah. "She is safe here, but if you lose her beyond this farm, you will likely not see her again."

"Okay, sorry," Kindle defensively grumbled, "I just got scared."

Azildor closed Nasah into her pen then gave both Kindle and Tad a serious look. "Do not allow fear to lead you. It will never take you where you need to go." He paused and his face relaxed somewhat. "Go on to the house."

Glad to escape his reproach, Kindle didn't hesitate to obey. She hurriedly trotted out of the barn then waited for Tad to come alongside her. Hungry to know about Natzal but not wanting to let on that she already knew he had it, Kindle waited a few steps before saying, "I don't know if Azildor told you, but he's gunna let us take Nasah. He gave her to me this morning."

Tad grunted.

"You think he's gunna give us anything else?" she pushed, hoping that would be enough to get him talking. Tad just shrugged, though, and Kindle couldn't help rolling her eyes. "You know, he gave Ella some arrows, so maybe he'll give us a sword or something like that. That would be cool, wouldn't it?"

"Yeah," he responded, and out of the corner of her eye, Kindle saw him grin slightly.

"What?" she urged and he dropped his smile.

"What?"

"You smiled," Kindle coyly said and noticed he was running his thumb along something on his side. "What's that?"

Tad shook his head and murmured, "You sure are annoying." Then, in one swift move, he whipped out the weapon, tossed it to his left hand, and held it out for her to see. It definitely wasn't the sword she had expected. In fact, everything from its short, hooked blade to its ornamented hilt was unlike anything she had ever seen. The dagger's shiny metal blade ended in a smooth, sharp, curved point, but closer to where it joined the handle, one side was serrated and the other side, which was partially etched with some sort of scribbling, shaped into up-hooked teeth. It looked deadly and beautiful all at once, and the hilt only added to its double-edged splendor with its two golden side hooks, deep sapphire plating winding around its middle, and jewels adorning the nub under Tad's hand. The further they moved from the torchlight emitting from the barn, the less Kindle could examine it, and finally as darkness swallowed it, Tad spun it back into its sheath.

"Pretty sweet, huh?" he bragged and stuffed his hands in his pockets.

"Yeah," Kindle agreed then, remembering she wasn't supposed to know about it, asked, "Did Azildor give it to you? Or did it come from the library?"

"Azildor gave it to me. He said…." Tad stopped short, and Kindle sensed he was regretting his words.

"What?" she urged, trying her best to *not* sound annoying.

He didn't continue, though, and Kindle had to employ all of her self-control to keep from pestering him for an answer. When they reached the house, Tad didn't enter the warm entry hall but stood staring off into the night. Kindle almost left him alone but changed her mind and turned back to face him.

"What?" he demanded after a long while of trying to ignore her.

"I dunno," Kindle honestly replied, "I just figured I'd stay out here too."

He gave her an agitated, sidelong glare. "Why?'

"I dunno. Why ever you're out here, I guess."

"Maybe I want you to leave me alone," he retorted but not seriously enough for Kindle to feel offended.

"You know you're gunna be stuck with me for a long time on this journey or trip or whatever it is. You might as well get used to me being around to annoy you."

The side of Tad's mouth perked up, and the snort he gave almost sounded like a laugh. "I'm already used to you being annoying."

"Good." Kindle smiled and tried to jam her hands in her pockets but switched to crossing her arms to avoid looking silly. As she did, a thought suddenly jumped in her mind.

"I've still got your necklace," she told him.

"Really? It didn't fall out of those stupid excuses for pockets?"

"Ugh, no. I didn't keep it in my pocket." She rolled her eyes as she bent down to fish around in her boot. Kindle slid it out and held it out for him to see. "Here, do you want it back?"

He eyed it with disgust and replied, "I don't care."

"Oh, c'mon, it's bugging my leg—" Kindle started to argue, but a noise from the surrounding darkness silenced her. She knew Tad had heard it as well because he also swung his head around to search for its maker.

"Tad, Kindle, what are you doing out here?" they heard Azildor ask and then saw him materialize out of the night. Neither of them answered, but Azildor didn't seem to care.

"Is that Tad's necklace?" He nodded at Kindle's hand.

"Oh, yeah, I—"

"Why do you have it? Give it back to him," Azildor forcefully commanded, and Kindle wrinkled her nose as she handed the chain to Tad.

"Sorry," she grumbled, quite put out by his tone, "I was just keeping it for him until—"

"No," Azildor interrupted, his voice still harsh, "You each must wear your own mark and no one else's."

"Chill," Tad snorted, and Kindle and Azildor both stared at him in surprise. "She wasn't wearing it. It was in her boot. And she only had it because I told her I wasn't gunna wear the stupid thing, okay?"

With narrowed eyes, Azildor looked back and forth at them. "Put it on, Tad. It is yours and you must wear it. Kindle, how long have you carried it? Since the night I met you both on the tower?"

"No, ever since that first time we went to the library," she begrudgingly replied.

Azildor gave each of them one more quick, probing glance then directed, "Go inside."

Kindle spun and marched away from him. She intended to stalk over to the chairs and complain about Azildor's rotten mood with Tad, but her plan changed when she saw everyone sitting at the table. As Azildor and Tad entered behind her, all eyes turned on them and the light chatter and smiles at the table faded.

"Come sit down you three, dinner's ready," Naam called in her usual pleasant tone, but Kindle could tell from her expression that she felt something was wrong.

For the first time since she had arrived at the Chokmah's house, the meal was almost entirely silent. Every one of the children except Sophia seemed to sense that their father was upset and acted so as not to bring any notice to themselves. After the quiet eating ceased, Masso began to follow Adin and Binah to the sink, but Azildor, with one quiet finger, directed him outside. Once they disappeared, everyone dispersed from the table and Naam and began whispering to one another. Kindle, Tad, Andrew, and Ella all retreated downstairs.

"Now *what* did you two do to him?' Ella questioned before they had reached the bottom of the stairs. "It was as if he brought a thunderstorm in with him."

"I didn't do anything!" Kindle exasperatedly insisted, "He just got all mad about nothing."

"I stomped Masso's face," Tad casually laughed, and Ella made a sound of protest to his back.

"Tad, that is awful—"

"Nah, it was pretty sweet."

"Tad!" Ella shook her head at the ceiling. "Well, at least that solves *that* mystery."

"No, it doesn't," snapped Kindle, determined to voice how she had been wronged. "He wasn't mad about that—he was mad because Nasah ran off and I had Tad's necklace in my boot."

"Nasah?" murmured Andrew, but no one paid attention to him.

"Nah, you should of seen him. He was pretty—" Tad laughed at the same time Ella waved a hand for quiet.

"Kin, you *lost* Nasah?! And what was Tad's necklace doing in your boot? Wait—was Tad riding Nasah?"

"Oh, shut up! Shut up! Everybody shut up!" cried Kindle, and finally they all stopped talking and stared at her. "Okay," she sighed and then as concisely as possible explained her incident with Nasah and Azildor's reaction to Tad's necklace being in her boot. "And I don't know what the big deal was about it. He was all like, 'Don't wear anybody else's necklace'!" she finished in a very rude imitation of Azildor's voice.

"That *is* odd…," Ella thoughtfully mused. "Are you sure he wasn't miffed at Tad for—"

"Nah, not then." Tad shook his head from his mattress.

"Hm… Andrew?" Ella turned to him, but he shrugged and shook his head. "Well, we'll just have to ask him about it tomorrow," she decisively concluded and flumped down on her bed.

"What? No." Kindle frowned. "I'm *not* gunna bring it up."

"Alright. *I'll* ask him. I don't mind one bit."

"No!" argued Kindle. "*Nobody's* gunna ask him about it because I think I know what we can do. It was, like, the first night we were here, and Masso and the twins and Navon went and listened at the top of the stairs. Azildor and Naam talk when they think everybody else is asleep, and if we do that, we could hear them, and I'm sure they'll talk about it tonight."

"That is eavesdropping, Kindle," Ella disapprovingly interjected.

"Not if it's about you," she argued, but Ella resolutely waved her head back and forth.

"No. It is wrong and you are not going to do it."

"I'm in," Tad piped up, and Ella gave him a motherly glare.

"No! I will not allow you two to debase yourselves, and if I have to sit up all night watching you both to keep you from acting like a pack of rascals, then I will."

"You're pretty lame," Tad mumbled. Ella gave him slightly confused stare.

"He means you're not any fun," Andrew explained for her.

"Well, if listening to conversations I'm not part of is fun, then no I am not. Kindle, really, don't bother with that. Just go on to sleep, and we'll ask him about it tomorrow, alright?"

Kindle huffed and dropped back on her pillow. "Okay, fine. Whatever."

She yanked her blanket over her head as she heard Ella sigh in a satisfied way. Before long, Kindle heard everyone else descend the stairs and make their way to bed. After what seemed like ages of careful listening and pinching her arm to keep herself awake, Kindle slowly poked her head out from under the blanket. Her intention had never been to go to sleep but to just make sure Ella did fall asleep. Seeing Ella was as lifeless as everyone else, Kindle carefully eased up out of bed and started weaving through the sea of sleepers. She was almost to the stairs when a hand grabbed her arm. Kindle almost let out a terrified scream, but at the same second another hand trapped it in her mouth and Tad's voice whispered, "Scared?"

Relieved that it was him but still annoyed, Kindle yanked his hand off her face and hissed, "You didn't have to sneak up on me, you jerk."

He quietly laughed. Rolling her eyes, she dragged him up the steps behind her.

"Just stay quiet, okay?" she ordered and cocked her head to the skin above their heads.

"I believe so," Azildor was saying.

"Then … they're not safe wherever they go, are they?" Naam replied with deep concern in her voice. "What do you think it is?"

"I don't know. From how she described it, though, something dark."

"Azildor, you don't think that … that…." Naam's voice trailed off as if she couldn't stand to finish her thought.

"No. The evil king himself would surely not have let them live. It was something dark but not powerful."

Naam sighed.

"They will be alright, Naam. The creature has only shown itself once. It may not plague them again."

"But it knew where the mark was. You said it yourself."

"We cannot fear for their safety, that will not aid them—"

"I know, it's just that they've become like our own children, Azildor, and if we could protect them—"

"Then we would be robbing Anelthalien of its protection."

A long pause opened, and Kindle and Tad exchanged inquisitive glances.

"I know," Naam finally sighed. "You're sure they'll be alright?"

"You know better than I do that they have a greater power on their side."

"I do. And that's what worries me."

"They will be alright. When they leave, they will be ready."

Quiet filled the air, and after several minutes, Kindle motioned Tad down the stairs.

"Dude—" Tad started but Kindle shushed him.

"Tomorrow," she whispered, jabbing a finger at the sleeper nearest to them.

He nodded with his odd half evil, half giddy smile on his face and then they split ways and returned to their mattresses.

A NOBLER MISSION

The next day provided them no chance to even think about the words they had overheard. After waking them up earlier than usual and rushing them through their bowls of mush, Naam sent all four of them to meet Azildor in the barn. He immediately assigned a job to each of them and kept them busy all day. Kindle, Tad, Ella, and Andrew hardly crossed one another's path while they completed the feeding, watering, picking, and other tasks that Azildor endlessly doled out. Every so often, though, he would call them all together to give a lesson about traveling through Anelthalien on their own. By the end of the day, Kindle's head was bursting with ways to find food, how to build a fire, techniques of trading with minas, the currency of Anelthalien, and much, much more. Her body felt just as fully run-down when they finally returned to the house for supper because Azildor had insisted that all of them, even Andrew who was more worn out than anyone else, practice their weapon skills. All of them were so tired that night after dinner that they listlessly wandered down the stairs and collapsed into deep sleep.

When Kindle awoke the next morning to Naam's voice chiming that they had another full day ahead, she groaned. The last thing she wanted was to move her horribly sore body out of bed, especially to just repeat the day that had caused her to become so sore. Once she and the other three did manage to lug themselves up to breakfast, though, they all had to face the fact that their day was going to consist of the same work as the previous one.

Azildor directed them to the same jobs but stopped their progress less often. The last time he called for them, when the sky was verging on darkness, Kindle pulled her basket brimming with corm to him then dropped down beside it.

"Ugh. Can we please not practice tonight? Can we just be done?" she moaned as Tad, Ella, and Andrew joined them.

"I will not ask you to train tonight," Azildor responded. "I can see you are weary."

"Awesome," Tad mumbled and also took a seat on the ground.

"We are not finished, though," the farmer continued, and Kindle felt the tremor of protest rising around her, but his next sentence extinguished it. "Tonight is our last night together, and I ask that you listen to my words."

Kindle and Tad let out a collective sigh of relief, and Ella, Andrew, and Azildor sat beside them.

"You four have worked hard and grown much since I met you at the edge of Danica Woods," he began, and Kindle peered over her shoulder to try to see the spot across the now green, bountiful field where she had last seen Missi.

"You are ready to leave this place and take on the task you have been chosen for. Tomorrow you will leave early and head southeast to the small village of Assula. It is not on your map, but you will find it on the first small curve of the woods. Do you know what I speak of, Andrew?"

He nodded his blonde head.

"Good. You may be able to make the trip by nightfall, but unless the need arises, it would be wise not to lodge there."

"Why?" Ella curiously asked.

"The people in the village are … very distant from outsiders," he carefully replied. "They do not take well to anyone they do not know. Stay outside the village then in the morning trade some crops for as many minas as possible. As strangers and children, they will try to cheat you—"

"We're not kids," Tad argued and Azildor shook his head at him.

"They will see you as children, Tad. Every person, town, and city you encounter will see you this way and will very likely reject you, so you must learn to control your temper."

"What? Nobody's gunna like us because we're kids?" Kindle cried in disbelief.

"Plenty of children live in Garrick and—" Ella also began to object, but Azildor raised a hand to stop them.

"No, not for that reason. This is what I must tell you: your journey to discover the evil throne and destroy it, the good and evil thrones, the necklaces you wear, and even the creators who made them and this whole land are all a laughable myth or completely unknown to almost all of Anelthalien. No one will easily believe you. They will likely call you absurd for even mentioning any of it."

"So we don't tell 'em. What's the big deal?" Tad shrugged.

Azildor's face became very serious. "You *must* tell them—you must tell everyone you encounter. If you hear nothing else, hear this: your arrival is the sign that the current thousand years is drawing to a close and a new evil king is preparing to take the throne. I can feel the earth groaning and am almost certain that the new king will unleash evil and destruction unlike any we have ever known. If you tell no one of this coming fate, they will do nothing to guard against it and will be annihilated in their apathetic ignorance."

Kindle, Ella, and Tad started talking all at once.

"How long do we have? Do we really have to tell *everybody*? How long . . .?" Kindle began to fret.

"Everything will honestly be destroyed? Where will we live?" asked Ella, leaning forward as Tad accused, "You said all we had to do was get rid of the stupid rock!"

"Stop," Azildor ordered with calm force, and they turned expectant eyes on him. "I do not know how long you have until the new ruler takes the evil throne; that is why you must leave tomorrow and make haste to Letum.

Arriving there and destroying the evil throne *is* your goal, but if you do not meet that goal and do not ready the rest of Anelthalien to stand against the evil king, then you all will surely perish with the rest of us."

"So, what, telling everybody is just some plan B in case we fail?" Tad sneered. "You don't really believe we can do it, huh?"

"Tad." Azildor turned to him, but Tad angrily glared away. "Evil never sleeps. It is always roaming the land for unsuspecting victims. If you succeed but awaken no one to their disease of ignorance, then Anelthalien will remain prey to the next evil that will guide them blindly to their death. This land will always have an enemy that wishes to ensnare it but will not always have heroes who wish to deliver it."

Tad's eyes then his face slid back to Azildor.

"I believe in you, Tad. And Kindle, Ella, Andrew, I believe in you as well. It is the people of Anelthalien who have chosen to follow a lie for so long that I do not have faith in to independently perceive their error."

After a long pause, Andrew, staring hard at his thumbs, asked, "What do we tell people?"

"Tell them that their lives are in danger and then, if they will listen, tell them that an evil king who is lurking in the shadows is preparing to attack."

"What if they don't listen?" Andrew questioned.

"Then their fate is out of your hands. You cannot help those who choose to ignore help."

"But... can't we do anything?" Ella looked both deep in thought and grieved but suddenly brightened. "If they see our necklaces—" she lifted up her own green charm, "—the marks of the makers, then surely people will believe us."

"Ella, did you know that mark when you found it?"

Her face fell. "No, I didn't."

"And neither will almost everyone in Anelthalien. They—"

"Then how do *you* know about these, huh?" Tad interrupted.

Azildor gave him a stern look but answered, "You forget I am an elf and one of the last in Anelthalien." He let his eyes carefully examine them before continuing, "The life of an elf is a long one. Fewer generations have passed in my family than in the families of the men living all through this land. That is less life between myself and the past. And, as you saw with the Cifra, the beings formed by the makers treasure their history and heritage and pass it along. My father told me all that I have shared with you about the makers, spirits, Great War, and Bellalux just as my grandfather told him and my great-grandfather, who served Bellalux's queen, told him."

"Wait—didn't you say that was a *thousand* years ago?" Kindle asked, trying to figure the math in her tired brain. She gave up the task and wondered aloud, "How old *are* you?"

He smiled slightly. "Old enough that I do not count the years. But that does not matter. What is necessary for your journey is that you understand that the rest of Anelthalien is unlike the Cifra or my family. It does not remember its past or its makers and lives as if neither ever existed. Because of this, your journey will be difficult and much doubt about it will plague you. When those times come, remember what you have learned or received or heard from me and my family—all that is true, noble, right, and pure— and put it into practice. Do not forget our time together." He let his hard stare travel over each one of their faces then peered up at the now dark sky. "Naam will have dinner ready soon. Go on to the house after you take these baskets to the barn. Tell her to begin without me if need be; I may be late," Azildor instructed then swiftly carried himself to the barn.

For a while none of them moved from their repose on the grass. Kindle wondered if Ella, Andrew, and Tad were also stirring together all that Azildor had said or if they were just too worn out to move. Finally though, just when Kindle was considering sleeping right where she was, Andrew let out a long, exhausted sigh and pushed himself up from the ground. His movement inspired the rest of them. Ella creakily rose up beside him as Kindle loudly groaned and tried to flop onto her back, but Tad caught her elbow.

"I'm not getting stuck with your basket too," he grumbled at her and fully pulled her to her feet.

"Ugh." She shook her sleepiness away then teased, "You couldn't carry both anyway."

"Pft. They're not heavy," Tad snorted and then did grab her basket as well and strutted off toward the barn.

Ella laughed, "Kin, did you do that on purpose?"

"No. What? What'd I do?"

"Oh, Kindle. Don't worry over it. Here, take a handle of Andrew's."

Kindle, confused but too tired to care, mindlessly obeyed Ella and they all headed to the barn together.

STILLNESS

The dinner Naam prepared that night was more like a feast. Never before had the table been so full of so many different dishes to try, and even when everyone had devoured more than enough, an abundance still garnished the table. Even though the food was festive, the mood was somewhat subdued. Yirah and Yirun's nightly fabricated story wasn't as unbelievable as usual, Navon and Masso avoided catching one another's eye, and at one point Binah burst out in tears and ran around the table to squeeze Andrew. Kindle could only guess that Naam had told all of her children that it would be their last night with her, Ella, Andrew, and Tad. Seeing all of them so deflated made her also remember how much she didn't want to leave.

After the chores had been completed, they all moved into the living room area to wait for Azildor to return. Kindle wanted to say something to them, maybe to promise she would come back and see them again or to tell them to not cry, but she envisioned all of those options only increasing the difficultly of everything, so she kept silent. It usually would have been beyond her ability to not say a word to anyone, but Kindle was so exhausted from the past two days that she didn't mind simply existing on the floor. Every now and then she allowed her eyelids to close and finally let them remain that way.

"Kindle," Naam's voice called but Kindle ignored it.

Then, much louder and closer, Tad yelled, "Hey!"

"Huh!" she yelled back, jolting awake.

"Told you I could," bragged Tad as he grinned.

Kindle took a blurry, dazed survey of the room around her. All of the Chokmah children had disappeared, but Azildor was standing among her, her three companions, and Naam.

"We go to bed now?" she mumbled but Azildor shook his head.

"Sit up, Kindle. Naam and I have something for each of you."

Ella slid off her chair and helped Kindle twist over and up to sit cross-legged on the floor. Her hands were incredibly warm, and Kindle wondered if she had tucked down into sleep as well.

"Now, this isn't much, but I hope it will help you all," Naam modestly said as she lifted a pile of multicolored cloth into her lap. "Tad, this is yours." She handed him part of her load. "It's a shirt and pants," she explained at his confused expression. "I made each of you a new outfit for your journey. I thought it would be good to have something sturdier and that fit in a bit better. Here…." She started passing each of them a different colored shirt paired with brown or black pants. Kindle watched Andrew pluck up a boxy, yellow hooded shirt and couldn't help but fear that hers would be just as ugly. To her surprise, though, when she unfolded her red shirt, it resembled the t-shirt she wore except it was longer and had long sleeves.

"Thanks!" She smiled, relieved she didn't have to fake appreciation then lifted her black pants to see they were actually leggings.

"They're the same color as our necklaces, aren't they?" asked Ella, and Kindle stared around to see that she was right.

"Yes." Naam seemed truly pleased at her observation. "I thought that would be nice." Naam's smile faltered, and Kindle followed her gaze to see Tad still frowning at his unfolded clothes.

"Tad, is something wrong?" Naam gently asked. "It's alright if you don't—"

"Why're you givin' us stuff?" he interrupted, and Naam blinked several times before answering.

"I just wanted to make sure you were taken care of. It's the least I could do for you all."

Tad eyed her, then the clothes, and finally slowly nodded as if still disbelieving.

"Thank you," Andrew suddenly said in an odd voice, and everyone turned to him. His head was bowed, but Kindle could still tell his face was red. She quickly looked away, embarrassed by his emotion, but Naam wrapped him in a motherly hug.

"I have your swords," Azildor announced, diverting them from the tenderness of the moment. He placed a cloth bundle on the floor and untied the knot binding it together. In it four beautiful swords lay snug in leather sheaths on a stack of shields.

"These also bear the colors of your marks," he informed them as he tossed the top one, a shorter, thinner sword with emeralds entwined in its swirling hilt, to Ella. "A rapier—it will do well with your quick aim and need to switch from long to short range. Tad, Kindle," he continued as he presented them with similarly-shaped weapons, "long swords. They are sturdy and forged to last." Azildor held the last sword out to Andrew, who just stared doubtfully at it.

"I can't—" he began but Azildor cut him off.

"Sometimes the appearance of strength is enough to dissuade an enemy. You may not have the skill to use this in a battle, but I trust that you do have the mind to use it wisely. It is a saber—unassuming but just as deadly as the others."

Andrew nodded and took it from him.

"And shields?" asked Ella as she pointed her sword at the stack.

"Yes. They as well have the color of each of your marks." Instead of handing them out, though, Azildor pulled the cloth back over them and said, "Tonight you do not require them. Tonight you require rest."

"Yes, you all have an early start tomorrow." Naam rose and spread her arms to sweep them to the corner. "Take those clothes with you and change into them in the morning. You can just leave the swords here—no one's going to bother them. Now...," she sighed heavily and caught Kindle and Ella in a hug. "This is the last night you'll sleep under our roof, so sleep well, alright?" She released the girls and then lifted the fur blanket from the basement opening. Kindle wanted to say something really wonderful that would make the moment magical just like people in movies always did but couldn't think of any words. All she could think to do was send a smile, which felt nervous and not at all magical, back at Naam as she trooped down the stairs behind the others.

When Kindle turned her face to the dim room below, she saw all of the Chokmah children waiting at the bottom of the steps to say their good-byes. As she approached them, Kindle wished she had a way to avoid them. Once the children started admiring their new clothes and sighing about how amazing their adventure would be, though, Kindle was glad to have their company. After everyone, even Binah, had run out of questions, Ella announced that they all really had to get some sleep, and the group dispersed.

A whole mixture of anticipation, nerves, excitement, and a million other emotions made sleeping difficult, though, and so when Kindle heard Naam's footsteps on the stairs, she pulled her cover over her eyes and vainly hoped for the coming wake-up call to go away. She could not avoid Naam's coaxing, though, and before long, Kindle, Ella, Andrew, and Tad were all outfitted in their new clothes sitting behind a bowl of mush. As they ate, Naam busily walked around the house with the bags the Cifra had given them. To Kindle, it seemed like Naam was trying to stuff everything possible into the sacks. The sight was growing more interesting each time she packed another item into a seemingly full bag, but Azildor appeared in the entryway, and Kindle remembered she should focus on eating her mush instead. She scooped a big spoonful in her mouth and watched Naam and Azildor pass by one another, talking with their eyes and nods. As Naam disappeared outside, Azildor came and sat among them.

"You are almost ready to depart," he quietly told them, and Kindle wondered if he knew his children often eavesdropped on him and Naam. Kindle dipped her face to hide any guilt on it, but his next word made it jump back up.

"Kindle—"

"Huh?' She tried to sound unaware but anticipated a lecture.

"—Nasah is saddled and laden down with some provisions. She has one feed bag, but the plants along your way will provide her with plenty of food."

"Oh, okay, cool." She smiled, relieved.

"Ella, I have filled your quiver. Remember to always keep your bow by your side and to retrieve any arrow you can."

Ella nodded, and Azildor continued to Andrew, "Your map, Andrew—do you have it? Good. Always keep it at your side. Anelthalien is a vast land, and you cannot afford to spend time wandering. As I said, make for Assula today. Follow the line of Danica Woods, and you should reach it near night-fall but camp outside the town and ride through it in the early morning only to trade. Your next destination will be Iteraum—do you know it, son?"

Andrew's eyes darted around as if he was thinking, then he asked, "Should we keep following Danica until we see the river?"

"Yes, your mind is strong. Once you reach Iteraum, the river will be your guide until you reach Ignancia Forest. Then turn south and trace the trees until you meet the shore. It should guide you to Letum." He took a deep breath, and Kindle thought she saw a glimmer of worry cross his face.

"That doesn't sound too bad," she commented, hoping he would agree.

"No. If you stay on course, your way will always be clear, but do not assume it will always be easy. Remember all I have told you, though, and it will not be as long or as difficult as it could be. Alright?" He waited until he had scanned all of their faces before continuing. "I have only one more les-son for you; those swords you carry—do not use them to kill another man. I have taught you to use them to defend yourselves, and I expect you to use them only in that capacity."

"What?" Tad argued, "What if somebody's tryin' to kill us, huh? What're we supposed to do, just ask 'em to quit? And what about the evil guy? We just let him go?"

"Tad," Azildor softly but seriously replied, "first, it is not your choice who lives and who dies. The weight of that responsibility is beyond any man's strength. Second, if you live by the sword, you will die by it. You have only one enemy now, and that enemy knows nothing of you, but the moment you choose to use your abilities for anything more than defense, you will acquire many enemies. Too many to escape. Do you understand?"

"Yeah, I get you, but seriously, what do you expect us to do if somebody attacks us?"

"*Defend* yourself."

"Pft. Okay, whatever."

"No, Tad, this is not a flexible matter. You know how to disarm an attacker and wound without killing. You know that you have no need to kill anyone."

Tad huffed and glared at his mush.

"I need your word, Tad, that you will use your skills only for good. I need each of you to give your word."

"Yeah, okay. For good," Tad grumbled, and Ella then Kindle and Andrew followed with a promise.

Azildor nodded in a satisfied way then stood and motioned for them to do the same. They followed him out into the cool morning and Kindle immediately felt grateful for her warm leggings and long sleeves. She expected to travel to the barn, but Azildor led them behind the house. Naam was standing with Nasah and when she noticed them, began explaining what each of their bags contained. Before she could dive into detail, Azildor took her wildly gesturing hands and said, "Thank you for packing the bags. I am sure they will find what they need at the right time. They must go now."

Naam gave him a smile then turned it to them. "You all will be alright. Goodness, I know you have half of our farm in those bags to keep you well," she laughed to herself. "You ... you will be fine." Suddenly Naam lunged forward to deliver a round of hugs to each of them, ending with a reluctant, stiff Tad.

"You be good, young man. Alright?" She held him out at arm's length. "Be careful. Take care of yourself so I can see you again. That goes for all of you—be safe so I can see all of your faces again when this is all over." She pulled Tad back into another embrace. "You've all become so dear to me." Finally she fully released him and patted his shoulder. "Go on and be heroes."

Tad, who seemed completely lost as to what to do, squirmed his shoulders to straighten his shirt and mumbled, "Sure."

Kindle decided to save him from his awkwardness and asserted, "Yeah, we'll be careful, Naam. Thanks. So can I still ride Nasah with all that...." She pointed at all of the bundles situated on her horse's rump.

"Yes, she is quite capable of supporting two of you at your walking pace."

"Oh, okay," Kindle replied as she climbed into the saddle. "Well, uh, if anybody wants up here...."

"We'll let you know." Ella winked at her and handed Kindle her bag. Silence took over the group as Tad, Ella, and Andrew slung their packs over their heads. Kindle stared around from her vantage point and realized that they were truly about to leave all she had gotten used to. Somehow, Kindle had pictured this moment—the point when they actually started off on their own—to be something momentous and terrifying like jumping from a cliff into crashing waves, but now that she sat here in the reality of it, it was not. It was calm and quiet and much more like the minutes before she took a test in school—full of unwillingness to start but also an impatience to begin and get through it. She didn't feel prepared, but just like when everything suddenly hushed and a test paper floated onto her desk, Ella took a hold of Nasah's lead rope, and they had begun before she even knew it. Kindle almost turned back to wave good-bye one last time but decided that seeing Naam and Azildor again wouldn't ease the distance that was growing between them.

STILLNESS DISRUPTED

For a long time, they traveled in silence. Before the sun could rise and stir all of their sleepy minds, they reached the shade of the tree line of Danica Woods. The long, cool shadows that fell over them didn't help Kindle wake any quicker. Only when the sky fully settled on a beautiful bright blue did any of them make a sound. It was a musical string of words, and Kindle, almost asleep atop Nasah, gazed toward the forest, expecting to see Lady Luna or Missi drifting their way. At the thought of seeing one of the Cifra again, Kindle shook herself into full consciousness and peered around to discover who was singing. Seeing that ahead of her Tad and Andrew were also searching for the sound maker, she deduced it must actually be Ella.

"What'd you say, Ella?" Kindle asked as she stretched.

"Hm? Oh, I was only singing a bit. It passes the time better than all this quiet I think." Ella looked up at Kindle. "I sing all the time at the Lighthouse. Did I tell you that?"

"Um ... maybe. You mean that place where you live?"

Ella nodded, and Kindle noticed Andrew had inclined his ear to listen.

"Well, I do and almost every night. Everyone so enjoys it, and it does make the place quite cheerful. At least most of the time...." A pained look crossed her face, and Ella dipped her eyes to the ground, but the next second her smile returned. "It's just what I hear from the travelers—the songs, I mean—things they say about their trips and adventures and ... do you want to hear one?"

"Yeah, sure. Just, I've got to get down first. I'm so stiff," Kindle grumbled, trying to work the kinks out of her back. She reined Nasah to a halt then traded places with Ella. Once they had returned to their steady pace, Ella slowly started up a hum, which eventually broke into bright, melodic lyrics.

> "You've traveled far, you've traveled wide,
> And now you'd like to lay aside,
> All you've gleaned and all you've gained,
> So come in from the heavy rain,
> The Lighthouse will cheer your soul,
> There's no place that I'd rather go,
> There's really no place better,
> Oh-ho weary soul, come in from the weather,
> Oh-ho weary soul, there's really no place better."

To Kindle, Ella did sing very well. The hint of something like an Irish accent in her voice that Kindle enjoyed so much was amplified when she sang and really did make her sound like she belonged on the bar of a pub. Ella sang the same tune several times, varying the words in each new round, and listening to her truly did help the time slide by quicker. Andrew also seemed to enjoy her song; he let his pace slow until he was beside Nasah. Only after Ella had switched to another tune did Kindle realize that Tad hadn't joined their happy group. In fact, he seemed to have put more space between them and himself. Not wanting to have to find him later, Kindle jogged ahead to catch up with him.

"Hey," she said once she was level with him, "you have to slow down or you'll get too far ahead."

He didn't say anything but kept his same quick pace. Kindle rolled her eyes in a good-humored way. "C'mon, Tad, slow down. We have to keep together. You know what Azildor said about getting lost."

"I could find you guys from a mile away with her singing like that," he grumbled.

"What? Ella? You don't like her singing?"

"No. She's annoying."

"Uh…." Kindle wasn't sure how to respond. *She* didn't see how he could think Ella was annoying but knew arguing with him would be pointless.

"Um, I guess you could ask her to sing quieter or—"

"Aw, great," Tad groaned as Ella, with a wary Andrew sitting behind her, rode up beside them.

"I thought it would be better if we just caught you." She grinned, and Tad returned a mocking grimace. Ella ignored his rudeness. "No sense in turning round, hm? Oh! Kin, Tad, do you know this is Andrew's first horse ride? He said he's never ridden one, and I thought he should begin today. I only have taken Papa's horse to the—"

"Will you shut up?!" Tad suddenly erupted. "Arg! All you ever do is talk! Just shut up!"

Kindle bit her lip and took a sidestep away from Tad. She wanted to explain his anger to Ella, but the fear of him exploding at her kept her quiet. Surprisingly, though, Ella seemed unaffected by his rage.

"You don't have to yell. I know I talk often—I like to be sociable," she commented in a casual way. "You'd do well to be a bit more relational as well. We have to work together; we really should try to like one another."

"Yeah, well, I don't like you. I haven't liked you ever since you mouthed off to me at that bug place. You talk too much, and you think you know everything, and you think you can tell everybody what to do. It's *annoying*!"

Kindle and Andrew exchanged slightly terrified glances. She was sure he was also afraid a fight would break out at any second.

"Heh." Kindle tried to fake a grin but failed. "Guys, why don't we just like … not talk for a while?"

"No, Kindle, it's alright." Ella shrugged, still unshaken. "No strife was ever settled by avoiding it." She turned to Tad. "If I talk too long for your personal taste, that is perfectly fine, and I thank you for telling me. But I would like you to understand that I do not think I know everything and in no way mean to tell you what to do. If I could be true with you—"

"Are you really gunna talk more?" muttered Tad.

"Yes," she replied, still without an ounce of annoyance. "My whole life I've lived with my papa at the Lighthouse and we never had a mother, and since I was tall enough, I've been the head waitress. So I always felt I ought to be the one taking care of everyone and everything—seeing that the guests were always well and in good company, that every spoon and mug made it to its home each night, and everything that needed to be done. And there it was all well and good. They—Papa and Sara and the lot—needed me to know the place inside and out and to direct the floor. I don't mean to act that way, Tad, it's only that it's the way I've always known was right." She continued looking down at him for a short while, as if awaiting a response, but after a few minutes she turned her eyes ahead and almost whispered, "Who we are is hard to break. But we all may need to do just that at some time or another."

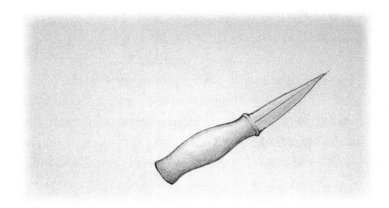

ASSULA

They stopped only once that day to dig through the bags to discover what kind of food Naam had packed. Once Andrew unearthed some bread and dried fruit, each of them took a handful to eat as they moved along. The incessant walking made Kindle's feet and legs incredibly tired, and she wished for a break until the sun started to sink. She knew the orange sunset hinted that they had to be close to Assula. When the sky grew dark, but they still had seen no sign of a town or any sort of life, though, Kindle began to worry. Every terrible possibility ran through her mind—they were lost, they had walked too slow, maybe the village was gone, or they had passed it…. She shook her head, and Tad looked down from Nasah's back at her.

"Tired?"

"No, I—it's just … we should be there by now, shouldn't we?"

Tad shrugged. "I don't know. Ask Einstein, he's the map."

Kindle squinted ahead at Ella and Andrew. She feared confirming her worries too much to approach them. "Yeah, I know he's got the map, but like, didn't Azildor say we'd be there when it got dark?"

He didn't reply. He didn't even look at her.

"Ugh. Are you ignoring me?" She couldn't handle being anxious *and* ignored. "You're such a—"

"I think I see it."

"What?"

"The village or whatever. There's a light." He pointed slightly to their left. Kindle took a moment to glare at him then searched for the light.

"I don't see it." She crossed her arms in agitation, sure he was joking. "I don't see anything."

He returned her glare. "It's because you're down there." Tad leaned forward and grabbed her wrist, pulling her away from the lead rope and up into the saddle behind him. Kindle immediately forgot to look for the light and became incredibly awkward. For some reason being so close to him made her brain jolt into a panic, and she felt overwhelmed by the options of where to put her hands.

"See?" Tad declared triumphantly, obviously unaware of her sudden conundrum.

"Uh . . .." She resolutely clamped her hands on her knees then peered into the night. "Oh! Yeah! Yeah, I see it!"

"Hey, guys!" Tad called to Ella and Andrew, "It's that way!"

Ella ran up to them. "Assula? Do you see it?"

"Yeah." Kindle stuck her head out from behind Tad. "It's just right over there. It doesn't look *too* far. I think we can get there in like…."

"We're not going there tonight," Andrew interrupted, and Kindle squished her pouty face at him.

"He's right." Ella nodded. "Azildor told us not to stay the night in the town. It might be best to bed down among the trees." She began to drift toward the edge of Danica Woods, but Tad's words froze her steps.

"Nah, I'm not sleepin' on the ground. I'm sleepin' in a bed."

Ella frowned. "Tad, I know you heard what Azildor said—it is dangerous in the town at night. We won't be welcome. We'll be much safer right here … and anyway, you know you will have to spend many nights on the ground while we're on our way—"

"Yeah, but not when there's a better place to sleep *right over there*. C'mon, it can't be that bad."

"Tad, no," Ella firmly commanded.

"Pft. Yeah," he blew back, and then before Kindle knew what was happening, Nasah shot away from Ella and Andrew, and she threw her arms around Tad's torso to keep from sliding off her horse.

"What're you doing!?" she yelled in surprise and annoyance.

"Proving her wrong," he laughed back.

"Ugh! Stop! Let me down! I'm not gunna be part of your—ahhh!" she shrieked as Tad steered Nasah into a sharp turn and Kindle slid sideways.

"What? You said you wanted off," Tad chortled.

Kindle squirmed back to safety. "You are such a jerk!" she cried, punching his back with each word. He laughed but slowed Nasah to a walk.

"Go ahead, get off and go back to your bestie where it's safe," he teased.

"No, you know what?" she replied sassily, "This is my horse. *You* get off *my* horse."

"Your horse, huh? Well, look who's driving it."

"Ugh," she huffed in frustration. "You're not seriously going to Assula, are you?"

"Yeah, why not?"

"Uh, because Azildor said not to, and Ella and Andrew aren't, and—"

"You scared?"

Kindle set her jaw. She was very much afraid, but he wasn't going to know it. "No. If you're going, I'm going."

"Okay," he replied in a way that could have been mocking or surprised. Kindle rolled her eyes but clamped her lips shut to keep herself from snapping something.

As they rode nearer to the village, Kindle saw that a tall wooden wall surrounded it. Each log had been cut to a threatening point at the top and altogether they created a fairly intimidating barrier.

"You sure this is a good idea? Like, I don't even see a way in," she prompted, hoping that would be enough to dissuade him.

"You pansying out?" he replied in a distant tone. Kindle could see he also was searching for some sort of break in the wall. "Boom. Right there," he suddenly bragged and steered Nasah to a small outcropping near the middle of the wall. It reminded Kindle of the little toll booths guards sat in except no mechanical arm stuck out from it. When they rode near it, a light appeared inside and a man's voice shouted, "Who's there?!"

"C'mon, Tad, this is stupid," Kindle urgently whispered. "He's not gunna let us in."

"I hear you out there! Lloyd?! That you?! Don't you be … ay! You ain't Lloyd!" A porky man in an old, floppy hat had poked his head and lantern out of the booth and was eyeing them suspiciously. "Who are you? Come on, let it out. I got a bow in here!"

"Dude, chill, I'm a trader," Tad lied, and Kindle had to restrain herself from banging her head onto her hand.

The man lifted his lantern higher. "You're mighty young to be a trader, boy. And who's that? You got a lass there?"

"She's my sister, Jamie. She's a trader too," he effortlessly spouted. Kindle hoped the man couldn't see them very well—she and Tad looked much too different to pass for siblings. For a moment the man considered them then shook his head.

"No. No. Shops ain't even open this time of night. If you're so set on trading, come back in the morning."

"See," Kindle hissed, "I told you."

"Ay! What you whispering out there? I told you I got a bow! I'll use it!"

Tad shook his head and made a loud, disgusted sound. "Are you really gunna make a girl sleep on the cold ground? That's low, man," he chided then began to turn Nasah, but the man stopped them.

"Ay boy, you didn't say nothing about needing a place to sleep. If that's all you're after … you got minas, don't you? Just because you got a lass don't mean you're staying free."

"Yeah, 'course we do. Pft, you think we're idiots?"

The guard grumbled something inaudible then consented, "I'll only open the gate a smidge, so get in and get in quick."

To the right of the booth, part of the log wall creaked back just enough to let them through.

"Hide your sword," Tad breathed to her.

"Wha—?"

"Get it on your right side or he's gunna see it."

"Oh." Kindle twisted her sword belt around her waist so that it was hidden as they dashed by the guard's lantern. As soon as Nasah cleared the gate, it snapped shut.

"Now get on and don't tell anybody I let you in after dark!" the guard called from his booth as his lantern light faded. Kindle adjusted her sword back to its proper home and lifted her eyes to take in the village. From where they sat, Kindle couldn't see much. The ground was mostly dirt, and the houses, which looked more like a sad variety of scraggly shacks, dotted the land in a completely disorganized manner. As they slowly rode forward, the village only became more jumbled. The houses all faced a different direction, and while some sat alone, others bunched together as if they were cold. A few windows let light shine on their path, but most were dark. Other than the feeble house lights, only one lantern on a pole almost as tall as the enclosing wall lit their surroundings. Now that she was in the village and could see how creepy and unwelcoming it was, Kindle felt even less confident about spending any time in it.

"Okay, you got in here, good job. Now can we leave? This place is weird."

Tad laughed to himself, "He had no idea…."

"Uh, duh he had no idea." She lowered her voice. "You lied to him. You didn't have to lie, you know."

"Calm down. What's the big deal? He's never gunna know."

"How do you know?" she griped, irritated at him. "We're probably gunna get killed."

He gave a self-satisfied snicker, which only irked her more.

"Do you even know where you're going?"

"Yeah." He pushed his chin forward, and Kindle leaned around him. Straight ahead a building that was much bigger—two stories and at least three times as long as most of the houses—and much less sorry than all the others was emitting light through most of its windows.

"You think that's an inn?" she asked sassily.

He shrugged and Kindle rolled her eyes. "So you *don't* know where we're going."

"Yeah, I do," he retorted just as snarkily. "I'm the driver, remember?"

She huffed in agitation but at the same time couldn't help smiling at his remark. For a moment, she was glad no one else, especially Ella, was around to see her enamored grin, but as she remembered Ella, Kindle frowned.

"You think Ella and Andrew are okay? I mean, like, you think she'll be mad?"

"Who cares?" he muttered, "Bet her and Andrew are having a great time without me to mess up everything."

Kindle bit her lip then said, "No, she's probably worried about us. Are— are we really going to stay the night here?" They had reached the well-lit building and Kindle could see it was really just as rickety as every other structure. From far away, the wooden porch hanging over just the bottom floor had shadowed the worn and dirty windows and planks lining the front of the lower level. As they rode right up to the porch, Kindle saw it was actually more like a line of uneven boards hanging over another row of planks lying on the ground. Kindle almost decided that the second story was the only redeeming part of the building until she stared up and realized that one of the windows was broken and some of the boards had holes in them. The structure was not just unpleasant to view, it also stank. She searched for the source of the foul odor and noticed that smoke was floating out of a courtyard enclosed by a metal frame attached to the end of the building. Tad dismounted, and Kindle could tell from his grimace he was enjoying the stink as much as her.

"Because it really doesn't look like a place to sleep," she resurged her argument, "and it stinks."

Tad didn't appear to be listening, though. He was pushing his face against a window to see inside.

"Quit!" Kindle gasped, jumped down from Nasah, and yanked the back of his shirt. "Somebody is gunna see you, and we are gunna get in trouble and get shot…."

"Kin. We're not gunna get shot," he bluntly reassured her then smirked, "Nobody around here has a gun. If they're gunna kill us, they'll cut our guts out."

"Ugh!" she snorted and smacked his shoulder. "That makes me feel *so* much better."

He gave her his devilish grin then headed for Nasah. "It looks like a bar in there." Tad dug through a bag for a moment then asked, "*Do* we have any minas?"

"You told that guard we did ... why?"

"Because we need some to buy a room."

Kindle groaned and made a sick face. Tad steadily glared back.

"We're just gunna go in and see if they have a place, okay? If they don't, we'll leave. Does *that* make you feel better, Miss Priss?"

Kindle chose to ignore the insult. "Yes."

"Okay, then help me find some minas."

It didn't take long for them to discover a small bag of coins, and then Kindle followed Tad through the flimsy door painted with the word "Smith's". The inside smelled much better than the outside but, in Kindle's opinion, *looked* much worse. The square space was occupied by a long, dusty wooden bar; some rough tables that were as haphazardly placed as the houses outside; and a few bearded men whose malevolent stares were full of distrust. Tad ignored them and made a beeline for the bar and its tender, a thin old man who looked oily and wily enough to be a used car salesman. The man's large white eyebrows arched in a haughty manner when Tad leaned on the counter in front of him.

"You guys got rooms?" Tad coolly asked, as if he inquired of strangers in sordid places every day. The bartender said nothing. He inspected Tad then Kindle while his tongue fished around in his teeth. Being eyed by him made Kindle want nothing more than to dash back out to Nasah and ride out of the village, but she tried to act just as natural as Tad. So she didn't have to face the creepy old man, Kindle crossed her arms and examined the dusty shelves and half empty bottles arranged along the back wall.

"Hey! I'm not gunna stand here all night. You got any place we can stay or—?" Tad demanded, but the old man cut him off with a scratchy squawk.

"Get out of here! I'm not selling you kids nothing!" He shooed them wildly, and Kindle stepped back, ready to follow his order, but Tad stood his ground.

"We're not kids and—!"

"He can't hear you!" called one of the men behind them. Kindle glanced back to see the largest man push back his chair and stomp up to them. He was the most intimidating thing about Assula Kindle had seen so far. Once he stood right next to them, Kindle could see that he was probably twice as tall and three times as wide as her. Since his shirt sleeves were rolled up past his elbows, it was clear that his size came from brute muscle. His girth was quite threatening on its own, but his bushy black beard and one long braid that traveled along his otherwise bald head amplified his frightening biker-pirate demeanor. Kindle was sure he had to be a giant, and from the way he stank and the layer of black soot that almost entirely covered him, she wondered if he might be the reason for the great stink in the outside courtyard.

"He can't hear you," he repeated in a bellowing voice that matched his stature. "He's about deaf in both ears." The giant, dirty man leaned around Tad and put his great, ugly face right in the bartender's.

"I'll handle them, Pops!" he shouted, and the old man, after eyeing them one more time, nodded and drifted down the bar.

"So, what do you kids want?" he demanded, frowning down at Tad.

"We're not kids!" Tad insisted angrily.

"I don't care who you are. I asked you what you're doing here. Because as far as I'm concerned, you got no business—"

"We're just passing through," Kindle burst out apologetically. She could see Tad was fuming and wanted to defuse the situation. "We just…just wanted to get some, like, water and…."

"We need a place to stay," Tad growled between his teeth, and Kindle knew her attempt to calm them had more than failed.

The man snickered out of the side of his mouth. "And what? You think we got a place?" He turned and called to the men still at his table, "The kid wants a cozy crib to sleep in!" The others heartily laughed, and Kindle glanced sideways at Tad. His sneer was full of hatred. The giant bent down level with them and in a mocking voice, teased, "We ain't got no place for you soft little kids, so why don't you bug off and ruin somebody else's ni—arrgh!"

The man reeled sideways from Tad's incredible left hook as Kindle shrieked and every other man in the bar jumped to his feet.

"Tad!" Kindle gasped in horror, now completely sure they were going to die.

"What now?!" Tad ferociously yelled as the giant blinked at him.

Much too soon, though, he gathered himself up to his full, terrifying height and growled, "You little brat."

The man pounced toward Tad, and at the same moment Kindle instinctively yanked him out of harm's way. She tried to keep pulling him to the door, but Tad shook out of her hold and grandly unsheathed his sword. For one second, it seemed like everyone froze and held their breath, then Kindle tackled his arm and shattered it all.

"Tad, no! You know what Azildor said!"

He shot an angry glare at her, snapped his arm free, and ran up to face the large man. At first, it seemed as if Tad outmatched him, but before Tad could take a swipe, the giant pulled a knife from his belt with one hand and smashed a chair against the bar with the other. He evilly grinned at them as he held up his metal and shattered, splintered weapons.

"Okay, kid. You want a fight? We'll fight and see just what you're made of," he threateningly laughed, and his friends let out an excited, wild roar. Without hesitation, Tad began swiping at every inch of the giant he could reach. Kindle bit her lip as she watched the huge man catch Tad's attacks with the destroyed chair and simultaneously jab with the pointy little knife. Her fear was sending her mind in so many directions that all she could do was stand gaping at them. Suddenly a wretched crack rent through the air, and she saw that Tad's sword had embedded itself in the giant's wooden weapon. They both yanked the conjoined mass back and forth, growling and snarling in frustration. Then Kindle saw what Tad couldn't; an evil smile crossed the man's soot-covered face, and as he released his chair and sent Tad stumbling backwards, he winked an eye to aim his knife.

"Tad! Look!" she screamed, and just as the knife spun out of the giant's hand, Tad spied it and twisted out of its path. Relief spread over her, but a second later something like stinging fire shot through her veins. Unwilling to check it and make it a reality but unable to ignore it, Kindle slowly dropped her wide eyes. The knife was lodged into her thigh. Such dread overwhelmed her that she simply stared at it. The sight wiped her of any sensation or thought besides shock and pain. Nothing else entered her mind until somewhere outside of her senses, the huge man said something and laughed. Then Kindle, feeling as if she had been submerged underwater, slowly raised her eyes and they met Tad's. They were full of fear and fire. He tore them away and hurled an enraged growl at his opponent but yanked his sword out of the chair and into its sheath. Even though it felt like a silent eternity in which her leg grew hotter and hotter, in a few tumultuous seconds, Tad had reached her side and grabbed her arm. The sudden movement exacerbated her pain, and she gasped as if finally breaking over the surface of the dizzy sea she had been drowning in. Tad halted at her chilling inhalation, glanced at her leg, then locked eyes with her.

"You get to Nasah," he commanded through bared teeth then swung her behind him as he drew his sword and sent one of the men into retreat. With his words echoing in her mind, Kindle stumbled to the door as quickly as she could. Once outside, Nasah trotted to her and bent her head, shaking it in what Kindle thought was agitation.

"Nasah, Nasah," Kindle repeated soothingly, hoping to calm herself as well as her horse. She tried to mount Nasah, but every time the pain in her leg surged unbearably.

"Nasah, I need up!" she cried, an overwhelming panic filling her. "I need up!"

Just then the door crashed open, and Tad came barreling out of it. Without a word, he swung up onto Nasah and pulled Kindle up in front of him. Before either of them could take the reins, Nasah shot off through the collection of dismal little shacks. In what seemed like no time, Nasah had slowed to a halt in front of the village gate. Kindle felt Tad jump off and saw him sprint over to the little guard booth. She hadn't realized it until he left her and the world began to spin, but he must have been the only thing keeping her in the saddle. Kind heard distant shouting, and suddenly an especially dizzying spin pushed her forward down on Nasah's neck.

"Ugh … Nasah," she groaned and tried to find a handhold but slipped away from the warmth of her horse's mane.

"We're out," Tad's angry voice said in her ear, and she let her eyes close to shut out the terrible pain.

FIRE AND FOLIAGE

"What happened?"

"What does it look like?"

"Oh, my—Andrew, Andrew, help me."

Kindle could feel hands moving her. She tried to continue to block out everything and remain in unconscious bliss, but a flood of fire in her leg threw open her eyes, and an involuntary yelp of pain escaped from her mouth.

"Oh! Kindle, it's alright," Ella breathed from her right side. "Andrew, be careful, don't let her leg—"

Before Ella could finish her command, Tad shouldered Andrew aside and took his place.

"He was managing," Ella quite coldly mumbled, and Kindle blinked up at her.

"Yeah, whatever," Tad grumbled in return.

Still in her icy tone, Ella directed, "Here, lay her by the fire so I can see…." Once they had carefully placed Kindle near a crackling bonfire, though, Ella regained most of her cheerfulness.

"Alright Kindle, I need to pull this out." Kindle raised her head to see Ella wrap her hand around the now very bloody knife. Looking at it made her feel even more lightheaded.

"It's going to hurt, but you will be better for it. Re—"

"Tie it off first," Andrew interrupted. Kindle saw him standing back but grimacing at her leg.

"What?" Ella took her hand from the knife.

"Tie something around her leg—above the...," he gulped and averted his eyes, "so she doesn't bleed out."

"Oh." Ella peered around. "I'll find something. Andrew, I need some grass, I think, or some leaves—lively green stuff whatever it is."

Andrew gave her a look that was as puzzled as Kindle felt, but he drifted out of the firelight on his quest. Ella also disappeared for a moment and returned with Nasah's lead rope. She quickly, tightly secured it around Kindle's thigh then without warning, yanked the knife out in one swipe. At first it felt good to be rid of it, as if it had been some giant splinter and its presence was the only reason for pain, but then a dull but persistent throbbing swelled through her leg. Kindle could tell Ella was busy doing something but knew she didn't want to watch. Instead, she turned her head to gaze at the fire char and snap the twigs feeding it. Soon Andrew returned.

"I found some grass."

"Thank you. Um, could you rip it? Just as small as you can."

"Like this?"

"Smaller, I think...."

"Whoa!" Kindle cried as something burning hot infiltrated her wound.

"It's going to burn; it's alright," Ella reassured her as Kindle tried to see what was happening. "That's fine, Andrew. Place it in my hands and pour some water on."

Kindle watched Andrew follow her orders. Ella held the odd mix in her cupped hands, staring very intently at it. Then—Kindle had to blink hard and check Andrew's expression to make sure she wasn't hallucinating—steam began to curl up from Ella's handful.

"Ella...?" Andrew slowly said, and Kindle knew he saw it as well. Ella didn't reply, though, but suddenly dumped the burning water onto Kindle's wound. Watching it happen, Kindle tensed, expecting it to hurt, but a warm, pleasant sensation overthrew the awful throbbing and then both feelings ebbed away.

Ella sighed as if she had just finished a race. "Is it better now, Kin? Do you feel alright?'

Kindle sat up without any dizziness and bent her leg toward the firelight to examine it. The rip in her leggings and the blood all around it clearly marked where the knife had been, but even when she pulled the tear wider, Kindle couldn't find a cut or any sign one had ever existed. Andrew, who had been observing her, quietly asked the question forming in her own mind.

"Ella ... what did you do?"

Instead of answering, though, she bowed her head to untie the rope still around Kindle's thigh.

"How'd you do that, Ella?" Kindle urged, trying to see her expression.

"Do you feel alright?" Ella pushed with a twinge of irritation in her words.

"Yeah." Kindle sat back, hurt by her friend's tone. "I'm fine. I just wanted to know what you did. You like—"

"You're better now. That's all that happened," Ella defensively broke into her sentence as she stood. "You two should bed down. You need to sleep." Without giving them another glance, Ella hurriedly stepped out of the ring of firelight.

Kindle frowned at Andrew. "You saw what she did, right?"

He nodded and sat down by her feet. "She made that water boil ... in her hands."

"I knew you saw it too!" She scooted closer to Andrew to show him her leg. "And there's not even a scar or anything."

He turned away but not because of the sight. Kindle had heard what had caught his attention also.

"What was that?" she whispered. Andrew didn't have to answer, though; Tad's voice suddenly echoed through the night.

"Shut up! If you wouldn't have been such a nag, I wouldn't have gone to that stupid place!"

"Oh, don't you even blame this on me," Ella retorted. "You knew long before the day began that Assula was dangerous, but of course you decided to be bull-headed and gallivant off in pursuit of your whims."

"Shut up, Ella."

"No, Tad, it is time you start listening to someone other than yourself. You can't just rampage about doing whatever you like. Azildor told us not to enter that village at night, and if you had listened to him, that would not have happened. I suppose you forgot *everything* he said and didn't bother to tell a soul about our quest, didn't you?" Ella briefly paused to let him answer, but from what Kindle could hear, he did not. "Hm! No? No, I didn't believe you could be so generous as to think of anyone but yourself. It wasn't enough to endanger Kindle, you had to doom a whole village."

"I know what I did, okay?! I don't need your fat mouth to tell me!" Tad yelled then his heavy footsteps neared the fire.

Just as he came into view, Ella shouted, "I don't think you do understand, Tad—that would take caring about someone other than yourself!"

"Ella!" Kindle cried, unable to stay silent any longer, "Get off his case! You don't even know what happened. He didn't *endanger* me. I told him I wanted to go too. It was *our* idea to go. And yeah, it was a bad idea, but you know what? Tad's the only reason we got out alive. If it wasn't for him, I'd be dead!"

Ella slid out of the darkness, frowning. "Kindle, don't be theatrical. If it wasn't for his foolishness, you would never have been hurt at all."

Kindle rolled her eyes and picked herself up so she could stomp away. She knew Ella was probably right; she just wanted Ella to feel awful about avoiding her and Andrew and yelling at Tad. When she had rounded the fire, Kindle found she was at the edge of Danica Woods. She marched under the trees until the fire was just visible then planted herself on a tree root. Before long a set of footsteps approached. Sure it was Ella, Kindle warned, "I'm not gunna talk to you unless you're done being rude to everybody."

The footsteps halted, then Tad's voice begrudgingly grumbled, "Oh. I guess you hate me too, huh?"

"Oh! No, sorry. I thought you were Ella," she replied apologetically. "I don't hate you."

"Oh." He still didn't move. "You okay?"

"Huh?" Kindle, even though she didn't believe he was heartless, was surprised that he would ask if she was okay. "Uh, yeah. Ella's just being, like, so dramatic. I dunno, it's stupid."

"I meant your leg."

"Oh! Yeah, it's fine. Ella fixed it. That's why she's all mad."

"What?"

"Yeah, she dumped some grass and water on it and made it totally fine, but then she got all weird when me and Andrew asked her how she did it."

He sniffed, "She's mad at me, not you guys."

"Well, she shouldn't be mad at anybody. *She's* the one who everybody should be mad at. Like, who does she think she is yelling at you like that, you know? Ugh."

"I'm used to it."

"You're—" she paused as she remembered what he had told her about his grandma. "Ugh, well that's dumb too. She shouldn't of yelled at you. You didn't do anything wrong."

"Yeah, I did. I almost got us killed. Remember? That was my fault because I don't care about anybody but myself. And I bet Ella could tell you a million other ways I screwed up."

"Uh, did you not hear what I said back there?" Kindle asked much more gently than she had intended, "You kind of, like, saved me. You're a—"

"What? Hero?" He snorted at the word. "No, I'm not."

Kindle was glad it was dark and he couldn't see her conflicted face. She wanted to remind him of what Azildor had said about being a hero but still wanted to keep her eavesdropping a secret.

"Well, I think you are," she decided to say then immediately felt her cheeks blush and blurted. "You know, like, you could of finished that guy, but you didn't. You got us out of there instead." She waited for a response, but when he didn't offer one, Kindle began to fear what he could be thinking about her. "You know what I mean?" She sounded just as anxious as she felt.

"Yeah," he finally grunted. Unsure of how to take his answer, Kindle backed into her thoughts. Endless possibilities of what she could say or do to ascertain his thoughts rifled through her brain, but even though some were tempting, none seemed fair, and so she let silence spread open between them. After a long while, Tad huffed an angry sigh.

"What?" asked Kindle, glad to have an opening to pick his mind.

"I'm leaving. I'm not staying with you guys. All I do is mess stuff up."

Kindle almost laughed at the absurdity of his statement, but his seriousness stopped her. "You're not leaving, Tad," she sighed, as if asking him rather than telling him. "We need your help."

"I can't help you guys or anybody. I'm worthless." His footsteps sounded, and Kindle jumped up to follow them.

"Tad, you're not—uff." She smashed into his back.

"What're you doing?" he demanded in an exasperated tone.

"Coming with you."

"No. You go save the world with Ella and Andrew. Just leave me alone." He tried to walk away again, but Kindle dodged ahead of him and stood in his way.

"No, I told you before, Tad, you're not worthless and I'm not going to let you go off alone."

He huffed an agitated, hot breath in her face. "I'm never gunna get rid of you, am I?"

She smiled devilishly, knowing she had won. "Nope."

Another frustrated huff fell out of him before he pivoted and began stalking back toward the fire.

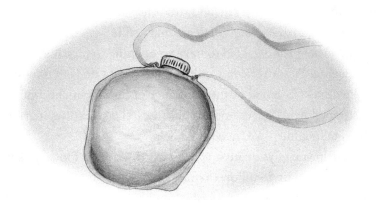

SKIRTING THE WALL

T he next morning, Kindle woke up slowly and reluctantly. When she and Tad had reached the fire the night before, Andrew had already fallen asleep on the ground, and so they each had found a spot and bedded down as well. Kindle thought she had picked the softest place possible, but now her aching, stiff body was assuring her otherwise. She rolled around, eager to find comfort and drift back to sleep, but between the light assaulting her eyelids and the distant conversation, she knew her battle was lost. Sitting up and staring around while she tried to stretch, Kindle saw all of their bags had been piled in the grass and Nasah had disappeared. Somewhat alarmed, Kindle gathered herself up and squinted all around.

"See dude, weird."

Kindle found Tad and glared at him. He and Andrew were sitting on the opposite side of the fire chewing on ears of corn.

"Where's Ella?" she demanded with her hands on her hips.

"Who cares?" Tad breezily laughed and chucked his bare corn cob into the low fire. Andrew gave him a sidelong look that was so subtly annoyed it made Kindle giggle.

"She went to Assula," Andrew answered. "She went when the sun was rising. She said it wouldn't take long."

"Well … how long's it been?" asked Kindle, staring at the faraway village.

"Oh, yeah, let me check my watch," Tad sarcastically snorted and held up a bare wrist.

Kindle rolled her eyes, causing Tad to laugh and slug Andrew.

Rubbing his shoulder, Andrew replied, "I don't know how long it's been, but she said we'd leave when she came back."

"That means breakfast." Tad grinned and tossed an ear of corn to her. After dusting it off, she took a bite and walked away from the boys. It was early enough that Tad's oddly playful mood irked her, and she knew it would be best for her to enjoy her breakfast alone. The fact that Ella had ridden off on Nasah also annoyed her. Before she had realized Ella was absent, she had been ready to forgive her for being so strange and rude, but now she wasn't sure if she wanted Ella to return. As she strolled around eating, Kindle prepared the perfect words to chew into Ella. A particularly vicious insult had popped into her thoughts when a neigh broke the peaceful morning and Ella rode up next to her.

"Good morning, Kindle!" she cheerfully called and then handed her a warm, wonderful smelling roll. "It's a morning bun and it's just been baked—at least that's what the shop lady said. I haven't ever eaten one, but it does smell lovely. Go on, eat it before those two see it and want one as well. I only bought one—that's all I felt right about buying with what little we have, but when I saw it, I thought you would so enjoy it and couldn't pass it."

Kindle stared up at Ella, then the bun, and felt her plan of attack shatter. "Thanks," she said weakly, now ashamed she had even tried to plot against Ella.

"Kindle, what's the matter?" Ella tilted her head in puzzlement as Kindle bit into her treat.

"Iff so bood!" she woefully cried through her mouthful then looked up at Ella. "Ib—" Kindle stopped to swallow. "I'm sorry Ella."

"Sorry? Whatever for? What's happened?"

"For yelling at you—you know, last night? I was just mad, you know? I—I just wanted you to quit yelling at Tad. I'm sorry."

"Oh, Kin, it's alright. We all had our tempers too high last night, and it's just as well you did give me my share of reproach. I know I was wrong to shout like that ... I don't believe I've ever scolded anyone so strongly. I just have never met a boy so hardheaded." Ella sighed and shook her head.

"He thinks you hate him," Kindle confided. "He thinks you think he's worthless and a screw-up."

"No, of course not. I don't think he's horrid or careless or anything that I may have shouted. Everyone makes mistakes, and his just happened at an especially unfortunate place and time, I suppose. I meant to and I still will talk to him ... or perhaps just a quick apology would suit him better."

Kindle nodded then grimaced up at Ella. "Just don't tell him I told you, okay? I just don't want him to get, like, mad that I told you."

"Kin, do you fancy him?" Ella quickly asked, and before Kindle could think, she blurted, "What? No! No, what?"

Ella slyly smiled, and Kindle took another bite of the bun to keep herself from saying anything else.

When they reached Tad and Andrew, the boys had already extinguished the fire and were waiting by all of the bags. Ella dished out a handful of her wares—some squares that looked and tasted like crackers—while they loaded Nasah. Then once it was decided Kindle would ride first, they started off in the direction that Andrew pointed. He reminded them that Iteraum would be their next stop and that it would take at least two days to reach it.

The two days' walking and scenery—Danica's towering trees on one side, endless green grass on the other—remained the same and left Kindle feeling drained of thought and motivation. If not for their ride shifts, which lasted only as long as it took for the one riding to become stiff or antsy, and Ella's endless stories, Kindle was sure that a combination of her boredom and aching feet would have knocked her over dead. In fact, Ella was the only one who seemed lively at all. She chattered on about how Iteraum was the only city that even came close to Garrick Kingdom in size and told every story she had ever heard about it. Kindle didn't mind her long-winded tales about the city's supposedly towering castle, rich people, and amazing royal family, but every so often she would catch up to Tad, who still seemed to despise Ella and refused to move anywhere near her even though Kindle had watched her apologize to him. Even when they camped that night, Tad made a point to shovel his dinner and stomp away to sleep as far from Ella as possible.

It made Kindle nervous that they camped a second night before seeing the city, but Andrew assured them that they were going the right way. He even seemed positive that he could hear the river that ran along the southern side of the city. Kindle hoped he was right but never heard the water even when everyone else fell asleep and all other noises hushed.

Before they dug through their bags for lunch the next morning, though, Iteraum's high city walls came into view. Seeing them roused true excitement in Kindle, and she urged Ella to tell her about all they could do once inside. Andrew listened silently until their banter slowed then interjected that they had to go to the river first.

"But isn't it on the *other side* of the city?" Kindle complained. "That will take forever. Why can't we just go in? I know Azildor didn't say we had to stay out of it."

"We need water," Andrew simply replied, and Ella reluctantly nodded.

"He's right, Kin," she sighed, "we've nearly dried up our supply."

"Why can't we just get some *in* Iteraum—the water will be better there anyway," argued Kindle, and Ella gave her a strange look.

"The river doesn't flow into the city, and it's all the same no matter where you draw it from."

"No, I mean, like, we'll just buy some or get it from a sink somewhere." Kindle saw Andrew grin at her comment and crossed her arms defensively. "What?"

"They won't have bottled water or sinks. I don't think plumbing exist here."

"It did at the Chokmah's. They had a sink."

"They had a well. That basin didn't have a faucet."

"Oh." Kindle frowned—she wasn't just wrong, she looked like an idiot. "Okay, fine. We'll go to the river. I'll go tell Tad," she grumbled and strode away from them. She knew that since Tad was riding Nasah behind them, he would be able to pick up on where they were heading on his own, but she didn't want to be around Andrew and Ella feeling humiliated.

"What?" he demanded when she met him. Tad's tone was rude, but by now she knew that was just what he always sounded like regardless of his mood.

"We're not going to Iteraum. Andrew said we have to go to the river first."

"That's stupid."

"Yeah, that's what I said, but I guess we're, like, out of water and the river's the only place to get it."

Tad mumbled, "Whatever." Then he glared at the growing city walls. Ella hadn't exaggerated when she told them how enormous Iteraum was; even though they still had a short distance to travel before they reached it, Kindle could tell that the light-grey stone walls towered higher than the fancy hotels featured in posh commercials on TV. The size of the city walls hardly seemed believable until they actually stood in their shadow. As they veered near the towering stone wall, Kindle gazed up at it and tried to guess how many stories high it could be but never fully decided on a number as they walked beside it. As the morning wore on into a warm afternoon, her mind trailed away to imagining what lay on the other side of the wall. The whole rest of the day she silently walked beside Nasah and Tad, mentally forming a plan of what she and Ella might do once inside Iteraum.

It wasn't until late in the evening when they finally passed the enormous corner of the wall that the river at the bottom of a slope pulled Kindle back to the present. Seeing the broad expanse of water, Kindle secretly rejoiced that Andrew had mandated they refill their water supply. Even the large jug Azildor had given them had been emptied during the day, and she could tell from everyone's vain attempts to persuade their dry canteens to yield just one more thirst-quenching drop that they were all parched.

Ella led them along the south wall of Iteraum until they found a flat spot to camp for the night. Kindle dropped her pack and headed down the steep but short hill to scoop up what she dreamed would be a refreshing, cool drink, but Ella suddenly stood in her way.

"I'll fill your canteen for you, Kin. You stay here and rest."

Before Kindle could object, Ella had swiped her canteen and jogged to the river bank. Kindle plopped down and watched her carefully tip each container to catch the current. She could hear Andrew and Tad setting up what they needed for the night behind her and knew she should help, but Ella's diligence held her captive. A curious thought was shaping in her mind when the boys walked up and threw it off track.

"Shouldn't we boil the water?" asked Andrew, frowning sickly at the river.

"What? You think the river's, like, dirty?" Kindle gazed up at him, hoping the disgust forming on her own face was for nothing. The river didn't appear dirty; in fact, it was one of the clearest rivers of its size that she had ever seen.

"I don't know. But boiling it would definitely make it safe."

"Hey, Ella!" Tad yelled with an evil grin. "Quit! That nasty water's gunna kill us!"

"Tad! She's just trying to help," gasped Kindle, silencing Andrew's mumbling about how he never said that the water would kill them. Ella gave them a passing glance but waited until the last canteen overflowed before joining them. She passed Kindle and Andrew their canteens, shoved Tad's at his chest, and in a voice strained between anger and pseudo-cheerfulness, said, "It is safe. No need to boil it or worry over it." A smile that was just as forced as her geniality flashed across her face before she trooped over to the pitiful attempt of a fire pit Andrew and Tad had created.

"We won't have a fire tonight," she curtly stated. "It could attract someone. Drink what you need and then bed down for the night."

"Pft. Okay, boss," Tad sarcastically grumbled then swigged a mouthful of water.

"It is only a suggestion," Ella, now done hiding her anger, huffed. "Do whatever you like." She snatched the water jug and started for the river.

"Whatever," Tad mischievously challenged, and Ella glared daggers at him but continued on her mission. Tad laughed but meandered up to the wall to do exactly what Ella had suggested.

"You're a jerk!" Kindle informatively called up to him then gulped some of her water. The warmth of the liquid that filled her mouth surprised her so much, she had to press the back of her hand on her lips to keep from spitting it out.

"Ugh, it's warm," she groaned in disgust once she had swallowed it. Andrew took a hesitant sip from his.

"It's hot," he gasped, blowing the heat out. "She *did* boil it."

Kindle shot a thoughtful look up at him. "You think? Just like she did at ... at...?"

"Assula," he finished her question and Kindle nodded.

"How? You think like ... I dunno, what do you think?"

"I don't know," Andrew whispered, shaking his head. He did look thoroughly perplexed.

"You should go ask her," Kindle urged as she stood and gave him a little push. "I bet she'll tell you if you ask."

"What?" He retreated against her hand. "I don't think—"

"She will," Kindle persisted, "She likes you—I mean, like, she likes to talk to you. You know?"

"Uh—"

"Okay. Okay, you go—" she nudged him forward again, "—and I'm gunna go to sleep. Okay? So ... go." Kindle ran him forward a few steps then spun and dashed to the fire pit. Quickly she lay down and flipped on her side to make sure Ella didn't suspect her of spying. Kindle planned to roll over after a few minutes to check Andrew's progress, but fatigue stealthily crept over her and knocked her into deep sleep.

UNDENIABLE INVITATION

Kindle awoke the next morning to something tickling her face. Half conscious, she tried to brush it away, but it persisted. In a burst of annoyance, she frantically rubbed her whole arm over her face then held her arm back to examine it. Nothing. The thought entered her sleepy mind that it probably had been a bug crawling over her. She shivered at the idea and tried not to dwell on it but began to feel imaginary legs creeping on her skin. Feverishly brushing off every inch of herself, she sat up to check for any little bugs, but saw none. Kindle huffed and rubbed her eyes. Now she was wide awake because of a silly itch, and as far as she could tell from the sky, it was still night. Her initial notion was to lie back down and try to fall asleep, but the ground repulsed her too much. After a quick survey of her companions, who all three were still asleep, she quietly searched through the bags until she found her old clothes then snuck down the slope and away along the river.

In her own home, Kindle begrudged waking up early and always wanted to hunker back under her covers. Every day, though, she would force herself out of bed to beat Mikey to the shower. Being the first one in their single upstairs bathroom meant hogging all of the hot water and taking her time to make her hair perfect. Kindle believed her morning shower was the one single good thing about mornings and so now hoped to find a place to bathe and perhaps wash away the feeling of bug legs on her skin. She knew a waterfall wasn't likely to pop into sight but hoped to at least find somewhere shallow but with a strong current. As dirty as she felt, though, Kindle was ready to settle for any sort of cleansing she could get, and once she had walked long enough to lose sight of the camp, she did settle for the first spot she saw a sign of a current near the bank. Not wanting to be caught unclothed, she quickly changed into her t-shirt and jean shorts and waded into the river. The water that enveloped her feet was colder than she had expected. For a moment Kindle wondered if her venture was a bad idea after all, but she left the doubt and determinedly sloshed deeper. Once the river ran around her torso, it didn't seem so cold, so she stopped and commenced her makeshift shower time. At first Kindle felt silly and embarrassed, trying to bathe her half-clothed self in a public place, but after she began to scrub some of the dirt away, triumph also washed away her awkwardness.

Just like her usual shower at her house, Kindle spent more time grooming herself than she intended and ended her bath only when she noticed the sky beginning to lighten. She flipped her wet hair out of the flowing river one last time and turned to the bank. Instead of wading back, though, she sank down so only her head stuck out of the water. An unfamiliar horse with a stranger on it was trotting her way. It was a shining black horse, huge and intimidating, and Kindle feared that the person on it would prove to be an enemy. A million escape plans tripped over one another in her mind, but none outshone another as achievable or even reasonable, and so she simply remained frozen, staring at the oncoming rider.

As the horse neared the spot on the bank where she had left her clothes, Kindle tried to examine the rider. He was difficult to see because his entire outfit matched the color of his horse. Only his face and brown hair gave away his presence and identity. He never looked fully her way, but his profile showed that he was too young to be a man but too old to be a kid. Kindle held her breath as he rode right past her pile on the bank. She almost let a sigh out in relief, but the rider halted his steed and curiously glanced back. He turned his horse then jumped down and paced over to her clothes. Kindle desperately hung on to her hope that he at least would not notice her, but a second later he shattered the hope. Upon spying her, he stumbled back a few steps as if shocked.

"Hello there!" he called in a voice accented like Ella's. "Are you alright?"

Kindle bit her lip and didn't say anything. He seemed friendly, but she still wanted to avoid stumbling into trouble.

"Are you in need of assistance?" he called and began to unlatch a boot. Kindle rolled her eyes, now sure no hope remained of pretending to not exist.

"Yeah, I'm fine!" she replied and stood up, sure he would laugh at her sopping wet ensemble. The boy suddenly blocked his eyes and averted his face.

"My apologies, I did not intend—!"

"Hey! It's fine. I'm not naked or anything," she laughed at his sudden embarrassment. Unconvinced, he maintained his stance until Kindle reached the bank and walked around him to prove her words.

"See?"

Hesitantly he lifted his face, and Kindle was sure she looked just as taken aback as he did. He was gorgeous. Kindle had never so immediately and thoroughly been assured of this fact about anyone else, but now, standing only a foot from him, she was positive the word had been created for him. It was as if his face had been chiseled from marble by some great sculptor; his bone structure was well defined and made him appear strong, mysterious, and soft all at once. To her, everything about him from his soft brown eyes and hair to his full lips struck her as perfect. Suddenly, Kindle felt immensely glad she had chosen to scrub the dirt and stink off herself.

"Yes, I see," he replied and shook her from her awed stupefaction.

"Heh—yeah," she laughed without really knowing why. Her head felt gaily light and thoughts eluded her.

"Are these your articles?" he asked, walking to her clothes but never taking his eyes from hers.

"Yeah … yeah, I was just, like, swimming, you know, and I didn't want to get those wet."

"Ah. Do you live in the city? I do not believe I have seen your face before."

"Oh, um, no ... I'm just kind of traveling. Well, not just me—I'm with a couple other people, but, you know, we're just ... just on our way somewhere else." Kindle knew Azildor had told them to explain their journey to everyone they met, but she dreaded that the full truth would turn her into a laughingstock in his eyes. She quelled her guilt by assuring it she would divulge the reason of their journey if he asked about it.

He nodded then smiled and said, "That is why I do not recognize you. I know I would not forget a face as lovely as yours."

In that moment, Kindle forgot everything Azildor had told her—and quite truthfully everything except the boy. She had always believed that her appearance was obnoxiously normal and plain, and so hearing such a complimentary remark from this gorgeous boy sent her spinning in girlish delight.

"Really?" she sighed, smiling.

"Of course. Tell me, what is your name? I must know."

"Kindle. Kindle McDonnell."

"Kindle," he repeated and held his hand out as if he wanted to shake hers. When she returned the gesture, though, he bowed slightly and placed a kiss on the back of her hand. "It is my pleasure to meet you. I am prince Adlic of Iteraum."

"Prince?" Kindle stumbled over the word, unable to believe it.

"Yes, at least until tomorrow evening. Then my father, King Diamas, will transfer his kingship to me at my coronation ball." He paused to gaze at the sand. "You say you do not live in the city, but perhaps you have caught wind of this?"

"Uh, no, sorry. I really don't live anywhere around here."

"Garrick?" he inquired, almost suspiciously.

"No, uh, it's really far away, you probably wouldn't know it ... but you're having a ball? Like a dance?"

"Yes, we will have music, dancing, and much festivity. My father insisted on a large celebration to honor my succession. I will be the youngest king Iteraum has ever seen, and my father hopes I will find a queen at the ball."

"Oh." Kindle's tone revealed her sudden inhibition.

Adlic grinned, "Yes, I was shocked as well. Marriage was not what I meant to gain with my kingship. But I must at the least humor his well-meaning intention and spend the evening dancing with the maidens that attend."

"Oh," she sighed, glad he was not about to ask her to marry him. "Well, that doesn't sound that bad, um, I mean—"

"No, it will not be so unappealing to simply delight the subjects of my city with my presence. I am sure, however, it would be much more enjoyable if you would attend. If it is not too forward to ask, would you perhaps grace me with your presence at the ball?"

Kindle took a moment to process his offer. "Uh, yeah. Yeah! I'd love to … but, uh…."

"What is it?"

"I dunno if I can. I mean, like, I don't know how long we're gunna stay here. The people I'm with probably won't want to stay until tomorrow night." Kindle dropped her head. "And anyway, I don't really have anything nice to wear."

"Even dressed as you are, you would be a gem brighter than the other maidens. As for your companions, perhaps I could speak with them to persuade—?"

"No, no, that's okay," Kindle hurriedly interrupted. She was sure Adlic would fail to convince Andrew, Ella, or especially Tad of anything. "I'll try and get them to stay until then, but…."

His smile began to fall, and she quickly changed her words.

"I'm sure they'll be okay with it. You know, once I tell them how great you are … uh, I'll see you then, okay?" Kindle gathered her dry clothes in a nervous flurry and then before he could answer, dashed back to camp.

A small spiral of smoke rising into the air told her that someone was awake, and when Kindle saw only Ella sitting by the small fire, she wanted to jump in exultation. She was sure if she could persuade Ella to stay in Iteraum for the ball, Andrew would follow her lead and regardless of what Tad wanted, his lone opinion wouldn't determine their schedule. Before Ella could dig into her for sneaking away without telling anyone, Kindle shushed her and excitedly recounted her encounter with Adlic.

"And then he asked if I'd come to the ball, Ella," she finished dreamily. "And he asked all sweet and it was just so … ah!"

Ella grinned, clearly also entranced. "Oh, Kin, that does sound lovely.

Was he really so handsome? Our washerwoman Sara said she heard from a friend how winning the prince was here, but I hardly believed it. So, however did you tell him you couldn't go?"

Kindle bowed her head and murmured, "I didn't."

"Kindle," Ella sighed in a reproachful tone but kept her grin. "He was so taken with you—how could you lie to him?"

"No, I didn't lie—I told him I didn't know if I could. I told him I'd ask you guys about it."

"Oh, Kin, you know we can't linger. We must get to Letum as quickly as possible."

Her words inspired a wonderful idea to blossom in Kindle's mind. "Yeah, I know, but remember how Azildor told us to tell everybody about the evil guy? I bet there's gunna be, like, everybody in the whole city at the ball, and it'd be so easy to just tell everybody right there. You know? And he acted like it was a really big deal, so maybe people from other places will be there too."

Ella gazed thoughtfully at her lap. "I don't know … that would keep us here for at least two full days."

"Oh, come on Ella, *please*. You know it'll be totally worth it. We'll get to tell a bunch of people and dance … *and* you'll get to see prince Adlic."

"Alright," Ella finally conceded, and Kindle shook her fists in excitement. Giggling at her glee, Ella tried to sternly say, "But we leave as soon as you've had your dance."

ITERAUM

O nce Tad and Andrew had eaten some breakfast, they set out around the wall of Iteraum to find its entrance. The ride to the high arched opening that welcomed them into the opposite side of the city took almost the whole day, but Kindle was so full of excitement that the morning and afternoon breezed by. Her elation peaked as they passed through the grand arch with another group of jolly travelers eagerly chatting about the coronation. Kindle had to stifle her temptation to join them and gush about Adlic and the ball. She knew Andrew and Tad were likely to oppose staying for it and wanted to put off that argument for as long as possible. Kindle did slide Ella a covert smile, though, and received a sly wink. Soon the happy troop trailed away, and Kindle distracted her jubilant mind by taking in the city around them.

The streets, which were paved with the same light-grey rocks that composed the walls, were packed with unending crowds of all sorts of people. Kindle wondered if most of them lived in Iteraum and were always mulling so leisurely up and down the wide streets. As they wove around the barricades of bodies, she caught a few conversations and decided that the hubbub had to be due to the citywide celebration. Every voice she heard was rambling about festivities, the king and prince, or the ball. She stared around, hungry for more information about anything happening, and noticed the crowds overwhelmed all of the streets that they passed. Even though people seemed to fill every inch of the huge city, Kindle was sure they could never become lost. All of the streets were tagged with names in large script and were so broad and orderly, it was as if they had been carefully planned on a grid. Also, like a beautiful, sparkling mountain, a white castle festooned with green flags stood right in the center of the entire city, assuring everyone of their location. Everything about the castle, the large shops lining the streets, and even the laughing crowd was cheerful and welcoming, and Kindle immediately decided that Iteraum was nearly as gorgeous as Adlic. Wide-eyed, she happily gazed around and saw from Tad's snarling frown he did not believe the same.

"Isn't this place wonderful?" she sighed, hoping to change his mood.

He stared at her as if he smelled something rotten. "If you like a bunch of people standing around like stupid cows."

Kindle tried her best to swallow her laughter as a woman searched for the origin of the insult. Once she had disappeared, Kindle giggled, "That wasn't nice. That lady thought you called her a cow."

"Yeah, so? She is. And so is everybody else around here."

Suddenly they emerged from the mob they had been swimming through and Ella led them under the awning of a corner building. She commanded them to wait while she went inside then left them standing against the stone wall.

"Stupid cows," Tad muttered to himself, glaring at the mob nearby. "Why's everybody standing around anyway?"

"I think some kind of celebration is going on," Andrew replied and Kindle blinked in surprise. She hadn't heard Ella say anything to him and wondered how he knew. As if he could sense her questions, Andrew continued, "I heard some people talking about a coronation and the prince here being famous. I guess him becoming king is the reason so many people are here."

"Yeah," Kindle quickly chimed in. "I heard somebody say they're gunna have a ball at the castle for it. We could go, you know, just to, like, tell every-body about how Anelthalien's in trouble and all that." She heard the slight desperation in her voice but hoped the boys would miss it.

Tad raised an eyebrow and snorted, "A ball?"

"We don't have to go. We could just tell everyone right here," Andrew pointed out, and Kindle bit her lip as he and Tad stared at the masses just feet from them. She tried to concoct another plan to trap them into attend-ing the ball, but after a few minutes, Kindle realized it was not necessary; neither Andrew nor Tad had said a word or moved an inch.

"So ... are you not gunna talk to anybody right now?" she asked, trying to not sound delighted.

Andrew didn't respond, but his worried, slightly widened eyes soaking in the vast number of strangers satisfied her question almost as well as Tad's grumbled, "Forget these cows."

Kindle turned to stroke Nasah so they couldn't see her pleased grin. Before long, Ella returned humming to herself.

"Alright you lot, I—" She rocked back on her heels and surveyed their faces. "Now what has gone on while I left you three? You two look utterly dismal." She flipped her hand between Tad and Andrew.

"We're going to the ball," Kindle replied in a singsong voice, and Ella's face fell into confusion.

"What? Is that why you're downcast?" she questioned Andrew.

Tad replied instead, though. "I'm not going to some stupid tutu show."

"Yes, you are." Ella brushed aside his rebellion. "Now, Andrew, is that what you're worrying over as well?"

"I'm not worried!" Tad defensively interjected, attracting a few startled looks from a nearby group. He snarled at them, and they hurriedly edged down the street. "And no, I'm *not* going." He crossed his arms. "What hap-pened to you not being so bossy, huh?"

"Whatever happened to you being decent?" Ella snapped then shook her head. "The woman in there told me that all the shops have closed for the evening festivities—something about a royal promenade—so we must stay until at least tomorrow morning if you plan on having any food for the journey, and…," her tone changed as she winked at Kindle, "the barmaid has said she would let us stay free if we help with service tomorrow evening."

"I'm not help—" Tad began to protest, but Ella cut him off.

"She said every place in the city is nearly full to bursting and what's left costs a year's wages or more. We can't pay that. Either you work or you bum about in the street." Ella returned his angry glare with an equally triumphant one. Slowly, one corner of her mouth lifted. "*Or*, you could escort Miss Kindle to the ball. There now, are you happy? I've not bossed you—I've informed you of your choices."

Tad looked far from happy. He silently seethed at her then grumbled an insult and stomped to the door. Before he could punch it open, though, Ella spoke again.

"They haven't a room inside."

"But I thought you said we're staying here," commented Kindle, nervous she had heard wrong.

"We are…." Her grin slid into an apologetic twist. "In the stable."

"Forget that," Tad snorted in disgust and angrily trounced off into the crowded street.

"Well that's fine if it doesn't suit him," Ella murmured to herself while Andrew and Kindle stared between her and the spot where Tad had disappeared.

"We're supposed to stay together," Andrew softly said and caused Ella to sigh and avoid his gaze. Kindle wanted to gripe at her but could tell she already felt bad.

"I'll go find him," Kindle mumbled and dove into the maze of people where Tad had entered it. She wove her way down the street trying to detect any sign of his blue shirt or dark hair but saw no one and nothing even remotely like him. After what seemed like much too long of a time, a twinge of panic crept on her and suggested her search had turned into an aimless, fruitless goose chase. Kindle halted and tried to determine where she stood.

Nothing looked familiar, and she really hadn't expected anything to, but as she slowly realized that she couldn't see the front gate, castle, or the building where Ella and Andrew were, hopeless desperation overcame her. Immediately she began to recall everything she had ever been told to do when lost. The idea to retrace her steps hit her first. Kindle turned a circle in the sea of people, then another, trying to remember which way she had come from, but the crowd shifted so constantly and sporadically that the street changed every second. Pushing that plan aside, she remembered that her mother had always told her to just stay put if she found herself lost. The advice, though, blew out of her mind like smoke.

Suddenly all she could think about was her mom, family, and home and how much she wished she could see them. Sadness then anger pooled in with her panic, and before she knew what she was doing, Kindle started down the street. She had no direction but simply wanted to go home— away from the people and shops and all of Anelthalien—and somehow the tramping made her feel better, as if it really was moving her further from the unfamiliar world surrounding her.

She continued pushing past unconcerned people for a long while. Remembering her real home made everything around her seem distant and fragile like a cardboard backdrop waiting to tip over. Compared to her home, which was so clear and fixed in her mind, the city felt so temporary and fake. She wished it would draw back and let her return to her real life. Visualizing an escape from Iteraum urged her antagonistic thoughts toward Anelthalien to grow louder. It was all fake—just a stupid dream like Tad had said—and it needed to end. A whole other world that no one knew about just could not exist. Surely it and everything in the whole land was an obnoxiously long dream she would stir out of at any moment.

Kindle was so wrapped in her thoughts she knocked into a smiling old man who cheerfully hailed her. Her feet refused to stop, but she did turn to see his happy face. It only deepened her new conviction that everything about Anelthalien was absurd. No one would be so happy in a world so apparently close to ending, but she was in a city full of exuberant people. It just did not make sense—the whole story about a good and evil throne *had* to be false. It had to be a myth Azildor had created just to scare them into being good or something like that.

Suddenly Kindle halted. The slowly thinning crowds, if they noticed her at all, hadn't seen it, but a tidal wave had just crashed over all of her inflamed thoughts. It had rolled up from the back of her mind where Azildor had placed it the last night they had spent with him. He had told them that they would start to think it was all a lie. Way back then he had known right now she would doubt it all. The massive force of the wave that had quieted her, though, was driven by what he had said right after that.

"Remember all that is true."

Then, in the beautiful safety of the Chokmah home, the truth had been so clear. Every word he had said about Anelthalien and its unseen struggle had made perfect, undeniable sense. Now, though, the stories he had told seemed more like a faraway mist.

Kindle gazed around at the sturdy stone buildings sparkling slightly in the setting sun's light. Then slowly, almost unconsciously, she let her fingers settle on the chain of her necklace. More than just feeling it, her fingertips *knew* it by now. Nothing about it was shaky or distant. It still hung around her neck exactly as it had since she had put it on. It, just like the solid world around her, was undeniably true and real. She bowed her head to examine the red jewel at the end of her chain and felt somewhat guilty for denying the little painted dragon on it. It had never left her, but she had forgotten it and all it proved.

"Sorry," she whispered at it then, feeling slightly embarrassed but also better, tucked it back under her shirt. As she did, a light snicker caught her attention, and she searched wildly for its maker.

"Talking to yourself, huh?" Tad laughed. Kindle wanted to roll her eyes at him but couldn't find the gumption against his oddly deriding but warm grin.

"No. I just…." She suddenly realized that all of the crowds had vacated the street around them and, besides herself, Tad was the only human nearby. "How'd you find me?" she decided to ask.

He shrugged. "I followed you."

"You—how'd you find me? And why did you just follow me? I've been looking for you for, like, ever. You could of told me you weren't lost."

"You're not hard to find." He leaned against the wall behind her and crossed his arms. "And what's it matter if I followed you? You're always doing it to me."

Kindle, unable to argue and still trying to reconstruct her thoughts, just bit her lip while vaguely squinting at his feet.

"What?" he finally grunted.

"This is real."

"What?" He squished his face in confusion.

"This—like, all of this and Anelthalien and all that stuff Azildor told us—it's really real."

"You're being weird."

"No—ugh." She fully faced him to explain. "It's just like . . . I was walking, and I started thinking about going home and then . . . I dunno, I guess I got mad and . . . and. . . ." She tried to find words that wouldn't reveal the wickedness and stupidity of her thoughts but couldn't. "And I started to think that it was all fake or a big lie or whatever. Like, I didn't believe the stuff about the thrones or our necklaces or that Anelthalien was real or anything, but . . . but it all is. It really is."

Tad simply continued to stare at her as if she was crazy.

"Don't you remember?" she pleaded, frustrated he didn't seem to comprehend the enormity of her epiphany. "Azildor told us we'd think like that. He said everybody else didn't believe any of it and we probably would too but we couldn't—we had to believe. He told us we had to remember what was really true. Remember?"

His eyes shifted. She could tell he was thinking. Leisurely he said, "Yeah, so?"

"So . . . Tad, I think that's why he got all mad about me having your necklace." She drew hers out and held it. "He wanted us all to wear our own because it's how we remember that everything we're doing isn't stupid or fake. Like, you get it? Our necklaces are supposed to remind us what we really have to do and keep us remembering all that stuff about the good and evil thrones and . . . and just everything that's really true." She stopped, completely out of words but hoping the ones she had spoken had manifested her wave of realization.

His face still held some apprehension, but he tugged out his own blue gem and stared at it.

"It's supposed to tell us what to do?"

"Yeah, but like, I mean ... I dunno. It's not gunna *talk,* but just it coming and finding us in our world and bringing us here and not letting us leave ... I mean, it just proves we're supposed to be here doing something important. Something to do with these. You know?"

"So ... they tell us to remember all that?" he flatly asked.

"Yeah. To remember what's true."

For a moment, Tad grinned at his necklace, and Kindle wondered if he also felt the same attachment and trust as she did to hers. All too soon, though, a snarl reoccupied his face, and he let the gem fall against his chest.

"Whatever," he mumbled without conviction.

"What? You don't believe me?" Kindle asked, afraid he not only thought she was dumb but also crazy.

His eyes ran over her face then glared down the street. "I dunno. Maybe. You know what everybody's doing over there?"

"Huh?" Kindle blinked around, trying to make sense of his answer, and saw what he meant. The crowds of people had gathered in one spot a long way down the street. At first it seemed odd that they would compact themselves even more, but then she considered an explanation.

"Didn't Ella say that a parade or something was going on?" Suddenly excitement of seeing Adlic fluttered in Kindle, and she cried, "C'mon, let's go see!"

Before Tad could reply or even move, Kindle sped away toward the mass of people. Tad caught her long before they reached the crowd but they arrived at the same time. Even though she was short of breath, Kindle hopped up and down, hoping to see over everyone's head.

"Can you see anything?!" she yelled to Tad over the enormous racket.

"No!" he shouted back then grabbed her arm and started pushing his way through the sea of bodies. Kindle was sure someone would shove them back for being so rude, but no one paid an ounce of attention to them. Soon they surfaced on the other side of the crowd. Even more cheering berated their ears now, but Kindle hardly noticed it; she was engrossed in the fleet of horses proudly marching a foot away from her. All of the horses calmly stepped in unison thanks to their golden blinders and wore gold and white ribbons in their manes and green streamers over their rumps. The men sitting atop the matching brown animals appeared just as aloof and synchronized as their steeds. Each rider held his stoic face straight ahead and was dressed in the same white-and-gold-buttoned riding uniform.

Kindle tired to spy what approached after the militant riders but could only see endless lines of the green crests bobbing on their golden helmets. She impatiently watched the parade for a while then turned to search for a friendly face. A girl, who could have been her age, stood cheering a few steps away. Kindle squeezed her way to the girl, tapped her shoulder, and yelled, "Who are these guys?!"

"The royal army of course!" she paused to explain before returning to her adoring shouting.

Kindle tapped her again. "Did prince Adlic already go by?!"

"No! Are you from another city or daft?! He and King Diamas are at the end!"

Kindle tried to grin as she nodded in understanding. The girl gave her a momentary look of puzzlement then turned back to the parade. Careful to stay on the sidewalk, Kindle made her way back to Tad.

"Did she say this stupid thing was gunna end soon?!" he yelled, annoyance saturating his face.

"Um…I dunno!" Kindle shrugged. "She said the king and the prince were at the end!"

He craned his neck but, just like her, must have seen nothing because he moodily plopped down on the ground. His sulking made Kindle shake her head. Even if he refused to enjoy the parade, she was still going to have fun and watch it.

The ranks of soldiers continued to ride by as the sky continued to darken. One by one they began lighting small lanterns, which they then hung on the ends of long batons. Soon the tiny, floating lights illuminated the whole street. The scene reminded Kindle of the night watchmen's path in Danica Woods, and she giggled to herself. The thought of the soldiers being bugs entertained her, and for a while she squinted and twisted her head different ways until she could almost imagine the men were white moths with funny green antennae drooping over their golden heads.

After the last horses finally passed, a myriad of men and women playing all sorts of instruments filed into view. Kindle recognized some flutes, trumpets, and hand harps but couldn't identify every instrument. Whatever they all were, they worked together to create a jovial march that led a great part of the crowd to clap along with its prominent beat. The beat boomed louder and louder, and soon two percussionists pounding large drums ended the band. Once all of the musicians had faded from her view and left the street empty, all the noise ebbed away to a wave of excited whispers. Then, as the next spectacle shone out of the night, everyone hushed.

A triangle of bright lanterns swinging from the tips of white flagpoles glided up the street. They emitted enough light to display the flags that hung under them and the men carrying the poles. The triangle of marchers halted almost level where Kindle stood, and she took the opportunity to examine the design on the flag nearest her. A white diamond outlined in gold lay in the center of an emerald green backdrop, which was also fenced with a gold border. She concluded that it had to be Iteraum's city symbol since the same rectangle had been stitched on all of the parading men and women's uniforms.

Suddenly, a loud voice called out, "Good citizens of beautiful and invincible Iteraum, fair ladies and strong men of Anelthalien, on behalf of the king, I welcome you!"

A round of cheers swelled then dropped into silence again.

"Now, behold and bend for the powerful King Diamas and your soon to be ruler, Prince Adlic!"

At the last word, a sea of lights blasted away the darkness, revealing an army of impressive-looking soldiers. Like the riding soldiers, these men wore the white-and-gold double-breasted uniforms, but the helmets situated on their heads appeared much more appropriate for battle. The swords that each soldier carried in his belt as well as in a band slung around his torso also gave the impression that they would fight if necessary. Kindle wasn't sure how they could actually draw their swords, though, since they each held a lantern aloft in one hand and a cloth that she figured must have been previously shielding it in the other. The lights illuminated the men very well, but she couldn't see most of them because, unlike the other group of riding soldiers, these men stood and not in rows but in numerous rings.

Each successive ring shrank until only a small circle of men stood around a richly dressed, smiling duo on horseback. Kindle recognized one as Adlic and guessed that the much older man beside him had to be King Diamas. She was so busy drinking in the marvelous scene that she didn't realize the crowd all around her had bowed, leaving her standing above everyone. Eyes started to expectantly slide to her. Just when she began to notice the soldiers glaring her way as well, Tad's fist slammed into the back of her leg and knocked her down on one knee. As soon as she crumpled, the loud voice grandly cried, "All hail King Diamas! All hail Prince Adlic!"

The crowd took up his words as a chant, and the royal procession resumed their slow march past Kindle and all of the onlookers.

"What was that for?" Kindle griped at Tad, rubbing her sore knee.

"The dude said to bow," he smirked. "I was helpin' you out."

"Ugh, thanks." She rolled her eyes.

"You should thank me. Them dudes were about to go all ninja on you— don't you know jerks like that kill people for not bowing?" He paused to glare at the back of the king's white head. "What were you doin' staring at 'em anyway? You got a thing for old dudes?"

"No," Kindle defensively replied and sat beside him to relieve her knee. She could feel her cheeks heating and tried to avoid Tad's suspicious glare but failed.

"Ha! You do!"

"No, I don't. I don't have a thing for old dudes. That's weird," she tried to firmly insist but smiled, and Tad caught it.

"It's that prince punk, isn't it?"

"He's not a punk!"

"Any dude dressed like that is a punk."

"Ugh, you're such a jerk. He is not a punk."

Tad sniffed but grinned. "You don't know."

"I do know!" Kindle felt a leg bump her arm and noticed that the crowd was dispersing. Not wanting to be trampled, she stood and saw that the parade had ended and the lights illuminating Adlic had disappeared.

"I do know," Kindle repeated as Tad also rose. "Because I met him this morning."

Tad's face clouded. "Whatever."

"It was before you and Andrew ever got up. He was riding his horse by the river, and he stopped to talk to me, and he was … nice. He even invited me to the ball." She straightened up importantly and huffed, "So see? He's not a punk."

"That's why you're going to the stupid—aw, great." His face fell into a sneer, but his eyes were glaring past her. Kindle turned and saw Ella and Andrew striding toward them.

"Kindle, you found him!" Ella happily sighed when she met them.

"She didn't find me—*I* found her," Tad corrected and Ella breezily shrugged.

"Well, who spotted who doesn't really matter as much as us being all together again. Now we must hurry back to the stables before Miss Becka locks the gate."

"Who?" Tad questioned.

"The barmaid, Tad. The woman who was gracious enough to let us stay in her stable for the night."

"Gracious," he sarcastically repeated. "Pft."

"Yes, gracious." Ella calmly nodded then turned to lead them to their home for the night. Obviously Ella had dropped her earlier anger, but Kindle could see Tad, who had rooted himself to the spot where he stood, had not.

"Come on," she emphatically mouthed back at him, and only after a long, begrudging exhale did he follow as well.

GILDED DARKNESS

Kindle expected sleeping in a barn to be a disgusting, uncomfortable experience, but once she finally settled down on the saddle blanket Ella had spread over some fresh hay, she decided it would not be so terrible after all. The bed of hay acted as a much better cushion than the ground they had been sleeping on, it smelled earthy and comforting, and it was warm. After lying down, Kindle believed she could drift off to sleep in a second, but Ella, who lay nearby, began chatting to her about the parade. She had watched it with Andrew across the street and had been dazzled by all of the sights. Even though Kindle wanted to fall asleep, she kept half-heartedly responding to Ella's whispers. Once Ella began gushing about just how handsome Adlic was, though, Kindle felt wide awake again and they fell into a fit of girlish giggles and exclamations until Tad yelled at them to shut up.

When the next morning dawned, giddy fluttering still bounced around Kindle's head. She wanted to continue her excited conversation with Ella but rolling over found Ella had disappeared. Looking across the stable, she saw Tad was still snoring but Andrew was searching Nasah's packs for some food. She joined him, and once they finally found the last of their corn, they meandered out onto the sidewalk that led them to the front of the inn. They wandered along the front of the building, examining the long window that announced the building to be the "Gilded Goose" and the almost empty streets until Andrew caught sight of Ella moving a table under the awning where they had huddled the day before. Upon seeing them, Ella called a pleasant morning greeting then immediately ran over a list of tasks that the barmaid, Miss Becka, had given them to finish before guests arrived for morning tea. From Andrew's face, Kindle knew that he was just as enthusiastic about scrubbing floors and arranging bouquets on each table. Despite his nauseous frown, though, Andrew tailed Ella into the inn, and after rolling her eyes at the ridiculous golden goose painted on the door, so did Kindle.

The trio cleaned and spruced the large dining area until merry customers arrived. When their voices and the tinkling bell on the door rang out, Miss Becka stuck her high, tight grey bun and sour, wrinkled face out from the kitchen and directed them to take orders. Kindle hated being shouted at by such an unpleasant woman. She tried to slip out of the door, but Ella snatched her back behind the bar to pour drinks. After that, the crowd kept thickening, and Ella, along with some other waitresses who eventually trickled in, brought her orders so quickly and constantly that the day flew by in a chaotic blur.

"What?" Kindle asked for what felt like the millionth time as she lined four more glasses on the bar.

"Hot tea, cold tea, twice each. And Kindle...."

"Hm?" she grunted, concentrating on her pouring.

"Kindle," Ella said again and leaned forward to snag her attention.

"More?" Kindle started to reach under the counter for another set of glasses, but Ella stopped her.

"No, no Kin, no more. You need to be on your way."

Kindle blinked, trying to fathom what Ella meant. "Huh?"

"The coronation ball, Kindle! You haven't forgotten, have you?"

"Oh! No—is it now?" Kindle shaded her eyes to peer outside. The bit of sky she could see was still bright blue.

"No, I asked round and it isn't until sunset, but you'll need time to dress and ride to the castle. One chap said from here it takes the whole afternoon to reach it. I know this city is enormous, but I don't—"

A beckoning yell from one of the diners caused Ella to shut her eyes and sigh. "One moment, sir! Hashing out things, you know!" she sweetly called back then returned her smile to Kindle. "Take Nasah, but Tad knows that. He's going with you—did I say that already? Well, no matter, he is and he already knows all this, so go on now and have your dance."

Kindle jogged around the bar and gave Ella a quick squeeze. "Oh, this is gunna be awesome!" she cried.

Ella laughed as she wormed out of the hug. "Yes, have a lovely time. Just remember us here and don't stay too late."

"Okay." Kindle nodded without really hearing Ella's last few words. She beamed one more time then wove her way through the crowded room. Halfway to the door, she heard Ella's voice call, "And Kindle, remember to tell everyone you see!"

For a millisecond Kindle slowed but chose to act as if she hadn't heard her friend over the din. Quickly she finished her dash to the door and left the noise behind. Assuming Tad and Nasah were waiting for her in the stable, Kindle rounded the inn and ran into the warm little structure. Before she could spy Tad, she heard him.

"Finally."

Following his voice upward, she saw he had managed to climb on a rafter and stretch out on his back. He tossed a rock in the air, caught it, then sat up and stared down at her.

"Ella said you're coming too," Kindle panted.

"Ella can go get hit by a truck," he grumbled almost inaudibly but jumped down beside her and said, "Yeah, but not because of her."

Kindle ignored his rudeness. She was too ecstatic to argue with him. "Okay, cool. Is Nasah saddled? We gotta leave, like, right n—"

"Chill, Miss Priss," Tad interrupted and threw a wrapped bundle at her. "Nasah's ready. We've been waitin' on you and we still are."

"What's this?" Kindle carefully pushed the soft package between her hands.

"It's a cheeseburger," he replied, his tone dripping with dull sarcasm.

Kindle gave him a glare but couldn't help but laugh as she untied the twine bow and unfolded the brown paper. Folded red cloth lay inside. Kindle lifted it out and twisted it until its shape made sense, and her eyes slowly widened.

"It's a dress!" she exclaimed.

"Nah, still a cheeseburger," Tad snickered.

Kindle gave him a suspicious look. "*You* got me a dress?"

"It wasn't my idea. And I wouldn't have done it if it was just you gettin' something." He grabbed something lying on Nasah's saddle and held it up for her to see. "Check it out. Genuine leather." The jacket in his hands was jet-black and looked like it could belong to a very suave military biker. Kindle didn't find it as wonderful as her dress but had to admit it did look sharp.

"Cool." She smiled down at her new outfit. "So you're gunna wear that and I'm gunna wear this?"

"Yeah, so get it on so we can go to this stupid thing," he demanded then slung his jacket over his shoulder and led Nasah outside. Once she was sure she was safely alone, Kindle emitted a quiet squeal and clapped her hands in excitement. She had been beyond overjoyed to just go to the ball, but now she had a dress to wear. After a quick change in one of the stalls, she did her best to examine how it looked. It was a simple dress—all red with little angled straps and a long, flowing skirt—but fit so well she almost believed she actually looked pretty in it. For a moment, she wished she could see her hair and fix it or at least not have to wear her boots. She had never worn anything nearly as formal and wanted to try to make herself match it. Knowing she really didn't have the time or ability to spruce up, though, Kindle willed herself to believe that she did look nice. Trying to smile, she walked outside to meet Tad. All of her insecurities about her appearance evaporated at his reaction. As if hit by a gust of wind, he tilted slightly back and blinked. Kindle shyly grinned and giggled as she watched his eyes run down, then up.

"What?" she asked as she stuffed her clothes into her pack.

He blinked one last time. "I dunno. You look different. It's weird."

Her confidence sank and she rolled her eyes. "Oh, thanks. I look weird."

"I didn't say you looked weird," he defensively retorted, but she ignored him. Instead of bickering with him, Kindle tried to elegantly seat herself on Nasah but ended up twisting her dress into a snare around her legs.

"Now you look weird," Tad chuckled and Kindle glared at him.

"Are you walking or riding?"

"I dunno. Depends if you can steer in that cocoon."

"Shut up," Kindle mumbled and kicked herself free as Tad easily swung himself in front of her. As she settled into the best side saddle position she could manage, Tad spurred Nasah into motion. Kindle was glad that their destination lay in an obvious direction so she didn't have to speak to Tad about if he knew the way or how far it was. His comment still stung, and she didn't want to give him a chance to insult her further. Determined to ignore him altogether, she watched the buildings and people passing instead.

Their path carried them past countless shops, inns, and homes, but after trotting by only a few streets, Kindle concluded that all of the buildings had been constructed to look similar. The almost white stone in the walls and on the street made up the majority of each boxy structure, and they all sat so close to one another that they seemed to meld into long blocks instead of separate shops and homes. Also, despite the function of the buildings, any wood or metal fixture on them had been painted gold or green. Everywhere she looked the two colors were exactly the same tone and matched the hues on the flags displayed all around. So many of the diamond flags flapped from doors, windows, and other nooks that Kindle wondered how she had missed them the day before. She almost asked Tad if they had actually filled the streets when they first walked through Iteraum but remembered her unspoken oath to excommunicate him for the ride and kept her thoughts to herself.

As they traveled along, the monotonous buildings interested her less and the growing crowds stole her attention. Unlike when they had first pushed through the sea of people, Kindle could see almost everyone from Nasah's back. Most of the people had fair skin and darker hair like Adlic but, in her opinion, were nowhere near as gorgeous. What most intrigued her about them was how they were all dressed exactly like the buildings in the city. The women wore long white dresses, and the men white shirts and trousers. Only the splashes of green and gold shawls, belts, buttons, and other accessories they wore set one apart from another. Their uniformity and the way they mulled aimlessly in clusters reminded Kindle of a herd of cows. Her thought reminded her of Tad's insults the previous day, and she secretly grinned. For just a moment, amusement at their ignorance to anything except their festive roaming in their city filled her, but then a strange sinking feeling flushed it away. All at once, a strong urge took over her to jump down and start warning them about the danger and death the evil ruler was crafting for them. She felt it imperative to run through the crowd and even shake a few people to illustrate just how clueless they were and how serious and real the threat to their city and lives was that she could almost see herself among them. However, the expressions that she imagined washing over their faces kept her planted. The thought of everyone staring at her like she had gone insane choked out her strange urge, and Kindle turned her eyes upward so she didn't have to face them all. Even though no one knew of the event that had just transpired in her mind, she still felt guilty about recoiling from it. She knew that she should have followed the compulsion, probably except for shaking people, and that she still could cry out from Nasah's back, but she felt much safer disregarding it. Trying to console herself, she assured her guilt that no one would listen to her if she acted crazy anyway and that she was planning to tell everyone at the ball.

For the rest of the ride, Kindle did her best to avoid anyone's gaze. She wanted to forget about how lost and unaware the citizens of Iteraum were, and seeing them herding down the street didn't help. In her determination to become oblivious to everything, Kindle lost track of time and space and almost tipped off Nasah when she noticed the castle standing right in front of them. From far away the extraordinarily tall towers had appeared to stand independently, but now she saw that the four slightly shorter, thinner, convex towers were anchored to the wide, concave middle one at its lowest tier and also with long, sloping flying buttresses at its four upper tiers. All of the towers were composed of beautiful, sparking white stone and stepped into narrower layers at each higher level. A large, fluttering green flag that Kindle was sure matched the ones strewn throughout the city grandly crowned each tower. Altogether, the castle looked like a humongous iced cake or the glorious topping of an icy mountain and enchanted Kindle out of her melancholy.

"Wow," she sighed, and Tad lifted an eyebrow back at her.

"What?"

"The castle—it's so pretty."

"How can you tell with all these idiots in the way?" he grumbled then yelled, "Hey! Move!"

Kindle peered around him to see a pair of short ladies shoot offended glares their way.

"Sorry! He didn't mean it!" called Kindle, smiling weakly.

"Yeah, I di—!" Tad began, but Kindle jabbed her finger into his ribs.

The ladies pushed ahead through the tight crowd, and Kindle sighed, "You can't yell at people like that. You'll get us thrown out of the ball."

"Who cares? I didn't want to come to this stupid thing anyway," he complained.

"Then why'd you come?" Kindle snapped back, but Tad didn't answer. "You don't have to go in, you know," Kindle said, hoping he would stay outside so he wouldn't dampen her spirits anymore. "You can just stay out here, and I'll meet you when it's over." She waited impatiently for his response, but he was busy trying to urge Nasah in any direction. When it finally became clear that their horse could not move, he flung the reins aside.

"Whatever. Go by yourself. There's too many idiots around here anyway."

Kindle gasped in excitement, "Seriously!?" She slid off Nasah and beamed up at him. "Okay, I'll find you when it's over. Okay?"

"Yeah," he mumbled, then as she turned away, she remembered why Ella had consented to her attending the ball.

"Tad?" she hesitantly asked.

"What?"

"We have to tell people about, you know, the whole evil king thing, so … tell people, okay? Or Ella will get mad again."

He grunted. Kindle took it as assent and dove into the sea of people.

Before she had gone very far, she thought she heard Tad tell someone, "Hey, all you idiots are gunna die."

Kindle tried to believe that he hadn't really said it and focused on squeezing a path to the castle.

CLOSE

When she finally reached the wide gate in the center of the huge, curved wall, Kindle bent her head back to digest the height of the castle before she stepped inside. A long, well-lit room, even more elegant and dazzling than the exterior of the castle, rolled out in front of her. Every inch of the floor, walls, and ceiling sparkled as if they were diamond rather than polished white stone due to the enormous golden chandeliers filled with thousands of candles that hung above. Gold ornamentation also ran down the walls like expensive ivy and decorated the edges of the long, thin green rug that began at her toes and spanned to the far end of the giant hall-like room. Where it ended, the wall caved back under a gold railed balcony flanked by two curving staircases. The decadence of the room almost left her breathless, and the person leaning on the balcony's rail finished stealing the air from her lungs.

Prince Adlic's high vantage point as well as his uniquely emerald green apparel set him apart from everyone else. Kindle grinned as she remembered what he had said at the river and slunk sideways to the edge of the crowd, content to just see him again. After a few minutes of indulging in his gorgeousness, though, Kindle dropped her eyes to her feet. She wondered if it was worth dancing with him and falling for him even more since she would probably never see him after the ball. Suddenly ready to scoot out of the hall, Kindle peered at him one last time. Her heart jumped. At the end of a slow scan of the crowd, Adlic's eyes had stopped at her corner, and he pushed back from the rail. Kindle hoped—and at the same time tried not to kid herself—that she had caused his unexpected reaction. To determine if she truly was the object of his interest, she sent a small wave his way. Adlic not only returned the gesture but beckoned her to make her way to him. Without hesitating, Kindle swept through the packed room as quickly as she could while still appearing composed. His acknowledgement of her out of the masses of people had catapulted her into an internal celebration of squealing and hopping, but she didn't want to expose her silly glee to anyone. Kindle took a few deep breaths as she made her way to the golden staircase and by the time she was face to face with Adlic, had calmed her excitement.

"Hi," she sighed, smiling.

"Hello, fair Kindle," he replied and bent to take her hand and kiss it. Kindle's heart fluttered, and she almost melted into a pool of giggles but restrained herself.

"You are the gem I believed you would be," he complimented her.

"Thanks." Kindle tried to think of something interesting to say, but her mind was drowned in bliss. Adlic peered out over the crowd spread below them, and following his gaze, Kindle realized that each head was slowly turning their way.

"My subjects anticipate my opening the floor with the first dance."

"Um, are you going to?"

"May I?" He offered his hand, and when Kindle took it, he led her down the stairs and to the head of the green carpet. The whole hall fell into whispers then silence.

"Citizens of Iteraum," Adlic proudly boomed, "I welcome you to the royal home and my coronation ball. Enjoy yourselves this night in honor of my father, knowing come the new dawn, I, Prince Adlic, will be your king!"

Cheers and applause broke out, but Adlic waved his free hand for quiet and everyone obeyed.

"I will now take the first dance and welcome every man and woman to do likewise."

Adlic grandly smiled and filled his chest with the renewed shouts before he turned to Kindle, bowed, then took his position as her dance partner. The fear of making a fool of herself suddenly burst over her elation like a water balloon. She had no idea how to dance.

"Uh, I don't really—" she began, but merry orchestra music sounded, and Adlic led her swirling down the carpet. Kindle swallowed her fear and quickly realized that as long as she followed and mimicked his steps, she could keep time with him. Focusing on where to move her feet also helped her escape the stares and whispers floating in her peripheral vision that would have otherwise driven her into an embarrassed hole. Soon, though, other couples began dancing as well until finally it seemed as if the white room had been filled with hundreds of white planets orbiting the ethereal space.

"So I see you convinced your fellow travelers to lend me the pleasure of this meeting," Adlic remarked as the music died.

"Yeah, well sort of... they didn't really mind like I thought they would. At least Ella didn't. And she's kind of our leader so...," Kindle finished with a shrug, hoping he would understand what she meant. Adlic nodded and opened his mouth to say something, but a new, cheerful tune interrupted him. Kindle wasn't sure she could last through another song, and so when Adlic took her hand again to dance, she gave an exhausted sigh. After a few lively steps that sent them closer to the wall, Adlic leaned in and whispered, "Would you rather we steal away and talk?"

Kindle nodded, relieved. A smile that seemed almost as pleased as her own spread across his face also, and still dancing, he deftly led them to the golden door nearest to the staircase. In a second, they both slipped through it and stood in a narrow, dim corridor.

"Come, let's walk to the garden," he suggested and in the silence his voice echoed. He led her a short way then turned to the left and traveled a little further before opening a door that Kindle hadn't noticed. When he ushered her through it, she took in the lovely little world around her with a long, slow gaze. They stood in a white stone colonnade that wrapped around all four sides of a green square that housed a tinkling fountain and a beautiful variety of colorful flowers. The grassy area seemed so serene that she wanted to pass between the tall white columns edging the walkway, but the fragile appearance of the foliage kept her still.

"Do you find this suits your taste?" asked Adlic.

"Oh, yeah, it's really pretty."

"Very good." He gave her a half-grin then started down the covered walkway.

"Tell me about these fellow travelers of yours, Kindle," he urged once they fell into the same pace. "I would like to hear the sort of company you entertain."

Kindle thought it strange he wanted to talk about other people but brushed away the notion. "Well, it's just me, Ella, Tad, and Andrew. We're all kind of the same age, but I think Ella's the oldest. She acts the oldest anyway. Like I said, she tells us what to do—she's really nice, though. She kind of acts like a mom. Me and Andrew don't really mind it—Andrew doesn't really say a lot—but she kind of makes Tad mad. But I guess he gets mad about a lot of stuff... but it's not, like, bad or anything. He's ... he's actually pretty cool sometimes." Kindle grinned to herself then checked Adlic's expression. He didn't share her cheerfulness but appeared deep in thought.

"Oh, I see," he slowly murmured then louder asked, "And from what city did you say you have come?"

"Oh, um, well...." Kindle wasn't sure how to respond. "I didn't really say. We met kind of north, um, west of here—of Iteraum, you know—but we all came from really different places."

"What brings you together then, if you were so distant? Perhaps it was the purpose of your journey?"

"Um ... yeah."

After a few moments of awkward silence, Adlic pressed, "And what sort of great purpose placed you each on the same path?"

"Well...," Kindle sighed. She very much wanted to answer honestly and tell him all about the evil throne they were going to destroy, but she also still feared that he wouldn't believe her. Finally she stopped to face him and rounded up a serious expression. "Okay, so I know this is probably gunna sound, like, crazy or something, but it's true. We're going to find this evil king and break his throne so nobody else becomes an evil king after him because they'd, like, end Anelthalien."

Adlic, wide-eyed, simply stared at her.

"I mean, the new evil guy would blow everything up or something, you know? And that's bad, so we're gunna stop him." Kindle dropped her head and shook it. "Please don't think I'm crazy. It's true—it really is." Her necklace caught her eye, and she plucked it off her chest. "And this is how we know. This—and Ella and Tad and Andrew have one too—they're makers' marks. The last good queen sent them to us so we'd know that it's us who's supposed to end the evil throne." She nervously lifted her eyes, and Adlic dipped his head in a nod.

"And—" he cleared his throat, "—and what else do you know of the necklaces?" He struggled to say the words, and Kindle furrowed her brow in concern.

"Are you okay?"

"Ye-yes. I-I may need some fresh night air," he confessed in a rush and linked his elbow around hers to guide her to the fountain. "Come, sit," he pushed, pulling her down on the short stone wall surrounding the pool, "and tell me about these necklaces."

His clear anxiety made Kindle feel achingly self-conscious. "Hey, I'm sorry—I know that all sounds, like, really weird and scary. I'll quit talking about—"

"No! Ah, excuse me. No, I-I do very much want to know more. Please, your necklace ... you say there are others?"

"Yeah, we each have one—me, Ella, Tad, and Andrew. Each one's different, like, different colors and the little dragon's different. Somebody told us that each one's a different maker's mark, so I guess that's why."

"Maker's mark...?"

"Yeah, their symbols, I guess. Um, don't you know about the four makers or anything like that?"

He shook his head.

"Oh." Kindle remembered that Azildor had told them almost everyone had forgotten most of the history of Anelthalien, but Adlic's ignorance still surprised her. "Well, they, like, *made* Anelthalien."

"Ah. And they made your necklaces as well?"

"Um, I think so...." She struggled to recall what the Cifra and Azildor had said about them. "No, um, there were, like, these elements or spirits or something and they made them ... I think. I dunno, I don't really remember, but, um, you want to go back to the ball?" Kindle asked, done with his interrogation. She had expected their conversation to center around each other, but now that she knew Adlic was clearly not interested in her, she wanted to leave.

"Is that all you know of the necklaces?" he asked as if he hadn't heard her question at all. Offended, Kindle stood up and crossed her arms.

"Yeah, I guess so. Is that all you care about? Did you even...." Her voice trailed off. A flicker of movement under the covered colonnade had pulled all of her attention away from the prince. She squinted hard into the shade but saw nothing. Adlic also flashed a peek in the direction of her gaze then jumped up beside her and almost frantically whispered, "What? Did you see something? What was it?"

"No." She dismissed it as a bird or a bug. "What's your pro—BLAK!" Without a word of explanation, Adlic had shoved her backwards into the fountain and bolted.

Still splashing and flailing, Kindle heard him yell, "I've done my part! Leave me be!" She managed to turn herself upright in time to see him finish his sprint to the door, wrench it open, and disappear.

"You jerk! Urgh!" she shouted in frustration and gathered up her heavy, wet skirt only to drop it when she moved to step out of the pool. Just on the other side of the low stone wall stood the hooded creature she had last seen tumbling off the Chokmahs' tower. Kindle wanted to run or scream, but every inch of her body had frozen into a tense block. The black cloak slowly, slightly rose then fell as the horrible wheezing issued from it and caused the hair on her neck to prickle. Her senses suddenly returned, and she gasped a breath as she started to ease away, but in a blink the creature pounced.

Everything went black as they toppled into the water and her own screams, along with the creature's, pierced her ears. Kindle kicked and swung with every bit of energy she had and finally launched the creature against the huge stone cup spitting water in the air. She took her moment of freedom to recollect her dress to free her legs and clambered out of the water. Gasping and coughing, she tried to run, but her tired limbs only allowed her to unsteadily stumble over to the nearest column. Kindle leaned against it to catch her breath, but shouts from somewhere unseen shocked her upright. The door Adlic had escaped through burst open, and the prince tripped backwards out of it, landing hard on the stone.

"Adlic!" Kindle cried, hoping he had returned to help her, but his wild stare and attempt to flee again told her otherwise. "Ad—!" she started to yell, but out of nowhere the hooded figure tackled her. Before she could react, it shoved her across the stone walkway and into the angle of the wall and floor so she couldn't escape. The creature pushed hard against her throat and though Kindle tired to make noise, her voice and breath were gone. With each panicked gasp, the cloaked creature wrapped its hold tighter and tighter, making it incrementally more impossible to breath.

When her head began to swim and she was sure she only had seconds before suffocation ended her life, a very quiet hissing voice whispered, "It is clossse."

The words chilled her bones and renewed her terror. She wanted to scream, but her lungs were empty now. Kindle closed her eyes and turned to try to suck in some of the precious air surrounding her. Suddenly all of the pressure around her neck and chest vanished, and she was drinking in oxygen. Loud, smacking footfalls sounded and roused her from her momentary bliss. Still dizzy and gasping, she rolled her head back to see someone running along the walkway to her. Fear almost sent her into helpless panic, but when a ray of moonlight illuminated his face, Kindle's heart jumped in joyous relief.

"Tad!" she cried as he raced past her. Kindle pushed herself up to see where he was headed and instinctively scooted backwards. Just a short distance from her feet, the cloaked creature lay in a heap with the hilt of Natzal sticking sideways out of it. Tad caught up his dagger then pivoted to face her.

"Go! Get outta here!" he yelled then returned his attention to the black mass at his feet.

Kindle wanted to obey him, but between her dizziness and fear, she felt paralyzed.

"C'mon!" Tad impatiently yelled to her without taking his eyes from the motionless creature. Using the wall for support, Kindle stood and started inching toward the door Adlic was near, still writhing in pain.

"Is it dead?" she cautiously asked.

Tad didn't voice a reply but planted a violent kick in the middle of the heap. He sniffed at it and turned to walk away. Just when she was about to grin at his victory, the cloak stirred and she let out a shriek. Tad spun around and met the horrible creature with Natzal. Kindle watched as the pair tumbled onto a bed of flowers and then separated, the creature rolling into a bush and Tad over more colorful petals. Tad recovered first and dove after his enemy. Pinning it under his knees, he commenced to stabbing it over and over. Kindle, sure blood would start flying everywhere, averted her eyes and returned to her escape route. Reluctant to leave without Tad, she stopped with her hand on the door, listening to his angry, savage grunts.

"Urgh ... Kindle," Adlic groaned and she gave him a curt glance.

"Help me—help me up. That buffoon attacked me."

"Well, you deserved it," she snapped and dared to peek Tad's way. He was still bent over, ferociously slinging with his knife.

"I did," Adlic admitted and Kindle glared at him. "I regret that I agreed to do you harm, but—but that monster vowed to take my life if I did not."

"What?" she questioned hatefully, snatching another glance at Tad's unaltered state.

"It threatened me—it commanded me to bring you here and lead you to speak about the necklaces. It said I must or it would kill me," he moaned pathetically, looking nauseated. "I had no choice."

Kindle's glare faltered. She still wanted to call him a scumbag but was too busy thinking, trying to remember. A shout from Tad derailed her train of thought, and Kindle spun to see him sprinting her way, followed by the gliding, cloaked creature.

"Go!" he yelled, and Kindle moved to run, but Adlic caught her foot.

"Oh! I beg you! Help me, do not leave me to that monster!" he cried. She hesitated. Kindle did not want to help him but knew it would be horrible to leave him to die. While she was wavering, Tad collided into them.

"Go! That freak thing won't die!" he shouted, grabbing her arm.

"Tad, we can't leave him—" she protested, but he yanked her out of Adlic's weak grasp and into the dim corridor.

"What do you care about him anyway? He was gunna let that thing kill you," Tad panted. They turned the corner then burst into the sparkling room and knocked into a dancing couple.

"Sorry!" Kindle gasped, steadying herself with the woman's arms. "Sorry!" She didn't wait for a reply but gathered her cumbersome skirt and ran after Tad.

"It's the prince's dancing partner!" someone shouted and a few people broke into cheers. Almost immediately, though, terrified screams replaced the happy sounds. Kindle knew what had caused it but didn't dare look back to make sure. She locked her focus on Tad and ran through the path he was creating as fast as she could. Neither of them stopped until Tad reached the street gate where he had tied Nasah. As soon as he was close enough, he sliced through the rope and held the nervous horse in place so Kindle could climb into the saddle. Once she was seated, he jumped up behind her, stole the reins, and sent them speeding down the empty street.

Soon the only sound in the dark street was Nasah's clopping hooves. Kindle summoned her courage to peer behind them. Nothing stirred. They had escaped the hooded figure. Tad met her stare and murmured, "Did we lose it?" She nodded. He huffed and grumbled, "I told you he was a punk."

Kindle, with no thought in her mind except exhausted relief, sighed, "Yeah. Thanks."

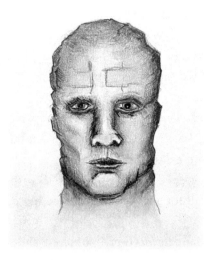

DRAWING NEAR

"**W**here have you been, you vile slug?" Menthoshine sneered. "I remember ordering you to return *quickly*. It has been days."

"Thingsss take time," Castrosphy hissed as he slid under the green light softly radiating from her orb. Menthoshine knocked him back from her throne.

"Must I repeat everything to you?!" she raged. "Keep your wretchedness away!" Menthoshine took a deep breath and glared at her staff. "Speak."

"Children in Iteraum. Ssstrange children."

"Children," she growled, "Castrosphy, do *not* tell me you wasted your time—"

"Four ssstrange children. Three sssmell of another kind. They hold ssstrange thingsss."

Menthoshine's eyes, piercing green slits, slipped in his direction. "You lie. You filthy roach, YOU LIE!"

"No liesss."